# WHISPERS
## *and* LIES

# WHISPERS
## *and* LIES

# Joy Fielding

**ATRIA** BOOKS

New York   London   Toronto   Sydney   Singapore

**This Large Print Book carries the
Seal of Approval of N.A.V.H.**

**ATRIA** BOOKS

1230 Avenue of the Americas
New York, NY 10020

ISBN: 0-7434-5134-1

First Atria Books large-print hardcover edition August 2002

10  9  8  7  6  5  4  3  2  1

**ATRIA** BOOKS is a trademark of Simon & Schuster, Inc.

For information regarding special discounts for bulk purchases, please contact Simon & Schuster Special Sales at 1-800-456-6798 or business@simonandschuster.com

Printed in the U.S.A

For Shannon,
my daughter, my helper, my friend.

# ACKNOWLEDGMENTS

As always, a special thank you to Owen Laster, Beverley Slopen, and Larry Mirkin, good friends as well as trusted advisors. Thank you also to Emily Bestler, the editor of my dreams, and her assistant Sarah Branham, for their assistance and good humor in the creation of this novel. I also count myself very lucky to have the support of Judith Curr, Louise Burke, Cathy Gruhn, Stephen Boldt, and all the other terrific people at Atria and Pocket who work so hard to make my books a success.

Writing this novel would have been very difficult without the help of Donna and Jack Frysinger, who gave generously of their time and energy to provide me with all the information I needed to bring the charming, oceanside city of Delray to life. I look forward to seeing you there soon.

My love to Warren, Shannon, Annie, Renee, Aurora and Rosie, and all my friends in Toronto and Palm Beach. Thank you for being patient, loyal, and always interesting (especially important for a writer). Note to Annie: You could be a little less interesting for a while.

And lastly, a special thank you to those readers who

have sent such wonderful messages to me via my Web site. While there's not enough time to thank you each in person, please know that your letters have meant more to me than I can ever adequately express. Your kind thoughts and good wishes buoy my spirits and make my day. Thank you.

# 1

She said her name was Alison Simms.

The name tumbled slowly, almost languorously, from her lips, the way honey slides from the blade of a knife. Her voice was soft, tentative, slightly girlish, although her handshake was firm and she looked me straight in the eye. I liked that. I liked **her,** I decided, almost on the spot, although I'm the first to admit that I'm not always the best judge of character. Still, my first impression of the amazingly tall young woman with the shoulder-length, strawberry-blond curls who stood tightly clasping my hand in the living room of my small two-bedroom home was positive. And first impressions are lasting impressions, as my mother used to say.

"This is a real pretty house," Alison said, her head

nodding up and down, as if agreeing with her own assessment, her eyes darting appreciatively between the overstuffed sofa and the two delicate Queen Anne chairs, the cushioned valances framing the windows and the sculpted area rug lying across the light hardwood floor. "I love pink and mauve together. It's my favorite color combination." Then she smiled, this enormous, wide, slightly goofy smile that made me want to smile right back. "I always wanted a pink and mauve wedding."

I had to laugh. It seemed such a wonderfully strange thing to say to someone you'd just met. She laughed with me, and I motioned toward the sofa for her to sit down. She immediately sank into the deep, down-filled cushions, her blue sundress all but disappearing inside the swirl of pink and mauve fabric flowers, and crossed one long, skinny leg over the other, the rest of her body folding itself artfully around her knees as she leaned toward me. I perched on the edge of the striped Queen Anne chair directly across from her, thinking that she reminded me of a pretty pink flamingo, a real one, not one of those awful plastic things you see stabbed into people's front lawns. "You're very tall," I commented lamely, thinking she'd probably heard that remark all her life.

"Five feet ten inches," she acknowledged graciously. "I look taller."

"Yes, you do," I agreed, although at barely five feet four inches, everyone looks tall to me. "Do you mind my asking how old you are?"

"Twenty-eight." A slight blush suddenly scraped her cheeks. "I look younger."

"Yes, you do," I said again. "You're lucky. I've always looked my age."

"How old are you? That is, if you don't mind . . ."

"Take a guess."

The sudden intensity of her gaze caught me off-guard. She scrutinized me as if I were an exotic specimen in a lab, trapped between two tiny pieces of glass, under an invisible microscope. Her clear green eyes burrowed into my tired brown ones, then moved across my face, examining each telltale line, weighing the evidence of my years. I have few illusions. I saw myself exactly the way I knew she must: a reasonably attractive woman with good cheekbones, large breasts, and a bad haircut.

"I don't know," she said. "Forty?"

"Exactly." I laughed. "Told you."

We fell silent, frozen in the warmth of the afternoon sun that surrounded us like a spotlight, highlighting small flecks of dust that danced in the air between us, like hundreds of tiny insects. She smiled, folded her hands together in her lap, the fingers of one hand playing carelessly with the fingers of the other. She wore no rings of any kind, and no polish, although her nails were long and cared-for. I could tell she was nervous. She wanted me to like her.

"Did you have any trouble finding the house?" I asked.

"No. Your directions were great: east on Atlantic,

south on Seventh Avenue, past the white church, between Second and Third Street. No problem at all. Except for the traffic. I didn't realize that Delray was such a busy place."

"Well, it's November," I reminded her. "The snow-birds are starting to arrive."

"Snowbirds?"

"Tourists," I explained. "You're obviously new to Florida."

She looked toward her sandaled feet. "I like this rug. You're very brave to have a white carpet in the living room."

"Not really. I don't do much entertaining."

"I guess your job keeps you pretty busy. I always thought it would be so great to be a nurse," she offered. "It must be very rewarding."

I laughed. "**Rewarding** is not exactly the word I would use."

"What word would you use?"

She seemed genuinely curious, something I found both refreshing and endearing. It had been so long since anyone had expressed any real interest in me that I guess I was flattered. But there was also something so touch-ingly naive about the question that I wanted to cross over to where she sat and hug her, as a mother hugs her child, and tell her that it was all right, she didn't have to work so hard, that the tiny cottage behind my house was hers to occupy, that the decision had been made the minute she walked through my front door.

"What word would I use to describe the nursing profession?" I repeated, mulling over several possibilities. "Exhausting," I said finally. "Exacting. Infuriating."

"Good words."

I laughed again, as I seemed to have done often in the short amount of time she'd been in my home. It would be nice having someone around who made me laugh, I remember thinking. "What sort of work do you do?" I asked.

Alison stood up, walked to the window, and stared out at the wide street, lined with several varieties of shady palms. Bettye McCoy, third wife of Richard McCoy, and some thirty years his junior, not an unusual occurrence in South Florida, was being pulled along the sidewalk by her two small white dogs. She was dressed from head to toe in beige Armani, and in her free hand she carried a small white plastic bag full of dog poop, a fashion irony seemingly lost on the third Mrs. McCoy. "Oh, would you just look at that. Aren't they just the sweetest things? What are they, poodles?"

"Bichons," I said, coming up beside her, the top of my head in line with the bottom of her chin. "The bimbos of the canine world."

It was Alison's turn to laugh. The sound filled the room, danced between us, like the flecks of dust in the afternoon sun. "They sure are cute though. Don't you think?"

"**Cute** is not exactly the word I would use," I told her, consciously echoing my earlier remark.

She smiled conspiratorially. "What word would you use?"

"Let me see," I said, warming to the game. "Yappy. Pesky. Destructive."

"Destructive? How could anything that sweet be destructive?"

"One of her dogs got into my garden a few months back, dug up all my hibiscus. Trust me, it was neither sweet nor cute." I backed away from the window, catching sight, as I did so, of a man's silhouette among the many outside shadows on the opposite corner of the street. "Is someone waiting for you?"

"For me? No. Why?"

I edged forward to have a better look, but the man, if he'd existed at all, had taken his shadow and disappeared. I looked down the street, but there was no one there.

"I thought I saw someone standing under that tree over there." I pointed with my chin.

"I don't see anyone."

"Well, I'm sure it was nothing. Would you like some coffee?"

"I'd love some." She followed me through the small dining area that stood perpendicular to the living room, and into the predominantly white kitchen at the back of the house. "Oh, would you just look at these," she exclaimed with obvious delight, gliding toward the rows of shelves that lined the wall beside the small breakfast nook, her arms extended, fingers fluttering eagerly in the air. "What are these? Where did you get them?"

My eyes quickly scanned the sixty-five china heads that gazed at us from five rows of wooden shelves. "They're called 'ladies' head vases,' " I explained. "My mother used to collect them. They're from the fifties, mostly made in Japan. They have holes in the tops of their heads, for flowers, I guess, although they don't hold a lot. When they first came out, they were worth maybe a couple of dollars."

"And now?"

"Apparently they're quite valuable. **Collectibles,** I believe, is the word they use."

"And what word would you use?" She waited eagerly, a mischievous smile twisting her full lips this way and that.

I didn't have to think very hard. "Junk," I said concisely.

"I think they're great," she protested. "Just look at the eyelashes on this one. Oh, and the earrings on this one. And the tiny string of pearls. Oh, and look at this one. Don't you just love the expression on her face?" She lifted one of the heads gingerly into her hands. The china figurine was about six inches tall, with arched painted eyebrows and pursed red lips, her light brown curls peeking out from under a pink and white turban, a pink rose at her throat. "She's not as ornate as some of the others, but she has such a superior look about her, you know, like some snooty society matron, looking down her nose at the rest of us."

"Actually, she looks like my mother," I said.

The china head almost slipped through Alison's fingers. "Oh my God, I'm so sorry." She quickly returned the head vase to its original position on the shelf, between two doe-eyed girls with ribbons in their hair. "I didn't mean . . ."

I laughed. "It's interesting you picked that one. It was her favorite. What do you take in your coffee?"

"Cream, three sugars?" she asked, as if she weren't sure, her eyes still on the china heads.

I poured us each a mug of the coffee I'd been brewing since she'd phoned from the hospital, said she'd seen my notice posted to the bulletin board at one of the nurses' stations, and could she come over as soon as possible.

"Does your mother still collect?"

"She died five years ago."

"I'm so sorry."

"Me too. I miss her. It's why I haven't been able to sell off any of her friends. How about a piece of cranberry-and-pumpkin cake?" I asked, changing the subject for fear of getting maudlin. "I just made it this morning."

"You can bake? Now I'm really impressed. I'm absolutely hopeless in the kitchen."

"Your mother never taught you to cook?"

"We weren't on the best of terms." Alison smiled, although unlike her other smiles, this one seemed more forced than genuine. "Anyway, I'd love a piece of cake. Cranberries are one of my very favorite things in the whole world."

Again, I laughed. "I don't think I've ever met anyone

who felt so passionately about cranberries. Could you hand me a knife?" I motioned toward a group of knives slid into the artfully arranged slots of a triangular chunk of wood that sat on the far end of the white tile countertop. Alison pulled out the top one, a foot-long monster with a tapered two-inch blade. "Whoa," I said. "Overkill, don't you think?"

She turned the knife over slowly in her hand, studying her reflection in the well-sharpened blade, gingerly running her finger along its side, temporarily lost in thought. Then she caught me looking at her and quickly replaced the knife with one of the smaller ones, watching intently as the knife sliced effortlessly through the large Bundt cake. Then it was my turn to watch as she wolfed it down, complimenting me all the while on its texture, its lightness, its taste. She finished it quickly, her entire focus on what she was doing, like a child.

Maybe I should have been more suspicious, or at the very least, more wary, especially after the experience with my last tenant. But likely it was precisely that experience that made me so susceptible to Alison's girlish charm. I wanted, really wanted, to believe she was exactly as she presented herself: a somewhat naive, lovely, sweet young woman.

**Sweet,** I think now.

Sweet is not exactly the word I would use.

**How could anything that sweet be destructive?** she'd asked.

Why wasn't I listening?

"You've obviously never had a problem with your weight," I observed as her fingers pressed down on several errant crumbs scattered across her plate before lifting them to her mouth.

"If anything, I have trouble keeping pounds on," she said. "I was always teased about it. Kids used to say things like, 'Skinny Minny, she grows like a weed.' And I was the last girl in my class to get boobs, such as they are, so I took a lot of flak for that. Now suddenly everybody wants to be thin, only I'm still catching flak. People accuse me of being anorexic. You should hear the things they say."

"People can be very insensitive," I agreed. "Where'd you go to school?"

"Nowhere special. I wasn't a very good student. I dropped out of college in my first year."

"To do what?"

"Let's see. I worked in a bank for a while, sold men's socks, was a hostess in a restaurant, a receptionist in a hair salon. Stuff like that. I never have any trouble finding a job. Do you think I could have some more coffee?"

I poured her a second cup, again adding cream and three heaping teaspoons of sugar. "Would you like to see the cottage?"

Instantly, she was on her feet, downing the coffee in one seamless gulp, wiping her lips with the back of her hand. "Can't wait. I just know it's going to be beautiful." She followed me to the back door, an eager puppy nipping at my heels. "Your notice said six hundred a month, right?"

"Will that be a problem? I require first and last month's rent up front."

"No problem. I intend to start looking for a job as soon as I get settled, and even if I don't find something right away, my grandmother left me some money when she died, so I'm actually in pretty good shape. Financially speaking," she added softly, strawberry-blond hair curling softly around the long oval of her face.

I had hair like that once, I thought, tucking several wayward waves of auburn hair behind one ear. "My last tenant was several months behind in her rent when she took off, that's why I have to ask . . ."

"Oh, I understand completely."

We crossed the small patch of lawn that separated the tiny cottage from the main house. I fished inside my jean pocket for the key to the front door, the heat of her gaze on my back rendering me unusually clumsy, so that the key fell from my hand and bounced on the grass. Alison immediately bent to pick it up, her fingers grazing mine as she returned it to the palm of my hand. I pushed open the cottage door and stood back to let her come inside.

A long sigh escaped her full lips. "It's even more beautiful than I thought it was going to be. It's like . . . magic." Alison danced around the tiny room in small, graceful circles, head arched back, arms outstretched, as if she could somehow capture the magic, draw it to her. She doesn't realize she **is** the magic, I thought, suddenly aware of how much I'd wanted her to like it, how much I wanted her to stay. "I'm so glad you kept the same colors as the main house," she was saying, briefly alighting, like a butterfly, on the small love seat, the large chair, the bentwood rocker in the corner. She admired the rug—mauve and white flowers woven into a pale pink background—and the framed prints on the wall—a group of Degas dancers preening back-stage before a recital, Monet's cathedral at sunset, Mary Cassatt's loving portrait of a mother and her child.

"The other rooms are back here." I opened the dou-ble set of French doors to reveal a tidy arrangement of galley kitchen, bathroom, and bedroom.

"It's perfect. It's absolutely perfect." She bounced up and down on the double bed, running eager palms across the antique white bedspread, before catching her reflection in the mirror above the white wicker dresser and instantly assuming a more ladylike demeanor. "I love everything. It's exactly the way I would have deco-rated it. Exactly."

"I used to live here," I told her, not sure why. I hadn't confided anything of the sort to my last tenant. "My mother lived in the main house. I lived back here."

A little half-smile played nervously with the corners of Alison's lips. "Does this mean we have a deal?"

"You can move in whenever you're ready."

She jumped to her feet. "I'm ready right now. All I have to do is go back to the motel and pack my suitcase. I can be back within the hour."

I nodded, only now becoming aware of the speed at which things had progressed. There was so much I didn't know about her. There were so many things we had yet to discuss. "We probably should talk about a few of the rules . . . ," I sidestepped.

"Rules?"

"No smoking, no loud parties, no roommates."

"No problem," she said eagerly. "I don't smoke, I don't party, I don't know anyone."

I dropped the key into her waiting palm, watched her fingers fold tightly over it.

"Thank you so much." Still clutching the key, she reached into her purse and counted out twelve crisp $100 bills, proudly handing them over. "Printed them fresh this morning," she said with a self-conscious smile.

I tried not to look shocked by the unexpected display of cash. "Would you like to come over for dinner after you get settled?" I heard myself ask, the invitation probably surprising me more than it did her.

"I'd like that very much."

After she was gone, I sat in the living room of the main house, marveling at my actions. I, Terry Painter, supposedly mature adult, who had spent my entire forty years being sensible and organized and anything but impulsive, had just rented out the small cottage behind my house to a virtual stranger, a young woman with no references beyond an ingratiating manner and a goofy smile, with no job and a purse full of cash. What, really, did I know about her? Nothing. Not where she came from. Not what had brought her to Delray. Not how long she was planning to stay. Not even what she'd been doing at the hospital when she saw my notice. Nothing really except her name.

She said her name was Alison Simms.

At the time, of course, I had no reason to doubt her.

# 2

She arrived for dinner at exactly seven o'clock, wearing a pair of black cotton pants and a sleeveless black sweater, with her hair pulled dramatically back and twisted into a long braid, so that she looked like an extended exclamation point. She was carrying a bouquet of freshly cut flowers in one hand and a bottle of red wine in the other. "It's an Italian Amarone, 1997," Alison announced proudly, then rolled her eyes. "Not that I know anything about wine, but the man in the liquor store assured me it was a very good year." She smiled, her lightly glossed lips overtaking the entire bottom half of her face, her mouth opening to reveal an acre of perfect teeth. My own lips immediately curled into a heartfelt smile of their own, although they stopped short of exposing the gentle overbite that not even years of expensive orthodontics had been able to correct completely. My mother had always claimed the overbite was the result of a stubborn childhood habit of sucking on the middle and fourth fingers of my left hand while simultaneously rubbing my nose with the tattered remains of a favorite baby blanket. But since my mother had virtually the same overbite, I'm inclined to believe this aesthetic deficiency is more genetic than willful.

Alison followed me through the living and dining rooms into the kitchen, where I unwrapped the flowers and filled a tall crystal vase with water. "Can I do anything to help?" Eager eyes ferreted into each corner of the room, as if memorizing each detail.

"Just pull up a chair, keep me company." I quickly deposited the flowers in the vase of lukewarm water, sniffing at the small pink roses, the delicate white daisies, the sprays of purple wildflowers. "They're beautiful. Thank you so much."

"My pleasure. Dinner smells wonderful."

"It's nothing fancy," I quickly demurred. "Just chicken. You eat chicken, don't you?"

"I eat everything. Put food in front of me and it's gone within seconds. I'm the world's fastest eater."

I smiled as I recalled the way she'd demolished the piece of cranberry-and-pumpkin cake I'd given her that afternoon. Had it only been a matter of hours ago that we'd met? For some reason, it seemed as if we'd known each other all our lives, that despite the difference in our ages, we'd been friends forever. I had to remind myself how little I actually knew about her. "So, tell me more about yourself," I said casually, searching through the kitchen drawers for a corkscrew.

"Not much to tell." She sank into one of the wicker chairs at the round glass kitchen table, although her posture remained erect, even alert, as if she were afraid of getting too comfortable.

"Where are you from?" I wasn't trying to pry. I was just curious, the way one is usually curious about a new acquaintance. I sensed a certain wariness on her part to talk about herself. Or maybe I didn't sense anything at all. Maybe the small talk we made in my kitchen that night before dinner was nothing more than it appeared to be, two people slowly and cautiously getting to know one another, asking normal questions, not overanalyzing the responses, moving from one topic to the next without any particular plan, no hidden agendas.

At least there were no hidden agendas on my part.

"Chicago," Alison answered.

"Really? I love Chicago. Where exactly?"

"Suburbs," she said vaguely. "How about you? Are you a native Floridian?"

I shook my head. "We moved here from Baltimore when I was fifteen. My father was in the waterproofing business. He thought Florida was the natural place to be, what with all the hurricanes and everything."

Alison's green eyes widened in alarm.

"Don't worry. Hurricane season is over." I laughed, finally locating the corkscrew at the back of the cutlery drawer. "That's the thing about Florida," I mused out loud. "On the surface, everything is so beautiful, so perfect. Paradise. But if you look a little closer, you'll see the deadly alligator lurking just below the water's smooth surface, you'll see the poisonous snake slithering through the emerald green grass, you'll hear the distant hurricane whispering through the leaves."

Alison smiled, the warmth of that smile filling the room, like steam from a kettle. "I could listen to you talk all night."

I waved the compliment aside, using my fingers as a fan, as if trying to protect myself from the heat. Knowing me, I probably blushed.

"Have you actually seen a hurricane?" Alison leaned forward in her chair.

"Several." I struggled to open the bottle of Amarone without breaking the cork in two. It had been a long time since I'd had to open a bottle of wine. I rarely entertained, and I'd never been much of a drinker. All it took was one glass of wine to start my head spinning. "Hurricane Andrew was the worst, of course. That one was something else. Makes you really respect Mother Nature when you witness something like that up close."

"What words would you use to describe it?" she asked, picking up the thread of our earlier game.

"Terrifying," I answered quickly. "Ferocious." I paused, twisting the corkscrew gently to the right, gradually feeling the cork surrender, begin its slow slide up the neck of the dark green bottle. I admit to being suffused with an almost childish sense of pride and accomplishment as I lifted the vanquished cork into the air. "Magnificent."

"I'll get the glasses." Alison was on her feet and in the dining room before I had time to tell her where the glasses were.

"They're in the cabinet," I called after her unnecessarily. It was almost as if she already knew where to look.

"Found them." She returned with two long-stemmed crystal goblets, holding out first one, then the other, as I filled each about a quarter of the way. "They're beautiful. Everything you have is so beautiful."

"Cheers," I said, clicking my glass gently against hers, marveling at the deep red of the wine.

"What are we drinking to?"

"Good health," the nurse in me responded immediately.

"And good friends," she added shyly.

"To new friends," I amended slightly, lifting my glass to my mouth, the rich aroma filling my head before I'd tasted a single drop.

"New beginnings," Alison whispered, her face disappearing into the roundness of the glass as she took a long, slow sip of the wine. "Mmm, this is yummy. What do you think?"

I quickly mulled over the adjectives experts generally employed when describing fine wine—**full-bodied, buttery, fruity,** occasionally even **whimsical.** Never **yummy.** What did they know? I thought, rolling the wine around in my mouth, the way I'd seen men do in fancy restaurants, feeling the flavor burst against my tongue. **"Yummy** is the perfect word," I agreed after swallowing. "Perfectly yummy."

Again the grin that transformed her face, engulfing her cheeks and swallowing her nose, so that it looked as if her eyes themselves were smiling. She took another long sip, then another. I followed her lead, and before long, it was time to refill our glasses. This time, I filled them almost halfway.

"So, what brought you from Chicago to Delray?" I asked.

"I was looking for a change." She might have stopped had it not been for the obvious questions on my face. "I don't know exactly." She stared absently at the rows of ladies' head vases on the shelves. "I guess I didn't particularly feel like going through another Chicago winter, and I had this friend who'd moved to Delray a few years back. I thought I could come down here and look her up."

"Did you?"

"Did I what?"

"Look her up."

Alison looked confused, as if unsure exactly what her answer should be.

That's the problem with lying.

A good liar is always one step ahead. She's always anticipating, answering one question with an ear to the next. She's on constant alert, always ready with a facile reply.

Of course, all a bad liar needs is an easy mark.

"I tried finding her," Alison said after a pause that lasted perhaps a beat too long. "That's what I was doing at the hospital when I saw your notice." The words flowed easier now. "She'd written that she was working at this private hospital called Mission Care in Delray, so I figured I'd surprise her, maybe take her to lunch, see if she was looking for a roommate. But personnel said she left a long time ago." Alison shrugged. Beautifully carved shoulders lifted up, then down. "Luckily I saw your notice."

"What's your friend's name? If she's a nurse, maybe I can find out where she went."

"She's not a nurse," Alison said quickly. "She was a secretary or something."

"What's her name?" I repeated. "I can ask around when I get to work tomorrow, see if anyone knows where she went."

"Don't bother." Alison ran a distracted finger along the rim of her wineglass. The glass made a slight purring sound, as if responding to a lover's gentle caress. "We weren't that close."

"And yet you left your home and traveled halfway across the country . . ."

Alison shrugged. "Her name is Rita Bishop. You know her?"

"Doesn't sound familiar."

She took a deep breath. Her shoulders relaxed. "I never liked the name Rita. Do you like it?"

"It's not one of my favorites," I admitted, allowing myself to be steered gently off-course.

"What **are** your favorites?"

"I don't think I ever really thought about it."

"I like Kelly," Alison said. "And Samantha. I think if I ever have a daughter, I'll name her one of those. And Joseph if I have a boy. Or maybe Max."

"You have it all planned out."

She stared thoughtfully into her goblet for several long seconds before taking another sip. "Do you have any children?" The question echoed against the side of the glass, barely escaped into the surrounding air.

"No. I'm afraid I never married."

"You don't have to get married to have babies."

"Maybe not today," I agreed. "But when I was growing up in Baltimore, trust me, it wasn't done." I opened the oven door, felt a warm rush of fragrant steam in my face. "Anyway, I hope you're hungry, because this chicken is ready to be devoured."

"Let's eat," Alison said with a wide smile.


ALISON WAS RIGHT. She was the fastest eater I'd ever seen. Within minutes, everything on her plate—roast chicken, mashed potatoes, pureed carrots, multiple stalks of asparagus—had disappeared. I'd barely swallowed my first forkful of chicken and she was already helping herself to seconds.

"This is so delicious. You are the best cook ever," she pronounced, her mouth full.

"I'm glad you like everything."

"Too bad I didn't bring another bottle of wine." Alison gave one of her rare frowns, glancing past the tapered white candles in the middle of the dining room table toward the now empty bottle of Amarone.

"Good thing you didn't. My shift starts at six in the morning. I'm supposed to be able to stand up straight."

"What made you decide to be a nurse?" Alison finished off what little wine clung to the sides of her glass.

"I lost my father and a favorite aunt to cancer before either reached fifty," I explained, trying not to see their ravaged faces in the bottom of my glass. "I felt so helpless, and I didn't like that, so I decided to go into medicine. My mother didn't have the money to send me to medical school, and I didn't have the grades for a full scholarship, so being a doctor was out. I settled for the next best thing. And I love it."

"Even though it's exhausting, exacting, and infuriating?" Alison laughed as she gently tossed my earlier words back at me.

"Even though," I repeated. "And being a nurse meant I was able to care for my mother after her stroke, that I was able to keep her at home, that she died in her own bed, not in some sterile hospital room."

"Is that why you never got married?" Alison asked.

"Because you were busy taking care of your mother?"

"No, I can't really blame her for that. Although I guess I can try," I said with a laugh. "I think I just assumed there was all this time, that eventually I'd meet someone, fall in love, get married, have a couple of beautiful babies, live happily ever after. Standard fantasy 101. It just didn't work out that way."

"There was never anyone special?"

"Not special enough, I guess."

"Well, time's not up yet. You never know . . ."

"I'm forty," I reminded her. "I know. So, what about you? No special someone in Chicago, waiting for you to come home?"

She shook her head. "No, not really." She volunteered nothing further.

"How did your parents feel about you moving so far away?"

Alison stopped eating, lay her fork neatly across her plate. "These dishes are really neat. I like the pattern. It's pretty, but it doesn't interfere with the food, you know what I mean?"

Strangely enough, I did. "Your parents don't know where you are, do they?" I asked tentatively, not wanting to trespass beyond invisible boundaries, but eager to know more.

"I'll call them after I find a job," she said, confirming my suspicions.

"Won't they be worried?"

"I doubt it." She paused, flipped her braid from one

shoulder to the other. "As you've probably figured out, we weren't on the best of terms." She paused, her eyes darting back and forth, as if reading from an invisible text. "Unfortunately, I had this older brother who was absolutely perfect. Star forward of the basketball team in high school, champion swimmer in college, graduated summa cum laude from Brown. And here I was, this tall, skinny kid who was constantly tripping over her big, clumsy feet. No way I could ever measure up, so at some point, I stopped trying. I turned into this major brat, insisted on doing my own thing, positive I had all the answers. You know the type."

"Typical teenager, by the sound of it."

Large green eyes radiated gratitude. "Thank you, but I don't think **typical** is the word they would use."

"And what word would they use?"

Sad grin widened into a smile as her eyes scanned the ceiling for proper adjectives. "Impossible," she said after a brief pause. "Incorrigible. In trouble all the time," she continued with a laugh, the words running together as one. "They were always kicking me out of the house. I left for good the day I turned eighteen."

"And did what?"

"Got married."

"You got married when you were eighteen?"

"What can I say?" She shrugged. "Standard fantasy 101."

I nodded understanding and reached for the bread basket, accidentally knocking my fork into my lap, where it deposited a large gob of gravy on my white pants before bouncing to the floor. Alison immediately rescued the fork and ran to the kitchen for some soda water, while I scrambled to my feet, instantly feeling the effect of so many glasses of wine.

Slowly, cautiously, I walked into the living room, trying to remember the last time a few glasses of wine had left me so inebriated. I approached the window and leaned my forehead against the cool glass.

That's when I saw him.

He was standing across the street, as still as the majestic royal palm he was leaning against, and even though it was too dark to make out who it was, I knew from his posture that he was staring at the house. I squinted into the darkness, tried to gather the light from the street-lamps into a spotlight and shine it on his face. But the effect was something less than I bargained for, and the man almost disappeared in the resultant blur. "Not a good idea," I muttered, deciding to confront the man directly, ask him what he was doing standing there in the dark, staring at my house.

I stumbled toward the front door, pulled it open. "You there," I called out, pointing an accusing finger at the night.

There was no one there.

I craned my neck, peered into the stubborn darkness, twisted my head from left to right, followed the road to the corner and back. I strained my ears for the sound of footsteps in hasty retreat, heard nothing.

In the time it had taken for me to get from the window to the door, the man had vanished. If he'd been there at all, I thought, recalling the apparition I thought I'd seen earlier.

"What are you doing?" Alison asked, coming up behind me.

I felt her breath on the back of my neck. "Just needed some fresh air."

"Are you okay?"

"A bit too okay. Did you put something in my drink?" I joked as Alison closed the front door, then led me back into the living room, where she sat me down on one of the Queen Anne chairs and began dabbing at the gravy stain on my pant leg with a wet cloth until I felt the dampness clear to my skin.

I reached down, stilled her hand. It lingered on my thigh. "Stain's gone."

She was instantly on her feet. "Sorry. There I go again, everything in extremes, that's the only way I seem to operate. Sorry."

"Why are you apologizing?" I asked, genuinely curious. "You didn't do anything wrong."

"I didn't? That's a relief." She laughed, sank down into the other chair, her face flushed.

"What happened with your marriage?" I asked gently, fighting a gnawing unease in my gut, a sensation that was undoubtedly trying to warn me that Alison Simms might not be the charmingly uncomplicated young woman she'd first appeared to be when I'd handed over the keys to the cottage at the back of my house.

"What usually happens when you get married at eighteen," she said simply, lowering her gaze to mine, no trace of a smile. "It didn't work out."

"I'm sorry."

"Me too. We tried. We really did. We split up and got back together a whole bunch of times, even after our divorce was final." She impatiently pushed the stray hairs away from her forehead. "Sometimes it's hard to stay away from someone, even when you know they're all wrong for you."

"And that's why you came to Florida?"

"Maybe," she acknowledged, then flashed the glorious smile that obliterated all traces of sadness or self-doubt. "What's for dessert?"

# 3

"I was fifteen when I lost my virginity," Alison was saying, pouring herself a second small glass of Baileys Irish Cream. We were sitting on the living room floor, our backs against the furniture, our legs splayed out carelessly in front of us, like two abandoned rag dolls. Alison had insisted on cleaning up after dinner, washing and drying the dishes by hand before returning everything to its proper place while I sat at the kitchen table and watched, marveling at the deftness of her touch, the speed with which she worked, the instinctive way she seemed to know where everything belonged, almost as if she'd been in the house before. She'd found the Baileys at the back of the dining room cabinet when she was returning the wineglasses to their shelf. I'd forgotten I even had it.

I don't know why we chose the floor over the sofa. Probably Alison simply plopped herself down and I followed suit. The same way with the Baileys. I'd certainly had no intention of having any more to drink, but suddenly the delicately sculpted liqueur glass was in my hand, and Alison was pouring and I was drinking, and there you have it. I suppose I could have said no, but the truth is I was having too good a time. You have to remember that my days were normally spent in the company of people who were old, ill, or in some form of acute distress. Alison was so young, so vibrant, so alive. She infused me with a sense of such profound well-being that whatever niggling doubts or petty reservations I may have had flew out the window, along with my common sense. Simply put, I was reluctant to see her leave, and if drinking a second glass of Baileys would prolong the evening, then a second glass of Baileys it would be. I eagerly proffered my glass for more. She promptly filled it. "I probably shouldn't have told you that," she said. "You'll think I'm a slut."

It took me a minute to realize that she was referring to her lost virginity. "Of course I don't think you're a slut," I said adamantly, as relief washed across Alison's face, like a paintbrush, almost as if she'd been waiting for me to exonerate her, to forgive her the sins of her sometimes errant past. "Besides, I've got you beat," I offered, trying to make her feel better, to prove I was hardly one to sit in judgment.

"What do you mean?" She leaned forward, lowered

her glass to the carpet. It disappeared inside the pink petal of a woven flower.

"I was only fourteen when I lost mine," I whispered guiltily, as if my mother might still be listening from the upstairs bedroom.

"Get out. I don't believe you."

"It's true." I found myself eager to convince her, to show her that she wasn't the only one with a past, with skeletons in her closet, however small and insubstantial they might be. Maybe I even wanted to shock her, just a little, to prove to her—and to myself—that I was more than I appeared at first glance, that underneath my middle-aged exterior beat the heart of a wild child.

Or maybe I was just drunk.

"His name was Roger Stillman," I continued without prodding, conjuring up the image of the lanky young man with light brown hair and large hazel eyes who'd seduced me with ridiculous ease back when I was in the ninth grade. "He was two grades ahead of me at school, so of course I was monstrously flattered that he even talked to me. He asked me to the movies, and I lied to my parents about where I was going, because my mother had decreed I was too young to date. So I said I was going to a friend's house to study for a test, and instead I met Roger at the movie theater. I remember it was one of the James Bond movies— don't ask me which one—and I was very excited because I'd never seen a James Bond movie before. Not that I saw much of that one either," I recalled, remembering Roger's tobacco-scented breath on my neck as I'd tried to follow the movie's convoluted plot, his lips grazing the side of my ear as I'd strained to make sense of all the double entendres, his hand sliding down my shoulder to the tops of my breasts as James coaxed yet another willing female into his bed. "We left before the movie finished. Roger had a car." I shrugged, as if that said it all.

"Whatever happened to Roger?"

"He dumped me. No surprises there."

Alison's face registered her displeasure. "Were you heartbroken?"

"Devastated, as only a fourteen-year-old girl can be. Especially after he bragged about his conquest to the entire school."

"He didn't!"

I laughed at Alison's spontaneous outburst of indignation. "He did. Roger, I'm afraid, was a rat of the first order."

"And whatever happened to the rat?"

"I have no idea. We moved to Florida the next year, and I never saw him again." I shook my head, watched the room spin. "God, I haven't thought about any of that in so long. That's one of the amazing things about being young."

"What is?"

"You think you'll never get over something, and then, the next minute, you've forgotten all about it."

Alison smiled, twisted her head across the top of her

spine, stretching her swanlike neck until the muscles groaned and released.

"Everything has such urgency. Everything is so important. And you think you have so much time," I said, almost forgetting I was speaking out loud as I watched her, mesmerized by the motion.

"Anyone interesting on the horizon?" Alison rolled her head from side to side.

"Not really. Well, there's this man," I confided, although I'd had no intention of doing so until I heard the words leave my mouth. "Josh Wylie. His mother is a patient at the hospital."

Alison's head returned to the middle of her shoulders. She said nothing, simply sat and waited for me to continue.

"That's it," I said. "He comes up once a week from Miami to see her. We've only spoken a few times. But he seems very nice, and . . ."

"And you wouldn't mind getting to know him," Alison said, finishing my sentence for me.

I nodded, deciding that was a mistake when the room continued bouncing around me like a rubber ball. Reluctantly, I struggled to my feet. "I think I'm going to have to call it a night."

Alison was immediately at my side, her hand warm on my arm. She seemed steady, as if the alcohol hadn't affected her at all. "Are you all right?"

"Fine," I said, though I wasn't. The floor kept shifting, and I had to balance against the side of the sofa to keep from falling over. I made an exaggerated show of checking my watch, but the numbers danced randomly across the dial, and I couldn't tell the small hand from the large. "It's late," I said anyway, "and I have to be up very early."

"I hope I didn't overstay my welcome."

"You didn't."

"You're sure?"

"Quite sure. I had a really nice evening." I suddenly had the strange sensation that she was about to kiss me good-night. "We'll do it again soon," I said, lowering my head and leading Alison through the living and dining rooms to the kitchen, where I promptly walked into the table and all but fell into her arms.

"You're sure you're okay?" she asked as I struggled to recapture my balance, if not my dignity. "Maybe I should stay and make sure you get into bed all right."

"I'm fine. Really. I'm fine," I repeated before she could ask again.

Alison was half out the door when she stopped suddenly, reached into the left pocket of her black pants, and spun around. The motion left me reeling. "I just remembered—I found this." She held out her hand.

Even with my head spinning and my focus blurred, I recognized the tiny gold heart at the center of the slender golden thread in Alison's open hand. "Where did you get this?" I reached for it, watching it unravel. The delicate necklace hung from my fingers like a forgotten strand of tinsel on a discarded Christmas tree.

"I found it under my bed," Alison said, unconsciously assuming ownership of the contents of the cottage.

"Why were you looking under the bed?"

Surprisingly, Alison blushed bright red. She shuffled uneasily from one foot to the other, the first time I'd seen her look truly uncomfortable in her own skin. When she finally answered me, I thought I must have misunderstood.

"What did you say?"

"Looking for bogeymen," she repeated sheepishly, lifting her eyes to mine with obvious reluctance.

"Bogeymen?"

"I know it's ridiculous. But I can't help myself. I've been doing it ever since I was a little girl and my brother convinced me there was a monster hiding underneath my bed who was going to eat me as soon as I fell asleep."

"You check underneath the bed for bogeymen?" I repeated, thoroughly, if inexplicably, charmed by the notion.

"I check the closets too. Just in case."

"Do you ever find anyone?"

"Not so far." She laughed, held out the necklace for me to take. "Here. Before I forget and take it home with me."

"It's not mine." I took a step back, almost tripping over my own feet, and watching the room rotate ninety degrees. Sixty-five ladies' head vases tilted on their shelves. "It belonged to Erica Hollander, my last tenant."

"The one who still owes you several months rent?"

"The one and only."

"Then I'd say it belongs to you now." Again Alison tried to hand over the necklace.

"You keep it." I wanted nothing more to do with Erica Hollander.

"Oh, I couldn't," Alison said, but her fist was already closing around it.

"Finders, keepers. Come on, take it. It's very . . . you."

Alison required no further coaxing. "It is, isn't it?" She laughed, wrapping the thin chain around her neck in one fluid gesture, securing the tiny clasp with ease. "How does it look?"

"Like it belongs there."

Alison patted the heart at her throat, strained to see her reflection in the darkness of the kitchen window. "I love it."

"Wear it in good health."

"You don't think she'll come back for it, do you?"

It was my turn to laugh. "Just let her try. Anyway, it's late. I have to get some sleep."

"Good night." Alison leaned forward, kissed my cheek. Her hair smelled of strawberries, her skin of baby powder. Like a newborn baby, I thought with a smile. "Thanks again," she said. "For everything."

"My pleasure." I opened the back door and took a quick glance around.

There was no one waiting, no one watching.

I breathed a sigh of relief and waited until Alison was

safely inside the cottage before closing the kitchen door. My hand brushed against the spot on my cheek where Alison's lips had grazed, as I pictured her walking through the small living area to the bedroom at the back. In my mind's eye, I watched her kneel to look under the bed, then check the closet for any stray monsters who might be lurking. I thought absently of the man I'd seen standing in front of the house. Had there been anyone there? And had he been watching me—or Alison?

Such a sweet girl, I remember thinking. So childlike. So innocent.

Not so innocent, I reminded myself as I painstakingly made my way up the stairs to my bedroom. A teenage hellion. Married at eighteen. Divorced soon after. Not to mention she could hold her liquor with the best of them.

I vaguely remember getting undressed and into my nightgown. Actually, I remember this only because I put the nightgown on backward the first time and had to take it off and put it on again. I don't remember washing my face or brushing my teeth, although I'm sure I did. I **do** remember the way my bare toes sank into the ivory broadloom as I walked toward my bed, as if I were wading through thick clumps of mud. I remember the heaviness in my thighs, as if my legs had been anchored to the floor. The queen-size bed that sat in the middle of the room seemed miles away. It took forever to reach it. A colossal effort was required for my arms to pull down the bulky white comforter. I remember watching it billow around me like a collapsing parachute as I climbed underneath the covers. I remember the pillow reaching up to catch my head before it fell.

I expected to fall asleep immediately. That's the way it always is in the movies. People drink too much, they get dizzy and disoriented, they pass out. Sometimes they get sick first. But I didn't get sick and I didn't pass out. I just lay there, my head spinning in the darkness, knowing I had to get up in a matter of hours, desperate for a sleep that stubbornly refused to come. I flipped from my left side to my right, tried lying on my back, and even my stomach, before I gave up and returned to my original position. I brought my knees to my chest, threw one leg atop the other, twisted my body into shapes that would have made a contortionist proud. Nothing worked. I thought of taking a sleeping pill and was almost half out of bed before I remembered it was a mistake to mix pills and alcohol. In any event, it was too late for sedatives. By the time they took effect, my alarm clock would be shaking me awake, and I'd spend most of the next day in a dreary fog, like the worst kind of rainy day.

I thought of reading, but I'd been struggling with the book on my night table for weeks and still hadn't made it past the fourth chapter. Besides, my brain was as tired as my eyes, and trying to digest anything at this hour would be an exercise in frustration and futility. No, I decided, I had no choice but to lie there in bed and wait patiently for sleep to come.

It didn't.

Half an hour later, I was still waiting. I took several long, deep breaths and improvised a half dozen yoga exercises I'd seen illustrated in a magazine, although I had no idea if I was doing them correctly. The hospital offered yoga classes, but I'd never quite gotten around to signing up. Just as I'd never quite gotten around to trying Pilates or transcendental meditation, or sending away for the AB-DOer I saw regularly advertised on TV. I made a silent vow to do all those things first thing in the morning, if only I could fall asleep right now.

No deal.

I thought of turning on the television across from my bed—undoubtedly there was a rerun of **Law & Order** on somewhere, but decided against it, choosing to replay Alison's visit instead. What on earth had possessed me to tell her the things I had, information I'd never shared with anyone before? Roger Stillman, for God's sake! Where had that come from? I hadn't even thought of him since I'd left Baltimore.

And what had she really told me?

That she'd lost her virginity at fifteen.

What else?

Not much, I realized. Alison may have opened memory's floodgates, but she'd remained resolutely outside them. No, I was the one who'd rushed eagerly inside, throwing caution and good sense to the wind. That was one of the more interesting things about Alison, I decided, as a low buzz settled behind my ears. She only

**seemed** to be confiding in you. What she was really doing was getting **you** to confide in **her**.

That's what I was thinking when I finally fell asleep. I don't remember drifting off. I **do** remember dreaming. Nothing substantial or particularly meaningful. Silly little vignettes: Roger Stillman imitating James Bond in the backseat of his car; Josh Wylie's mother smiling at me from her hospital bed, asking me to put the bouquet of yellow and orange roses her son had brought with him from Miami into a vase; my mother warning me I hadn't set my alarm clock.

It was this realization that I hadn't, in fact, remembered to set my alarm that woke me up at two minutes past four in the morning, sent me stretching toward the night table at the side of my bed. My hands reached out in the semidarkness, my eyes opening only with the greatest reluctance as my fingers searched for the clock radio.

It was at that moment that I saw the tall figure at the foot of my bed.

At first I thought it must be some sort of apparition, a trick my wine-saturated brain was playing on my senses, perhaps a dream that had failed to disperse upon waking, a haunting mixture of moonlight and shadows. It was only when the figure moved that I understood it was real.

And I screamed.

The scream sliced through the darkness like a blade through flesh, scraping at the surrounding air, leaving it tattered and bleeding. That this insane, inhuman sound could emanate from my body scared me almost as much as the figure moving slowly toward me, and I screamed again.

"I'm so sorry," a voice was whimpering. "I'm so sorry."

I'm not sure exactly when I realized the stranger in my room was Alison, whether it was the sound of her voice or the glint of the small gold heart at her throat. She was holding her head, as if she'd been struck, and swaying from side to side, as if she were a tree being buffeted by the wind. "I'm so sorry," she kept repeating. "I'm so sorry."

"What are you doing here?" I finally managed to get out, swallowing another scream that was rising in my throat, and stretching toward the lamp at the side of my bed.

"No!" she cried. "Please don't turn it on."

I froze, not sure what to do next. "What are you doing here?"

"I'm so sorry. I didn't mean to wake you up."

"What are you doing here?" I repeated over the loud pounding of my heart.

"My head . . ." She started pulling at her hair as if trying to pull it out by the roots. "I'm having a migraine."

I climbed out of bed, took several tentative steps toward her. "A migraine?"

"I guess all that red wine must have triggered something—" She stopped, as if unable to continue.

I reached her side, put my arm around her, lowered her to the side of my bed. She was wearing a long, white cotton nightgown not unlike my own, and her hair hung loose and free around a face wet with tears. "How did you get in the house?" I asked.

"The door wasn't locked."

"That's impossible. I always lock it." Although I'd been pretty woozy, I reminded myself. It was possible I'd forgotten to lock the door, just as I'd forgotten to set the alarm clock.

"It was open. I knocked first. You didn't answer. That's when I tried the door. I was hoping I could find something in your medicine cabinet without waking you up. I'm so sorry."

I glanced toward the bathroom. "The strongest thing I have is extra-strength Tylenol."

Alison nodded, as if to say anything was better than nothing.

I left her sitting on the edge of my bed while I ran into the bathroom and ferreted through the mostly useless items on the shelves of the medicine cabinet until I found the small bottle of pills. I shook four into the palm of my hand, filled a glass full of water, and returned with them to my bedroom.

"Take these," I instructed. "I'll try to get you something stronger in the morning."

"I'll be dead by morning," she said, and tried to laugh. But the laugh detoured into a moan as she swallowed the pills and buried her head against my shoulder, trying to block out what little light there was in the room.

"That'll teach both of us," I heard myself say in my mother's voice as I stroked her arm, rocked her gently back and forth, like a baby. "You'll sleep here tonight."

Alison offered no resistance as I led her around the side of the bed, pulled the covers around her. "What about you?" she asked, her eyes closed, the question an obvious afterthought.

"I'll sleep in the other room," I said.

But already Alison had pulled the comforter up over her head, and the only signs I had that she was there were a few strands of strawberry-blond hair that curled over the top of my pillow like a question mark.

# 4

Alison was still sleeping when I left the house the next morning.

I thought of waking her up, ushering her back to her own bed, but she looked so peaceful lying there, so vulnerable, her soft blush of strawberry-blond hair in marked contrast to her skin's still ghostly pallor, that I hated to disturb her. My experience with migraine sufferers was that, like most drunks, they needed twenty-four hours to sleep it off. I did the math, decided there was a good chance Alison would still be sleeping when I arrived back home at four o'clock that afternoon. What was the point in waking her?

Looking back, this was undoubtedly a mistake, although not my first mistake where Alison was concerned, and certainly not my last. No, it was only one of many errors in judgment I made about the girl who called herself Alison Simms. But hindsight is easy. Of course it was stupid to allow a virtual stranger to stay unattended in my house. Of course I was asking for trouble. All I can say in my defense is that it didn't feel that way at the time. At barely 6 A.M., with maybe a total of four hours of sleep, leaving Alison alone in the house that morning felt natural and right. What was there to worry about after all? That she'd abscond with my ancient nineteen-inch TV? That she'd commandeer a wheelbarrow to cart away my mother's collection of china head vases, perhaps hold a garage sale on my front lawn? That I'd come back to find the house and cottage burned to the ground?

Maybe I should have been more careful, more circumspect, less trusting.

But I wasn't.

Besides, what is it they say about letting sleeping dogs lie?

Anyway, I left Alison sleeping in my bed, like Goldilocks, I remember thinking, chuckling as I tiptoed down the stairs in my clunky white nurse's shoes, opening and closing the front door as silently as possible. My car, a five-year-old, black Nissan, was parked in the driveway beside the house. I cast a desultory glance down the empty street, hearing the faint hum of traffic several blocks away. The city was waking up, I thought, wishing I could trade my polyester white uniform for my white cotton nightgown and crawl back into bed. Luckily, I wasn't as tired as I'd feared I might be. In fact, I was feeling surprisingly well.

I backed the car onto the street, opening the windows to let in the cool morning air. November is a lovely time of year in South Florida. The temperature usually stays on the comfortable side of eighty; the oppressive humidity of the summer months is pretty much gone; the threat of extreme weather is over. Instead, the sky provides a continually shifting combination of sun and clouds, along with the occasional burst of welcome rain. And we get more than our fair share of absolutely flawless afternoons, days when the sun sits high in a borderless panorama of shiny Kodacolor blue. Today looked as if it might be that kind of day. Maybe when I got home, I'd see if Alison was feeling well enough to go for a walk on the beach. There's nothing like the ocean to heal the spirit and calm the troubled soul. Maybe it could work its magic on a migraine headache, I thought, glancing up at my bedroom window.

For a minute, I thought I saw the curtains move, and I hit the brake, inched my face closer to the glass of the car's front window. But on closer inspection, it appeared I'd been mistaken, that it was only the outside shadows of nearby trees that were dancing against my bedroom window, creating the illusion of movement from inside the house. I sat watching the window for several seconds, listening to the whispering of the palm fronds in the breeze. The curtains at my bedroom window hung undisturbed.

My foot transferred from brake to gas pedal, and I proceeded slowly for several blocks along Seventh Avenue until I reached Atlantic, where I turned left. The normally congested main thoroughfare of Delray is largely empty at this hour of the morning, one of the few perks of having to be at work so early, and I had an unencumbered view of the many smart shops, galleries, and restaurants that had redefined the city in recent years. To the surprise of many, myself included, Delray had become something of a "hot spot," a destination as opposed to a drive-through. I loved the unexpected changes, the aura of excitement, even if I was rarely part of it. Alison, I knew instinctively, would love it here.

I passed the tennis center on the north side of Atlantic, where every spring they hold the Citrix Open, past the Old School Square on the northwest corner of Atlantic and Swinton, continued on past the South County Courthouse and the Delray Beach Fire Station on my left. I took the underpass at I-95 to Jog Road, then headed south. Five minutes later I was at the hospital.

Mission Care is a small, private health facility housed in a five-story building, painted bubblegum pink, that specializes in chronic care. The majority of patients are elderly and in considerable distress, and as a result, they're often angry and upset. Who can blame them? They know they aren't going to get better, that they're never going home, that this is, in fact, their final resting place. Some have been here for years, lying in their narrow beds, blank eyes staring at blank ceilings, waiting for the nurse to bathe them or adjust their position, longing for visitors who rarely come, silently praying for death while stubbornly clinging to life.

It must be so depressing, people are always saying to me, to be constantly surrounded by the sick and the dying. And sometimes, I admit, it is. It's never easy to watch people suffer, to comfort a young woman stricken by MS in the prime of her life, to tend to a comatose child who will never wake up, to try calming an old man with Alzheimer's as he shouts obscenities at the son he no longer remembers.

And yet, some moments make it all worthwhile. Moments when the most banal act of kindness is rewarded by a smile so blinding it brings tears to your eyes, or by a whispered thank-you so sincere it makes you go weak at the knees. This is why I became a nurse, I understand in moments like these, and if that makes me a hopeless romantic or a silly sentimentalist, so be it.

Probably it is this quality that makes me such an easy target. I suffer from Anne Frank's delusion that people are basically good at heart.

I parked my car in the staff parking lot at the front of the hospital and made my way through the lobby, past the gift shop and pharmacy that wouldn't be open for another few hours, to the coffee shop that was already busy. I waited in line for a cup of tasteless black coffee and a fat-free, cranberry-studded muffin. I thought of

Alison, how much she loved cranberries. I had a recipe at the back of one of my drawers for banana-cranberry muffins. I decided to make a batch when I got home.

The administration offices were closed till nine, and I made a mental note to stop by later to inquire about Alison's friend, Rita Bishop. Even though Alison had told me not to bother, I thought it might be worth a try. Rita might have left a forwarding address. One of the secretaries might know where she'd gone.

I'd already finished my coffee and was halfway through my muffin when the doors of the excruciatingly slow-moving elevator finally opened onto the fourth floor. The nurses' station was already buzzing. "What's up?" I asked Margot King, a heavyset woman with copper-orange hair and blue contact lenses. Margot had been a nurse at Mission Care for more than ten years, and during that decade the color of her eyes had changed almost as often as the color of her hair. The only constant was the color of her uniform, which was a crisp Alpine white, and the color of her skin, which was a wondrous ebony black.

"Rape victim," Margot said, her voice a whisper.

"A rape victim? Why'd they bring her here?"

"The rape was three months ago. Guy beat her with a baseball bat, left her for dead. She's been in a coma ever since. Doesn't look like she's going home anytime soon. Her family decided to bring her here when Delray Medical Center needed the bed."

"How old?" I asked, bracing myself.

"Nineteen."

I sighed, my shoulders collapsing, as if someone had jumped on them from a great height. "Any more pleasant surprises?"

"Same old, same old. Mrs. Wylie's been asking for you."

"Already?"

"Since five o'clock. 'Where's my Terry? Where's my Terry?' " Margot repeated in Myra Wylie's frail voice.

"I'll look in on her." I started down the hall, stopped. "Is Caroline here yet?"

"Not till eleven."

"She gets migraines, doesn't she?"

"Oh, yeah. She suffers real bad from those damn things."

"When she gets in, will you tell her I need to see her?"

"Problems?"

"A friend," I said, continuing down the peach-colored hall toward Myra Wylie's room.

I slowly pushed open the door and peeked my head through, in case the frail, eighty-seven-year-old woman fighting both chronic leukemia and congenital heart disease might have drifted back to sleep.

"Terry!" Myra Wylie's voice wafted up from the center of her hospital bed, quivering into the air like smoke from a cigarette. "There's my Terry."

I approached the bed, patted the bony hand beneath the sterile white sheets, smiled at the graying face with the watery blue eyes. "How are you today, Myra?"

"Wonderful," she said, the same thing she said every time I asked, and I laughed. She laughed too, although the sound was weak and segued quickly into a cough.

Still, in those few seconds, I saw traces of the beautiful, vibrant woman Myra Wylie had been before her body began its slow, insidious betrayal. I could also make out the face of her son Josh in the sculpted lines of her cheekbones, the soft bow of her lips. Josh Wylie would be a very handsome old man, I couldn't help but think as I pulled up a chair and sat down beside his mother. "I understand you've been asking for me."

"I was thinking maybe we could do something different with my hair next time we wash it."

I smoothed the fine gray hair away from her face with my fingers. "What style do you think you'd like?"

"I don't know. Something more with it."

"With it?"

"Maybe a bob."

"A bob?" I fluffed out the fragile wisps of hair that framed Myra's face. Her skin was sinking, the heavy lines around her eyes and mouth becoming folds, caving in around her. Slowly, the living tissue was morphing into a death mask. How much longer did she have? "A bob," I repeated. "Sure. Why not?"

Myra smiled. "That cute little nurse with all the freckles was in last night. The young one, what's her name?"

"Sally?"

"Yes, Sally. She brought me my medicine and we got

to talking, and she asked me how old I was. You should have seen the look on her face when I told her I'm seventy-seven."

I searched Myra's eyes for signs she was teasing, saw none. "Myra," I told her gently. "You're not seventy-seven."

"I'm not?"

"You're **eighty**-seven."

"Eighty-seven?" There was a long pause as Myra's trembling hand reached for her heart. "That's a shock!"

I laughed, stroked her shoulder.

"Are you sure?"

"That's what it says on your chart. But we can check with your son next time he visits."

"I think that's a good idea." Myra's eyes fluttered to a close, her voice growing faint. "Because I think there has to be some mistake."

"We'll ask Josh on Friday." I eased out of my chair and walked to the door. When I turned back to check on her, she was sound asleep.

The rest of the morning was uneventful. I tended to patients, fed them their breakfast and lunch, changed soiled sheets, helped those who could still walk to the bathroom. I looked in on Sheena O'Connor, the nineteen-year-old rape victim who'd been transferred from Delray Medical Center, filling the room with idle chatter as I surveyed the scars and bruises that made a mockery of her once innocent face, but if she heard me, she gave no sign.

Normally, I eat lunch in the hospital cafeteria—the food is surprisingly good and you can't beat the price—but today I was anxious to check on Alison. I thought of phoning, but I didn't want to wake her in case she was still sleeping, and besides, I didn't think she'd answer my phone. So armed with two Imitrex tablets I'd bought from Caroline—"I'd give them to you, but they're so damned expensive!"—and the names of several doctors in the area I thought Alison should contact, I used my lunch hour to drive home and see how she was doing.

Pulling into my driveway, I saw a young man with a baseball cap pulled low on his forehead lurking behind a corner tree, in almost the same spot where I'd seen the man yesterday, but by the time I parked my car and came back to look, he was gone. I looked down the street in time to see him disappear around the corner and thought momentarily of going after him. Luckily I was distracted by the sound of barking dogs, and I turned back toward my house. Bettye McCoy was standing beside a neighbor's prized rosebush, pretending not to notice that one of her dogs was peeing all over it. I thought of asking her if she'd noticed any suspicious strangers in the area, but decided against it. Bettye McCoy had barely acknowledged my existence ever since I'd chased one of her precious Bichons out of my yard with a broomstick.

I slipped my shoes off at the front door, silently cursing the slight creaking noise the door made as I closed it, determining to oil it when I got home at the end of my shift. The house was eerily quiet except for the gentle hum of the air conditioner. A quick look around told me everything was in its correct place. Nothing had been disturbed.

I tiptoed up the stairs to my bedroom, coughed quietly so as not to scare Alison if she was awake, then opened the door.

The curtains were still pulled, so it took me a few seconds to determine that the room was empty and the bed neatly made. Goldilocks was no longer sleeping in my bed. "Alison?" I called out, checking the bathroom and the second bedroom before heading back downstairs. "Alison?" She was gone.

"Alison?" I called out again at the door to her cottage, knocking gently. No one answered. I tried peering in the windows, but I saw nothing. Nor could I hear anyone moving around inside. Was it possible Alison had felt well enough to go out? Or was she lying on her bathroom floor, her head pressed against the cold tiles for relief, too sick and weak to respond to my knock? Despite common sense telling me I was overreacting, I returned to the front door and knocked more forcefully. "Alison," I called loudly. "Alison, it's Terry. Are you all right?"

I waited only thirty more seconds before letting myself in. "Alison?" I called again once inside.

I knew the cottage was empty the minute I crossed the threshold, but still I persisted, repeatedly calling out Alison's name as I inched toward the bedroom.

The clothes she'd worn last night lay in a careless diagonal across the bedroom floor, discarded and abandoned where they fell. The bed was unmade and redolent with her scent, a potent mix of strawberries and baby powder still clinging to the rumpled sheets and crumpled pillows, but Alison herself was nowhere to be seen. I'm embarrassed to say I actually checked underneath the bed. Did I think the dreaded bogeyman had surfaced, snatched Alison while she lay sleeping? I don't know what I thought. Nor do I know what possessed me to check the small, walk-in closet. Did I think she was hiding inside? Truth to tell, I don't know what I was thinking. Probably I wasn't thinking at all.

Alison had little in the way of clothes. A few dresses, including the blue sundress she'd worn at our first meeting. Several pairs of jeans. A white blouse. A black leather jacket. Perhaps half a dozen T-shirts were stacked in one corner of the long, built-in shelf, some lacy underwear crammed into the other. Wellworn, black-and-white sneakers sat beside a pair of obviously new, silver sling-back heels. I lifted one shoe into my hand, wondering how anyone managed to walk in those damn things. I hadn't worn a heel that high in—well, I'd **never** worn a heel that high, I realized, glancing toward my stockinged feet, reaching down before I was even aware of what I was doing and slipping on first one shoe, then the other.

It was at that moment—standing there in Alison's

sexy shoes—that I heard movement in the next room and felt the vibration of footsteps as they drew near. I froze, not sure what to do. It was one thing to tell Alison that I'd been so concerned about her health I'd felt entitled to invade her privacy, but how was I going to explain being discovered in her closet, teetering precariously in her new, silver, sling-back, high-heeled shoes?

For one insane second, I actually thought of clicking those heels together and reciting, "There's no place like home; there's no place like home," in hopes that, like Dorothy in **The Wizard of Oz,** I would be transported miraculously back to my own living room. Or Kansas, for that matter. Anywhere but here, I thought, feeling Alison's presence in the doorway. "I'm so sorry," I said, waiting for her to appear. "Please forgive me."

Except no one was there. There was only me and my overactive imagination. Not to mention my guilt for being where I didn't belong. I stood in the closet, wobbling in those outrageous three-inch heels, waiting for my heartbeat to return to normal. Some criminal I'd make, I thought, kicking off the shoes and returning them to their place beside the tired-looking sneakers.

At that point, I should have gotten the hell out of there. Alison was obviously feeling better. There was no need to be concerned. Certainly no reason for me to be standing in the middle of what was now, after all, her place. And I was on my way out—I really was—when I saw it.

Her journal.

It was lying open on the top of the white wicker dresser, as if waiting to be read, almost as if Alison had left it that way deliberately, as if she'd been expecting me to drop by. I tried not to notice it, tried to walk by it without stopping to look, without **stooping** to look, I should probably say, but the damn thing drew me like a magnet. Almost against my will, I found my eyes dipping through the dramatic swirls and loops of Alison's elaborate scrawl, as if on some wild, visual roller-coaster ride.

**Sunday, November 4: Well, I did it. I'm actually here.**

I stopped, slammed the journal shut, then realized it had been open when I found it and quickly rifled through the pages looking for the last entry.

**Thursday, October 11: Lance says I'm crazy. He says to remember what happened last time.**

**Friday, October 26: I'm getting nervous. Maybe this isn't such a good idea after all.**

**Sunday, October 28: Lance keeps warning me against getting too attached. Maybe he's right. Maybe this whole plan is just too crazy.**

Back to the last entry without allowing my eyes to settle, the words to sink in.

**Sunday, November 4: Well, I did it. I'm actually here. I'm living in the cottage behind her house, and she's even invited me over for dinner. She seems nice, if not exactly what I was expecting.**

What did that mean?

What had she been expecting?

We'd spoken for less than a minute on the phone, scarcely enough time to form any impressions at all.

**Lance says I'm crazy. He says to remember what happened last time.**

Were these entries somehow related?

"I'm doing it again," I said out loud. Letting my imagination get the better of me. The snatches I'd read in Alison's journal could mean anything. Or nothing. The discomfort I was feeling had more to do with my own guilt for snooping through Alison's personal belongings than it did with her innocent scribblings. I pulled away from the diary as if it were a hissing snake.

And I did nothing. Not then, not later, not even after I returned home at the end of my shift and stopped by to see how Alison was doing, and she told me that, aside from a brief walk around the block, she'd spent pretty much the whole day in bed.

I left her with the Imitrex, a list of doctors in the area, and some homemade chicken soup, deciding to be pleasant, but to keep my distance—**not allow myself to get too attached,** as the mysterious Lance would undoubtedly advise—and somehow I managed to convince myself that as long as Alison paid her rent on time and followed my rules, everything would be fine.

# 5

By Friday, I had all but forgotten the diary. One of the other nurses was sick with a nasty flu, so I'd volunteered to take her shift as well as my own on both Wednesday and Thursday, and as a result, I didn't see Alison at all. I **did** receive a lovely note from her, thanking me for dinner and apologizing profusely for being such a nuisance. She assured me she was feeling much better and suggested going to a movie on the weekend, if I had any free time. I didn't respond, deciding to plead exhaustion if and when we actually connected. If I turned down enough such overtures, I reasoned, Alison would get the message, and our relationship would revert to what it should have been in the first place, landlord and tenant. I'd been too hasty in allowing Alison into my life.

"What are you thinking about, dear?" the voice beside me asked with marked concern.

"Hmm? What? Sorry," I said, returning to the present, casting unwanted memories aside, returning my full attention to the withered old woman connected to life by a series of tubes that force-fed nutrients into her collapsing veins.

Myra Wylie's eyes radiated quiet curiosity. "You were a million miles away."

"Sorry. Did I hurt you?" My hands dropped from the IV I'd been adjusting.

"No, dear. You couldn't hurt me if you tried. Stop apologizing. Is everything all right?"

"Everything's fine." I secured the blanket at her toes. "You're doing remarkably well."

"I meant with you. Is everything all right with you?"

"Everything's fine," I repeated, as if trying to reassure myself as well.

"You can talk to me, you know. If you have a problem."

I smiled gratefully. "I appreciate that."

"I mean it."

"I know you do."

"You look like you have very deep thoughts," Myra Wylie remarked, and I laughed out loud. "Don't laugh. Josh thinks so too."

I felt my pulse quicken. "Your son thinks I have deep thoughts?"

"That's what he said last time he was here."

I felt almost ridiculously flattered, like a teenage girl who's just found out the silly boy she has a crush on feels the same way about her. I checked my watch, noted the trembling in my fingers. "Well, it's almost noon. He should be here any minute."

"He thinks you're very nice."

Was I mistaken, or was there a playful glint in Myra's watery eyes? "Oh, he does, does he?"

"Josh deserves someone nice," Myra was saying, almost to herself. "He's divorced, you know. I've told you about that, haven't I?"

I nodded, eager for more details, but careful to look only mildly curious.

"She left him for her aerobics instructor. Can you imagine? Stupid woman." Myra Wylie's frail shoulders stiffened with righteous indignation. "Destroys the family. Breaks my son's heart. And for what? So she can march off into the sunset with some muscle-bound body-builder ten years her junior, who dumps her less than six months later—what did she expect?—and of course, **now** she sees the error of her ways, **now** she wants him back. But Josh is too smart for that, thank God. He'll never let that woman back into his life." Myra's voice began breaking up, like a bad radio signal, then dissolved into a worrisome combination of coughs and wheezes.

"Take deep breaths," I cautioned, watching Myra's breathing gradually return to normal. "That's better. You shouldn't let yourself get so upset. It's not worth it. It's all over now. They're divorced."

"He will never let that woman back into his life."

"Never," I repeated.

"He deserves someone nice."

"Absolutely."

"Someone like you," Myra said. Then: "You like children, don't you?"

"I love children." I followed her eyes to the two silver-framed pictures of her smiling grandchildren that sat on the movable nightstand beside her bed.

"Of course they're older now than when these pictures were taken. Jillian is fifteen, and Trevor is almost twelve."

"I know. We've met," I reminded her. "They're lovely children."

"They went through hell after Jan left."

"I'm sure it wasn't easy." It's never easy to lose your mother, I remember thinking. No matter how old you are, no matter what the circumstances. A mother is a mother is a mother, I thought, and almost laughed. So much for the depth of my thoughts. "I should get going. Is there anything I can do for you before your son gets here?"

"Comb my hair a little, if you don't mind?"

"It will be my pleasure." I ran a gentle comb across Myra's scalp, watching the delicate strands of gray hair immediately fall back into place, as if untouched. "You were right about the bob. It's very becoming."

"You think so?" A smile, eager as a child's, spread across her face.

"Now all the nurses are asking me to cut their hair. They say I missed my calling."

"I don't think you miss a thing." Myra reached out to squeeze my hand.

"I'll be back to say hello to your son," I said with a wink.

"Terry?" she called as I was about to leave the room. I swiveled around as she brought her fingers to her lips. "Maybe a little lipstick?"

I started back toward the bed.

"No. Not me," she said quickly. "You."

I laughed, shaking my head as I returned to the door. I was still laughing as I stepped into the hall and saw Alison standing in front of the nurses' station.

"Terry!" Alison rushed forward to greet me, arms extended, face flushed with pride. She was wearing her blue sundress and her hair fell in lush tendrils around her shoulders. Erica Hollander's necklace hung around her neck, the tiny gold heart resting at her collarbone, as if it had been there all her life.

"Alison! What are you doing here?" I looked toward Margot and Caroline, both of whom were busy behind the long, curving desk of the nurses' station, Margot on the phone, Caroline entering notes in a patient's chart. They glanced in our direction, pretending not to be paying attention.

"I did it! I did it!" Alison was jumping up and down, like a small child.

I brought my finger to my lips in a silent signal for

her to settle down and lower her voice. "Did what?"

"I got a job," she squealed, unable to contain herself. "At the Lorelli Gallery. On Atlantic Avenue. Four days a week, some Saturdays, some evenings. Shift work," she said, beaming. "Like you."

"That's great," I heard myself say, her enthusiasm catchy despite my effort to remain detached. "What exactly will you be doing?"

"Selling mostly. Of course, I don't know much about art, but Fern said she'd teach me everything I need to know. Fern's my boss. Fern Lorelli. She seems very nice. Do you know her?"

I started to shake my head, but Alison had already moved on.

"I told her I didn't know much about art, because I figured I should be honest, right? I didn't want her to give me the job under false pretenses. I mean, she'd find out soon enough anyway, right? But she said not to worry, she'd handle the art, that I should stick mostly to the jewelry and gift items they sell, although if I do manage to sell one of the paintings, I'd get a commission. Five percent. Isn't that great?"

"It's great," I agreed.

"Some of those paintings sell for thousands of dollars, so that'd be fantastic, if I sold one of them. But mostly I'll be behind the cash register. Me and this other girl who works there. Denise Nickson, I think her name is. She's Fern's niece. And what else? Oh—I get twelve dollars an hour, and I start on Monday. Isn't that great?"

"It's great," I said again.

"I couldn't wait to tell you, so I came right over."

"Congratulations."

"Can I take you to lunch?"

"Lunch?"

"To celebrate. My treat."

I shifted uneasily from one foot to the other. Technically, I was on my lunch break right now, and my stomach had been making hungry noises for the past hour. "I can't. Things are so busy here today. . . ."

"Dinner, then."

"I can't. I'm working a double shift."

"Tomorrow night," she persisted. "That's even better. It's a Saturday, so you can sleep in the next morning. You're not busy tomorrow night, are you?"

"No," I said, realizing that Alison wouldn't settle for less than a definite date, even if she had to go through every day from now till Christmas. "But really, it isn't necessary for you to take me out."

"Of course it is," Alison insisted. "Besides, I want to. To thank you for all you've done for me."

"I haven't done anything."

"Are you kidding? You gave me the best place in the whole wide world to live, you cooked me dinner, you made me feel welcome. You even took care of me when I got sick. I owe you big time, Terry Painter."

"You don't owe me anything but the rent," I said, struggling to keep my distance, feeling myself sway reluctantly back into her orbit, falling under her spell.

**You gave me the best place in the whole wide world to live.** Who says things like that? How could you not be charmed?

Besides, what was I so worried about? What could I possibly have to fear, especially from someone like Alison? Even assuming the worst, that she was some sort of clever con artist, what could she possibly be after? I had little in the way of material goods—my small house, its tiny adjacent cottage, negligible savings, my mother's silly collection of ladies' head vases. So what? Small potatoes, all of it. This was Florida, for heaven's sake. Forty minutes north were the oceanside mansions of Palm Beach and Hobe Sound; forty minutes south were the palatial homes of Miami's infamous South Beach. Florida was synonymous with money, with wealthy old men just waiting to be taken advantage of by beautiful young girls. Hell, it's what was keeping them alive. It didn't make sense that Alison would waste her time with me.

I realize now that there are times when our brains will simply not allow us to accept the evidence our own eyes present, that the desire for self-delusion outweighs the instinct for self-preservation, that no matter how old we are or how wise we think we've become, we are never really convinced of our own mortality. Besides, since when do things have to make sense?

"So, are we on?" Alison's big, loopy grin widened with expectation.

"We're on," I heard myself reply.

"Great." She spun around in a full circle, the skirt of her sundress swirling around her knees. "Anywhere in particular you'd like to go?"

I shook my head. "Surprise me."

She rubbed the gold heart at her throat. "I love surprises."

As if on cue, the fire alarm sounded. It turned out to be a false alarm, but in the few minutes it took to make sure everything was okay, chaos reigned. When I returned to the nurses' station after reassuring several panicky patients that the hospital was not about to become a blazing inferno, Alison was gone.

"Everybody okay?" Margot asked.

"Mr. Austin said, fire or no fire, he wasn't going anywhere without his teeth." I laughed, picturing the feisty old man in room 411.

"Pretty girl you were talking to earlier," Margot remarked.

"My new tenant."

"Really? Well, I hope you have better luck this time around."

THE NEXT HOUR PASSED IN RELATIVE CALM. There were no more fire alarms, no unexpected visitors. After a brief lunch in the cafeteria, I kept busy checking pulses, delivering pain medication, helping patients to and from the bathroom, comforting them as they railed against their fate. At some point I found myself at the door to Sheena O'Connor's room. I hesitated briefly, then pushed the door open and stepped inside.

The teenager lay in the middle of her bed, staring at the ceiling with eyes wide with terror. Was she seeing the man who'd raped and beaten her senseless, then left her for dead? I approached the bed, reached out, and touched her hand, but if she felt my touch at all, she gave no sign. "It's okay," I whispered. "You're safe now."

I pulled up a chair, sat down beside her, the words to an old Irish lullaby suddenly dancing inside my head. It took a few seconds for me to find the tune, and next thing I knew I was singing—softly, gently, as one sings to a newborn baby—"**Too-ra-loo-ra-loo-ra . . . too-ra-loo-ra-lie . . .**"

I don't know what made me think of that particular song. I couldn't remember my mother ever singing it to me. Maybe it was the name O'Connor. Maybe I thought Sheena's mother might have sung it to her, that the song might stir something deep in the girl's subconscious, remind her of a time when she felt secure and protected, a time when no harm could befall her.

"**Too-ra-loo-ra-loo-ra,**" I sang, my voice gaining strength with each repetition of the simple sounds. "**Too-ra-loo-ra-lie . . .**"

Sheena remained motionless.

"**Too-ra-loo-ra-loo-ra . . . that's an Irish lullaby.**"

"And it's a very lovely one," a man's voice said from the doorway.

I recognized the voice without having to turn around. I swallowed the sounds in my throat and willed my face not to betray me as I turned toward the doorway. Josh Wylie, tall and almost carelessly handsome, with salt-and-pepper hair and his mother's blue eyes, stood watching me. "How long have you been standing there?"

"Long enough to realize you have a beautiful voice."

I gripped the railing at Sheena's bedside to steady myself as I rose to my feet. "Thank you." I walked across the room, my heart wobbling, although my feet were surprisingly steady. Josh Wylie backed into the hallway as I approached, and I shut the door to Sheena's room behind me.

"What's the matter with her?" Josh asked as we started down the corridor.

I related the gruesome details of the assault. "She's in a coma. Her eyes are open, but she doesn't see anything."

"Will she be that way forever?"

"Nobody knows."

"What a shame." Josh shook his head sadly. "So, how's my mother doing?" He smiled, a warm upturn of his lips that underlined the sparkle in his eyes. "I understand you cut her hair."

"Just a few snips here and there. She seems to like it."

"She's crazy about it. She's crazy about **you**," Josh emphasized. "Thinks you're the greatest thing since sliced bread."

"The feeling's mutual."

"Thinks I should take you out to lunch the next time I visit."

"What?"

"Lunch, next Friday. If you're free. If you're hungry . . ."

"I'm always hungry," I said, grateful when he laughed. "Lunch next Friday sounds great." I thought of Alison. Two surprising invitations in one day.

"Okay, then, next Friday it is." We reached the nurses' station. "Till then, I leave my mother in your capable and creative hands."

"Drive carefully," I called as Josh stepped inside the waiting elevator.

"And no uniform. This isn't a business lunch." He waved as the elevator door drew slowly closed.

**This isn't a business lunch,** I repeated silently, mentally raiding my closet, trying to decide what to wear, wondering whether to splurge on a new outfit. It was only then that I became aware of a slight commotion behind me. "Problems?" I asked, spinning around on my heels, seeing Margot and Caroline making exaggerated sweeps of the desk with their hands and eyes.

"Caroline's wallet is missing from her purse," Margot said.

I came around to the inside of the nurses' station, began my own head sweep. "You're sure? It's not in a pocket somewhere?"

"I've looked everywhere," Caroline moaned, brushing chin-length, brown hair away from her long face, emptying the contents of her purse onto the floor. At the best of times, Caroline looked vaguely depressed. Now she looked positively distraught.

"Maybe you left it in another purse. I did that once," I offered gamely, although I'd never done any such thing.

"No, I had it with me this morning. I know, because I bought a cup of coffee and a Danish downstairs."

"Maybe you left it on the counter after you paid."

Caroline shook her head. "I'm sure I put it back in my purse." She looked up and down the corridor, tears filling her dejected brown eyes. "Damn it. I had over a hundred dollars in there."

I thought of Alison. She'd been here when the fire alarm had sounded and the nursing station had been left temporarily unattended. And she'd been gone by the time everything had settled down. Was it possible she'd helped herself to Caroline's wallet?

Why would I think that?

Surely it was much more logical to assume that Caroline had left her wallet in the cafeteria. "I think you should call downstairs," I advised, opening and closing drawers, checking each small compartment behind the desk, then peeking into my own purse to make sure nothing was missing.

"I'll call the cafeteria," Caroline agreed grudgingly, "but I know it's not there. Somebody took it. Somebody took it."

# 6

Saturday night, the phone rang just as I was stepping out of the shower. I wrapped one large white towel around my body, threw another one across my shoulders, and padded across my bedroom floor toward the phone, wondering if Alison was calling to cancel our dinner. I lifted the phone to my ear and pushed my wet hair away from my cheek. "Hello?"

"I'd like to speak to Erica Hollander," the male voice announced without further preamble.

It took half a second for the name to register on my brain. "Erica Hollander is no longer my tenant," I said coolly, my eyes following several wayward trickles of water as they ran down my legs to the ivory carpet. Anxiety simultaneously trickled through my insides.

"Do you know where I can reach her?" The voice carried traces of a soft Southern twang. I didn't think I'd heard it before.

"I'm afraid I have no idea where she is."

"When did she leave?"

I thought back to the last time I'd seen Erica. "It was the end of August."

"She didn't leave a forwarding address?"

"She didn't leave a thing, and that includes the two months' rent she owed me. Who's calling?"

The answer to my question was a resounding click in my ear.

I dropped the receiver into its carriage, then plopped down on my bed, taking a series of long, deep breaths, trying to push unpleasant memories of Erica Hollander out of my head. But she was as stubborn in her absence as she'd been in her presence, and she refused to be so easily dismissed.

Erica Hollander was young, like Alison, and like Alison, willowy and tall, though not quite as tall, not quite as willowy. Her hair was a luxurious dark brown and hung straight to her shoulders, and she was continually tossing it from side to side, the way you see them do in those annoying television commercials that equate a good shampoo with a good orgasm. But her face, while pretty enough in a certain light, hovered perilously close to plain. Only her nose, a nose that was long and thin and veered suddenly to the left, gave her any character at all. It was her one distinguishing feature. Of course, she hated it. "I'm saving up to have it done," she'd told me on more than one occasion.

"Your nose is beautiful," I'd assured her, ever the mother hen.

"It's awful. I'm saving up to have it done."

I'd listened to her whine about her nose; I'd listened to her brag about her boyfriend—"Charlie's so handsome, Charlie's so smart"—who was spending a year working in Tokyo; I'd listened when she stopped bragging and started whining—"Charlie didn't call this week, Charlie better watch his step"—and I'd reserved judgment when she got involved with some guy she'd met at Elwood's, a well-known biker hangout on Atlantic Avenue. I'd even lent her money to buy a used portable computer. All because I thought we were friends. It never occurred to me that she'd skip out in the middle of the night, still owing me for the computer, not to mention several months in back rent.

Smart, handsome Charlie in Tokyo couldn't accept that his girlfriend had dumped him as unceremoniously as she'd dumped me and had plagued me with increasingly unpleasant phone calls from Japan, demanding to know her whereabouts. He'd even notified the police, who basically corroborated my story, but even that wasn't enough to satisfy him. He'd continued harassing me long-distance until I'd threatened to call his employer. And then suddenly, the phone calls stopped.

Until tonight.

I shook my head, amazed that though Erica

Hollander had been gone for almost three months, she was still causing me grief. She'd been my first tenant and, I'd vowed after she'd taken off, my last.

What had happened to change my mind?

Truth be told, I missed having someone around. I don't have a lot of friends. There are my co-workers, women like Margot and Caroline, but we rarely socialize away from the hospital. Caroline has a demanding husband, and Margot has four kids to look after. And I've always been a little reserved. This shyness, coupled with my tendency to throw myself into my work, has made it hard for me to meet new people. Plus, my mother was sick for so long before she died, and between caring for my patients at the hospital and caring for her at home, well, there are only so many hours in a day.

Besides, something insidious happens to women in our society when they turn forty, especially if they're not married. We get lost in a heavy, free-floating haze. It becomes difficult to see us. People know we're there; it's just that we've become a little fuzzy, so blurred around the edges we've begun blending into the surrounding scenery. It's not that we're invisible exactly—people actually step around us to avoid confronting us—but the truth is we are no longer **seen**. And if you aren't seen, you aren't heard.

That's what happens to women over forty.

We lose our voice.

Maybe that's why we seem so angry. Maybe it's not

hormones after all. Maybe we just want someone to pay attention.

Anyway, I started thinking about how nice it had been when Erica Hollander had first moved in, how much fun it had been having someone around, even if we didn't see each other all that much. I don't know. Somehow, just the fact that someone was sharing my space had made me feel less alone. So I decided to try it again. What is it they say about second marriages? That they're a triumph of hope over experience?

At any rate, I was determined not to make the same mistakes the second time around. That's why I'd decided against advertising for a tenant in the newspaper, choosing instead to post a number of discreet notices around the hospital. I reasoned that, this way, I was more likely to attract someone older, more responsible. Maybe a professional, perhaps even a woman like myself.

Instead I got Alison.

The phone rang, bringing me back to the present. I became aware of the air conditioner blowing against the back of my neck, like a lover's cool breath. I shuddered with the chill.

"Hi, it's me," Alison chirped as I lifted the receiver to my ear. "Didn't you hear me knock?"

The towel at my breast came loose and fell to the floor as I rose to my feet. "What? No. Where are you?"

"At your kitchen door. I'm on my cell. Is everything all right?"

"Fine. I'm just running a little late. Can I pick you up in ten minutes?"

"No problem."

Securing my towel around me, I walked to my bedroom window and watched from behind the white lace curtain as Alison ambled back toward the cottage. She was wearing a slinky, navy dress I didn't remember seeing in her closet, and her silver sling-back shoes, which she had no trouble walking in at all. I watched as she tucked her cell phone inside the silver purse dangling from her shoulder, only to withdraw it again almost immediately, several loose bills escaping their cramped confines and wafting toward the ground. Alison immediately scooped up the money and stuffed it back inside her small silver bag. I quickly recalled the handful of $100 bills Alison had given me for first and last month's rent, then found myself thinking about the $100 that had gone missing from Caroline's purse. Was it possible Alison had taken it?

"That's ridiculous," I said out loud, watching Alison punch a series of numbers into her cell phone. Alison had no need to steal money from strangers. I watched her whisper something into the receiver, then laugh. Suddenly she spun around, almost as if she'd known I was watching her. I flattened myself against the wall and didn't move again until I heard the cottage door open and close.

Fifteen minutes later, I was at her door, wearing a calf-length, pale yellow, sleeveless dress with a pronounced décolletage that I'd bought a year ago, but had never had the nerve to wear. "Sorry I took so long. I couldn't get my hair to sit right."

"You look fabulous." Alison regarded me with the practiced eye of women who are used to looking in mirrors. "You just need a little trim," she announced after a pause. "I could do it for you. Don't forget I worked for a few months in a hairdressing salon."

"You were a receptionist," I reminded her.

She laughed. "Yeah, but I watched and I learned, and I'm really pretty good. You want me to give it a try after dinner?"

I thought of the improvised bob I'd given Myra Wylie earlier in the week. Was I as brave as she was? "Where are you taking me?"

"It's this new place right across from the Lorelli Gallery. I already called them and said we'd be a bit late."

The restaurant was called Barrington's, and like many restaurants in South Florida, it was much bigger on the inside than it appeared from the street. The main room was decorated like a French bistro, lots of Tiffany lamps and leaded-glass windows, along with Toulouse-Lautrec posters of dancers from the Moulin Rouge suspended from pale yellow walls that were an exact—and unfortunate—match with my dress. Were it not for my ample cleavage, I might have vanished altogether.

The waiter brought over a basket of bread, the wine list, and two large menus, before reciting by heart the list of the night's specials. His eyes moved back and forth between Alison's face and my chest. Together, I remember thinking, we could rule the world.

"Dolphin!" Alison wailed in horror at one of the waiter's suggestions.

"Not Flipper," I explained quickly. "This dolphin's a fish, not a mammal. It's sometimes called mahi mahi."

"I like the sound of that much better."

"How's the salmon?" I asked.

"Tasty," the waiter said, looking at Alison. "But kind of boring," he said, looking at me.

"What about the swordfish?" Alison asked.

"Wonderful," the waiter enthused. "They grill it in a light Dijon mustard sauce. And it comes with sautéed vegetables and little red potatoes."

"Sounds great. I'll have that."

"I'll have the salmon," I offered, risking the young man's scorn, daring to be dull.

"Some wine?"

Alison motioned to me with her hand, as if giving me the floor. "Some wine?" she repeated.

"I think I'll skip the wine tonight."

"You can't skip the wine. This is a celebration. We have to have wine."

"Remember what happened last time," I cautioned.

She looked confused, as if she'd forgotten all about her recent migraine. "We'll have white wine, not red," she pronounced upon reflection. "That should be all right."

The waiter pointed out the choice of wines, and Alison followed his recommendation. Something from

Chile, I believe. It was good, and it was cold, and it quickly gave me a pleasant buzz. Service was slow, and I'd already finished my glass by the time the food arrived. Alison poured me another, and I didn't object, although I noticed she'd only taken a few sips of her own drink. "Ooh, this is yummy delicious," she enthused, biting into the swordfish. "How's yours?"

"Yummy." I laughed at the sound.

"So, did you see your friend this week?" Alison asked suddenly.

"My friend?"

"Josh Wylie." Alison stole a look around the crowded restaurant, as if he might be there, as if she might recognize him if he were.

The salmon stuck in my throat. "How do you know about Josh Wylie?"

Alison swallowed one forkful of swordfish, then another. "You told me about him."

"I did?"

"Dinner at your house. I asked if you were interested in anyone, and you said there was this guy"—she lowered her voice, her eyes doing another slow spin around the room—"Josh Wylie, whose mother is one of your patients. Right?" She popped two small potatoes into her mouth, speared another forkful of fish.

"Right."

"So, did you see him?"

"Yes, I did. As a matter of fact, he's taking me to lunch next Friday."

Alison's eyes widened with delight. "Way to go, Terry!"

I laughed. "It's not a big deal," I cautioned, as much to myself as to Alison. "He probably just wants to talk about his mother."

"If he wanted to talk about his mother, he'd do it in the waiting room. Trust me, he's interested."

I shrugged, hoping she was right. "We'll see."

Alison waved my hesitation aside. "You'll have to tell me all about it." She clapped her hands together, as if congratulating me for a job well done, then finished off the last of her swordfish in three quick swallows. "This is so exciting. I can't wait till next Friday."

I don't remember much else about the meal, except that Alison insisted on ordering dessert, and that I ate more than I should have.

"Come on," I remember her saying as she pushed the large piece of banana-cream cake toward me. "You only live once."

After dinner, Alison was eager to show me the Lorelli Gallery. She grabbed my hand and all but pulled me across the busy street. I heard a car whiz by behind me, felt its exhaust on my bare calves. "Watch where you're going, lady," the driver yelled out.

"Be careful," Alison admonished as if I'd been crossing the street all by myself.

On weekends, the gallery stayed open till ten o'clock, hoping to attract tourists and passersby. I counted four people inside the well-lit store, including the spike-haired young woman behind the counter. The walls were covered with colorful paintings, mostly by artists I didn't recognize, although there was a typical Motherwell painting of a woman with large red lips and a prominent nipple, and three paintings of pears were stacked one on top of the other, by an artist whose name I could never remember no matter how many times I saw his work. I found my attention drawn to a small, rectangular painting of a woman, her face hidden behind a large hat, as she sunned herself on a pink, sandy beach.

"That's my favorite," Alison said, then lowered her voice. "It would go great in your living room, don't you think? On the wall behind the sofa?"

"It's beautiful."

Alison pulled me toward the center of the room, almost knocking over a sculpture of a large fiberglass frog. "Whoops." She giggled. "Isn't that the most hideous thing you've ever seen?"

I agreed it was.

"Fern says she can't keep the damn things in the store, they sell so fast. Can you believe it? Denise, hi," she continued in the same breath. "This is Terry Painter, my landlady. My friend," she added with a smile.

The girl behind the counter looked up from the fashion magazine she was perusing, extraordinary violet eyes overwhelming the rest of her small face. "Nice to meet you," she said, her voice surprisingly husky, the words emerging slowly from between small but full lips, as if she weren't quite sure whether meeting me was nice or not. She was dressed all in black, which made her look thinner than she already was, although her breasts were high and disproportionately large for her narrow frame.

"I don't think they're real," Alison would later say.

"I'm wondering how much that painting is," I said, glancing toward the painting of the girl on the pink, sandy beach, her face hidden by her wide-brimmed hat.

Denise raised bored violet eyes to the far wall. Then she reached under the counter and pulled out a plastic-covered sheet of paper to scan the typed list. "That one's fifteen hundred dollars."

"The wall behind the sofa in your living room," Alison said again. "What do you think?"

"I think you don't start work till Monday," I reminded her.

Alison's face broke into a wide smile. "I'm gonna be great at this, aren't I?"

I laughed, directing my attention to the display of jewelry in the glass counter that occupied the middle of the store. I found myself staring at a pair of long silver earrings in the shape of cupids.

"Aren't those great?" Alison knew exactly what pair I was looking at. "How much are these?" She poked at the glass above the earrings.

Denise opened the back of the case, lifted the earrings out, held them toward me. Deep purple nails protruded over the ends of long, tapered fingers. "Two hundred dollars."

I backed away, lifted my hands in the air. "Too rich for my blood."

Alison quickly scooped up the earrings. "Nonsense. She'll take them."

"No," I countered. "Two hundred dollars is way too much."

"My treat."

"What? No!"

"Yes." Alison gently removed the thin gold loops I was wearing and replaced them with the long silver cupids. "You gave me a heart," she said, patting the tiny gold heart at her throat. "Now it's my turn."

"It's hardly the same thing."

"I won't take no for an answer. Besides, I get an employee discount. How much with my discount?" she asked Denise.

The young woman shrugged. "Take them. They're yours. Fern'll never miss them."

"What do you mean?" I asked, immediately preparing to take them off.

"She's just kidding," Alison said, already returning several loose $100 bills to her purse. She quickly ushered me to the front of the store. "Fern's her aunt," she reminded me, as if this should be explanation enough.

"Does she know her niece is a thief?"

"Don't worry. I'll settle with Fern on Monday."

"You promise?"

Alison smiled, tucked my hair behind my ears to better admire my new earrings. "I promise."

# 7

Don't you look lovely!" Myra Wylie lifted her head from the pillow, gnarled fingers, like turkey claws, beckoning me toward her bed.

I ran self-conscious hands across the front of my yellow dress as I approached. Myra had asked to see what I'd be wearing for lunch with her son, so I'd used her bathroom to change out of my nurse's uniform and into my street clothes. I'd decided on the same dress I'd worn to dinner with Alison the previous week.

"Thank you, dear." Myra lowered her head back to the pillow, although her eyes remained on me. "It was very sweet of you to show me your dress. I get a taste of what I missed by not having had a daughter. That former daughter-in-law of mine was for the birds. She was no fun at all. But you . . ."

"Me?" I prompted, eager to hear more.

"You're very good to me."

"Why wouldn't I be?"

"People aren't always kind," Myra said, her eyes on some distant memory.

"You make it very easy," I told her truthfully, pulling up a chair and sitting down beside her, stealing a glance at my watch. It was almost twelve-thirty.

"Don't worry," Myra said with a knowing smile. "He won't be late."

I leaned forward, pretended to be tucking in the blue cotton sheet that served as a bedspread.

"Those are lovely," Myra said. "Are they new?"

Her bony fingers were twisting toward the dangling cupids at my ears. "Yes, they are. A friend gave them to me." I wondered if Alison had settled with her boss, as she'd promised.

"A boyfriend?" Worry clouded Myra's eyes, like fresh cataracts.

"No. Actually, they were a gift from my new tenant." Again I pictured Alison. She'd started work on Monday, and except for one quick call to say she was loving every minute of her new job, I hadn't spoken to her all week. "Besides, I'm a little old for boyfriends, don't you think?"

"We're never too old for boyfriends."

"What's this about boyfriends?" the male voice boomed from the doorway.

"There he is," Myra said, all girlish flutter. "How are you, darling?" She held out her arms. I stepped out of the way and watched Josh fold inside them.

"Perfect," he said, looking right at me.

"Was the traffic bad?"

"It was miserable."

"You should take the turnpike."

"Yes, I should." He straightened up and smiled at me. "We have this same discussion every week."

"You should listen to your mother," I told him.

"Yes, I should."

"Doesn't Terry look beautiful?" Myra asked.

I looked to the floor to hide the blush I could feel spreading across my face. Not because I was embarrassed by the compliment, but because I'd been thinking exactly the same thing about her son. I don't think I'd realized before how deep were the dimples at his cheeks, how pronounced the muscles that bulged beneath his short-sleeved shirt. It was all I could do to keep from crossing my legs and screaming out loud. I hadn't felt this way in years.

"She looks very beautiful," Josh dutifully replied.

"Do you like her earrings?"

Josh lifted his fingers to my ear, his hand grazing the side of my cheek. "I like them very much."

I felt a rush of heat, as if he'd struck a match, held it against my flesh. "You're a troublemaker, you know that?" I told Myra, who looked inordinately pleased with herself.

"You ready?" Josh asked.

I nodded.

"I expect a full report after lunch," Myra called after us.

"I'll take notes," I called back as Josh ushered me into the hall.

"How would you like to have lunch by the ocean?" he asked.

"You read my mind."

WE WENT TO LUNA ROSA, an upscale eatery located on South Ocean Boulevard, directly across from the beach. The restaurant was one of my favorites, an easy walk from my house, although Josh had no way of knowing that. He'd reserved a table outside, and we sat along the narrow sidewalk, soaking in the ocean air, and watching the constant parade of people pass by our chairs.

"So, tell me, when did all this happen?" Josh's voice rose easily above the conflicting sounds of surf and automobiles.

"When did what happen?" I watched a young woman in a turquoise thong bikini as she ran barefoot across the road, then disappeared into a burst of sunlight.

Josh waved large, expressive hands into the air. "This. The Delray I remember was all pineapple fields and jungle."

I laughed. "You don't get out much, do you?"

"I guess not."

"Delray's changed a lot in the past ten years." I felt an unexpected surge of pride. "We've just been awarded our second All-American City designation by the National Civic League, and a few years back we were named 'the best-run town in Florida.' " I smiled. "How do you like them pineapples?"

He laughed, his eyes on mine. "Looks like I should visit more often."

"I'm sure your mother would like that."

"And you?"

I grabbed my ice water, took a long sip. "I'd like that too."

The waiter approached with our orders. Crab cakes for Josh, a seafood salad for me.

"Your mother's quite a character," I said, taking a mouthful of calamari, seeking safer ground. I'd never been a good flirt, and I was even worse when it came to playing games. I tended to blurt out whatever thought was on the tip of my tongue.

"Yes, she is. She's filled you in on the sordid family history, I take it."

"She told me you're divorced."

"I'm sure her description was considerably more colorful than that."

"Maybe just a little." I took another sip of ice water. Sensibly, I'd declined Josh's offer of a glass of wine. It was important to keep a clear head, to stay in control. Besides, I had barely an hour before I had to be back at work. I leaned back in the uncomfortable folding chair, listened to the sound of the waves somersaulting toward the shore, echoing the tumult taking place inside my body. God, what was the matter with me? I hadn't felt so overwhelmed, so smitten, so damn **girlish,** since I was fourteen years old.

I wanted to grab Josh Wylie by the collar of his white linen shirt and yank him across the table. **I haven't had sex in five years,** I wanted to shout. **Can we just skip all this verbal foreplay and get on with the real thing?**

But of course I didn't. I just sat there smiling at him. My mother would have been proud.

"She tells me you never married," Josh said, cutting into his crab cakes, unaware of the more interesting conversation taking place inside my head.

"She's right."

"Hard to believe."

"Really? Why?"

"Because you're a beautiful, intelligent woman, and I would have thought some guy would have snapped you up long ago."

"You would have thought," I agreed with a laugh.

"You have something against marriage?"

"Not a thing." I wondered why I always seemed to be explaining my single status. "As I told Alison, it wasn't any conscious decision on my part."

"Who's Alison?"

"What? Oh, my new tenant."

"Any regrets?"

"Regrets? About Alison?"

Josh smiled. "About life in general."

I released a long, deep breath. "A few. You?"

"A few."

We finished the rest of our meal, talking easily, laughing often, as the waves swept our unspoken regrets back and forth along the water's edge.

AFTER LUNCH, Josh removed his socks and shoes and rolled his black linen trousers up around his knees, while I slipped off my sandals, and we walked along the beach. The ocean repeatedly rushed toward us, only to pull away upon contact. Like an eager lover tormented by second thoughts, it charged only to retreat. It seduced you with its monstrous beauty, then abandoned you, breathless and alone, on the shore. The eternal dance, I thought, the water cold as it licked at my toes.

"Aren't we just the luckiest people alive?" Josh said with an appreciative laugh.

"We are." I pushed my face toward the sky, squinting into the sun.

"I remember when I was a kid," he continued. "My father used to take me to the beach every Saturday afternoon while my mother was having her hair done."

"You're from Florida originally?" I wasn't sure why I asked that. I already knew everything there was to know about Josh's background: that he'd been born in Boynton Beach, weighing a hefty nine pounds, two ounces; that his parents had lived at 212 Hibiscus Drive all their married life; that his mother had continued to live there after her husband's death a decade ago; that she'd refused her son's offer to move her down to Miami so that she could be closer to her grandchildren; that she'd continued to live in that little house she loved until she got too sick to look after it anymore; that she'd personally selected Mission Care over fancier facilities in Miami, insisting that she got nosebleeds south of Delray; that her son drove up at least once a week to see her; that he was still reeling from his divorce after seventeen years of marriage to his college sweetheart; that he was the single father of two lovely but confused children; that he was lonely; that he deserved a second chance at happiness; that I was more than prepared to provide him with that chance.

That I was completely out of my mind, I thought, realizing that I hadn't heard a single word he'd said in the last two minutes. What was the matter with me? Was I so starved for male companionship that a pleasant lunch instantly spawned fantasies of happily ever after? I needed to slow down, calm down, cool down. Before I ruined everything.

Deliberately, I allowed myself to be distracted by the sight of two boys, maybe five or six years old, in matching bright red bathing suits, tumbling over each other as

they rolled, like runaway logs, into the water, before disappearing underneath a succession of increasingly large
waves. I looked around the crowded beach. An elderly
couple was relaxing under a red-and-white-striped
umbrella; a young man was erecting a sand castle with
his toddler son; two teenagers carelessly tossed a neon-
pink Frisbee back and forth; a middle-aged woman, her
large stomach protruding over a tiny bikini bottom,
swung her arms with careless abandon as she marched
along beside the ocean; a younger woman was soaking
up the sun, breast implants proudly pointing toward
the cloudless sky. No one was supervising the two boys,
I realized, holding my breath as the boys' heads
appeared above the water, only to disappear again under
the next big wave.

"Do you see anyone watching those boys?" I asked
Josh, hard pellets of sunshine bouncing off my eyes as I
continued scanning the beach.

Josh's eyes joined in the search. "I'm sure there's
someone," he said unconvincingly, as one of the young-
sters began waving his arms in the air.

A fresh wave immediately slapped them down. This
wave was immediately followed by a much larger one. A
small voice rode the wave to shore. "Help!" the voice
cried, wobbling like unsteady knees on a surfboard.

"Help!" I echoed loudly, motioning frantically to the
lifeguard farther down the beach, but he was busy chat-
ting up a teenage girl in a black-and-white string bikini,
the girl's long, lean legs stretching all the way up to her

baseball cap. I've had nightmares about drowning all my life, maybe because I never learned how to swim. I couldn't just stand there waiting for disaster to strike. I had to do something. "We have to do something," I shouted as Josh raced toward the lifeguard.

"Help! Help!" the small voice pleaded, now joined by a second voice, more plaintive than the first. Their cries skipped along the surface of the water like a stone, only to disappear beneath yet another rush of deadly white foam.

"Somebody do something!" I shouted at the people around me, but although a small crowd was starting to gather, nobody moved.

Without further thought, I dropped my purse and shoes to the sand and jumped into the surf after the boys, the cold water reaching between my thighs and whipping my dress around my legs. An unexpected undertow suddenly anchored my legs to the sand, and I struggled to maintain my balance, my hands circling my body like rusty propellers.

"Help!" the boys continued crying, their heads bobbing like apples in a bucket as I resolutely pushed myself forward, only to feel my legs collapse beneath me like the folding chair I'd been sitting on only moments before.

"I'm coming," I called out, the bitter taste of salt washing over my tongue as the ocean spilled into my mouth. "Hang on," I urged as the ground under my toes suddenly disappeared, as if I'd stepped off a steep cliff, and I fought to keep my head above water. My hands reached blindly for something to grab on to, accidentally smacking against what felt like a rock, but proved to be a small head. Hair curled between my fingers, like seaweed.

Whether through determination, good fortune, or just plain, dumb luck, I managed to get my hands around first one boy, then the other, and somehow catapulted their kicking frames toward the shore in time for anxious arms to reach them. I heard a series of excited, high-pitched exhortations—"Didn't I tell you to stay put until I got back? Look at you! You almost drowned!"—and then the water once again wrapped itself around my torso, like a hungry boa constrictor, and carried me back out to sea.

So this is what it feels like to drown, I remember thinking as the water covered my head like a heavy blanket, sneaking into all my private cavities, an impatient lover who would no longer be denied. "Terry," the water whispered seductively. Then louder, more insistent. "Terry . . . Terry."

"Terry!"

The voice exploded in my ear as determined hands reached under my arms to pull me toward the sky. My head burst through the surface of the water like a fist through glass.

"My God, are you all right?" Strong arms pushed me toward the shore where I collapsed onto my hands and knees.

Water clung to my eyes, like shards of glass, and I

struggled to open them. Slivers of breath escaped my lungs in a series of short, painful spasms.

"Are you all right?" Josh's face formed around the edges of the words.

I nodded, coughed, sucked furiously at the air. "The boys . . . ?"

"They're fine."

"Thank God."

Josh's fingers pushed the hair out of my eyes, smoothed the water from my cheeks. "You're a hero, Terry Painter."

"I'm an idiot," I muttered. "I can't swim."

"So I noticed."

"You're not supposed to go in the water without a bathing suit," a little girl admonished from somewhere beside me.

I looked down at my once seductive dress, now wrapped around me like a bruised yellow tent. "Look at me," I wailed. "I look like an overripe banana."

Josh laughed. "Good enough to eat," I thought I heard him say, although in the ensuing commotion I couldn't be sure. A crowd was gathering. Unfamiliar voices were exclaiming their gratitude; strange hands were patting my back.

"Way to go!" someone enthused in passing.

"Are you okay?" a young woman asked, long legs approaching cautiously. I recognized the black-and-white string bikini and the baseball cap, knew she was the girl I'd seen earlier, talking to the lifeguard.

"I'm fine." I noted the lifeguard was standing directly behind her, and that he was suitably tall, blond, and muscular. The expression on his bland, bronzed face wavered between gratitude and resentment.

"I just wanted to thank you," the girl continued. "Those are my brothers. My mother would have killed me if anything had happened to them."

"You should keep a closer eye on them."

She nodded, glanced up the beach to where the boys were wrestling in the sand. "Yeah, well, I told them . . ." Her voice disappeared into a passing breeze. "Anyway, thanks again." She looked past me at Josh.

"You interested in a job?" the lifeguard joked uneasily.

"Just do yours," I told him, but he was already backing away, and he dismissed my admonishment with a wave of his hand, as if swatting at a pesky insect.

"My purse!" I said, suddenly remembering I'd dropped it on the shore. "My shoes . . ."

"Right here." Josh lifted them into the air, like a proud fisherman displaying his catch of the day.

"My God, look at you!" I exclaimed, realizing he was almost as wet as I was.

"We're quite a pair," he said, leaning his face toward mine.

I held my breath, didn't move. Was he going to kiss me?

A clump of hair promptly fell into my eyes, and I brushed it aside impatiently, feeling particles of sand attach themselves to my eyelashes, like globs of errant mascara. Great, I thought, trying to picture myself through his eyes. A regular beauty queen, I could almost hear my mother say.

"Terry?" a familiar voice asked from miles above my head.

I looked up, shielded my eyes. Alison loomed between me and the sun like a giant eclipse.

"Terry?" she said again, crouching down beside me. "My God, I can't believe it's you!"

"Alison! What are you doing here?"

"I have the day off. What's going on? Somebody said you saved two little boys from drowning."

"She was magnificent," Josh said proudly.

"Until I almost drowned myself."

"My God, are you all right?"

"She's magnificent," Josh repeated, extending his hand toward Alison. "I'm Josh Wylie, by the way."

Alison took his hand, shook it vigorously. "Alison Simms."

"Alison's my new tenant," I qualified.

"Pleasure to meet you, Alison."

"You too." Almost reluctantly, she relinquished his hand. "So, has Terry invited you over for Thanksgiving yet?"

"Alison!"

"Terry's only the best cook in the whole wide world. You're not busy, are you?"

"Well, no, but . . ."

"Good. Then it's settled. Don't worry, Terry," Alison cautioned, "I'll help."

I'm not sure exactly what happened after that. I remember wanting to wring Alison's lovely, swanlike neck. I also wanted to throw my arms around her and jump up and down with joy. At any rate, perhaps sensing my ambivalance, Alison muttered something about meeting with me later to discuss all the necessary details, then made a hasty retreat, disappearing into a swirl of pink sand. Josh drove me to my house, waiting in the car while I ran upstairs, towel-dried my hair, and changed out of my wet clothes. Then he drove me back to work. Neither one of us said anything until he pulled up in front of the hospital. Then we turned simultaneously toward one another.

"Josh . . ."

"Terry . . ."

"You don't have to come to dinner on Thanksgiving."

"You don't have to invite me."

"No, I'd love to invite you."

"Then I'd love to come."

"Really?"

"Jan's taking the kids that night, so I have no particular plans."

"Well, it wouldn't be anything fancy. . . ."

"I don't need fancy if I have the best cook in the whole wide world."

I laughed. "Well, that might be a slight exaggeration."

"She's quite a character, isn't she?"

"Yes, she is."

"A real whirling dervish. Slightly fey, very charm-ing."

Charming, fey, I think now. Not the words I would use to describe her.

**What words would you use?** I hear Alison whisper slyly in my ear.

"You'll explain to my mother why I didn't come back to see her?" Josh asked, indicating his wet clothes.

"Can I leave out the part where I almost drowned?"

Josh laughed. "What time next Thursday?"

I quickly mulled over everything I had to do to pre-pare. It had been years since I'd cooked anyone Thanksgiving dinner. I couldn't remember the last time I'd bought a turkey. It's not something you normally buy when you're cooking for one. "Seven o'clock?"

"Seven o'clock," he repeated. "I'm thankful already."

I stepped out of the car and skipped up the hospital's front steps, turning back as I pulled open the door. My hero, I thought, watching Josh drive away, my head pleasantly dizzy with anticipation, the sound of the surf still ringing in my ears.

# 8

"Okay, so are you ready for your whole new look?"

Alison, wearing blue shorts, a white halter top, and hot-pink nail polish on her bare toes, stood outside my kitchen door, her arms loaded with an interesting array of bottles and tubes. Her hair was pulled back into a ponytail. She looked about twelve.

My own hair was freshly washed, as per her instructions, and wrapped in a white towel that matched my white terry-cloth robe. "What's all this?" I stepped back to let her inside.

"Creams, oils, emulsions." She deposited the various items on my kitchen table and arranged them to her satisfaction. "What's an emulsion anyway?"

I thought back to my years at nursing school. "Any

colloidal suspension of one liquid in another liquid," I said, almost by rote, startled by how easily such long-forgotten nuggets resurfaced.

"Colloidal?"

"A colloid is a gelatinous substance which when dissolved in a liquid will not diffuse readily through either vegetable or animal membranes."

Alison looked at me as if I were some new form of alien species. "Could you try that again?"

"It's a liquid preparation that's the color and consistency of milk," I said plainly.

She smiled, lifted a medium-sized glass bottle of white cream into her hands. "That would be this one."

"How can you buy products when you don't know what they are?"

"Nobody knows what they are. That's why they cost so much."

I laughed, thinking she was probably right. "What else have you got here?"

"Let's see. There's a pore-purifying microbead face wash, and an alpha hydroxy exfoliating peel-off masque—that's **masque** spelled with a **que,** which means it's **really** expensive. Then there's a botanical, gentle facial-buffing cream, another botanical cream with collagen and woodmallow. What's that? Never mind," she said in the same breath. "Then we have a soothing eye-contour mask—this one spelled with a **k,** so it's probably not as good—a milky refiner, not to be confused with the aforementioned milky emulsion, an oil-free moisturizing lotion, and a tube of concentrated apricot oil. Did you happen to catch my casual use of the word **aforementioned?**"

"I did."

"Were you impressed?"

"I was."

"Good." She dug into the right-side pocket of her blue shorts, pulled out several small bottles of nail polish. "Very Cherry and Luscious Lilac. Your choice." From her left-side pocket emerged cotton balls, emery boards, and assorted tiny implements of torture. Then she reached behind her and extricated a large pair of scissors from her back pocket, waving them before my eyes like a magic wand. "For Madame's new do."

"I'm not so sure about that," I wavered, pulling the towel off my head.

"Don't worry. I'm not going to do anything drastic. Just even it up a bit, maybe take an inch off the bottom. You said you have cucumbers?"

"In the fridge," I told her, trying to keep up with the conversation.

"Good. Then what say we get started?"

What could I do? Alison was so enthusiastic, so confident, so persuasive, I really didn't have a choice.

**You want to be gorgeous for Thanksgiving, don't you?** I can still hear her ask.

And the truth was, I **did** want to be gorgeous for Thanksgiving. I wanted to be drop-dead, knock-'em-

down-and-drag-'em-out gorgeous for Thanksgiving.
For Josh.

**Not that you aren't gorgeous already,** Alison had
quickly amended.

All week I'd been walking around in a stupid haze,
singing along with the radio, humming merrily off-key
as I doled out medications, even waving a pleasant
"Hello" to Bettye McCoy as she hurried those over-
grown furballs past my house. And why? All because
some guy I liked had been nice to me.

No, more than nice.

Interested.

Interested in me.

**He's only using you,** I could almost hear my
mother say. **He'll break your heart.**

Yes, he probably will, I agreed.

But I didn't care. It didn't matter that Josh was still
carrying a torch for his ex-wife, that he had two kids and
a dying mother, that a serious involvement was probably the last thing he was looking for. It didn't matter
that we'd had only one real date, a **lunch** date at that,
and that I'd almost drowned during it. What mattered
was that he was interested.

**Good enough to eat,** he'd said.

I felt an almost forgotten tingle between my legs.

**What do you really know about this man?** my
mother asked.

Not much, I was forced to admit.

That didn't matter either. Josh Wylie could have

been an ax murderer for all I cared. Sadistic killer or not, he made me feel things I hadn't felt in years. He resurrected emotions so long and deeply repressed I'd forgotten I had them. At forty, I felt like one of those silly teenage girls you see giggling in the mall with her friends: **And then he said; and then he said.** I was fourteen again, in love with Roger Stillman.

**And look what happened there,** my mother reminded me.

"We'll do your hair first," Alison was saying now, a comb appearing from out of nowhere to drag the wet tangles of my hair across my ears and forehead. Alison sat me down and knelt in front of me, her palm turning my chin from one side to the other as she studied my face. She smiled, as if privy to my innermost thoughts. Could she see Josh Wylie in the reflection of my eyes?

I heard the scissors, felt the blades snipping at the air around my head, moving closer. "I'll clean up later," she announced as I felt first one tug, then another, and watched in horror as several wet clumps of hair fell to the white tile of the kitchen floor.

"Oh, God," I moaned.

"Close your eyes," Alison instructed. "Have faith."

With my eyes closed, the sound of cutting was even more intense. It was as if those scissors were slicing through all my protective outer layers, snipping away my secrets, sapping my strength. Samson and Delilah, I thought dramatically, taking a series of long, deep breaths, deciding to roll with the punches, go with the flow.

"I'll wait till after your facial to blow it dry properly. We can go into the living room now," she instructed as I stepped over the hair lying across the white tiles, like a small area rug. "Don't look," she said as a shudder shook my shoulders. "Have faith. Trust me."

I'd already laid a bedsheet across the living room sofa in preparation for my "night at the spa," as Alison had laughingly referred to it, and now I stood paralyzed in front of it, waiting for Alison to tell me what to do.

"Okay. Lie down, with your head at this end, and your feet . . . here. That's good. I want you to be really comfortable. You're going to enjoy this," Alison said as if she wasn't sure. "Now, you get cozy, and I'll bring all the stuff I need in here."

"The cucumber slices are in the fridge," I reminded her, closing my eyes, my fingers darting about my neck, feeling for hair.

"You didn't have to slice them," Alison called back from the kitchen. "I would have done that."

I heard her rifling around in the fridge, heard the tap running, listened to the sounds of cupboard doors opening and closing. What was she looking for?

In less than a minute, Alison was back. "We'll start with the exfoliating masque."

"Is that with a **que** or a **k**?"

She laughed. "The expensive one."

"Oh, good."

"Okay, so close your eyes, relax, think pleasant thoughts."

I felt something cold and slimy being spread across my face, like molasses on a slice of bread.

"This might feel a bit weird as it starts to harden."

"Feels weird now."

"You won't be able to talk," she warned, slathering the product around the outlines of my lips. "So it's best if you stay still."

Did I have a choice? Already it felt as if my face were encased in cement. A death mask, I remember thinking. Death **masque,** I amended, and might have laughed were it not for the stiffening of the muscles around my mouth. "For how long?" I asked through barely parted lips.

"Twenty minutes."

"Twenty minutes?" I opened my eyes, started to sit up.

Firm hands settled me back down. "Relax. The night is young, and we're just getting started. Close your eyes. I'm going to put the cucumbers on them."

"What are the cucumbers for?" I asked, although I was no longer able to pronounce the hard c's and the noun emerged as more of a verbal blur than an actual word.

"They reduce swelling. What kind of nurse are you that you don't know that?" she teased. Then: "Keep still. It was a rhetorical question." She fitted the cucumber slices gently into the empty circles around my eyes. Instantly, the room darkened, as if I were wearing sunglasses. "You like that word, **rhetorical?**"

"Good word," I managed to say without moving my mouth.

"I'm trying to learn three new words every day."

"Oh?" That was an easy one.

"Yeah, it's kind of fun. I just open up the dictionary and point to a word, and if I don't know what it means, I write it down and memorize the definition."

"Such as?"

"Well, let's see. Today I learned three very interesting words: **ineffable,** which means incapable of being expressed or described, like ineffable happiness, you know, so great you can't describe it. That's one. Then there's **epiphany,** which was a real shock because I thought I knew what that one meant, but I was wrong. I was **really** wrong. Do you know what it means?"

"A revelation of some sort," I managed to squeeze out, although the effort required all my concentration.

"An epiphany is 'the sudden, intuitive perception or insight into the reality or essential meaning of something,' " she recited, then paused. I could feel her shaking her head. "Do you want to know what I thought it meant?"

I nodded my chin, careful not to disturb the cucumbers at my eyes.

"Promise you won't laugh."

I grunted. I couldn't have laughed if I'd tried.

"Well, I saw this movie on TV when I was a kid. It was about a man who, for some unknown reason, turned into a chicken. And it was called **Epiphany.** So I assumed that an epiphany was when someone changed into a chicken. I actually grew up believing that. God, can you imagine if I'd tried to use it in a conversation?"

I shook my head, albeit gently. There was something so vulnerable about her, something so terribly raw, as if she were sitting there with all her nerve endings exposed. I wished I could take her in my arms and comfort her like the big overgrown child she was. "What's the third word?" I asked instead.

"**Meros.** It's a flat surface between two channels of a triglyph."

"What's a triglyph?"

"I have no idea." She laughed. "I only do three words, remember. Now that's enough talking. I want you to relax and just enjoy being pampered. Something tells me you don't pamper yourself nearly enough."

She was right. Being pampered was new to me. I'd worked hard all my life, first at school, then at my chosen profession, and even at home, looking after my mother. In some ways, I was grateful that I hadn't had an easy ride, that my mother hadn't spoiled me more. It made me that much more appreciative of the things I did have, more sensitive and caring toward others.

"Okay," Alison was saying. "So while this masque hardens, I'm going to start on your pedicure. I'll be right back. Take deep breaths. Let your whole body relax."

A sudden silence filled the room. I heard her moving about the kitchen. What was she doing? I wondered, taking one deep breath, then another, feeling the tension of the day seep slowly from my limbs.

"You have really strong toenails." Alison's fingers suddenly pulled on the big toe of my right foot.

I realized I hadn't heard her come back into the room. Was it possible I'd fallen asleep? For how long?

"I'm going to cut them now, so try not to move."

My feet squirmed under her touch.

"Don't move," she warned again.

I heard the rapid snipping of the nail clippers as her fingers flitted expertly from one toe to the next. **This little piggy went to market,** I recited silently, then stopped because I couldn't remember what had happened to the next little piggy.

"Now comes the best part," she announced, gently massaging my tired feet with lotion. The smell of apricots drifted toward my nostrils. "Feels good, huh?"

"Feels wonderful," I agreed, although I'm not sure I said the words out loud.

"Why, Terry Painter, I think you're actually beginning to enjoy this."

I nodded, tried to smile, felt tiny fissures at my cheeks, as if my flesh had turned to stone.

"My husband used to give the best foot massages," Alison said, although from the sudden faraway tone in her voice, I knew she was speaking more to herself than to me. "It's probably why I married him. Certainly it would explain why I kept going back to him. He had the best hands. Once he started massaging my feet, I was a goner."

I understood what she meant. Alison had obviously learned a great deal from her former spouse. Her hands were magic. In less than two minutes, I too was a goner.

"I still miss him," Alison continued. "I know I shouldn't, but I can't help myself. He's so cute. You should see him. All the girls take one look at him and faint dead away. Which, of course, was part of the problem. He had no willpower whatsoever. 'Course, neither did I. He'd cheat on me, and I'd swear there was no way I was going to forgive him, no way I was ever going to take his sorry ass back, and then there he'd be one night, standing at my door, and he'd look so damn good, and of course I'd let him in. 'We're just gonna talk,' I'd say, and he'd agree, and we'd go sit on the sofa, and the next minute, he'd start rubbing my feet, and that was that. Back to square one."

I thought I should probably comment, assure her she wasn't the only woman in the world to fall for the wrong guy, or to forgive him too many times. But the truth was that, even had my face been free of its cosmetic constraints, I couldn't have found the strength to speak. Her little-girl voice was like a lullaby, singing me to sleep. I breathed deeply, the room growing ever darker as I drifted in and out of consciousness.

The next thing I remember was the sound of footsteps overhead. I opened my eyes, found myself staring at the white underside of two slices of cucumber. I removed them, my eyes adjusting quickly to the surrounding darkness. I felt my face, still hidden beneath a layer of hard alpha hydroxy. When had Alison turned off the light? How long had I been asleep?

Again I heard the sound of movement overhead, the opening and closing of drawers. Was she in my bedroom? I wondered, pushing myself to my feet and turning on the nearby lamp. What was she doing? Bright red toenails winked at me from beside the soft, white cotton balls wedged between each toe. Very Cherry, I remembered as I walked on my heels toward the stairs.

She was in the guest room, standing in front of the bookshelf that occupied most of the wall opposite the old burgundy velvet sofa bed. Her back was to me. Obviously, she hadn't heard me come up.

"What are you doing?" I asked, the masque around my mouth cracking like glass.

Alison spun around, the book in her hand dropping to the floor, landing on her toes. She gasped, although I'm not sure whether it was from pain or surprise. "Oh my God, you scared me."

"What are you doing?" I asked again, the cracks in my masque lengthening, reaching for my eyes.

Hesitation flickered briefly across her face, like a candle flame caught in an unexpected breeze. "Well, first I came up to look for these," she said, recovering quickly as she pulled a pair of tweezers from her pocket. "I realized I forgot mine, and you were snoring away, it was so cute, I didn't want to wake you up. I figured you must have a pair somewhere, but I had to go through practically every drawer in the bathroom till I found them. Why don't you keep them in the medicine cabinet like everyone else?"

"I thought I did," I answered lamely.

She shook her head. "They were next to your hot rollers, underneath the sink." She returned my tweezers to her pocket. "And then I was on my way back downstairs when I saw all the books, and I thought I'd take a second and look up word number four in the dictionary." She bent down to retrieve the large book with its glossy red-and-yellow cover, held it up for me to see. "A triglyph is a structural member of a Doric frieze," she announced triumphantly. "Please don't ask me what a Doric frieze is."

It was then that I caught sight of my reflection in the window and saw my newly shorn hair sticking out at weird angles from around my mummified face. "Oh, God, I look like the bogeyman."

Alison winced. "Don't even joke about that." She replaced the book on the shelf, laced her arm through mine. "Let's get that masque off your face. We still have lots more to do."

"I think I've had about all the pampering I can take."

"Nonsense. I'm just getting started."

# 9

I took Thanksgiving off.

This was unusual because, since my mother's death five years ago, I'd worked every Thanksgiving. In fact I worked every holiday, and that included Christmas Day and New Year's Eve. Why not? I reasoned. Unlike Margot and Caroline, I had no family waiting for me at home, no one to bemoan my absence or complain they didn't see enough of me. And the residents of Mission Care still needed looking after, holiday or not. It was truly sad how few visitors some of them received, how perfunctory many of those visits were. If I could make the holidays less lonely for these people, many of whom I'd come to like and admire, then I was more than happy to do it. Besides, it was a trade-off: I was doing it as much for me as for them. I didn't want to spend the holidays alone any more than they did.

But this Thanksgiving was different. I wasn't going to be alone. I was having a dinner party, a slightly bigger dinner party than I'd first anticipated. Aside from Josh and Alison, the guest list now included Alison's co-worker, Denise Nickson. Alison had asked if we could include her, and although I was reluctant—I didn't really trust Denise after the incident with the earrings—Alison assured me that she was smart, funny, and basically good at heart. So, against my better judgment, I agreed to include her. Besides, with Denise around to talk to Alison, I reasoned I'd have more time to concentrate on Josh.

"Something smells absolutely fabulous." Alison swept into the kitchen from the dining room, where she'd been setting the table. She was wearing her blue sundress, and her hair, secured behind one ear by a delicate, blue dragonfly clip, hung in a wondrous rush around her shoulders. On her feet were her silver slingback shoes. I still couldn't look at them without feeling a jolt of anxiety. "This turkey is going to be yummy delicious."

"I hope you're right."

"What else can I do to help?"

"The table's set?"

"Wait till you see it. It looks like something out of **Gourmet** magazine. I put the roses Josh sent in the middle, between the candles."

I blushed and turned back toward the stove, pretended to be watching the pot of small red potatoes that were boiling at a brisk and steady pace. Believe it or not, no one had ever sent me flowers before. "I think we're all set to go," I said, running through my mental checklist—turkey, stuffing, marshmallow-covered yams, small red potatoes, homemade cranberry sauce, a pear-and-walnut salad with Gorgonzola dressing.

"We have enough food for an army," Alison remarked, throwing her hands into the air, as if she were tossing confetti. It was a gesture of pure joy, and it made me laugh out loud. "You're so pretty when you laugh," Alison said.

I smiled my appreciation, thinking that if I looked especially nice tonight, it was all because of her. Not only was the haircut she'd given me the best, most flattering haircut I'd ever had—it fell about my face in soft amber waves that stopped just below my chin—but my skin still glowed from the facial she'd administered, and the makeup she'd selected and meticulously applied several hours earlier had somehow managed to be both dramatic and natural. My fingernails matched my toe-nails, Very Cherry going very well with my navy slacks and newly purchased white silk shirt. My silver cupid earrings dangled from my ears. Tonight, I told myself, was going to be a very special night.

The doorbell rang.

"My God," I said. "What time is it?"

Alison checked her watch. "Only six-thirty.

Somebody's very anxious to get here." Big eyes widened in anticipation.

"Do I really look okay?" I pulled my blue-and-white-checkered apron up over my head, careful not to disturb my hair, ran my tongue across the muted red of my lips.

"You look fantastic. Just relax. Take a deep breath."

I took one deep breath, then another for good luck, before proceeding out of the kitchen. Even before I reached the front door, I could hear giggling from outside. Clearly it was Denise, and not Josh, who'd been anxious to get here. Just as clearly, she wasn't alone. Had she and Josh arrived at the same time? I wondered, pulling open the door.

Denise, wearing a pink T-shirt with orange letters that said DUMP HIM, and a pair of tight black jeans, her dark hair spiking rudely around the pale triangle of her face, was standing on the outside landing, skinny arms wrapped around an equally scrawny young man with short brown hair, light brown eyes, and a strong, hawk-like nose. The face was vaguely sinister, although it softened a bit when he smiled. Still, he filled me with unease.

"We're here," Denise announced gaily. "I know we're early, but . . ." She laughed, as if she'd said something funny. "This is K.C.," she said, and laughed again.

Was she drunk? I wondered. High? "Casey?"

"K.C.," the young man explained, biting off each letter. He was about the same age as Alison, I estimated.

"Short for Kenneth Charles. But nobody ever calls me that."

I nodded, wondered who he was and what he was doing in my house.

"Denise?" Alison asked from behind me.

"Hi, you." Denise pushed past me into the living room of my home. "Wow. Nice house. Alison, meet K.C."

"Casey?"

"K.C.," the young man explained again. "Short for Kenneth Charles."

"But nobody ever calls him that," I added, thinking he must get awfully tired of having to explain himself.

"I didn't realize you were bringing a date," Alison said, nervous eyes flitting in my direction.

"Is it a problem? I just assumed it would be all right. Everybody always makes way too much food on Thanksgiving."

"If it's a problem," the young man interjected quickly, "I can go. I don't want to put anybody out."

"No," I heard myself say. "Denise is right. There's more than enough food. We can't very well toss you out on the street on Thanksgiving, can we?" I wasn't being especially magnanimous. It was more that I suddenly decided Josh might be more comfortable if another man was present.

"I'll set another place," Alison volunteered, disappearing into the dining room as I ushered Denise and K.C. toward the sofa and chairs.

"Can I get you something to drink?" I offered.

"Vodka?" Denise asked.

"Beer?" asked K.C.

I had neither, so they settled for white wine. We sat in my living room, sipping on our drinks—Alison and I were sticking to water for the time being—and making awkward conversation. Denise seemed neither particularly smart nor funny, and K.C., who said little, had a way of looking right through you, even in repose, that was quite unsettling. Tonight is going to be a disaster, I thought, almost praying Josh would call to cancel.

"So, where'd you two meet?" Alison asked.

"At the store." Denise shrugged, her eyes zeroing in on the large painting of lush pink and red peonies that hung on the wall across from the sofa. "That's a nice painting."

"Thank you."

"I don't usually like stuff like that. You know, flowers and fruit and stuff."

"Still life," I said.

"Yeah. I usually don't like it. I like art with more of an edge, you know? But this is kinda nice. Where'd you get it?"

"It was my mother's."

"Yeah? And what—you inherited it after she died?" Denise was seemingly oblivious to the fact this might be none of her business. "Along with the house and everything?"

I said nothing, not sure how to respond.

"I've been trying to talk Terry into buying that paint-ing of the woman with the large sun hat on the beach," Alison chipped in, as if aware of my discomfort.

"You're an only child?" Denise pressed, ignoring her.

"Yes, I'm afraid so."

"No, you're lucky," Denise protested. "I have two sis-ters. We hate each other's guts. And Alison has a brother she never talks to. What about you, K.C.? You have any brothers or sisters you can't stand?"

"One of each," he said.

"And where are they tonight?" I asked.

"Back in Houston, I guess."

"I didn't know you were from Texas," Denise said. "I've always wanted to go to Texas."

"It doesn't sound like you've known each other very long," I remarked.

"We met last night." Denise giggled, the incongru-ously childish sound emerging from between deep-purple lips. "Actually, I'd seen him in the store a few times, but we didn't talk until last night."

"I thought you looked familiar," Alison suddenly exclaimed. "You were in on Monday. You asked about the frog sculpture."

K.C. looked vaguely embarrassed. "I was trying to pick you up," he admitted with a laugh.

"Oh, nice talk!" Denise said. "And what? It didn't work, so you came back last night and hit on me?"

"It doesn't mean I don't love you," K.C. said with a sly grin.

Denise laughed. "Isn't he cute? I think he's so cute." She reached over, scraped clawlike fingers across his skinny thigh. "The thing about art," she continued, as if this were the most logical of continua, her eyes back on the floral painting, "is that it's such a lie. Don't you think?"

"I'm not sure I follow," I answered.

"Take these flowers," Denise said. "Or the woman with the hat on the beach. I mean, when have you ever seen flowers this big and lush in real life, or sand that pink? It doesn't exist."

"It exists in the artist's imagination," I argued.

"My point exactly."

"Just because art is subjective doesn't make it a lie. Sometimes an artist's interpretation of something is ultimately more real than the thing itself. The artist is forcing you to view the subject in a new and different light, to arrive at a greater truth."

Denise waved my theories away with a careless hand. The wine sloshed around in her glass, veering dangerously toward the rim. "Artists distort, they enhance, they leave things out." She shrugged. "That makes them liars in my book."

"You got something against liars?" K.C. asked.

I heard a car pull into the driveway, listened to the sound of footsteps on the outside path, was already on my feet when the doorbell rang. I couldn't help but notice the look of anticipation on Alison's face as I walked to the door.

"You look great," she called after me, giving me two encouraging thumbs-up.

I laughed and opened the door, then had to lean against it in case my legs gave out and I fell over the large leafy plant to my right. Josh Wylie was wearing a blue silk shirt and carrying a bottle of Dom Pérignon. He looked absolutely gorgeous, and it was all I could do to keep from throwing myself into his arms. Calm down, I told myself. You're forty years old, not fourteen. Relax. Take deep breaths.

"Am I late?" Josh asked as I closed the door after him, then stood rooted to the floor, as if I'd been planted.

"No. You're perfect. Perfectly on time," I qualified quickly, letting go of the doorframe and accepting the bottle of Dom Pérignon. "You didn't have to bring champagne. Your flowers were more than enough."

"Ooh, champagne." Denise was suddenly at my side, lifting the bottle from my hands. "I'm Denise, and I love champagne." She extended her free hand.

"Denise Nickson, this is Josh Wylie," I said. "Denise works in the gallery with Alison."

Alison waved hello from the sofa.

"It's my aunt's gallery," Denise explained. "So I'm kind of a part-owner, I guess. This is my friend K.C."

"Nice to meet you, Casey."

"K.C.," we corrected in unison.

"Stands for Kenneth Charles," he said.

"But nobody calls him that," Alison said.

"You must get awfully tired of having to explain that

to everyone," Josh said, and I smiled, hearing my own thoughts resonating through his words.

What can I say about that night?

My initial reservations were quickly dispelled in a wave of champagne and friendly banter. Despite the disparity in our ages and interests, the five of us made for a lively and interesting group. The food was delicious, the conversation effortless, the mood relaxed and happy.

"So what exactly does an investment counselor do?" Denise asked Josh at one point, the cranberry sauce on her fork competing with the stubborn purple of her lips. "And don't say he counsels people on their investments."

"I'm afraid there's not much else I can say," Josh demurred.

"Are you counseling Terry on her investments?" K.C. asked.

I laughed. "First I'd have to have some money to invest."

"Oh, come on. You must have lots of money kicking around," Denise protested. "I mean, you work, you own your own house, you have a tenant. Plus I'm sure you have a nice pension."

"Which I don't collect till I retire," I told her, a slight twinge of discomfort worming its way into my gut. How had we come to be discussing my finances?

"What about you, K.C.?" Josh asked. "What is it you do?"

"Computer programmer." K.C. helped himself to

another slice of turkey, another heaping spoonful of yams.

"Another job I'll never understand," Denise said. "Do you have a computer, Terry?"

"No," I answered. "I've never really needed one."

"How can you survive without E-mail?"

"You'd be suprised what you can survive without." I stared into my lap, trying not to picture Josh slamming me against the wall of my bedroom, eager fingers unbuttoning my blouse.

"You have no relatives across the country you need to keep in touch with?" Denise asked.

I shook my head, caught sight of K.C. as he leaned forward, cold eyes focused on me intently. Snake eyes, I thought with a shudder.

"Okay, so what are we all thankful for?" Alison suddenly asked. "Three things. Everybody."

"Oh, God," Denise groaned. "This is so **Oprah.**"

"You first, K.C.," Alison instructed. "Three things you're thankful for."

K.C. lifted his glass into the air. "Good food. Good champagne." He smiled, snake eyes slithering between Alison and Denise. "Bad women."

They laughed.

"Denise?"

Denise made a face that said this sort of game was beneath her, but that she'd indulge us anyway because she was such a good sport. "Let's see. I'm thankful the gallery was closed today and I didn't have to work. I'm thankful my aunt is visiting her daughter in New York and I didn't have to spend Thanksgiving with her. And"—she looked directly at me—"I'm thankful you're as good a cook as Alison said you were."

"Amen to that," Josh said, raising his glass in a toast.

"Okay, Josh," Alison directed, "your turn."

Josh paused, as if giving the matter careful thought. "I'm thankful for my children. I'm thankful for the wonderful care my mother gets each day. And for that, and for tonight, I'm especially thankful to—and for— our lovely hostess. Thank you, Terry Painter. You're a godsend."

"Thank **you**," I whispered, dangerously close to tears.

"I'm thankful for Terry too," Alison said as I felt my cheeks grow warm. "Thankful that's she's given me a place to stay and welcomed me so warmly into her life. Secondly, I'm thankful for my instincts that told me to come here in the first place. And thirdly, I'm thankful for the chance I've been given to start over again."

"Aren't you a little young to be starting over?" Josh asked.

"Your turn." Alison blushed, swiveled toward me.

"I'm thankful for my health," I began.

Denise groaned. "That's like wishing for world peace."

"And I'm thankful for all your kind words," I continued, ignoring her. I looked from Alison to Josh, then back to Alison. "And I'm thankful for new friends and new opportunities. I consider myself very lucky."

"We're the lucky ones," Alison said.

"Does anyone here believe in God?" Denise asked suddenly.

And then everybody was speaking at once, as the conversation veered from philosophic to sophomoric to downright moronic and then back again. Not surprisingly, Alison was among the believers. Surprisingly, so was Denise. K.C. was an atheist, Josh an agnostic. As for me, I'd always wanted to believe, and on a good day, I did.

Today, I decided, perhaps prematurely, had been a good day.

# 10

At ten o'clock, Josh announced it was time for him to be heading back to Miami.

He was right. It was time to call it a night. We'd polished off the homemade pumpkin pie, drunk all the champagne, finished the last of the Baileys. Alison had cleared the table, hand-washed the dishes, and led us in an impromptu game of charades, which she'd handily won. "I'm very good at games," she'd said proudly.

"I'll walk you to your car," I told Josh, feeling a slight twinge in my stomach, like a poke in the ribs, as I rose from the living room sofa and followed him to the door.

"Nice meeting you, Josh," Denise called after him.

"See you again soon, I hope," Alison said.

K.C. said nothing, although I detected a slight nod of

his head that meant either good-bye or that he was too drunk to do more.

No one else made a move to leave. Clearly, Josh and I were the only two people in the room who understood the value of timing.

The warm air embraced us, like a lazy lover, as we stepped outside and gazed up at a sky heavy with stars. The smell of the ocean filtered through the night air like silver threads through a dark tapestry, lingering like an expensive perfume. "Beautiful night," I remarked, walking beside Josh to his car.

"Lovely evening all around."

"I'm so glad you could make it."

"So am I." He looked down the empty street. "Feel like taking a little walk? Just to the corner," he added when I hesitated.

I'm not sure why I hesitated. In truth, I wanted nothing more than to prolong my time with Josh for as long as humanly possible. Probably I was leery of leaving my other guests alone in the house for too long. "Sure," I heard myself say, ignoring my concerns, falling into step beside him. My arm brushed against his. I felt a jolt, like a small but potent electrical charge, shoot through my body.

"I was hoping for a few minutes alone with you," Josh said.

"Do you want to talk about your mother?"

He laughed, stopped walking. "You think I want to get you alone so I can talk about my mother?"

I looked toward the sidewalk, afraid I was so transparent my thoughts were visible on my forehead. I felt his hand at my chin, a succession of increasingly powerful shocks raising my eyes back to his, as I watched his face tilt toward mine. If he gets any closer, I thought, he's liable to be electrocuted.

"I'd really like to kiss you right now," he said.

A loud sigh escaped my lips as he moved closer. My heart was pounding right through my clothes, like a baby kicking in its mother's womb. Except it wasn't my heart, I realized with a sudden gasp. It was my stomach. And it wasn't passion. It was pain. My God, was I going to be sick? Was he going to kiss me and then shrink back in horror while I threw up all over him? Certainly that was one way of ensuring tonight would be a night to remember, I decided, as his lips settled gently on mine.

"Very nice," he whispered, kissing away my fears, his arms wrapping around me like a cloak.

Instantly I relaxed. **Come back into the house,** I wanted to say. **Come back and tell the others they have to leave. Stay and make love to me all night. You can drive back to Miami in the morning.**

Except, of course, I said no such thing. Instead I kissed him again and again, then stood there grinning like an idiot until it became obvious he wasn't going to kiss me anymore, and we turned back, walking hand in hand toward his car, my mind racing with my heart, my intestines doing a slow rope burn against the inside of my stomach. I was thinking that it doesn't matter how old we are, fourteen or forty, we're ageless when it comes to love.

"Thanks again for a wonderful evening," Josh said when we reached his car.

"Thank **you** for the champagne and the roses."

"I'm glad you liked them."

"They're beautiful."

"So are you."

He kissed me again, this time on the cheek, his eyelashes fluttering against my skin, like butterfly wings. "I'll see you next week," he said, climbing into his car.

I watched in silence as he backed his car onto the street, heading toward Atlantic Avenue. When he reached the stop sign at the corner, he waved without looking back, as if he knew I was still watching him. I waved back, but by then he was already halfway down the next block.

It took several minutes before I was able to move. Truthfully, it was as much the tingling on my lips and cheek as the renewed cramping in my gut that rendered me immobile. Too much rich food and excitement for an old lady, I decided when I was finally able to put one foot in front of the other. I returned to the house, prepared to tell the others that the party was officially over, but my living room was empty. Had everyone cleared out while I was gone?

It was then I heard the sound of careless laughter bouncing above my head like a rubber ball. What were they doing upstairs? I wondered, temporarily forgetting about the pains in my stomach. "Alison," I called from the foot of the stairs.

Immediately Alison's head popped into view at the top of the landing. "Josh leave?"

"What are you doing up there?" I asked, ignoring her question.

Denise suddenly appeared beside Alison. "My fault. I asked for a tour of the house."

"There's not much to see." I watched the two young women make their way down the stairs, K.C. nipping at their heels like a large, uncoordinated golden retriever.

"It's like a little dollhouse," Denise pronounced.

"I'm sorry," Alison whispered in my ear. "She was up the stairs before I could stop her."

Whatever annoyance I was feeling was replaced by a sharp jab to my solar plexus. I grimaced, grabbed my side.

"Something wrong?" Alison asked.

I shook my head. "I think I should have skipped that second helping of pie," I muttered, hoping I wouldn't have to say more.

"Okay, guys," Alison announced immediately. "Party's over. Time to pack it in."

We said our good-byes at the front door. Alison kissed me on the cheek. I think Denise hugged me. K.C. mumbled something about being slightly inebriated, then almost fell into the leafy branches of the large, white oleander that sat to the right of the front door. Then they were gone, and the house was quiet, save for the whispering of the leaves.

\*     \*     \*

SURPRISINGLY, I had no trouble falling asleep.

My stomach seemed to settle down the minute every-one left, so I attributed the discomfort to all the excite-ment: the elaborate dinner; a house full of new people; my first kiss in forever; Josh; Josh; Josh. "Yes!" I said in Alison's voice. Then again, watching her clap her hands together and jump up and down with glee. "Yes, yes, yes!"

And then I must have fallen asleep, because the next thing I knew I was dreaming. Wild dreams. Crazy dreams. Dreams where I was running around the house in helpless circles, trying to find Alison, to warn her of danger, although the danger was nonspecific, unde-fined. At one point, I was climbing up the stairs when K.C. jumped out at me from the shadows, long legs fly-ing, karate-style, through the air toward my stomach.

I gasped, doubled forward in my bed, barely made it to the bathroom, where I threw up, copiously and repeatedly. But even a thorough purging of the night's dinner provided little relief. I sat on the tile floor, my head spinning, painful spasms shooting through my body like pinballs, wondering whether it was possible I was having an attack of appendicitis. Unlikely, I knew. It was much more likely to be a simple case of overindul-gence, or perhaps even food poisoning. I wondered if any of my guests had gotten sick.

Oh, God, poor Josh, I thought, pushing myself to my feet and creeping slowly, my back hunched, like a dod-dering old woman, toward my bedroom window. I pulled back the lace curtains, stared at the cottage behind my house, surprised to see the lights still on. I glanced at the clock beside my bed. It was almost three in the morning, awfully late for Alison to be up. Was she sick as well? I pulled on my housecoat and gingerly made my way down the stairs.

I unlocked the kitchen door and tiptoed outside, the grass cool on my bare feet. A sudden rush of nausea almost overwhelmed me, and I gulped frantically at the fresh air until the feeling subsided. I took several long, deep breaths before continuing toward the cottage door. It was then I heard the sound of laughter from inside the cottage. Clearly, Alison wasn't sick. Nor was she alone.

I returned to the house, relieved that Alison was okay, that it appeared no one else had gotten sick. My reputation as a cook was safe, I thought, and might have laughed had it not been for the renewed spasms that catapulted me toward the kitchen sink. Dozens of ceramic eyes looked down disapprovingly from the shelves above my head, the pitiless, blank stares of the china ladies passing silent judgment on my condition. **Serves you right,** the women shouted through pouting, painted lips. **That'll teach you to have too good a time.**

I was halfway up the stairs when the phone rang.

Who would be calling me at this hour? I wondered, moving as quickly as my stomach would permit. Alison? Had she seen me outside the cottage door? I pushed my bent frame toward the phone beside my bed, answered it at the start of its fifth ring. "Hello?"

"Have a nice evening?" the voice asked.

Not Alison. A man. "Who is this?"

"I have a message for you from Erica Hollander."

"What!"

"She says you better watch your step."

"Who is this?" The phone went dead in my hands. "Hello? Hello?" I slammed down the receiver, too angry to speak, too weak to try. I fell back on the bed, hands shaking, heart pounding, my brain alternating between trying to place the voice and to put it out of my mind altogether. What did his strange message mean? Of course, sleep was no longer an option. I spent the balance of the night rolling from one side of the bed to the other, either too hot or too cold, my teeth chattering or my forehead bathed in sweat, my arms securing the blankets tightly under my chin, my feet kicking them angrily back to the foot of the bed. For hours I lay on my back observing the moonlight slither through the lace of my curtains, watching the darkness bleed from the sky until it grew light. Whenever it looked as if I might be granted a few minutes respite, a not-quite-familiar voice would sneak up beside me and whisper in my ear: **I have a message for you from Erica Hollander. She says you better watch your step.**

At around eight o'clock, I pushed myself out of bed. I was still nauseous and weak, but at least my stomach was no longer threatening to burst from my body. My forehead felt a little warm to the touch, and my hands were still trembling. I decided to make some tea, maybe eat a piece of toast, although, at the thought of food, my stomach lurched. Maybe just tea, I decided, about to head downstairs when I heard voices outside my window.

I shuffled toward the sound and pulled back the curtains, careful to stay out of sight. Alison was standing in the open doorway of the cottage talking to Denise, both still dressed in last night's clothes. Denise was doing most of the talking, although I couldn't make out what she was saying. The look on Alison's face, however, told me she was paying close attention.

"Come on, sleepyhead," Denise suddenly shouted toward the inside of the cottage. "Time to get your bony ass out of there."

Seconds later, K.C. stood in the doorway. His shirt hung open and his blue jeans rode dangerously low on his skinny hips, emphasizing the line of dark hair that spiraled from the center of his bare chest down past his belly button, then disappeared beneath the buckle of his black leather belt. His short brown hair was matted and uncombed, and sleep clung to his eyes as carelessly as the half-smoked cigarette that dangled from his lips.

I watched him toss the cigarette into my bed of pink and white impatiens, then lean toward Alison and whisper something in her ear, his fingers playing with the gold necklace at her throat as his eyes glanced toward my bedroom window. Was he talking about me? I wondered, careful to keep out of sight. Did he know I was there?

Alison pushed him playfully aside, waving after them as he and Denise ambled along the side of the house to the street. My eyes followed after them until they disappeared into the shadow of a nearby tree. When I looked back, I saw Alison staring up at me, a strange look on her face. She waved, signaled that she was coming over. Seconds later, looking remarkably fresh and rested for someone who'd been up all night, she was at the kitchen door.

"Are you all right?" she asked as soon as she saw me.

"I was sick last night." I promptly collapsed into one of the kitchen chairs.

"Sick? You mean like throwing-up sick?"

"I mean like throwing-up sick."

"Oh, yuck! That's awful. I hate throwing up. It's my least favorite thing in the whole world."

"I can't say I'm overly fond of it myself."

"You know how some people tell you that throwing up will make you feel better? Not me. I'd rather feel sick as a dog for weeks on end than throw up. That's why it was always such a joke to me when people thought I was bulimic. As if I would ever do anything to make myself vomit. I mean, yuck!"

I could almost see the exclamation point.

"I remember when I was a little girl," she continued, "and I got sick one night after eating too much red licorice, and every night after that, when I'd climb into bed, I'd ask my mother if I was going to be all right. And she'd roll her eyes and say yes, but I wasn't convinced, so I'd make her promise. Even still, I'd grit my teeth until I fell asleep."

"You didn't believe your mother?"

Alison shrugged, her eyes circling the kitchen. "You want some tea?"

"I'd love some."

She busied herself with the mechanics of making tea. She filled the kettle with water, dropped a tea bag into a mug, got the milk out of the fridge. "You probably drank too much champagne," she ventured, eyes glued to the kettle.

"A watched pot never boils," I told her.

"What?"

" 'A watched pot never boils.' One of my mother's little aphorisms."

"Aphorism? Good word. That's like, what, a saying?"

"More or less."

Alison obligingly looked away from the kettle and toward the window. "So I guess you saw me talking to Denise and K.C." It was more statement than question.

I nodded, said nothing.

"They wanted to see the cottage." She paused, studied her bare feet. "Anyway, we stayed up pretty late talking, and next thing I knew, Denise was curled up in my bed and K.C. was passed out on the floor." The teakettle whistled its readiness. Alison jumped at the sound, then laughed. "Looks like your mother was right. I just had to stop watching it."

"Mother knows best." I chose my next words carefully. "Did you call your family to wish them a happy Thanksgiving?"

"No." Alison poured my tea. "Not quite ready to do that yet. Here. Drink this. It'll make you feel better."

"I hope so." I took a tentative sip.

"So, did you enjoy last night? I mean, aside from the throwing-up part."

I laughed, understanding the subject of her family was closed, at least for now. "I had a wonderful time."

"I think Josh really likes you."

"You do?"

"I could tell by the way he looked at you. He thinks you're something special."

"He's a very nice man." I took another sip of my tea, felt it burn the tip of my tongue, pulled back.

"Careful," Alison warned too late. "It's hot."

"So, what are you up to today? Going to the beach with your friends?"

"Not a chance. I'm going to stay right here and make sure you're okay."

"Oh, no. I don't want you to do that."

Alison pulled up a chair, plunked down beside me. "You took care of me when I got sick, didn't you?"

"Yes, but . . ."

"No buts." She smiled. "It's settled. I'm not going anywhere."

NOT LONG AFTER I FINISHED THE TEA, my nausea returned, and I suffered through an agonizing round of dry heaves. Surprisingly, Alison made a wonderful nurse, holding a cool compress to my head and not leaving my side until I was safely tucked back in bed. "Sleep," I can still hear her repeating as she stroked my hair. "Sleep . . . sleep."

Whether it was from exhaustion, the sound of her voice, or the touch of her hand, within minutes I was sound asleep. This time, no dreams plagued me. I slept soundly, deeply, for several hours. When I opened my eyes, it was almost noon.

I sat up in bed, twisting my neck from side to side to get rid of the stiffness that had settled in. Then I heard a voice talking quietly from the second bedroom and realized it was Alison. "I didn't call to fight," I heard her say as I climbed out of bed, steadying myself against the wall as I shuffled toward the door.

"Everything is going exactly as planned," she continued as I stepped into the hall, drew closer. "You're just going to have to trust that I know what I'm doing."

I must have made a sound because she suddenly spun around in her seat, went ghostly white.

"Terry! How long have you been standing there? Are you all right?" The words tumbled from her mouth in a frantic rush, like sand from a broken hourglass. "Look, I have to go," she said into the portable phone at her ear, before stuffing it unceremoniously into the pocket of her white shorts. She jumped to her feet and quickly ushered me toward the sofa, then sat so close to me our knees were touching. "My brother," she explained, patting the phone in her pocket. "I decided you were right, that the least I could do was call my family and wish them a happy holiday, let them know I'm okay."

"It didn't go well?"

"About as well as expected. Anyway, how are you? You look a hundred percent better."

"I feel better," I said without much conviction. What had Alison been talking to her brother about? What, I wondered, was going exactly as planned? "What have you been doing all morning?" I asked instead.

"First I went home, took a shower, changed my clothes. Then"—a huge grin swept across Alison's face, temporarily obliterating my concerns—"I found this." She grabbed a large, leather-bound photo album from the pillow beside her, balanced it across her lap. "I hope you don't mind. I stumbled across it when I was looking for something to read." She flipped it open. "Are these your parents?"

I found myself staring at an old black-and-white photograph of a smiling young couple at a public swimming pool, my father's skinny legs sticking out from underneath a pair of dark, oversize swim trunks, loafers on his feet, a straw hat on his head, my mother sitting beside him in a modest gingham bathing suit, hands clasped primly in her lap, hair piled high on her head, large, white sunglasses swamping her small face. How long had it been since I'd looked at these pictures? The album had been tucked away at the back of the highest shelf. How had Alison simply stumbled across it? "That's them," I said, brushing an invisible hair away from my mother's face, feeling her swat my hand aside. "They weren't married yet."

As Alison steadily turned the pages, I watched my parents grow up before my eyes, from shy young lovers to self-conscious newlyweds to nervous parents. "This one's my favorite." Alison pointed to a picture of my mother pressing a sad-eyed baby to her cheek. "Look at how cute you were."

"Cute, my ass. Just look at those bags under my eyes." I shook my head in dismay. "My mother claimed I didn't sleep through the night until I was three years old. And I peed in my pants until I was seven. No wonder they decided not to have any more kids."

Alison laughed, studied each page in turn. "Which one's you?" she asked suddenly, indicating a large photograph of a bunch of small children arranged in neat little rows, like pansies in a garden—my senior kindergarten class.

I pointed to a little girl in a white dress, frowning from the back row.

"You don't look very happy."

"I never liked having my picture taken."

"No? I love it. Oh, look at this one. Is this you?" Alison's index finger landed on a little girl in a plaid jumper, scowling beside her third-grade teacher.

"That's me all right."

"Would you just look at that face." Alison laughed. "You have the same expression in every picture, even as a teenager. Which one's Roger Stillman?"

"What?"

"Roger Stillman. Is he in any of these pictures?"

"No. He was a few grades ahead of me," I reminded her.

"Too bad. I would have liked to see what he looked like. What do you think happened to him?"

"I have no idea."

"Do you ever think of just picking up the phone and calling him? Saying, 'Hi, Roger Stillman, this is Terry Painter. Remember me?' "

"Never," I said, louder than I'd intended.

"Do you think he still lives in Baltimore?"

I shrugged my lack of interest, flipped to another page, saw my parents, now in glorious color, posed together on the front lawn of their first house in Delray Beach. They looked a little stiff, as if aware there were difficult times ahead. "Would you mind making me another cup of tea?" I asked.

"It would be my supreme pleasure." Alison pushed herself off the sofa. "How about some toast and jam to go with it?"

"Why not?"

"That's the spirit."

I leaned my head against the burgundy velvet of the sofa, closed my eyes, the sound of Alison's voice soft against my ear. **Everything is going exactly as planned,** she purred. And then another voice: **I have a message for you from Erica Hollander,** the stranger whispered in my ear. **She says you better watch your step.**

But I was too tired, too weak, to listen.

# 11

The weeks between Thanksgiving and Christmas were especially busy, both at the hospital and at home. In the five years since my mother's death, I hadn't bothered much with the festive trappings of the holiday season. Indeed, I'd gone out of my way to ignore the holidays, often working overtime and volunteering for the graveyard shift. But Alison was determined to change that.

"What do you mean you're working on Christmas?" she wailed.

"It's just another day."

"No, it's not. It's Christmas. Can't you switch with somebody else?"

I shook my head. It was late afternoon and I was

working in my garden. Alison was pacing restlessly back and forth on the lawn behind me.

"But that really sucks!" she protested, looking and sounding at least a decade younger than her twenty-eight years. "I mean, I was kind of hoping we could have Christmas together."

"We could do Christmas Eve."

Immediately her face brightened. "That's right. Lots of families open their presents on Christmas Eve, don't they? I guess that would be okay. Can I go with you to pick out a tree?"

"A tree?" I couldn't remember the last time I'd had a Christmas tree.

"You have to have a tree! What's Christmas without a tree? And we'll get decorations and little white lights. My treat, of course. It's the least I can do. It'll be so great. Can we do that?"

How could I say no? In the weeks since I'd been sick, Alison had become a regular—and increasingly welcome—part of my day. We spoke often on the phone from our respective places of work, had dinner together two or three times a week, occasionally went to the movies or for a leisurely stroll along the beach. No matter how busy our schedules, Alison found time for us to be together. And despite my initial reservations about tenants in general, and Alison in particular, she simply ran roughshod over any misgivings I might have had. I was powerless where she was concerned, I realized as we drove along Military Trail some days later, a tall Scotch pine protruding from the half-open trunk of my car. Alison had managed, in the space of only several months, to become an integral part of my life, and despite the twelve-year difference in our ages, probably the closest friend I'd ever had.

"Is this not the most absolutely gorgeous tree in the whole wide world?" she asked after we'd finished attaching the last of the delicate, pink bows to its long, sharp branches. We stood back to admire our handiwork.

"It's absolutely the most gorgeous tree in the whole wide world," I concurred, and she hugged me.

"This is going to be the best Christmas ever," Alison declared as Christmas Eve drew closer, and she added yet another present to the growing pile under the tree that she'd stationed in the corner of my living room.

"I think she's homesick," I confided to Margot at work. "I mean, you should see what she's done to the house. There are decorations everywhere, mountains of holly sprigs, and I can't move without bumping into one of these weird little Santas she has everywhere."

"Sounds like she's taking over," Margot observed with a laugh. "How long before she moves in and you go back to living in the cottage?" She reached for a patient's file, answered the ringing phone beside her.

"I think she's just homesick," I repeated, vaguely annoyed with Margot, although I wasn't sure why.

Margot held out the phone. "For you."

"Terry Painter," I announced, expecting to hear Alison's voice. Had she somehow sensed we were talking about her?

"Terry, it's Josh Wylie."

My heart sank.

"I really hate to do this to you again," he was saying as I lowered my chin to my chest, silently mouthing the words along with him. "Something's come up, and I'm going to have to cancel our lunch. I'm really sorry."

"So am I," I said truthfully. This was the third lunch date Josh had canceled in as many weeks. Aside from a few quick exchanges when he'd dropped by to visit his mother, we hadn't seen each other since Thanksgiving.

"How about dinner?" he surprised me now by asking. "I have to be up your way later and I have a little something for you."

"You have something for me?"

" 'Tis the season. It's just a little token of my appreciation. For being so nice to my mother," he added quickly. "How about I pick you up at seven o'clock?"

"Seven o'clock would be fine."

"Seven o'clock it is." He clicked off without saying good-bye.

"Somebody looks awfully pleased with herself," Margot said with a sly wink.

I said nothing, my mind already on the night ahead. So what if Josh had canceled three lunch dates in a row. One dinner equaled three lunches any day. Not only that, but he had a gift for me—a small token of his appreciation, he'd said. **For being so nice to my mother.** I tried to imagine what it could be. A bottle of perfume? Some fancy soaps? Maybe a silk scarf or even a small brooch? No, it was way too early for jewelry. Our relationship—if a few kisses and several canceled lunch dates could be called a relationship—was still in the beginning stages. It wouldn't be appropriate, as my mother might have said, for him to be showering me with extravagant gifts. It didn't matter. Whatever Josh gave me would be wonderful. I wondered what I could get him in return, deciding to ask Myra for her advice. Her condition had deteriorated in the last few weeks, and she was understandably depressed. Perhaps news of my upcoming dinner date with her son might cheer her up.

But Myra was asleep when I entered her room, so after checking her IV and adjusting her blankets, I left. "I'm having dinner with your son tonight," I said from the doorway. "Wish me luck."

But the only response I got was an involuntary whistle that escaped Myra's lips as she exhaled. I closed the door and stepped into the hall, where I was almost run over by one of the orderlies. "What's going on?" I called after him as he raced down the hall.

"Patient in 423 came out of her coma," he called back excitedly.

"Sheena O'Connor?" I asked, but the young man had already disappeared around a corner. "My God, I don't believe it."

I hurried to room 423, pushed open the door. The room was overflowing with doctors and assorted medical personnel, everyone moving about purposefully, their actions both condensed and exaggerated, as if the scene were being enacted in both slow motion and fast-forward simultaneously. I caught a glimpse of the pale young woman who was the calm at the center of the storm. She was sitting up in bed, still attached to a myriad of tubes, and our eyes connected for only the briefest of seconds as I was backing out of the room.

"Wait!" Her tiny voice pierced the air.

I froze as half a dozen bodies swiveled in my direction, half a dozen faces found my own.

"I know you," the girl said. "You're the one who's been singing to me, aren't you?"

"You heard me?" I approached the bed, the doctors and nurses who surrounded her clearing a path for me.

"I heard you," Sheena said softly, leaning back against her pillow, large, dark eyes fluttering to a close.

"It's a miracle," a hushed voice whispered from a corner of the room.

"Has anyone notified her family?" someone asked.

"Her parents are on their way."

"Should we call the police?"

"They've already been notified."

"It's a miracle," someone else said. "A true Christmas miracle."

I COULDN'T WAIT TO SHARE THE NEWS of Sheena's miraculous recovery with Alison, so I decided to stop off at the gallery where she worked. Maybe Alison could help me select a gift for Josh, something **appropriate**, I thought, feeling giddy and euphoric, as I pulled into a just vacated parking space right on Atlantic Avenue. Another miracle!

I didn't see Alison when I entered the store. Nor did I see Denise. Indeed, the gallery appeared to be deserted. How on earth did they stay in business? I wondered, looking around, noting that the painting of the woman with the wide-brimmed sun hat no longer occupied its usual place on the far wall. I felt a pang of regret. Alison had been right about it being the perfect painting for my living room. It was too bad I hadn't taken her advice and scooped it up when I had the chance. Obviously, someone much more decisive than I had done just that.

My life was a collection of missed opportunites, I thought glumly, deciding that was about to change.

Starting with tonight.

Starting with Josh.

"Hello?" I called out. "Alison?"

"Can I help you?"

I turned to see an attractive woman approximately my own age walking toward me, her high heels clicking against the hardwood floor.

"I'm sorry. I was in my office. Have you been waiting long?"

"Just got here."

The woman smiled, although the skin around her mouth was pulled so tight it was hard to tell whether she was happy or in pain. Reflexively, I brought my hand to my cheek, pushed at the fine lines around my eyes. "Is there something in particular you're looking for?" she asked.

"Actually, I'm looking for someone who works here. Alison Simms."

The woman's smile became a tense, straight line. "Alison no longer works here," she said curtly.

"She doesn't?"

"She left last week."

"She left? Why?"

"I'm afraid I had to let her go."

"You had to let her go?" I repeated, feeling like a parrot. "Why?"

"Perhaps you should ask her."

Alison hadn't said a word about being let go. She **had** told me that her boss had requested she not receive any more calls at work. Dear God, was I the reason she'd lost her job? "And this happened last week?" I heard myself ask, my mind reeling.

"Is there anything **I** can help you with?" Fern Lorelli was clearly anxious to move on.

I muttered something about needing a Christmas gift for a friend and eventually purchased an attractively masculine ballpoint pen I thought Josh might like, but my heart wasn't in it. Why had Alison been fired? More importantly, why hadn't she told me? I made up my mind to ask her as soon as I got home.

My phone was ringing as I pulled into the driveway. I ran into the house, the bells Alison had hung on the front door jingling as I raced into the kitchen and grabbed for the phone. I dropped the small bag containing my new purchase on the counter beside three small plastic Santas, all of whom stared at the bag with bemused curiosity. "Hello?"

A soft male voice slithered through the phone wire like a snake. "Buy anything for me?"

My breath froze in my lungs, even as my eyes darted nervously toward the back window. Had someone been following me? Was I being watched? Why? I wondered, my arms folding protectively across my chest, as if I were standing in my kitchen completely naked. "Who is this? What do you want?"

My answer was a sly chuckle, followed by silence and the familiar drone of the dial tone.

"Damn it!" I hung up and immediately pressed *69. But whoever was calling had blocked the trace. I slammed the phone into its carriage.

It rang again almost immediately.

"Look, I don't know what your problem is," I said instead of hello. "But if you don't stop bothering me, I'm going to call the police."

"Terry?"

"Josh!"

"I know I broke our lunch date, but do you really think the police are necessary?"

"I'm so sorry. I've been getting these crank calls. . . . It's nothing." I sighed, shook thoughts of other voices out of my head.

"Rough day?"

"Actually, no," I said, regrouping, refocusing. "It was a great day." I wondered briefly why he was calling. Surely it wasn't to talk about my day. "You remember Sheena O'Connor? She came out of her coma this afternoon," I prattled on, almost afraid to let him speak. "It was incredible. Everyone's calling it a Christmas miracle."

"It must have been very exciting."

"It was amazing. And the best part was that she'd heard me singing to her while she was comatose. Isn't that incredible?" I asked, sounding just like Alison, aware I'd used superlatives three times in as many seconds. "Anyway, I'll tell you all about it tonight."

An awful silence followed. For the second time that day, my heart sank, my happiness crashing to the floor with such force I felt the room shake beneath my feet.

"I feel like such a jerk," Josh was saying.

"Is there a problem?" I opened the nearest drawer and stuffed the gift bag from Lorelli Gallery inside it. Clearly, I wasn't going to be seeing Josh Wylie anytime soon.

"It's Jillian," he said, referring to his daughter. "She came home from school and said she wasn't feeling very well."

"Does she have a fever?"

"I don't think so, but I just wouldn't feel comfortable about leaving her. I'm so sorry. I can't believe I'm doing this to you twice in one day. Maybe you **should** call the police."

"Some days are like that," I said gamely, slamming the cupboard drawer shut, watching the three Santas collapse against each other, like dominoes.

"I feel really terrible about this."

"You'll make it up to me," I ventured bravely.

"Absolutely. As soon as I get back from California."

"You're going away?"

"Just for a couple of weeks. The kids have cousins in San Francisco. We leave the day after tomorrow, get back January third."

So much for New Year's Eve, I thought.

"I hope you don't hate me."

"These things happen."

"I **will** make it up to you."

"Have a wonderful trip," I said. "And tell Jillian I hope she feels better soon."

"I will."

"See you next year," I said cheerily, then hung up the phone before I burst into tears. "Damn it!" I swore. "Damn it. Damn it. Damn it!"

There was a knock on the kitchen door. I gasped, budding tears coating my eyes, leaving a filmy residue.

"I'm sorry," Alison apologized over the sound of jingling bells as I opened the door to let her in. "I didn't mean to scare you."

I caught a glimpse of strawberry curls, white shorts, and long, tanned legs, before turning away.

"Terry, what's wrong?"

"Why didn't you tell me you lost your job?" I demanded, swiping at my eyes with the back of my hand, refusing to look at her.

I could almost feel the color drain from Alison's face. "What?"

"I dropped into the gallery this afternoon. I spoke to Fern Lorelli."

"Oh."

"She said she had to let you go."

Silence. Then: "What else did she say?"

"Not much."

"She didn't say why?"

Wiping the last errant tears from my eyes, I pivoted around to face her. Alison's gaze immediately dropped to the floor. "She said I should ask you."

Alison nodded, still unable to look me in the eye. "I was going to tell you."

"But you didn't."

"I thought I'd wait until I found another job. I didn't want you worrying about the rent. I didn't want to ruin Christmas."

"Why were you let go?"

Slowly Alison lifted her gaze to mine. "I didn't do anything wrong," her voice implored. "Apparently there was some money missing. Certain figures didn't add up. . . . I swear it wasn't me."

"It was just easier for her to fire you than confront her own niece," I offered after a pause, biting down on my tongue to keep from adding, **I told you so.**

"You don't have to worry about anything. Honestly. I have enough money."

"I'm not worried about the money."

"Then what is it? Are you worried about me? Don't be," she said before I could respond. "I'm sorry I didn't tell you. I won't lie to you ever again. I promise. Please don't be angry with me."

"I'm not angry."

"You're sure?"

I nodded, realizing it was true, that if I was angry with anyone, it was with myself. For being such a damn fool.

"I have a great idea," Alison suddenly announced, running from the room.

Seconds later, I heard her foraging around under the Christmas tree, and seconds after that she was back, a brightly, if somewhat sloppily, wrapped gift in her hands. She extended it toward me. "Since we're opening the presents early anyway, it won't hurt to open this one now. Ignore the wrapping. I actually took a course in gift-wrapping once, would you believe? Go on. Open it. It'll make you feel better."

"What is it?"

"Open it."

I tore the wrapping off the brown cardboard box, opened it. Large dark eyes stared up at me from under a shroud of translucent bubble wrap. Slowly, carefully, I lifted the head vase into the air. The china lady sported an elaborate blond coif, a large blue bow at her throat, and mock diamond studs in her ears. "She's beautiful. Where did you find her?"

"At the flea market over by Woolbright. Isn't she great? I mean, I know you think they're junk and every-thing, but I couldn't resist. I saw her, and I thought it was kind of like a sign or something."

"A sign?"

"Like I was meant to find her, and you were meant to have her. Fate," she said with an embarrassed roll of her eyes. "I mean, the other heads were more your mother's. This one's, well . . . she's all yours. Your first-born, so to speak. Do you like her?"

"I like her very much."

Alison squealed with delight. "She's in mint condi-tion. Check the eyelashes."

"She's perfect." I turned the china head over in my hands. "Thank you."

"Feel better?"

"Much."

"Where are you going to put her?" Alison glanced toward the five shelves of ladies' heads.

"This one's pretty special. I think I'll keep her in my room."

Alison beamed, as if I'd just paid her the highest of compliments. "So, I guess I'll see you later?"

"Later," I agreed, hearing the bells jingle as the kitchen door closed behind her. I wandered into the dining area, smiling at the sprigs of holly and pine that lay across the top of the cabinet, at the apple-cheeked Santa Claus who stood in the middle of the dining room table, at the papier-mâché reindeer that leaned against the wall.

The living room was more of the same: more Santas, more reindeer, at least a dozen elves. If there was a space, something Christmassy was in it. And then there was the tree itself—tall and full and smelling of the forest, its branches swathed in pink bows and small white lights, presents swelling from beneath its base. Just looking at it buoyed my spirits. And it was all Alison's doing, I recognized, cradling the china head vase in my hands as if it were indeed my firstborn child.

Alison was the true Christmas miracle, I decided.

What was I doing moping around the house because some guy had stood me up? Just think of all the things I had to be grateful for.

**Name three,** I heard Alison urge.

"My health," I said reflexively, then groaned. "Sheena O'Connor's amazing recovery." My God, she'd actually heard me sing to her! "Alison," I whispered, then again, louder, more forcefully: "Alison."

I looked down at the china head in my hands, my heart full of remorse. I was no better than Fern Lorelli, I thought with disgust. I'd used Alison as a scapegoat, transferred my anger and disappointment with someone else to her.

How could I have let her leave without giving her something in return? I reached under the tree and selected a small parcel wrapped in silver foil. Then I carried it back into the kitchen, leaving the china head on the kitchen table, next to the Santa Claus salt-and-pepper shakers Alison had picked up at Target. The sound of jingle bells followed me across the small patch of yard to the cottage door.

I heard the voices as I was about to knock.

"I told you to let me handle this," Alison was saying, her voice an angry hiss, intense enough to be heard from outside.

"I'm just here to help."

"I don't need your help. I know what I'm doing."

"Since when?"

I turned to leave, my shoulder accidentally brushing against the bells hanging from the bronze knocker, setting them jangling. Almost immediately, the door opened, and Alison stood before me with questioning eyes. "Terry!"

Instinctively, I thrust the gift toward her. "I wanted you to have this."

"Oh, that's so sweet." She glanced toward the interior of the cottage. "You didn't have to."

"I know, but I thought . . . " What did I think? "Is someone here?" I ventured meekly.

There was a moment's strained silence as a handsome young man materialized behind Alison, as if waved there by a magic wand. He was several inches taller than Alison, with fair skin, curly, dark hair, and the disturbingly blue eyes of a Siamese cat. Well-defined biceps bulged from beneath the short sleeves of a black T-shirt that stretched tightly across his chest.

"That would be me," the young man said, smiling. He reached around Alison and extended his hand.

"Terry," Alison said, her gaze drifting toward the grass, the second time this afternoon she'd been too embarrassed to look me in the eyes, "I'd like you to meet Lance Palmay. My brother."

# 12

A pleasure to meet you," Lance said, his hand-shake surprisingly gentle.

"I called him after Thanksgiving. Remember?" Alison asked.

I nodded, recalling the one-sided conversation I'd overheard the morning I was so desperately sick.

**Everything is going exactly as planned. You're just going to have to trust that I know what I'm doing.**

"Lance decided he needed to fly down and see for himself how I'm making out."

"Looks like she's managing just fine," Lance pronounced.

"That's why I came over before, to tell you about Lance," Alison explained, inviting me inside the cottage with a sweep of her hand. "We got kind of sidetracked. . . ."

I'm not sure what I expected to see when I stepped inside—a tinsel-covered wonderland, a veritable army of toys, a re-creation of the North Pole? But surprisingly, the cottage bore only a few traces of Christmas— a large red candle, surrounded by a few careless sprigs of holly, on the glass coffee table in front of the deep purple love seat, a lonely Santa Claus doll lying facedown on the bentwood rocker. That was it.

"Do you want a cold drink?" Alison offered.

I shook my head, watched as Lance flopped down on the large floral-print chair. He looks way too comfortable, I thought, masking the unkind thought with a clearing of my throat. "When did you get in?"

"Plane got into Fort Lauderdale around twelve-thirty." He smiled at Alison. "I rented a car at the airport. White Lincoln Town Car, no less. It's parked across the street. You must have seen it. Surprised old sleepyhead here as she was getting out of bed."

Alison's eyes narrowed as her shoulders tensed.

"Where are you staying?" I asked.

The two exchanged wary glances.

"We were just talking about that," Alison began.

"I thought I could stay here for a few days," Lance said as if the decision had already been made.

"Here?" I repeated when I could think of nothing else to say.

"Of course if you have any objections . . . ," Alison said quickly.

"Why would she object?" Lance asked, looking right at me.

"But where would you sleep?" The sofa was far too short for the elongated legs of a former high school basketball player, the double bed way too small to accommodate a brother and sister comfortably.

"This is a pretty neat chair." Lance pounded its oversize arms. "And I can always throw a pillow on the floor."

"Is it all right?" Alison asked me again. "Because honestly, if it isn't, Lance can find a motel."

"At this time of year? Without a reservation? I wouldn't count on it."

"I don't want you to be uncomfortable," Alison said.

"Absolutely not," Lance concurred. "If my staying here would make you feel uncomfortable in any way . . ."

"It's **your** comfort I'm concerned with."

"Don't worry about me."

"I'll pay you extra," Alison volunteered.

"Don't be silly. That's not the point."

"Terry had a bad experience with her last tenant," Alison told her brother.

"How so?"

"Too long a story." I shook my head. "Well, okay then, I guess it's okay. A few days, you said?"

"Absolutely," Alison agreed.

"Christmas . . . New Year's, tops," Lance said, effortlessly stretching the few days to ten.

"Well . . ."

"Can I open my present now?" Alison asked eagerly. Without waiting for my reply, she tore off the silver wrapping paper, her eyes widening with delight when she saw what was inside. "A wallet! Oh, that's so great. I need a wallet. How'd you know that?"

I laughed, picturing the loose bills that were always tumbling around inside her purse.

"We are just so tuned in to each other, don't you think?" Alison stated more than asked, turning the honey-colored leather wallet over in her hands, caressing its smooth sides. "It's amazing. Don't you think?"

"I think it's a very nice wallet," Lance said. "Terry is obviously a woman of impeccable taste."

Was he being sarcastic? I couldn't tell.

"I should go." I turned toward the door.

"You'll come with us for dinner, won't you?" Alison asked.

"I don't think so. I'm not very hungry. You guys go, get reacquainted."

"Okay," Alison agreed reluctantly, "but only if you promise to spend the day with us tomorrow."

"Tomorrow?"

"I know you're not working tomorrow, and I want to show Lance all around Delray."

"You don't need me for that."

"Yeah, I do. Please. It won't be the same without you."

"You know it's pointless to argue," Lance said with a laugh.

He was right, and we all knew it.

"You have to come," Alison persisted. "Please. It'll be so fun. Please. Please. Say you'll at least think about it."

"I'll think about it," I said.


OF COURSE, in the end I agreed to go. What other choice did I have? It's pointless to say that I was being dangerously naive, even reckless, that I was deluding myself into thinking that everything was going to be all right, that Alison and her brother were exactly the people they represented themselves to be. I've said all these things to myself, and much more besides. But I continued to rationalize my doubts away. I convinced myself Alison was sincere in her reasons for not telling me she'd been fired, and that, of course, she'd had nothing to do with any money that might be missing from the gallery.

And what of the conversation I'd overheard at the cottage door?

**I told you to let me handle this.**

Handle what?

**I'm just here to help.**

**I don't need your help. I know what I'm doing.**

What did it mean?

Nothing, I assured myself that night. Alison and her brother could have been talking about anything. What self-conscious paranoia made me think their conversation had anything to do with me? Not everything was

about me, as my mother might have said. Whatever
Alison and her brother had been arguing about probably didn't concern me at all.

**Handle what?**

I was too tired to try figuring it out. And the truth
was, I didn't want to. I didn't want to believe that Alison
was anything other than the beautiful free spirit who'd
brought magic into my otherwise mundane existence.
Why would I assume she had ulterior motives or that
she might be planning anything sinister? Why couldn't
her brother's visit be as unexpected and spontaneous as
they claimed?

So I made a conscious decision to ignore the warning
bells that were jingling like mad in my head, much like
the bells Alison had hung from our doors. I rationalized
away my instincts, reminded myself that Lance Palmay
would be gone in a few days, scolded myself for being so
suspicious, so uptight. Then I made a cup of tea and carried it into the living room, where I curled up on the
sofa with a new book, the white lights of the Christmas
tree winking behind me, the smell of pine needles competing with the aroma of white oleander. I took a sip of
the soothingly hot liquid, read a few pages, read them
again when they failed to register, then slowly drifted
off to sleep, the book slipping from my hands to the
floor, as old ghosts rushed toward me from the darkness
and distant voices whispered in my ears.

In my dream I was kissing Roger Stillman in the
backseat of his old red Thunderbird, his hands groping

me under my sweater and skirt. A succession of increasingly loud moans escaped his lips as he triumphantly
rolled my panties down over my hips and climbed on
top of me. "Are you wearing a rubber?" I asked him, feeling my flesh tear as he pushed his way roughly inside
me. I cried out, opening my eyes, eyes that had been
tightly closed throughout most of our encounter, and
that's when I saw the policeman staring at us through
the car window, his flashlight illuminating the careless
sprinkling of dark hairs across the top of Roger's bare
buttocks. I screamed, but Roger continued humping
away, like an unwelcome dog on a human leg. Any leg,
any human, I realized, pushing him off me, watching
him effortlessly morph into Alison's brother, Lance
Palmay.

"Could you step out of the car, please?" the police
officer directed, and Roger/Lance complied with an easy
smile.

I struggled with my clothing, trying to push my skirt
down over the panties twisted around my knees, but the
policeman was already climbing into the backseat,
assuming Roger's former position on top of me, his flashlight directed at my eyes so that I couldn't see his face, his
large penis pushing its way toward my mouth. "You've
been a bad girl," he was saying in Josh Wylie's soothing
baritone. "I'm going to have to tell your mother."

"Please don't do that," I begged as his monstrous
organ forced my lips apart. "Please don't tell my
mother."

"Tell me what?" my mother asked, suddenly materializing on the seat beside me.

Which is when I woke up.

"Well, that was fun," I muttered, my heart pounding as I looked around the room, dark except for the flickering white lights of the tree behind me. I checked my watch, discovered I'd been sleeping for several hours, which meant I'd probably be up half the night. I rolled my head back, letting it drop lazily from one shoulder to the other, and waited for my heartbeat to return to normal. I realized, with equal amounts of shame and surprise, that the dream had excited me in spite of its peculiarities. In spite of my mother.

Or maybe because of her.

I marveled at the appearance of Roger Stillman in my dream. I didn't think I'd ever dreamed about him before, even during the heat of what might have been described, rather generously, as our relationship. And why the link to Alison's brother? Yes, they were both tall and good-looking, but so what? My subconscious had obviously intuited a deeper connection, even if my conscious mind had yet to determine what that connection might be.

I wiped a trickle of perspiration from the side of my neck, massaged the tenderness at my shoulders, my hand falling across my breast, the way Roger Stillman's hand had done, my nipples hardening at the memory of his fingers reaching underneath my blouse to unhook the clasp at the front of my bra. I felt my bare breasts rush into his waiting hands, recalled the way he fumbled with my pliant flesh, manipulating it like cookie dough, his eager mouth sucking on my nipples, as ferociously as a starving infant.

I remembered my mother's barely concealed disgust each time she looked at my maturing body, as if my breasts were a deliberate act of rebellion on my part, something for which I should be duly ashamed.

"Go away, Mother," I whispered now, lying back on the sofa, recalling how clumsily Roger had pulled on the zipper of my pants before pushing his hand down the front of my panties. I thought of Josh's hands, imagined his fingers in place of Roger's, felt them dancing around my most secret folds before disappearing inside me.

I cried out, my own fingers unable to follow my mind's lead, to provide my body the relief it craved. Instead I flipped onto my stomach and pressed myself against the hard edge of the sofa, its soft pillows muffling my embarrassed cries, my body shaking with a series of mild convulsions.

Instantly, my mother's shame swept over me.

I pushed myself to my feet and looked around, half-expecting my mother to be sitting in one of the Queen Anne chairs, watching me, as she had watched me in my dream. But the room was mercifully empty of ghosts.

I walked to the window, stared out at the street, watched large palm leaves dance in the shadows of the tall streetlight. I pressed my head against the glass, clasping my hands tightly behind my back. I caught a flicker of movement across the street, a shadow where before had been nothing. Was someone there? Dear God, had anyone seen me?

**Someone's always watching,** my mother admonished as I rushed to the front door, threw it open, and stared into the night.

Bettye McCoy and her two idiot dogs were rounding the corner and coming this way. I watched them approach, totally oblivious to my presence in the darkened doorway. She was wearing a pair of tight blue jeans and a cropped red sweater, with matching red heels. A red headband held her thick blond hair in place. Like an aging and surgically enhanced Alice in Wonderland, I thought cruelly, listening to her heels click against the pavement as she was pulled along by her two dogs. Of course the dogs stopped every few seconds to sniff at each and every bush, repeatedly lifting their legs to mark their territory. Just do your business and move on, I thought, watching in growing dismay as one of the dogs suddenly spun around and lifted his rump into the air, dropping several unwelcome deposits in the middle of the sidewalk at the end of my walkway. I waited for Bettye McCoy to scoop the droppings into her waiting plastic bag, but instead she only smirked, then tucked the empty bag back inside her jeans pocket before walking away.

I reacted without thinking. "Excuse me!" I ran down

the front path, stopping just short of the neat pile of fresh excrement. "Excuse me," I called again when Bettye McCoy failed to take notice.

Her dogs began to bark and pull at their leashes. "I'm sorry," Bettye McCoy said, reluctantly turning around. "Were you addressing me?"

"Do you see anyone else?"

"Is there something I can do for you?" Bettye McCoy arched one disdainful eyebrow.

"You can clean up after your dogs."

"I always clean up after my dogs."

"Not tonight, you didn't." I pointed at the small pile of dog feces by my feet.

"My dogs didn't do that."

I could scarcely believe my ears. "What are you talking about? I watched him do it." I pointed at the smaller of the two white dogs, who looked as if he were in danger of strangling on his leash.

"It's not Corky's," Bettye McCoy insisted. "Corky didn't do it."

"I was standing right in the doorway. I saw the whole thing."

"Corky didn't do it."

"Look. Why don't you just admit your dog did it, clean it up, and be on your way. Don't treat me like an idiot."

"You **are** an idiot," Bettye McCoy muttered, not quite under her breath.

I couldn't believe my ears. "What did you say?"

"I said you're an idiot," Bettye McCoy repeated brazenly. "First you chase poor Cedric out of your yard with a broom, and now you accuse Corky of pooping on your precious sidewalk. You know what you need, don't you?"

"Suppose you tell me."

"Get a man, lady, and stop picking on my dogs!"

"Keep them off my property or I'll lay them flat," I countered, our voices bouncing off the trees, echoing through the leaves. From out of the corner of my eye, I saw Alison and her brother walking up the street.

"Terry!" Alison rushed to my side.

"What's going on here?" Lance asked, trying to keep the bemusement in his eyes from spreading to the rest of his face.

"The woman's a lunatic," Bettye McCoy shouted, already in retreat.

"She wouldn't clean up after her dog," I said, understanding how hopeless I must sound.

"Her dog did this?" Lance pointed to the dog feces he'd narrowly missed stepping in.

I nodded, then watched in shock as he scooped the offending dog poo into his hands, then hurled it, with stunning accuracy, at Bettye McCoy's head. It splattered against her blond hair, clinging to the back of her head, like mud.

Bettye McCoy stopped, her shoulders rising around her ears as she spun around to face us, her face mirroring the openmouthed amazement of my own.

"You better close your mouth," Lance warned. "There might be more."

"You're all crazy," Bettye McCoy stammered, backing up and getting entwined in the dogs' leashes, almost losing her balance, then bursting into tears. "All of you."

We watched as she extricated herself from the dogs' leashes, a small turd dropping from her hair to her right shoulder, then falling toward the ground, landing on the toe of one red shoe. A final outraged squeal escaped Bettye McCoy's lips as she kicked off her shoes, gathered one yapping dog under each arm, then ran to the end of the block and disappeared.

"Think she'll call the police?" Alison asked.

"Oh, I don't think she'd want to chance this story making the rounds." I looked at Lance, who was grinning like the proverbial Cheshire cat. Had he really picked up a dog turd with his bare hands and hurled it at my tormentor? My hero, I thought with a laugh. "Thank you."

"Anytime."

We returned to the house in silence. "How was dinner?" I asked before I went inside.

"Not nearly as exciting as what was going on here," Alison said. "God, I can't leave you alone for a minute. Speaking of which, have you decided about tomorrow?"

I smiled, then laughed out loud. "What time do you want me to be ready?"

# 13

Lance knocked on my kitchen door at ten minutes after noon the following day. He was all in black; I was all in white. We looked like opposing pawns on a chessboard. "I thought you said eleven o'clock," I said, trying to keep my mother out of my voice.

"Slept in," he said without apology. "You ready to go?"

"Where's Alison?"

"Still in bed. Migraine."

"Oh, no! Is she all right?"

"Should be fine in a few hours."

A verbal minimalist, I decided, watching his eyes swallow my kitchen whole. "I better go check."

"Not necessary." Lance grabbed my floppy straw bag

from the kitchen table, slung it over my shoulder. "Alison instructed me to take you to lunch, said she'll join us as soon as she can stand up straight."

"I think I should check on her first," I protested, remembering how sick Alison had been with her last migraine, but Lance was already ushering me out the door, guiding me away from the cottage and around the side of the house.

"She'll be fine," he said, giving my elbow an extra squeeze as we reached the street. "Stop worrying."

"I just don't feel right about going."

"Come on. It'll give us a chance to get better acquainted."

I looked up and down the sun-soaked street. Shadows, like puddles, spilled across the road from the high trees. Waves of heat, like ocean surf, rolled up from the pavement. Several houses down, a large snowy egret stood, straight and still as stone, on a manicured front lawn. "Anywhere in mind?"

"The Everglades?"

"What!"

"Just joking. Nature's not my thing. Thought we'd try Elwood's. We can walk, and we don't have to worry about snakes."

"Don't be too sure." Elwood's was a converted filling station turned biker hangout that specialized in barbecue and Elvis memorabilia. It was located on Atlantic Avenue several blocks west of the Lorelli Gallery. "How do you know about Elwood's?"

"Alison pointed it out last night. Thought it looked interesting."

I shrugged, recalling the last time I'd been to Elwood's had been with Erica Hollander. I was about to suggest an alternative, but I decided against it, instinctively understanding that to argue with Alison's brother would be as pointless as arguing with Alison herself. Taking no for an answer was clearly not a family trait.

"It's unusual to be this hot in December," I remarked idly as we fell into step beside one another, the heat wrapping itself around my shoulders like a scratchy shawl. But Lance wasn't paying attention, his eyes flitting restlessly from one side of the street to the other, as if half-expecting someone to jump out at us from behind a neatly trimmed hedge. "Looking for anything in particular?"

"What kind of tree is that?" he asked suddenly, his finger brushing against the tip of my nose as he pointed to the squat palm tree in the middle of my neighbor's front yard. "Looks like it has a bunch of penises hanging from it."

"I beg your pardon!"

Lance bounded across my neighbor's lawn, kneeling beside the tree in question, and pointed at the numerous protuberances of various lengths that hung from its trunk. "You don't think they look like a bunch of uncircumcised dicks? Take a good look."

"You're crazy." Reluctantly I rolled my eyes toward the tree. "Oh, my God. You're right."

Lance laughed so loud, he startled the nearby egret, who soared gracefully into the air, like a giant paper plane. "Ain't nature grand?"

"They're called screw palms," I whispered.

"What?"

"You heard me."

"You're kidding me, right?"

"Honestly. That's their name."

"Screw palms?"

"I couldn't possibly make up something like that."

Lance shook his head, grabbed my elbow, picked up the pace of our walk. "Come on," he said, laughing. "All this talk about screwing is making me hungry."

"YOU SHOULD HAVE SEEN this city twenty years ago," I was saying between bites of my hamburger. "Half these storefronts were vacant, the school system was a disaster, race relations were a mess. About the only business that was doing well was the drug trade."

"Really?" It was the first time since I'd started my verbal tour of Delray that Lance had shown any real interest. "And how's the drug trade doing these days?" he asked, surveying the line of motorcycles parked outside the large front patio where we were sitting. "I mean, where would a person go if he were interested in such things?"

"Jail, most likely," I said as Lance's lips curled into a grudging smile.

"Cute. You're very cute."

My turn to smile. **Cute** had never been a word used to describe me.

We watched a middle-aged man whose ragged, gray ponytail extended halfway down the back of his black leather jacket as he wiggled his sagging gut between two chairs. Grandpas on wheels, I thought, taking another bite of my burger, wondering how anyone could wear leather in this heat. "Now, of course, the city's completely changed."

"And what changed it exactly?"

I paused, trying to choose between the short and long answers, deciding on the short. "Money."

Lance laughed. "Ah, yes. Money makes the world go round."

"I thought it was love."

"That's because you're a hopeless romantic."

"I am?"

"You're not?"

"Maybe," I admitted, squirming under his sudden scrutiny. "Maybe I am a romantic."

"Don't forget hopeless." He reached across the table and peeled several sweat-dampened hairs away from my forehead with a gentle but confident hand, as if he were teasing a bra strap off my shoulder.

I lowered my gaze to the table, the tips of Lance's fingers lingering on my flesh even after he'd removed his hand. "What about you?"

He lifted a sauce-coated sparerib from his plate to

his mouth, tearing the meat off with one neat tug. "Well," he said with a wink, "I love money. Does that qualify?"

I took a sip of my beer, held the ice-cold glass against my throat, trying to ignore the perspiration trickling into the deep vee of my white T-shirt.

"Wow! Would you look at those babies!" Lance exclaimed, and I saw that Lance's attention had been captured by the two shiny black motorcycles with chrome-plated monkey-hanger handlebars that had just pulled up in front of the restaurant. "Aren't they beauties?"

"Harley-Davidsons?" I asked, pulling out the only brand with which I was familiar, trying to sound interested.

Lance shook his head. "Yamaha 750cc Viragos." He punctuated his sentence with an appreciative whistle.

"You obviously know a lot about motorcycles."

"A bit." He raised another barbecued rib to his lips, then slowly and meticulously stripped it bare.

I thought of Alison. She would have polished off those ribs in a heartbeat. "Maybe we should call Alison. See how she's doing."

Lance patted his cell phone, which lay on the table next to his plate. "She knows my number."

"It's been over an hour."

"She'll call."

I rubbed the back of my neck, the sweat coating my fingers like shellac. "Has your family been very worried about her?"

He shrugged. "Nah. They pretty much know what to expect by now."

"Which is?"

"Alison's gonna do what Alison's gonna do. No point arguing. No point getting in her face about it."

"But you obviously felt concerned enough to fly down here and see for yourself."

"Just checking to make sure she's okay. I mean, she comes to Florida, doesn't know a soul . . . "

"She knew Rita Bishop," I said, recalling the name of Alison's friend.

"Who?"

"Rita Bishop." I wondered if I had the name correct.

Lance looked confused, although he tried to hide it by tearing into another rib. "Oh, yeah, Rita. Whatever happened to her anyway?"

I realized I'd forgotten to ask personnel to find out where she'd gone. "I don't know. Alison couldn't locate her."

"Typical." Lance released a deep breath of air. "It's hot," he said, as if noticing the temperature for the first time.

"I think it's sweet that you were concerned about your sister. I didn't think you were that close."

"Close enough to worry." He shrugged, an increasingly familiar gesture. "What can I say? Maybe I'm a romantic after all."

I couldn't help but smile. I liked Lance for worrying about Alison's welfare. "It's nice you could take the time off work."

"No problem when you're self-employed."

"What is it you do?" I tried to remember if Alison had ever mentioned her brother's occupation.

Lance looked surprised by the question. He coughed, ran his hand through his hair. "Systems analyst," he said, so quietly I almost didn't hear him.

My turn to be surprised. "They teach that sort of thing at Brown?"

"Brown?"

"Alison said you graduated summa cum laude."

He laughed, coughed a second time. "Long time ago. A lot of beer under the bridge since then." He hoisted his mug into the space between us, finished what was left in his glass, and swiveled around in his chair, looking for the waiter. "You ready for another one?"

My own mug was still half-full. "I'm fine for the moment."

"Another draft," Lance called to a bald and heavily tattooed waiter resting against the far wall. FEAR was stamped in large blue letters along his right forearm; NO MAN was imprinted on the other. Charming, I thought, noticing a man nursing a beer at a small round table in the corner, a red bandanna wrapped around his forehead like a blood-soaked strip of gauze. Long, calloused fingers stroked a beard that was dark and scruffy. The man was staring at me, I realized, thinking there was something disturbingly familiar about him, trying to remember if and when I'd seen him before.

"How's your burger?" Lance asked, swatting a

buzzing insect away from his head as he squinted into the sunlight.

"It's fine."

"Just fine? My ribs were fantastic. I'm thinking of ordering another pound."

I glanced at his empty plate. "Are you serious?"

"I'm always serious about what I put in my mouth." His tongue lapped some errant sauce from his upper lip.

Was he flirting with me? Or was the heat starting to affect my brain? **Should have worn a hat,** I could almost hear my mother say.

I looked away, my eyes pulled back toward the man with the red bandanna. He cocked his head to one side, then raised his beer mug in a silent toast, as if he'd been expecting me to look his way again. Where had I seen him before?

"So, tell me what you think of my baby sister," Lance instructed as the waiter approached with his beer. Lance gulped at its large head, chewed it as if it were solid food.

"I think she's great."

"She involved with anyone special these days?"

"Not to my knowledge."

"She tell you about her ex-husband?"

"Just that he was a mistake."

Lance laughed, shook his head.

"You don't agree?"

"Seemed like a nice enough guy to me. But, hey, what do I know? She's the one who lived with him. Although Alison doesn't always know what's good for her," he added, his face darkening as a cloud passed by overhead.

"I don't think I agree with that."

"I don't think you know Alison as well as I do."

"Maybe not," I conceded, deciding to shift the focus of the conversation away from Alison. "What about you? Any sweet young thing on the horizon?"

"Not really." Lance allowed a slow smile to creep across his lips. "Actually, I've always had a thing for older women."

I laughed. "You should drop by the hospital one day. I'll introduce you to some of my patients."

Lance stretched his neck back over the top of his spine and poured half his beer down his throat. "So, what's the story on this guy who sings here every Thursday night?" he asked, as if this were the most logical of follow-ups.

I glanced at the large cardboard cutout of a Las Vegas–styled Elvis impersonator—long sideburns, rhinestone-studded, white jumpsuit, flowing cape, classic karate pose—that greeted patrons at the door to the restaurant's interior. "He's a Delray policeman, believe it or not."

"Is he any good?"

"Very good." I'd heard him the time I was here with Erica. I gasped, suddenly realizing where I'd seen the man with the red bandanna before. I'd seen him with Erica Hollander. My eyes shot toward the corner of the patio, but the man was no longer there.

"Something wrong?" Lance asked, signaling the waiter for another half order of ribs and two more beers. Clearly we weren't going anywhere anytime soon.

"Will you excuse me a minute?" I was already out of my chair and heading for the washrooms at the back of the restaurant before he could answer. I needed to splash some cold water on my face. The heat was definitely getting to me.

The interior of the restaurant was soothingly dark and, while not exactly cold, considerably cooler than outside. I passed the large bar, its barstools constructed from the old hoists of the former gas station. Most people ate outside, but a few wooden tables hugged by leatherette furniture were scattered around the room for those who preferred not to see what they were eating. "The pig place," people called Elwood's, with affection. I wondered, as I brushed by another potbellied biker, if they were referring to the menu or the clientele.

I spent the next few minutes in the washroom, trying to convince myself that my mind was playing tricks on me, that the heat plus my overly active imagination had deceived me into thinking that the man with the red bandanna and scruffy goatee was anything but an overly familiar stereotype. Of course I didn't know him. Of course I'd never seen him with Erica.

Except even as I was trying to convince myself I was seeing bogeymen who didn't exist, I knew the truth—that I **had** seen the man before, seen him with Erica, and

not just once, but several times. And not only here, I
realized, as a series of suppressed images assaulted my
already spinning brain, but much closer to home.
Hadn't I seen him coming out of the cottage on several
mornings with his arm around Erica's waist? Hadn't I
heard the unmistakable sounds of a motorcycle disappearing down the middle of a darkened street on several
evenings? And did the fact he was back mean Erica was
back as well?

I sprinkled water on my neck, dabbed a few drops
behind my ears, as if it were perfume, stared at myself in
the grimy mirror over the sink. My mother stared back.
"Dear God," I said out loud, realizing how much her
features were starting to intrude upon my own.

Except for the eyes in the back of her head, I thought
ruefully, remembering her terrifying admonition when
I was a little girl. **There's no point in trying to fool
me,** she'd warned. **I see everything. I have eyes in the
back of my head.**

Too bad I hadn't inherited those, I thought, returning to the patio. My table was empty, and I looked
around for Lance.

I saw the man with the red bandanna first. He was
standing by the row of motorcycles parked along the
curb, one hand resting on a pair of steel handlebars, and
he and Lance were having an obviously serious conversation. I watched the man lean forward to whisper
something in Lance's ear, before climbing on his bike
and backing out into traffic, acknowledging me with a

barely perceptible nod of his head. Lance remained where he was, as still as the cardboard-imitation Elvis, his fists clenched tightly at his sides.

"What was that about?" I asked when Lance returned to the table.

"What was what about?"

"That guy you were talking to."

"What about him?"

"How do you know him?"

"I don't know him." Lance's eyes squinted into the sunlight.

"You were talking to him."

"I'm a friendly guy."

"Don't play games with me, Lance."

"What kind of games?" Lance leaned back in his seat, ran his tongue along his lower lip.

"Look, that guy you were talking to is bad news. He was involved with my previous tenant. I think he's been phoning me," I said, realizing this was true.

"You **think**? You don't know?" Lance looked amused.

"I'm not sure," I backpedaled, beginning to doubt my instincts.

"Sorry, sweetheart, I don't have a clue what you're talking about."

"Why were you talking to him?"

"Why is it so important?"

"What were you talking about?" I pressed, my voice rising in frustration.

"Hey," Lance said softly, his hand reaching across the table to stroke my arm. "No need to get upset. It was nothing. I was just telling him how much I liked his bike. That's all it was. You okay?"

I nodded, somewhat mollified. Already I was starting to feel foolish about my outburst.

Lance picked up his cell phone. "Time to give Alison a call."

# 14

Alison joined us at Elwood's within minutes of Lance's call, her migraine blissfully vanquished. "Those pills you gave me were a godsend," she told me repeatedly, looking radiant in her blue sundress, as she simultaneously wolfed down an order of spareribs and chewed on a mouthful of french fries. I marveled that she managed to do so with such grace. I also marveled that her headache had had no effect on her appetite. Indeed, she seemed in better shape than I did. "Are you okay?" she asked me as Lance was settling the bill.

"Me? I'm fine."

"You're so quiet."

"Terry thought she saw some guy who was involved with her last tenant," Lance interjected.

"Really? Who?"

I shook my head. "It probably wasn't him. Must be the heat," I demurred, now almost convinced I'd been mistaken.

"It's a scorcher all right." Alison looked around the patio, still crowded at almost three o'clock. "Okay, so where should we go now?"

I suggested a visit to the Morikami Museum and Japanese Gardens, something I thought would be both soothing and interesting, but Alison said she wasn't in the mood for museums and Lance reiterated that nature wasn't his thing. So instead we went for a long walk along the Intracoastal Waterway and took a boat ride on the **Ramblin' Rose II,** then sat on the seawall at twilight and watched the bridge as it opened for a small parade of magnificent yachts on their way to the Bahamas.

"Did you know that alligators move really fast?" Alison asked later, apropos of nothing at all, as we strolled along Seventh Avenue, heading for home. "And that if you're ever being chased by one, you should run in a zigzag, because alligators can only move in a straight line?"

"I'll keep that in mind," I said.

"What's the difference between alligators and crocodiles?" Lance asked.

"Crocs are nastier," Alison said with the sweetest of smiles. She stretched her arms toward the sky, as if reaching for the full moon that dangled precariously overhead. "I'm starving."

"You just ate," I reminded her.

"That was hours ago. I'm famished. Come on, let's go to Boston's."

"I'm game," Lance said.

"You two go. I'm exhausted."

"Come on, Terry. You can't poop out on us now."

"Sorry, Alison. I have to be up really early in the morning. What I need now is a cup of herbal tea, a soothing bubble bath, and my nice comfortable bed."

"Let Terry go," Lance urged his sister softly.

"Did you have a good time?" Alison stared at me expectantly, the fat yellow moon reflected in eyes as eager as a child's. "Three words."

"Yes," I answered truthfully, dismissing any lingering concerns about the man in the red bandanna. I'd done my best to forget about him during the long afternoon, but like a bad penny, he kept popping up. "Yes. Yes. Yes," I said, banishing his image altogether.

Alison wrapped me in a tight embrace, several loose tendrils of her hair tickling my cheek, sneaking between my lips. "See you later, alligator," she said, kissing my forehead.

"In a while, crocodile," I answered back, watching them until they turned the corner and were swallowed by the night. I could hear Alison laughing in the dark, and I wondered briefly what she found so amusing. The echo of her laughter pursued me down the street, bouncing off my back like sharpened stones.

**What's the difference between alligators and crocodiles?** Lance had asked.

**Crocs are nastier,** Alison had replied.

My house was in total darkness. Normally I leave at least one light on, but Lance had ushered me out so quickly, I'd obviously forgotten. Proceeding cautiously, my eyes scanning the ground in case Bettye McCoy had returned with the dogs from hell, I zigzagged up my front path, mindful of hungry alligators that might have strayed dangerously off course.

Feeling both relieved and foolish—foolishly relieved?—I unlocked the front door and flicked on the light switch, my eyes sweeping across the sofa, the Queen Anne chairs, the painting of peonies on the wall beside the window, the Christmas tree in the corner, the numerous presents beneath it, the daunting parade of Santas and reindeer and elves Alison had lovingly assembled.

"Merry Christmas, everybody," I said, locking the door behind me and heading for the kitchen. "And an especially merry Christmas to you, dear ladies," I greeted the sixty-five china heads regarding me with indifferent eyes. "I trust you were good little girls while I was away." I filled the kettle with water, made myself a cup of ginger-peach tea, and carried it up the stairs to the bathroom, where I stripped naked and poured myself a bath. I climbed inside and leaned my head against the cool enamel, jasmine-scented bubbles covering me like a blanket.

I remembered how once, when I was a little girl, my mother had found me in the tub, my legs akimbo, the water lapping against the insides of my thighs, as I giggled with childish abandon. The spanking I'd received that night was worse than any other she'd administered over the years, partly because I was soaking wet, and partly because I had no idea why I was being punished. I kept begging her to tell me what I'd done wrong, but my mother never said a word. To this day, I can feel the sting of her fingers on my bare buttocks, like the bite of thousands of tiny wasps, my wet skin a magnifying glass, reflecting and enlarging my pain and humiliation. More than anything, I remember the sound of those slaps as they resonated against my bare bottom, then ricocheted off the walls. Even now there are nights, when I close my eyes to sleep, that I hear it.

I shook my head free of such unpleasant thoughts and slid down in the tub, dragging my head under the water's surface, my hair floating around my head, like seaweed. Immediately, another unpleasant memory attached itself to the insides of my closed eyelids: three little gray-and-white kittens, abandoned strays I'd found shivering in a corner of our garage, all mangy and mewing and "probably riddled with ringworm," as my mother had proclaimed before wresting them from my arms and drowning them in a pail of water in the backyard.

I tried unsuccessfully not to see the kittens as I lay in the tub, an inch of water covering my face, like a shroud. What was the matter with me? Why was my mother so much in my thoughts these days?

It seemed that ever since Alison's arrival, my
mother had once again taken up residence in not only
the house, but my brain. Probably it was all the questions Alison asked, the photographs we'd looked
through together. They were responsible for my
strange dreams, these unscheduled trips down memory lane. I hadn't thought of those damn kittens in
years. Why now, for God's sake? Hadn't I made peace
with my mother during those long, awful days of her
illness? Hadn't she begged my forgiveness? Hadn't I
gratefully bestowed it?

My mother was such a formidable presence,
although I'm at a loss to say exactly why. At only five
feet two inches tall, it was hardly her physical stature
that made her so imposing. Indeed, her disproportionately large bosom gave her a pigeonlike shape that was
almost comic, and her features were surprisingly small
and nondescript.

I think what truly set her apart was the way she carried herself, proud shoulders rigid, stubborn head held
high, so that her tiny, upturned nose always seemed to
be looking down at you from a great height.

That posture infused all aspects of her life. She was
definite in her opinions, even on subjects she knew little
about. Her temper was quick, her tongue sharp. I
learned early that there was no point in trying to press
my side of things, that only one side mattered.

Certainly my father was rarely consulted. If he had
any opinions, he kept them to himself. I'd learned early

to count on him for nothing, and in that way, he never disappointed me. If he had any regrets, they died with him.

My mother became even angrier after my father died, lashing out at me at the slightest provocation. **You're a stupid, stupid girl!** I can still hear her shout whenever I've done something particularly foolish.

Later, of course, when age rounded those stubborn shoulders and infirmity softened her more abrasive edges, she became gradually less formidable, less self-righteous, less prone to poisonous outbursts. Or maybe she just became less. After her stroke, my mother literally shrank to half her former size.

And a strange thing happened.

In becoming less, she became more, as the architect Mies van der Rohe might have said—more tolerant, more grateful, more vulnerable. Her shadow shrank to something approximating human size.

**You know that everything I did, I did for your benefit,** she said often in those last months of her life.

I know that, I told her. **Of course I know that.**

**I didn't mean to be cruel.**

I know.

**It's the way I was raised. My mother was the same with me.**

You were a good mother, I said.

**I made a lot of mistakes.**

We all make mistakes.

**Can you forgive me?**

**Of course I forgive you.** I kissed the flaky, dry skin of her forehead. **You're my mother. I love you.**

**I love you too,** she whispered.

Or maybe she didn't. Maybe I just wanted to hear her say the words so badly that I imagined she said them.

Why was she returning to haunt me now?

I pushed my head above the water's surface, felt the tiny soap bubbles evaporating on my skin. Was there something she was trying to tell me? Was she trying to warn me, to protect me, in death, the way she never had during her lifetime?

Protect me from what?

I pulled the plug with my toes, listening as the water gulped its way musically down the drain. It took a moment for me to become aware of other sounds, another moment for me to understand exactly what those sounds were. Bells, I realized, hearing a downstairs door open and close, as my heart slid down the drain with the last of the bubbles.

Someone was in the house.

I stepped softly from the tub, gathering my robe around me as I stretched over to lock the bathroom door. But the lock had been broken for the better part of a year, and the closest thing I had to a weapon was the blunt blade of a disposable razor. I might have laughed had I not been so terrified.

"Hello? Is someone there?" I called as I peeked out the bathroom door and stepped into the hall. "Alison? Is that you?" I waited for someone to respond, my wet feet leaving footprints on the hardwood floor as I ventured to the top of the stairs. "Alison? Lance? Is that you?"

Nothing.

Was it possible I'd been mistaken?

I did a quick check of the bedrooms before inching my way down the stairs toward the living room, half-expecting someone to lunge out of the shadows with each step I took. But no one lunged and nothing in the living room appeared to have been disturbed. Everything was in its proper place, exactly as it had been earlier.

I jiggled the front door handle and breathed a deep sigh of relief at finding the door securely locked. "Hello?" I called again as I headed toward the kitchen. "Is anybody here?" But the kitchen was as empty as the rest of the house. "So now I'm hearing things," I muttered, my shoulders relaxing as I reached for the back door.

It fell open at my touch.

"Oh, my God." I stepped back in mounting horror as the warm night air pushed its way rudely inside the kitchen. "Stay calm." Hadn't I just checked every room in the house and found nothing?

**You didn't check the closets,** I heard Alison say. **You didn't look under the bed.**

**You're a stupid, stupid girl!** my mother added for good measure.

"There are no such things as bogeymen," I told them loudly, deciding it was entirely possible I'd neglected to lock the back door when I'd left the house. I pictured Lance, unapologetic and an hour late, slipping my purse over my shoulder and ushering me outside, his hand on my elbow. I hadn't turned on any lights and I hadn't locked the kitchen door.

"I didn't lock the door!" I informed the rows of ladies' heads. "I didn't lock the door," I repeated, locking it now, laughing at my foolishness. "There are no such things as bogeymen."

The phone rang.

"Don't you know it's dangerous to leave your door unlocked?" the voice asked before I had a chance to say hello. "You never know who might drop by."

I spun around, my hand sweeping across the counter and knocking against the block of knives. I pulled the largest of the knives out of its slot, waved it in the air like a flag. "Who is this?"

"Sweet dreams, Terry. Take care of yourself."

"Hello? Hello? Damn it! Who is this?" I slammed the phone back into its cradle, then immediately picked it up again, punched in 911.

"Emergency," a woman's voice stated after several minutes on hold.

"Well, it's not exactly an emergency," I qualified.

"This is 911, ma'am. If it's not an emergency, you should call your local police station."

"Well, I'm not sure exactly."

"Ma'am, is this an emergency or isn't it?"

"No," I admitted, lowering the knife to my side.

"Please call your local police station if you have a problem."

"Thank you. I'll do that."

Except I didn't. What was I going to say, after all? That I suspected someone had broken into my house, except that I'd left the door unlocked and nothing had been taken? That I'd received a vaguely menacing call from an anonymous man whose words, on their surface, were decidedly more solicitous than threatening. **Don't you know it's dangerous to leave your door unlocked? You never know who might drop by. Sweet dreams. Take care of yourself.**

Sure. That would bring the police running.

I returned the phone to its cradle and sank into a kitchen chair, trying to decide my next move. Should I call the police anyway, risk their derision, or worse, their indifference? If only I had something more concrete to offer them, to prove I wasn't some lonely, middle-aged woman with a too active imagination and way too much time on her hands. If only I was sure about the voice on the other end of the phone.

I played the words back in my head, like a recording. **Sweet dreams, Terry. Take care of yourself.** But while there was something familiar about the speaker, I couldn't be sure it belonged to Erica's biker friend, the man I'd seen talking to Lance at Elwood's, the seriousness of their expressions indicative of more than a shared interest in motorcycles. Was there some connection between the two men? Between Lance and Erica? Between Erica and Alison?

Was it just a coincidence these phone calls had

started around the time Alison had turned up on my doorstep?

What the hell was going on?

And then I saw him.

He was standing outside the kitchen window, his forehead pressed against the windowpane, the red of his bandanna bleeding into the glass.

"Oh, my God."

And then, as suddenly as his image had appeared, it vanished, absorbed by the night like a blotter.

Had I seen anyone at all?

I rushed to the window, peered out at the night.

I saw nothing.

No one.

I rifled through a kitchen drawer for the spare set of keys to the cottage. **You're a stupid, stupid girl**, my mother admonished, and for once, I had to agree with her. But I needed some answers, and those answers could very well be found in Alison's journal. I estimated I had at least half an hour before Alison and her brother returned home. More than enough time if I moved quickly.

Clutching the keys tightly, I threw open the door and stepped outside, my bare feet slipping into the night air, like a pair of slippers.

"Are you crazy? What are you doing?" I mumbled as I locked the door behind me and approached the cottage, hand extended, key pointing at the lock. I was almost at the door when I heard a twig snap behind me.

I gasped, spun around.

"Hi, there," a disembodied voice said from the darkness. Slowly, almost magically, a man materialized out of nothing to take shape in my backyard. With deliberate care, he stepped into the moon's spotlight. He was tall, skinny, clean-shaven. There was no scraggly beard, no red bandanna. "Remember me?"

"K.C.," I whispered.

"Short for Kenneth Charles, but nobody ever . . . hell, you know the rest."

"What are you doing here?"

"I came to see Alison."

"She's not home."

"Really? Then where are you going?"

I slipped the key to the cottage into the side pocket of my robe, wondering if he'd noticed. "I thought I heard something. I was just checking to make sure everything was all right." I wondered why I was bothering to explain myself to someone I barely knew.

"It was probably just me."

"Did you just phone me?" I asked, my voice sharper than I'd intended.

K.C. produced a cell phone from his pocket, smiled lazily. "Was I supposed to?"

"You didn't answer my question."

"No, I didn't phone you." His eyes narrowed. "Are you okay?"

"I'm fine."

"You seem a little on edge."

"No," I said, forcing a yawn. "Just a little tired, I guess. Busy day." I looked down, realized my robe had fallen open. I quickly secured the two sides of the robe together, ignoring the growing smile on K.C.'s face. "I'll tell Alison you stopped by."

"If you don't mind, I think I'll wait till she gets back."

"Suit yourself." I turned back toward the house.

"Terry?" he called after me.

I stopped, turned around.

"I just wanted to thank you again for the lovely Thanksgiving dinner."

"I'm glad you enjoyed it."

"You don't find many people these days who are so willing to open their homes to strangers."

Or so stupid, I heard my mother say, the key to the cottage weighing heavily in my pocket. "I was happy to do it." Again I turned toward the house.

"Terry?" he called a second time.

Again I stopped, although this time I didn't turn around.

"Take care of yourself," he said, as I stepped inside the house and locked the door behind me.

# 15

"Merry Christmas!" Alison jumped into the air at precisely the stroke of midnight, clapping her hands with childish abandon.

"Merry Christmas," Lance echoed, clicking his glass of eggnog against Alison's, then mine.

"God bless us, everyone," I added, taking a tiny sip of the thick liquid, pungent fumes of nutmeg swirling through my nostrils.

The evening had been pleasant, filled with good food and happy chatter. Just the three of us. No uninvited guests. No apparitions in the glass. No unexpected phone calls. I'd asked Alison about K.C. She claimed not to have seen or heard from him since Thanksgiving. When I told her about my encounter with him, she'd shrugged and said, "That's odd. I wonder what he wanted." Ultimately I decided I'd probably blown the whole incident out of proportion and pushed it to the back of my mind.

"Where's that from?" Alison was asking now.

"Where's what from?"

"What you just said. 'God bless us, everyone.' That sounds so familiar."

"Charles Dickens," I told her. **A Christmas Carol.**"

"That's right," Lance said. "We saw the movie. Remember? Bill Murray was in it."

"You should read the book."

Lance shrugged his indifference. "Don't read much."

"Why is that?"

"Not really interested."

"Lance had his fill of books at Brown," Alison was quick to explain.

"What **does** interest you?" I pressed.

Lance glanced across the table at his sister before returning his attention to me. **"You** interest me."

"I do?"

"Yes, lady, you certainly do."

I laughed. "Now you're mocking me."

"On the contrary. I find you fascinating."

It was my turn to glance at Alison. She seemed to be holding her breath. "And what exactly is it about me that fascinates you?"

He shook his head. "I'm not sure exactly. What is it they say about still waters running deep?"

Now I was the one holding my breath. "Just that they do."

"Guess I'd like to be around when they get all churned up." Lance took another sip of eggnog, the pale yellow cream creating a thin mustache across his upper lip. He ran a lazy tongue across it, his eyes fastened on mine.

"I don't read nearly as much as I should," Alison piped in.

"You don't read at all."

A flush of embarrassment stained Alison's cheeks, turning them almost the same color as her sweater. "Maybe you could recommend some good books for me, Terry. Something to get me started again."

"Sure. Although I probably don't read as much as I should either."

"We should all read more," Alison agreed.

"There's lots of things we should do," Lance said cryptically.

"Name three," I said, and Alison smiled, although the smile was tentative, as if she was afraid of what her brother might say.

"We should stop procrastinating," Lance said.

"Procrastinating," Alison repeated with a strained laugh. "Good word."

"Procrastinating over what?" I asked.

Lance ignored my question. "We should stop playing games."

"What kind of games?" I asked, watching the smile harden on Alison's face.

"We should shit or get off the pot." Lance finished the eggnog in his glass, then tossed his napkin onto the table, as if challenging his sister to a duel.

"Am I missing something here?"

Alison leaped to her feet. "Speaking of getting off the pot, can we open the presents now?" She was in the living room and at the tree before I could answer.

"Open this one first," she was saying, holding a small gift bag toward me as I approached. "It's from me. It's just little. I thought we could start with the small gifts first. Save the best ones for last." I carefully withdrew a small crystal rock from its tissue. "It's a paperweight. I thought it was so pretty."

"I think it's lovely. Thank you." I sat down next to Alison on the floor, my mind still on our previous exchange—procrastinating over what? What kind of games?—as I ran my fingers along the jagged pink surface of the crystal. "I love it."

"Really?"

"It's beautiful." I motioned toward a small, square box wrapped in red and green. "Your turn."

Eager hands tore at the wrapping paper. "What is it?"

"Open it and find out."

"This is so exciting. Isn't this so exciting?" Alison discarded the last of the paper and ripped open the box. "Would you just look at this! Lance, look. Nail polish. Six bottles, all in fabulous colors."

"Be still my heart," Lance said from the sofa.

"Vanilla Milkshake, Mango Madness, Wild-flower . . . These are so great."

"Use them well."

"We'll do another spa day."

"Now **that** sounds like fun," Lance said. "Can I come?"

"Only if you let us paint your toes with Mango Madness," I told him.

"Lady, you can paint whatever part of my anatomy your little heart desires." Lance flopped over the sofa and joined us on the floor. "Anything for me under there?"

Alison made a prolonged show of searching under the tree. "No, I'm afraid it doesn't look like there's anything for you. Oh, wait. Here's something." She extended an oblong box wrapped in gold. "It's a golf shirt," she announced before the package was half-unwrapped. "It's an extra-large because the salesman said they fit small. What do you think? Do you think it'll fit?"

Lance held the beige-and-black golf shirt against the navy one he was wearing. "Looks good. What do you think, Terry?"

"I think your sister has very good taste."

Lance laughed. "First time she's ever been accused of that."

"Very funny." Alison pointed at the design that criss-crossed the lightweight fabric. "Those are golf tees, in case you didn't know."

"Looks like I'll have to stick around," Lance said casually. "Take up golf."

Alison dropped her eyes to the floor. "Here's something for Terry." She read the sticker, glanced warily at her brother. "From Lance," she said with obvious surprise. "You didn't tell me you were buying Terry a present."

"What? You think I was raised in a barn?"

I opened the gift, my hands trembling with the knowledge I hadn't bought anything for him. Inside was a long, lilac-colored nightgown, its lace bodice scooped provocatively low.

"Oh, my," Alison said.

"It's silk."

"It's lovely. But I really can't accept something like this," I said in my mother's voice.

**Totally inappropriate,** I heard her agree.

"What are you talking about? Of course you can. Why don't you try it on right now, model it for us." Lance's fingers slipped under the long slit that ran up the side of the nightgown. I shivered, as if his hand were on my leg.

"I think you should save it for when Josh comes home," Alison said, eyes still on her brother.

"Josh?" Lance sat up straight, his interest clearly piqued. "First I'm hearing of any Josh."

"He's a friend of Terry's."

"Sounds like more than a friend."

"His mother is one of my patients," I qualified, not

really wanting to discuss Josh with Alison's brother, wondering what Josh was doing at that moment. It was three hours earlier in California. Probably he was attending some big family dinner, or maybe he was out doing some last-minute shopping. Did he miss me? Had he thought about me at all?

"What's the matter with his mother?"

I pictured Myra Wylie asleep in her narrow hospital bed. "Everything," I said sadly.

Lance shrugged. "She exceeded her expiration date, did she?"

"What?"

"Lance thinks people should be stamped with a 'best before' date. You know, like dairy products."

I laughed in spite of myself.

"You ever consider pulling the plug on some of these people?"

"What!"

"I think you'd be doing most of them a favor. And yourself too, come to think of it."

"Now you've really lost me."

"Well, I'm just thinking out loud here, but I bet you get pretty close to some of these lonely old biddies. Am I right?"

I nodded, not sure where this conversation was going.

"And a few of them probably have a little something stashed away," Lance continued. "I bet it wouldn't be that difficult to get them to include you in their wills, have them sign over the bulk of their estates to you, their humble caregiver. Then after a suitable period of time, enough so as not to arouse undue suspicion, you just give nature a little push. You know, a stray air bubble in their IV; an extra dose of something to help them sleep. Hell, I don't have to tell you. You're the nurse. You'd know exactly how to do it. Wouldn't you?"

I looked for the familiar mischievous twinkle in his eyes, but he stared back at me with eyes as cold and humorless as a corpse's. Was he serious?

"What do you think, Terry?" he pressed. "Sounds like a plan to me."

"I think plans like that are the reason our jails are so overcrowded."

"Lance is just kidding," Alison said.

"Am I?"

"Is money really so important to you?"

"It's pretty important."

"So important you'd actually consider taking some-one's life?"

"Guess that would depend."

"Lance is just joking," Alison interrupted again. "Enough, Lance. Terry doesn't understand your sense of humor."

"I think she understands me very well."

"It's my turn to open another present," Alison said, pulling a gift from under the tree with such force she almost knocked the whole thing over. "Look. It's from Denise."

"Where **is** Denise these days?" I asked, as eager as Alison to move on.

"She's spending Christmas with her folks up north. But she'll be back in time for New Year's. Speaking of which, I guess we should start making plans for New Year's Eve."

"I'm working New Year's Eve," I told her.

"You're not!"

"I'm afraid so."

"But it's the start of a whole new year. I can't believe you're working. It's not fair!"

I laughed. "Open your present."

Alison quietly unwrapped her gift and held out a pair of pink, heart-shaped earrings. I couldn't help but wonder if Denise had paid for them or simply helped herself to more of her aunt's inventory. Alison said nothing. She closed the small cardboard box and lowered it to the floor.

"Don't you like them?"

"They're very nice."

"Poor Alison's all upset because you won't be celebrating New Year's Eve with us."

"I'm just disappointed."

"Don't be. It's just another night," I said, although I didn't really believe it. Hadn't I been equally disappointed when Josh had announced he'd be out of town. "I just realized I forgot to put Lance's present under the tree." I scrambled to my feet, ran into the kitchen, retrieved the bag with the ballpoint pen I'd originally intended for Josh—what the hell? I'd buy him some-thing better, something more personal—then headed back to the living room.

"What's the matter with you?" I heard Alison hiss as I approached.

"Lighten up," Lance said.

"What are you trying to pull?"

"I'm just having fun with her."

"I don't like it."

"Relax."

"I'm warning you . . ."

"Is that an ultimatum? Because we both know how much I love ultimatums."

"Here it is," I said, announcing my presence before I walked back into the room.

Lance reached across the top of the sofa to take the small bag dangling from my fingers. "Just what I wanted," he said without a trace of irony as he extricated the thick, black pen from its layers of tissue. "Thank you, Terry. I'm touched." He stood up, walked around the sofa, and extended his hand.

I took it, expecting a small handshake of gratitude, but instead he pulled me toward him, bringing his face so close to mine I tasted his breath in my mouth. I turned my cheek, but it was almost as if he'd anticipated my reaction, and he turned with me, catching me fully on the lips. "What are you doing?" I asked, attempting a smile but breaking away, the taste of him lingering.

He looked surprised, as if he had no idea what I was

talking about. Had he thought I wouldn't notice? "It's a great pen," he said.

"Okay, you guys," Alison called. "There's still lots to go here. My turn."

"It's always your turn." Lance resumed his place on the sofa.

Alison pulled a baseball cap with a logo from the Houston Astros out of a bag without examining the card. "Look. It's from K.C. Isn't that sweet?" She put the hat on her head. "He dropped by this afternoon," she explained before I had time to ask. "He told me he came over the other night to give it to me, but I wasn't home," she continued unprompted. "That's why he was here."

I nodded, although I couldn't recall any gift in K.C.'s hands. "What do you know about him?" I asked, straining to sound casual.

"Not much. Why?"

"Just curious."

"He thinks you don't like him."

"He's right."

"Why is that?"

"I don't trust him, I guess."

"Seemed like a nice enough guy to me," Lance interjected.

"I think he's nice too," Alison agreed.

"Name three things you like about him," I challenged.

Alison smiled. "Let's see. I like his accent."

K.C.'s gentle Texas twang slammed against my ears.
"I like his eyes."

I hated K.C.'s eyes, I thought, seeing them laughing at me through the darkness of the other night.

"I like that he bought me a present."

"What three things do you like about **me?**" Lance asked suddenly, turning to me.

"I'm not sure I like anything about you at all."

He laughed, although it was the truth, and I think he knew that. "Sure you do," he insisted anyway. "Think."

"I can't."

"No more presents till you come up with something."

"Okay," I said, giving up. "I like that you threw dog poop at Bettye McCoy."

He laughed. "Are you saying you like my spunk?"

"I think she's saying you're full of you know what," Alison corrected.

"What else do you like?" Lance asked, ignoring his sister.

"I like your taste in nightgowns," I admitted, watching my mother shake her head in the reflection from the front window.

"You like the way I taste," Lance translated, blue eyes dancing.

I shook my head, declined comment. "I like your belt," I said finally.

"You like my belt?"

"It's a very nice belt."

Lance Palmay glanced down at the black leather belt

that was secured around his slender waist by a large silver buckle. "You like my belt," he repeated wondrously. "Anyone ever tell you that you're a very strange woman, Terry Painter?"

We opened the remainder of the gifts in relative silence. A T-shirt from me to Alison, a photograph album from Alison to me. Some movie tickets, a box of shortbread cookies, a travel alarm clock, a pair of fluffy pink slippers. "Last one," I said, reaching under the tree and extricating a small package with a large white bow.

"What is it?" Alison looked almost afraid to open it.

"I hope you like it." I watched as she gently lifted off the bow and discarded the paper, removing the lid from the top of the box. "I thought it was time for you to have a necklace of your own," I said as she held up the thin gold necklace that spelled out her name.

Tears formed in Alison's eyes, fell freely down her face. Silently, she reached up and removed the heart necklace, replacing it with the new one. "It's beautiful. I'll never take it off."

I laughed, but tears were in my own eyes as well.

Alison suddenly got up and reached to the very back of the tree, pulling out a long, thin, rectangular present wrapped in dark green paper. "It's for you," she said, laying it across my lap.

Even before I unwrapped it, I knew what it was. "This is too much," I whispered, staring at the painting of a woman in a large-brimmed hat relaxing on a beach of pink sand. "This is way too much."

"You like it, don't you?"

"Of course I like it. I **love** it. But it's way too expensive."

"I got my employee discount. This was before I got canned, of course."

We both laughed, although we were crying too.

"Even so . . ."

"Even so, nothing. It belongs here. Right here." Alison pointed to the blank space on the wall behind the sofa. "Lance'll help you hang it. He's good at hanging stuff."

"Are you suggesting I'm well hung?" Lance asked as he pushed himself to his feet.

"Lance!"

But I barely heard them. "Nobody's ever done anything like this for me before," I whispered. Whatever reservations I harbored, whatever questions remained unanswered, whatever doubts still lingered, they vanished in that instant.

"Me neither," Alison said, stroking the gold at her neck, then extending her arms toward me

"Careful, you two," Lance said. "I might get jealous."

Alison ignored him, wrapping me in an almost suffocating embrace. I felt the wetness of her tears on my cheeks, the pounding of her heart against my own. At that moment it was impossible to tell where I left off and she began.

"Merry Christmas, Terry," she cried softly.

"Merry Christmas, Alison."

# 16

"Merry Christmas," I called as I pushed open the door to Myra Wylie's hospital room.

It was just past eight o'clock in the morning, and Myra Wylie was lying in her bed, her head turned toward the window. She made no move to turn around, even as I closed the door behind me and cautiously approached, holding my breath. I'd been through this routine already twice this morning, and both times had found Myra Wylie sleeping soundly. I hadn't disturbed her. How often did the poor woman get a good night's sleep anymore?

I remembered that my mother's last months had been marked by extreme restlessness. She'd tossed and turned in her bed all night, hardly closing her eyes at all. If Christmas had managed to bring a measure of peace to Myra Wylie's tortured existence, then who was I to disturb her?

Except that there was something different about her posture this morning, something worrisome about the way her shoulders slumped against their covers, something unsettling in the angle of her head. "Myra?" I reached for the skeletal hand beneath the sheet, praying for a pulse.

"It's all right," she said, her voice clear but dull, as if it had been stripped of its natural shine by a harsh abrasive. "I'm not dead yet."

**Lance thinks people should be stamped with a "best before" date,** I heard Alison say.

Immediately I rushed around to the other side of the bed, positioned myself directly in front of her, and realized instantly that she'd been crying. "Myra, what's the matter? Has something happened? Are you in pain? What's wrong?"

"Nothing's wrong."

"Something's obviously upset you."

She shrugged, the tiny gesture upsetting her delicate equilibrium, throwing her frail body into a series of exaggerated spasms. I grabbed a glass of water from the night table, extended the straw to her lips, watched as she coaxed the tepid liquid into her mouth.

"Do you want me to call a doctor?"

Myra shook her head, said nothing.

"What is it? You can tell me."

"I'm just a silly old woman," Myra said, really looking at me for the first time since I'd walked into the room. She tried to smile, but the attempt disappeared into a prolonged set of twitches that made her jaw quiver like a ventriloquist's dummy.

"No, you're not." I smoothed several fine wisps of hair—more like threads really—away from her forehead. "I think you're just feeling a little sorry for yourself, that's all."

"I'm a silly old woman."

"I brought you a present." I watched her eyes fill instantly with a child's delight. We're never too old for presents, I thought, pulling a small package out of the pocket of my uniform.

She struggled with the wrapping for several seconds, then gave up and handed the present back to me. "You open it," she instructed eagerly, and I discarded the paper to reveal a pair of bright, red-and-green Christmas socks.

"So your feet will stay nice and warm."

She brought her hand to her heart, as pleased as if I'd brought her diamonds. "Will you put them on for me?"

"It will be my pleasure." I lifted up the bottom of the sheets, felt her toes ice-cold against the palms of my hands. "How's that?" I asked, slipping on first one sock, then the other.

"Wonderful. Just wonderful."

"Merry Christmas, Myra."

A shadow, like a large palm frond, passed across her face. "I don't have anything for you."

"I wasn't expecting anything."

The shadow disappeared as quickly as it had come, her eyes noticeably brightening. "I might have some money in my purse." She nodded toward the end table. "You could take as much as you want, buy yourself something nice from me."

**I bet you get pretty close to some of these lonely old biddies,** I heard Lance say. **I bet it wouldn't be too difficult to get them to include you in their wills, have them sign over the bulk of their estates to you.**

He was right, I realized in that instant. It wouldn't be difficult at all.

And once I had their money, then what? Was I expected to sign over my own estate to Alison? Was that the plan?

Was I the lonely old biddy to whom he'd been referring? Was I the real target here?

Why not? I had a home, a cottage, a retirement savings plan.

**Sounds like a plan to me,** I heard Lance say.

**Everything is going exactly as planned,** I recalled Alison telling her brother over the phone after Thanksgiving.

What was the matter with me? I wondered impatiently. Where were these thoughts coming from? Hadn't I made a conscious decision to banish such silliness from my mind?

"Terry," Myra was saying. "Terry, dear, what's the matter?"

Instantly, I snapped back into the here and now. "I'm sorry. Did you say something?"

"I asked if you could get my purse from the drawer."

"Myra, Josh took your purse home with him months ago. Don't you remember?"

She shook her head, dislodged several fresh tears.

"You miss Josh, don't you? That's why you're so depressed."

Myra buried her cheek into the side of her pillow.

"I miss him too," I said, trying to sound upbeat and cheerful. "But he'll be back real soon."

She nodded.

I checked my watch. "It's only five o'clock in the morning in California. I'm sure he's planning to phone you as soon as he wakes up."

"He called last night."

"He did? That's great. How is he?"

"Fine. He's fine." Myra's voice was curiously flat, as if someone had rolled over it with a tire.

"Myra, are you sure you're okay? Does something hurt you?"

"Nothing hurts. You're here. My feet are warm. What more could I want?"

"How about a piece of marzipan?" I pulled a miniature marzipan banana out of my pocket.

"Oh—I love marzipan. How did you know?"

"One marzipan lover can always spot another." I unwrapped the marzipan candy, placed it between her lips, felt her nibble at it like a squirrel.

"It's delicious." Her hand reached toward my face. I leaned forward, felt her fingers trembling against my cheek. "Thank you, dear."

"Anytime."

"Terry . . ."

"Yes?"

She lifted her mouth to my ear. "You've been so kind. The daughter I never had."

**You've been so kind,** I repeated silently back at her. **The mother I never had.**

"I want you to know how grateful I am for everything you've done for me."

"I know."

"I love you."

"I love you too," I whispered, burying my tears in the soft threads of her silver hair.

There was a knock on the door, and I turned, half-expecting to find Josh standing there. If this were the movies, I thought, then Josh Wylie would have flown in as a surprise gift for his mother on Christmas morning. He would have seen me standing beside her bed, recognized me as the great love of his life, and instantly dropped to his knees, begging me to be his wife. But as this wasn't the movies, when I turned toward the knock I saw, not a love-struck suitor, but an indifferent, gum-chewing orderly. "Yes?"

"Phone call for you at the nurses' station."

"For me? Are you sure?"

"Beverley said to tell you it was important."

Who would be calling me at work on Christmas morning? It had to be Alison. Had something happened? Was anything wrong?

"You go, dear," Myra said. "I'll see you later."

"You're sure you're all right?"

"I'm always all right when you're around."

"Then I'll be back before you know it."

I left the room and headed for the nurses' station. "Line two," Beverley said as soon as she saw me. "He said it couldn't wait."

"He?" Josh? I wondered. Calling from San Francisco to wish me a merry Christmas, to say he missed me, to tell me he was coming home early? Or maybe Lance, I second-guessed, calling to tell me there'd been an accident, that Alison had been critically injured. "Hello?"

"Merry Christmas."

"Merry Christmas to you," I repeated, disappointed it wasn't Josh, relieved it wasn't Lance.

"Erica sends her love, says she's sorry she couldn't be with you for the holidays."

"Who are you?" I shouted, unmindful of the people walking by. "Enough is enough! I don't know what your game is but—"

"Terry!" Beverley cautioned from somewhere beside me, lifting a silencing finger to her mouth.

I dropped the receiver angrily into its cradle. "Sorry. I didn't mean to raise my voice."

"Who was that?"

"I don't know."

"You don't know?"

"I've been getting these nuisance calls."

Beverley nodded. "You don't have to tell me about those," she said, chubby fingers carelessly tapping the desk as she leafed through a small stack of patients' files. She was thrice-divorced and at least twice her fighting weight. Her hair was too short, too permed, and too many shades of blond. Clearly, this was a woman only comfortable with extremes, possibly the reason for the three divorces, I thought, but then, who was I to judge? I'd always felt vaguely sorry for her. Now I wondered if she felt the same about me. "After my last divorce," Beverley was saying, "my ex-husband called me fifty times a day. Fifty! I changed my number four times, didn't do any good. I finally had to sic the police on him."

"I guess I might have to do that."

"Kind of hard when you don't know who it is. You have no idea . . . ?"

A smiling trio appeared before my eyes—Lance and K.C. flanking the man with the red bandanna. "No," I said.

"Too bad. He sounded so sexy, the way he said your name. Real slow. Kind of like he was purring. I thought it might be, you know, someone special." She shrugged, returning her attention to the stack of papers in front of her. "Probably just some stupid kid getting his jollies."

"Well, if anybody else calls, just tell him . . . I don't know. Use your imagination."

"Don't worry. I'll think of something."

I heard her laughing as I walked down the hall, no

clear idea where I was headed until I found myself in front of Sheena O'Connor's door. I peeked inside, saw her sitting up and talking animatedly on the phone. I was about to withdraw when her voice stopped me.

"No, wait." She waved me inside the room. "Come in. I'll just be another minute."

While she finished her conversation, I checked on the many flower arrangements and poinsettias that filled the room, watering the several that were in dire need, and silently counting the others, stopping at fifteen. **We love you, Mom and Dad. Merry Christmas, Munchkin, from Aunt Kathy and Uncle Steve. Way to go, Love Annie.** I paused the longest at the two dozen long-stemmed yellow roses, recalling the roses Josh had sent me for Thanksgiving, wondering if there'd be a surprise bouquet waiting for me when I got home.

"Smells like a funeral parlor in here." Sheena laughed as she replaced the receiver.

She looks beautiful, I thought, brown eyes as soft as sable against the whiteness of her skin. Her face was still swollen from the beating she'd received and her subsequent corrective surgery, but the deep scratches around her mouth had faded into fine lines, and the only sign her nose had been broken was a slight curvature to the left, an imperfection I rather liked, but one she probably wouldn't.

"I think it smells nice," I said truthfully.

"I guess." She nodded toward the phone. "That was my parents. They're on their way over with a truckful of presents."

"I bet they are."

"I just wish I could go home."

"I would think you'll be going home very soon. You've made remarkable progress."

"Why don't you sit down," Sheena suggested. "Talk to me for a while. Unless you're busy . . ."

I pulled up a nearby chair, plopped down into it. "I'm not busy."

"How come you're working today? Doesn't your family mind?"

"They don't mind," I said, deciding Sheena wasn't really interested in the details of my life story. She was just making pleasant conversation as a way of passing the time before her own family arrived.

"Are you married?" she asked unexpectedly, glancing at my bare ring finger.

I pictured Josh, his warm eyes and warmer lips. I felt his mouth graze mine as his eyelids fluttered against my cheek. "Yes," I told her. "I am."

"Do you have any kids? I bet you have lots of kids."

"I have a daughter," I heard myself say, and almost gasped at my audacity. What was I doing? I tried picturing Alison as she must have looked as a little girl. "She's older than you are."

"Just the one child?"

"Just the one."

"I'm surprised. I would have thought you'd have at least three."

"Really? Why?"

"Just 'cause I think you'd be a really good mother." She smiled shyly. "I remember the way you sang to me. How did that song go?"

**"Too-ra-loo-ra-loo-ra,"** I sang softly. **"Too-ra-loo-ra-lie . . ."**

"That's it. It was so beautiful. It was calling to me."

I stopped singing. "What was it like?"

"Being in a coma?"

I nodded.

She shook her head. "I guess it was like being asleep. I don't really remember anything specific. Mostly voices off in the distance, like if I was dreaming, except there were no pictures. And then the sound of someone singing. You," she said, and smiled. "You brought me back."

"Do you remember anything about the attack?"

A shiver swept the smile from Sheena's face.

"I'm sorry," I apologized immediately. "I shouldn't have asked."

"No, that's all right," Sheena said quickly. "The police have asked me about it a hundred times. I wish I had something to tell them. But the truth is, I don't remember a thing about the attack itself. I just remember that I was lying in my backyard, working on my tan. My parents were out and my sister was at the beach. I was waiting for a phone call—this guy I liked at school—so I didn't want to leave the house. I stretched a blanket across the grass and lay down on my stomach. I remember undoing the back of my bikini top. It's pretty secluded in my backyard. I didn't think anyone could see me. I was almost dozing off when I heard it." She stopped, her eyes coming to rest on a large red poinsettia behind my head.

"Heard what?"

"There was this sound. The leaves were rustling. No," she corrected immediately. "It wasn't as strong as that. It was quieter."

"They were whispering," I said, my own voice hushed.

"Yes! That's exactly what it was." Her eyes fastened on mine. "I remember thinking it was so strange that the leaves would be moving when there was no wind at all. And then I felt someone standing over me, and it was too late."

"I'm so sorry."

"My instincts were trying to warn me, but I didn't listen."

I nodded. How often we ignore our instincts, I was thinking. How often we ignore the whispering of the leaves.

"Will you sing to me again?" Sheena asked, lying back against her pillow and closing her eyes.

"**Too-ra-loo-ra-loo-ra,**" I began softly.

"**Too-ra-loo-ra-lie,**" Sheena sang with me.

"**Too-ra-loo-ra-loo-ra,**" we sang together, our voices steadily gaining strength. And I was able, for a few fleeting minutes, to pretend that the leaves had stopped whispering, and all was right with the world.

# 17

H e called again," Beverley said as I returned to the nurses' station at the end of my shift.

I didn't have to ask whom she meant. "When?"

Beverley glanced at the large, round clock on the wall. "About forty minutes ago. I told him you were dead."

I laughed in spite of myself. "What did he say?"

"Said he'd catch you later." She shrugged, as if to ask, What can you do? "Holiday season brings out all the crazies, I guess."

"I guess," I repeated, moving like an automaton toward the elevators, pressing the button repeatedly until the doors opened. Was that all it was?

**My instincts were trying to warn me,** I heard Sheena O'Connor repeat, **but I didn't listen.**

The elevator was already pretty full, and I had to squeeze in between two middle-aged men, one of whom smelled of liquor, the other of poor personal hygiene. I watched the doors drag to a close and steadied my feet as the elevator lurched into its slow, almost painful descent. "Merry Christmas," one of the men said, the smell of whiskey overwhelming the small space, like fumes of poisonous gas.

I held my breath, nodded, and prayed the elevator wouldn't stop at every floor. Of course it did, and even more people crowded inside. "Merry Christmas," the man beside me greeted each new occupant, at one point even attempting a courtly bow. He promptly lost his balance and fell against me, his hand brushing against my breast as he tried to right himself. "Sorry about that," he said with a stupid grin as I fought back the urge to throw up all over him. Unlike Alison, I had no phobias in that department.

The elevator finally reached the lobby, bouncing several times on its arrival, as if it were surprised it had landed in one piece, and its doors yawned open. Everyone folded together as one, pouring from the elevator like water from a glass. I felt a hand on my rear end and initially dismissed the intrusion as an unavoidable consequence of so many people being squished together like sardines, until I felt stray fingers trying to worm their way between my legs. I angrily swatted the hand away and glared at the drunk beside me, whose stupid grin had now settled across his entire face. "Jerk,"

I muttered. I stepped into the lobby, releasing the trapped air from my lungs and brushing another phantom hand from my backside, feeling its illusion linger, invisible fingers continuing to probe.

"Terry," a voice said from somewhere behind me, and I found myself staring at an attractive, olive-skinned woman about five years younger than I, whose name stubbornly refused to materialize. "Luisa," she said, as if sensing my predicament. "From Admitting. I thought I recognized you when you got in the elevator, but it was so crowded . . ."

"And smelly."

She laughed. "Wasn't that awful? Were you working today?"

I nodded. "You?"

She shook her head. Several black curls fell across her wide forehead. "No. I was visiting my grandmother. She tripped on a tiny crack in the sidewalk last week and broke her hip. Can you believe it?"

"I'm sorry."

"This getting older is for the birds."

I thought of my mother, of Myra Wylie, of all the sick and helpless men and women who'd exceeded their "best before" dates.

"Well, have a merry Christmas," Luisa said. "And if I don't see you before, have a healthy and happy New Year."

"The same to you." I watched her turn and walk away. "Luisa," I called out suddenly, the unexpected urgency in my voice stopping us both dead in our tracks. Luisa eyed me quizzically as I ran to catch up to her. "Sorry, I just remembered something I need to ask you about."

Luisa said nothing, waited for me to continue.

"A friend of mine is trying to locate a woman who used to work here. Rita Bishop." Why was I bringing this up now? I wondered. Hadn't Alison herself told me not to bother?

Luisa raised thick, black eyebrows, furrowed her wide brow. "Name doesn't ring a bell."

"She left about six, seven months ago."

"Do you know what department she worked in?"

"I think she was a secretary or something."

"Well, I've been here for three years and I've never heard of any Rita Bishop, but that doesn't necessarily mean anything. Would you like me to check the files?"

"I don't want to put you to any trouble."

"It'll only take a minute."

I followed Luisa to the main office, waited while she unlocked the door. This is silly, I told myself, watching while she flipped on the lights and quickly activated the computer on her desk.

But my conversation with Sheena O'Connor had left me a little unsettled. **My instincts were trying to warn me,** she'd said, and I'd nodded understanding, realizing how successfully I'd buried my own instincts, feeling them stubbornly reasserting themselves now, refusing to be ignored any longer.

"I'm pulling up the personnel files," Luisa explained, her eyes on the screen. "I don't see anyone by that name. You said she left about six or seven months ago?"

"Maybe eight," I qualified.

"Well, I can't find anyone by that name at all." Luisa paused, typed in some further information. "You said Rita Bishop, right?"

"Right."

"I show a Sally Pope."

I laughed. "Close, but no cigar."

"Let me check something else." She pressed a few more keys. "I'll enter her name, let the computer run a search."

I nodded, although I already knew what the outcome of that search would be. Mission Care would have no record of Rita Bishop ever having worked here. In fact, it was highly doubtful that anyone named Rita Bishop worked anywhere, that she existed at all. Alison hadn't shown up at Mission Care looking for an old friend named Rita Bishop. She'd shown up at Mission Care looking for me.

There was no other plausible explanation.

The only remaining question was why.

"No." Luisa shook her head. "There's nothing. I'm not sure where else to look."

"That's okay. Don't bother."

"Sorry." Luisa shut off the computer. "There's an assisted-living community not far from here called Manor Care. Maybe your friend got the name confused."

"Maybe," I said hopefully, grasping at proverbial straws, still trying to ignore my instincts, to silence the whispering of the leaves by convincing myself that Alison was exactly whom she claimed to be, that she hadn't lied to me, that she wasn't lying to me still. "Thanks for trying," I told Luisa, offering her a lift home. But she had her own car, and we wished each other a final merry Christmas in the parking lot. Ten minutes later, I was still sitting in my car, trying to figure out what it all meant, and more importantly, what I was going to do next.

IT WAS ALREADY DARK when I pulled my car into my driveway. Lance's white Lincoln Town Car was parked on the street, and I debated whether to knock on the cottage door and confront Alison and her brother with my latest discovery. Except that I was confused and exhausted and vulnerable, and Alison always had a plausible explanation for everything. Besides, what exactly was I so upset about? That I was being played for a fool? Or that I still hadn't figured out what the game was?

One thing was clear: I wasn't some random victim. I'd obviously been researched carefully, chosen for a specific purpose, although the reason I'd been selected continued to elude me. A lot of time and money—I thought of the expensive painting Alison had presented me with at midnight—had gone into whatever plan she and her brother had concocted. But why? What could they possibly want with me? What could they possibly expect **from** me? And what, if anything, did Erica Hollander have to do with any of it?

I got out of the car, fished in my purse for my keys, reconsidered calling the police. And saying what exactly? That I'd rented out the small cottage behind my house to a young woman I now suspected of being a con artist? Or worse.

**And what has this young woman done to arouse your suspicions?** I could hear them ask. **Has she asked you for money? Is she behind in her rent?**

**Well, no. She pays her rent exactly on time, and she's never asked me for a thing. In fact, she's bought me expensive presents and gone out of her way to be nice to me.**

**Well, that's certainly suspicious. No wonder you called us.**

**You don't understand. I'm afraid.**

**Afraid of what exactly?**

**I don't know.**

**Listen, lady, it's your house. If you don't like her, ask her to leave.**

Exactly. So simple. Ask her to leave. That's all I had to do. So, why didn't I? What was stopping me? Was I trying to persuade myself that, despite mounting evidence to the contrary, there was a simple and perfectly reasonable answer for each and every deception, that nothing had happened that couldn't be neatly explained away? Was I still trying to convince myself that there were no ulterior motives, no grand conspiracy, no risk to my safety and well-being?

**I can't ask her to leave.**

**Why not?**

**Because I don't want her to go,** I acknowledged silently.

It was her brother I wanted gone, and in another week, he would be. Happy New Year indeed! Then we could go back to the way it had been in the beginning. We could go back to pretending that Alison wasn't pretending, that she was everything she had initially represented herself to be.

At that moment, I tripped across the image of Sheena O'Connor, who appeared before me, stretched out on a blanket across my front lawn. I watched her reach behind her back to untie the top of her bikini, then turn her profile lazily toward the indifferent moon overhead. I heard the cool breeze rustling through the trees, listened to the subtle whispers warning her of danger, saw her wave them away with a careless toss of her hand, as if brushing off a pesky mosquito.

Could I really afford to be so cavalier?

The only solution was to talk to Alison. If she could provide me with a plausible explanation for what was going on, I would consider the matter settled. If not, I'd have to insist she leave.

Before I could change my mind, I marched around the side of the house and stepped up to the cottage door, knocking forcefully. Immediately, I thought better of it. I was being too hasty, too foolhardy, too naive. At the very least, I should tell someone of my concerns. If not the police, then maybe Josh or someone at work.

Except that Josh was out of town and my coworkers had their own problems to deal with. Besides, it was Christmas. I thought of all the lovely gifts Alison had given me, the beautiful painting, the china head vase. Christmas Day was hardly the time to question her sincerity, to accuse her of sinister plans and nefarious motives.

**Nefarious,** I could hear her say. **Good word.**

There was plenty of time to confront her, I decided, turning to leave.

"Door's open," Lance called from inside the cottage.

Reluctantly, I pushed open the door. What other choice did I have? I stepped over the threshold and shut the door behind me, glancing past the empty living room toward the rumpled bed in the next room. **You made your bed,** I heard my mother say.

"What's the matter? You forget your key?" Lance asked, emerging from the bathroom, wearing nothing but a towel around his slender waist. His hair was wet. Beads of water glistened from his sculpted chest.

"Oh."

"Oh yourself," he said with a mischievous smile.

"I'm sorry. I didn't realize . . ."

"Didn't realize what? That I was naked?" He took two steps toward me.

I took two steps back. "I've obviously interrupted you."

"Shower's all finished." Lance lifted muscular arms into the air. "See? Clean all over." He turned, the towel lifting slightly as he spun around, exposing a flash of inner thigh.

I pretended not to notice. "Is Alison here?" Silly question, I thought, biting down on my tongue. Obviously, she wasn't.

"She went for a walk."

"A walk?"

"Said she needed some air."

"Is she feeling all right?"

"Sure. Why wouldn't she be?"

"No migraine?"

He laughed. "She's fine." He took another step toward me. "Is there anything I can do for you? Keep you entertained until Alison gets back?"

I backed up until I felt the door handle press against the small of my back. "No. I just wanted to thank her again for the beautiful painting."

"I can come over," he offered, his right thumb hooking into the top of his towel. "Hang it for you right now."

"It can wait till morning."

"Some things are better hung at night." His tongue darted between newly parted lips.

"Some things are better left to the imagination," I countered.

"And I bet you have quite the imagination."

"What makes you say that?"

His eyes traveled down my white sweater and black pants, lingering on my breasts, stopping on my crotch. "I've been watching you."

"You've been watching me," I repeated, afraid to say more. I felt an unwanted tingle between my legs.

"Just trying to figure you out."

I lifted my hands into the air. Two can play this game, I thought, curiously emboldened. "What you see is what you get."

"Is that so?"

I nodded as he edged closer, so close now I felt the dampness of his recent shower on my skin.

"No secrets?" he asked provocatively.

I shook my head, his breath brushing against the side of my cheek like a furtive kiss. "I'm very boring, I'm afraid."

"What exactly is it you're afraid of?"

I almost laughed, would have had he not been standing so close. "What **exactly,**" I repeated in a voice not quite my own, "do you want from me?"

"What do **you** want from **me?**"

This time I did laugh, immediately tasting his breath on mine. "I've never been very good at games."

"I love games," Lance countered. "You ever see a cat playing with a mouse? Cat gets the poor mouse cornered, no question the mouse is gonna bite the dust, but the cat isn't satisfied with just the kill. The kill's the least interesting part, as far as the cat's concerned. No, the cat likes to play a while first."

"Is that what you're doing? Playing with me?"

"Is that what **you're** doing?" he repeated slowly. "Playing with **me?**"

I heard footsteps behind me, felt the doorknob turn against the small of my back, and suddenly the door opened, and I was propelled into Lance's waiting arms. Immediately, he grabbed my hand, slid it beneath the towel at his waist. I felt the wet curls of his pubic hair as his organ stiffened against my unwilling fingers. Without pausing to consider my actions, I reached up with my free hand and slapped him hard across the face. "Okay, that's it. I want you out of here right now."

"Terry!" Alison exclaimed, stepping inside as I struggled to compose myself. "What's the matter?" She looked at her brother. "What's going on here? What did you say to Terry? What have you done?"

"Just a slight misunderstanding," Lance said, flopping down on the large chair and extending one leg across its overstuffed arm, so that his entire expanse of inner thigh was clearly visible. His cheek was red where I'd slapped him. "Isn't that right, Terry?"

"I was just telling your brother that I think it's time he found another place to stay."

Alison's expression vacillated between confusion and anger as her eyes traveled back and forth between us. "Whatever he's done, please let me apologize—"

"Hey," Lance interrupted, bringing both legs to the floor. "You don't have to apologize for me. I was walking out of the shower when she came waltzing in."

"I knocked," I offered quickly. "Lance said to come in, the door was open."

"You don't have to explain," Alison said, staring at

her brother. "Whatever you said or did, I want you to apologize right now."

"I didn't do anything."

"Apologize anyway."

Lance glared at his sister, although by the time he turned to me, his face had softened, and he managed to look suitably contrite. "I'm sorry, Terry," he said quietly and with conviction. "I thought we were just having some fun. I guess sometimes I get carried away. I really **am** sorry."

I nodded, silently accepting his apology. "I should go."

"I'll be out of your hair in a few days. How's that?" Lance asked as I opened the cottage door.

Again I nodded, stepping outside and closing the door behind me, hoping to overhear snatches of their conversation, but there was nothing. In the ensuing silence, I stumbled toward my back door, the night air cool against my skin, still damp from contact with Lance's body, my fingers tingling with unwanted echoes of the feel of his flesh. **You ever see a cat playing with a mouse?** I heard him whisper in my ear.

"The cat isn't satisfied with just the kill," I acknowledged out loud as, moments later, I stepped into my own shower, tried washing the smell of him from my fingertips.

**The cat likes to play a while first.**

# 18

"The last time I made love was on New Year's Eve," Myra Wylie said, her voice heavy with age and infirmity, although a youthful glint was in her eyes. I pulled my chair closer to her bedside and leaned forward, eager to catch each word. "It was ten years ago. Steve and I—Steve was my husband—had been invited to this ghastly party, you know, one of those overblown affairs where there are too many people, most of them strangers, and everybody drinks too much, and laughs too loud, and makes a great show of having a good time, but they're really pretty miserable. You know the kind of party I mean."

I nodded, although I had no real idea what she was talking about. I'd never been to one of those parties. I'd never had a date for New Year's Eve.

"Well, I wasn't in a great mood because I didn't want to go to the damn party, and Steve knew that, but it was at the home of one of his former business partners, and he didn't think we could say no. You know how it is."

I didn't, but I agreed anyway.

"So, I got all dolled up in my fancy new dress, and Steve put on his tuxedo. He always looked so handsome in his tuxedo. Not that I told him how handsome he looked." Myra's eyes grew wistful, filled with tears. "I should have told him."

I grabbed a tissue from the night table beside Myra's bed and dabbed gently at the rolling waves of flesh beneath her eyes. "I'm sure he knew how you felt about him."

"Oh, he knew. But I should have told him anyway. It never hurts to tell someone he's loved."

"So you went to the party," I encouraged when she failed to continue.

"We went to the party," Myra repeated, picking up the thread of her earlier musings, "and it was every bit as awful as I knew it was going to be, so I guess there was a certain satisfaction in that. And we drank too much champagne, and laughed too loud at jokes that were only mildly funny, and pretended to be having the best time of our lives, just like everybody else, and at midnight, we yelled, 'Happy New Year,' like a bunch of drunken old idiots, and kissed everyone in sight. Pretty soon after that, we left for home. I was very nervous. I was always on the lookout for drunk drivers—I had an uncle who'd been killed by one when I was a little girl—

and this being New Year's Eve, well . . ." She coughed, gasped for air. I lifted the nearby glass of water to her lips.

"All out of champagne, I'm afraid," I said, watching her gulp it down.

"Tastes even better." She finished the last of the water, lay back against her pillows. "Shouldn't get so excited. It's all this talk about sex, I guess."

"I must have missed something," I said, and she laughed.

"I haven't gotten to the good part yet." She cleared her throat. "Not that there was much of a good part."

"No?"

"Not that it was bad," she qualified. "What is it they say about sex? When it's good, it's really good, and when it's bad, it's still good? It was that kind of bad. Do you follow?"

Again I nodded, although my own experiences with sex had been decidedly more bad than good.

"Well, we got home around twelve-thirty, maybe later. I guess it doesn't matter. The point is that it was later than we were used to staying up, and we were exhausted. I don't know why we felt we had to have sex that night just because it was New Year's Eve. I mean, we weren't kids anymore. We were in our late seventies, for heaven's sake. It wasn't like we weren't going to see each other the next morning. It wasn't like we hadn't been having sex for almost half a century." She stopped. "Am I making you uncomfortable?"

I shook my head.

"I'm glad. Because I'm rather enjoying talking about

this. I never have before, you know. Out loud, that is. You're sure you don't mind?"

"I'm sure."

"It's been my experience that young people don't like to hear about old people having sex. They think it's, I don't know . . . yicky," she settled on finally.

I laughed. "Yicky?"

**Good word,** I heard Alison say.

I quickly pushed thoughts of Alison from my mind. I'd seen almost nothing of either her or her brother since the episode in the cottage. Alison had come over early the next morning to apologize again for her brother's inappropriate behavior, and to assure me he'd be leaving in a matter of days. But Lance's rented white Lincoln was still parked in my driveway when I'd left for work this evening, and the painting Alison had bought me for Christmas remained on my living room floor, waiting to be hung.

"Children, especially, don't like to think of their parents having sex, even when they're older and should know better. They prefer to think of their conception as some sort of miracle birth, or that their parents only did it that once or maybe twice and stopped altogether once they'd completed their families. But, God, Steve and I did it all the time. Sorry, I can see by the look on your face that was rather indelicate."

"No, of course not," I stammered, pushing some nonexistent hairs away from my forehead, trying to arrange my features into a placid mask. I was thinking of my own parents, how certain I'd always been that my birth had been a freak of nature, or that sex had been something they'd tried once, disliked intensely, and had never attempted again, that that was the reason I was an only child. Now Myra was telling me this wasn't necessarily the case.

"Too much information," Myra joked. "That's what Josh always says."

"He'll be home soon."

"Yes." She looked toward the window. "Where was I?"

"You were having sex all the time."

Myra all but hooted with glee. It was the most animated I'd ever seen her. "Oh, I was such a bad girl." She laughed even harder. "Can I tell you something I've never told anyone?"

"Of course." I held my breath, almost afraid of what she was about to say.

"Steve wasn't the only man I ever had sex with."

I said nothing, although truthfully, I was almost relieved. Myra Wylie was so full of surprises tonight, I hadn't been sure what she was about to confide.

"No, there were several others before him. And this was in the days before birth control, when girls who had sex before marriage were considered loose women, although, of course, that never stopped anyone from doing it. Well, you know . . ."

I nodded. This time I **did** know.

"Anyway, there were several young men before I met Steve, although I told him he was the first, and he believed me."

"Were you **his** first?"

She leaned forward, cupped withered hands around her mouth, lowered her voice, as if afraid her late husband might be eavesdropping at the door. "I think I was." A smile pulled at her powdery skin. "Steve was such a natural lover. Much better than the other boys I'd been with."

"And were there others after you got married?" I ventured.

"Heavens, no! Once I'd made that commitment, that was it. Not that there weren't opportunities. But after I got married, I never really looked at other men in that way. I had my Stevie, and he kept me plenty busy." Her voice trailed off. She stared at the ceiling. For a minute, I thought she might have fallen asleep. "So on New Year's Eve," she started up again, her eyes flickering across the ceiling as if her past were being projected on it, "we got home and went to bed, and we kissed each other and wished each other a happy New Year, and Steve said, 'What do you think? Are you too tired?' And I was, but I didn't want to say so, so instead I said, 'No. I'm okay. How about you?' So, of course, he said he was okay too, and we made love, although neither of us really felt like it, and it was a bit of an effort, if you know what I mean."

Again I nodded, hoping she wouldn't go into details.

"But we managed. I think we felt we should, it being the New Year and everything. Sort of like on your anniversary or your birthday. You just feel you **should**. Anyway, we made love and then we fell asleep. Sex always puts me right to sleep." She laughed. "And later, I was so glad we'd made love that night because it turned out to be the last time we ever did. Steve had a heart attack the following week and died a month after that."

"You must miss him a great deal."

"There isn't a day goes by that I don't think about him. But I guess I'll be seeing him again pretty soon," she said brightly.

"Well, let's hope not too soon." I patted her arm and stood up, straightening her covers, although there was no need. I checked my watch. Another twenty minutes and it would be a brand-new year.

"Will you sit with me until midnight?" she asked. "Then I promise to go to sleep like a good little girl."

I sat back down, watched Myra's eyes flutter to a close.

"I'm not asleep," she warned. "Just resting my eyes."

"I'm not going anywhere," I assured her, watching the steady rise and fall of her chest beneath the covers, noting the satisfied smile that lingered in the folds of her ancient face.

At seventy-seven, she'd still been sexually active. At eighty-seven, the thought of sex still made her smile. I was envious, I realized. When had sex ever made me smile? When had it brought me anything but embarrassment and shame?

My first time had been fast and uncomfortable and not particularly pleasant. I remember Roger Stillman trying to pry my legs apart, the few hurried grabs at my breasts that served as foreplay. And then the sudden jolt of pain as his body pushed into mine, the unexpected weight of his torso as he collapsed on top of me when it was over.

The last time I'd had sex hadn't been much of an improvement, I thought with a shudder, again envying the dying old woman lying in bed before me. She'd been so open, so honest with me. What would she think if I were to be equally open and honest with her?

Could I tell her that the last time I'd had sex—real sex, not just the hint of it with Josh or the threat of it with Lance—had been the night my mother died? I shook my head in disbelief. Dear God, how could I have done anything so vile? What on earth had possessed me?

In truth, I'd all but pushed the details of that night out of my mind altogether. But Myra's memories had unleashed a flood of my own. I sat back in my chair, stared at the window, saw the ghosts of my past etched in the dark mirror of glass.

I watched myself as I sat stiffly by my mother's bedside, her death obvious in the grayness of her pallor, and the stillness that had settled over her body like a fine coating of wax. Her eyes and mouth were open, and I reached out to close them, her skin already cool against my fingers. Even in death, there remained a hint of the anger that had fueled her life. Even with her eyes closed and her breath stopped, a certain ferocity clung to her features. She was still a force to be reckoned with, I remember thinking as I bent down to kiss her lips, surprised to find them so soft and pliant. When had I ever experienced softness from those lips? Had she ever kissed me as a baby, a toddler, a child? Had those lips ever brushed across my forehead to check if I was feverish? Had they ever whispered "I love you" while I slept?

The sad fact was that I'd hated my mother almost as much as I'd loved her, that I'd spent my entire life trying to please her, to make up for whatever wrongs, both real and imaginary, I'd committed. After she'd suffered her stroke, I'd tried everything in my power to nurse her back to health, and when it became obvious to both of us she wouldn't get better, I'd continued to do my best to make sure she was as comfortable as possible. I'd sacrificed so much of my life for her, and suddenly she was gone, and I had nothing. No one. I was left with an emptiness so overwhelming I didn't know what to do.

I remember pacing back and forth at the foot of her bed. Back and forth. Back and forth. I could feel her watching me through closed, dead eyes, casting her continuing disapproval across my shoulders like a heavy cloak. **What kind of nurse are you that you couldn't keep your own mother alive?** I could hear her demand through cold, dead lips. And it was true, I conceded. I'd failed her. Again. As I'd always failed her.

"I'm so sorry," I cried out loud. "So sorry."

Sorry, sorry, sorry.

**A sorry excuse for a nurse. A sorrier excuse for a daughter.**

I don't remember leaving the house, although at some point I obviously did. I must have showered and

changed my clothes, although I have no memory of having done so. I **do** remember being in a bar on Atlantic
Avenue, throwing back several glasses of tequila, and
flirting with the handsomely nondescript bartender until
he abandoned me for a girl who kept tossing her long
blond hair from one shoulder to the other at the far end
of the bar. I then turned my attention to another generi-
cally handsome man, this one wearing a bright Hawaiian
shirt, who casually slipped his wedding band into the
pocket of his tight jeans as he sidled up beside me.

"I don't think I've seen you in here before," he said.

Yes, he actually said that. Maybe because it was true,
maybe because he was too lazy to think of anything more
original, maybe because he sensed I was such an easy mark
that nothing was to be gained by being more creative.

"It's my first time," I told him, trying—and failing—
to toss my hair over my shoulder like the blonde at the
end of the bar.

"First time, huh?" He signaled the bartender to refill
our drinks. "I like first times. Don't you?"

I gave him what I hoped would pass as a mysterious
smile and said nothing. Instead I pushed my shoulders
back and crossed my legs, his eyes tracing each move. I
was wearing a striped jersey that accentuated the swell
of my bosom, and strappy sandals that dangled provocatively from my bare toes. He was tall and slender, with
hair as black as coal and eyes the color of cool mint. He
did most of the talking—about what I don't remember.
I'm sure he told me his name, but I've successfully

blocked it out. Jack, John, Jerrod. Something with a **J**. I don't think I told him mine. I'm not sure he asked.

We had a few more drinks, and he suggested going somewhere more private. Without another word, I slid from my barstool and walked to the door. Surprisingly, I had no trouble walking, despite all the liquor in my system. In fact, I didn't feel the least bit drunk, although afterward, I convinced myself I'd been very drunk indeed. But as much as I'd like to blame what happened that night on a combination of grief and alcohol, I'm no longer sure I can do that. The truth is that I wasn't drunk that night, at least not so drunk I wasn't responsible for my actions. The truth is that I knew **exactly** what I was doing when I agreed to leave that bar for somewhere more private, when I let Jack or John or Jerrod feel me up as we stumbled toward his car, when I whispered that I lived just around the corner.

He parked on the street in front of my house, and I led him around the side to the cottage at the back. "Who lives in the main house?" he asked as I opened the cottage door and began turning on the lights.

"My mother," I told him, glancing toward her bedroom window.

"Aren't you afraid she'll see us with all these lights on?"

"She's a very sound sleeper," I said, pulling off my jersey in front of the window, hearing my mother's silent gasp.

After that, we said little. But if I'd been expecting

great sex, I was sorely disappointed. If I'd been looking for some kind of release, I got nothing of the sort. Instead I got a lot of grunting and thrashing about to no particular purpose, and when it was over—too fast, yet not nearly fast enough—I couldn't wait for Jack or John or Jerrod to put on his tight jeans and Hawaiian shirt and leave.

"I'll call you," he said on his way out the door.

I nodded, looking up at my mother's room, feeling the crushing weight of her disapproval, as heavy as the weight of the man who'd just left my bed. I took a shower and got dressed, then I called for an ambulance and returned to the main house, where I sat dutifully by my mother's side until it arrived. Then I wiped that night from my mind as if it had never happened and refused to think of it again.

Until now.

I glanced at my watch. It was midnight. "Happy New Year," I whispered, kissing Myra's warm cheek.

"Happy New Year," she repeated, opening her eyes briefly, her thin lashes brushing against my skin.

Seconds later, she was asleep, and once again, I was alone.

# 19

I thought I heard something when I stepped into the hallway. I stopped, looked around, saw nothing but an empty corridor. I stood there, my hand still on the door to Myra's room, my head cocked to one side, like an attentive puppy, my ears on full alert for any errant sounds—a stray step, a heavy breath—anything at all out of the ordinary.

But there was nothing.

I shook my head and started down the hall, looking in on my patients as I passed each joyless room. Most were asleep, or pretending to be. Only Eliot Winchell, a middle-aged man saddled with the brain of a toddler as the result of a seemingly harmless spill from a bicycle, was awake. He waved when he saw me.

"Happy New Year, Mr. Winchell," I said, automatically checking his pulse. "Is there anything I can get for you?"

He smiled his eerie child's smile and said nothing.

"Do you need to go to the bathroom?"

He shook his head, smiled wider, the white of his teeth flashing in the semidarkness of the room.

"Then try to get some sleep now, Mr. Winchell. You have a very busy day ahead of you." I doubted this was true, but what difference did it make? One day would be pretty much the same as the next for Eliot Winchell for the rest of his life. "Why weren't you wearing your helmet, Eliot?" I scolded in my mother's voice, watching the child's smile vanish abruptly from his face. "Get some sleep," I said, softening, patting his arm, and making sure his covers were secure. "I'll see you tomorrow."

I heard the noise as soon as I stepped back into the hall.

I spun around, my eyes darting back and forth, up and down the brightly lit corridor. But again, there was nothing. I held my breath, waited, tried unsuccessfully to figure out exactly what it was I thought I'd heard. But there was nothing I could put my finger on, nothing but a vague sense of disquiet.

"It's nothing," I said out loud as I walked past Sheena O'Connor's former room. Sheena O'Connor was no longer a patient at Mission Care. Her doctors felt she'd recovered sufficiently to release her, and her parents had arrived to take her home the day before yesterday.

"Isn't it great? I'll be home for New Year's," she'd exclaimed.

"You take good care of yourself," I urged.

"You'll keep in touch, won't you? You'll come visit me?"

"Of course I will," I said, but I think we both knew that once she left the hospital, I'd never see her again.

She hugged me. "I'm gonna call you every time I can't sleep," she warned. "Have you sing to me."

"You won't have any trouble sleeping."

What was she doing now? I wondered, returning to the nurses' station, realizing I missed having someone to sing to.

On holidays, the hospital retained only a skeletal staff. Beverley and I were the only nurses on the floor. Truthfully, I would have preferred total solitude. Then I wouldn't have to spend the first moments of the New Year mired in boring small talk or pretend to be interested in Beverley's mind-numbingly stupid problems. I wouldn't be expected to offer advice I knew would never be followed. I could simply enjoy this time alone. Chances were slight there'd be an emergency, and doctors were on call if I needed them. **A glorified baby-sitter, that's all you are,** I heard my mother whisper.

"Did you hear something?" I asked Beverley, drowning out the sound of my mother's voice.

"Like what?" Beverley looked up from the double issue of **People** she was perusing and listened. "I don't hear anything."

I shrugged, unconvinced. The silence of the night pounded against my head like a hammer.

"Just your imagination working overtime," Beverley pronounced.

God knows I have plenty of imagination, I thought. Yes, sir—lots of imagination.

And no life.

The people dying in their beds just down the hall had more life than I did. Myra Wylie, for God's sake, at eighty-seven and sick with leukemia and heart disease, still grew wistful at the very thought of sex. Ten years ago, **ten years ago,** she'd still been sexually active! And here was I, almost half her age, with only a tiny fraction of her life experience. What was I waiting for? How much of my life was I going to waste?

I'd never made New Year's resolutions before, but I made one now. Come hell or high water, this year was going to be different. Josh would be back from California in a few days, and I was going to be ready for him.

"Who would you sleep with if you had the chance?" Beverley startled me by asking, as if privy to my thoughts. "Tom Cruise or Russell Crowe?" She held up the magazine, tapped fake, orange nails against the appropriate pictures.

"Is George Clooney an option?"

She laughed, and I listened in mounting fear as the laugh spun circles around us. "Don't tell me you didn't hear that."

"I heard it." Beverley dropped the magazine to the counter and rose to her feet. "Probably Larry Foster in 415. He has that weird little laugh. I'll go check on him."

"Maybe we should call security."

Fake, orange nails waved my concerns aside as Beverley headed down the hall.

I picked up the **People** magazine and flipped through its pages, trying to pretend there was no cause for alarm by concentrating on which stars had undergone plastic surgery in the last year. "You, definitely," I said, pointing to the picture of an aging starlet who, except for an exaggerated mane of curly blond hair, barely resembled her former self. In fact, it was only after I read the name beneath the photograph that I realized who she was.

That's when I heard the sound again.

The magazine dropped from my hands and slid off my lap as I jumped to my feet. "Who's there?" I demanded, eyes straying toward the alarm button on the wall.

A figure emerged from behind a nearby pillar and sauntered slowly toward me, his fingers hooked into the pockets of his black jeans, a cruel smile tugging at his lips. Tall, skinny, dressed all in black, his brown eyes laughed at me from atop his hawklike nose. I didn't need a name beneath a photograph to identify him.

"K.C.!"

"Happy New Year, Terry."

I fought to get air into my lungs. "What are you doing here? How did you get past security?"

"You mean my friend Sylvester?"

"What did you do to him?"

The smile disappeared from his mouth. "You mean after I slit his throat?"

My voice fell to my knees. "Oh, my God!"

K.C. laughed, slapped his thigh in disbelief. "What—you think I'm serious? You think I'd hurt my friend Sylvester? What kind of people have you been hanging out with, lady? Of course I didn't hurt him. I just explained how unfair I thought it was you had to miss out on all the festivities and said I wanted to surprise you with a party of your own. Sylvester was very understanding, especially when I presented him with a nice bottle of ten-year-old Scotch. What's the matter, Terry? You don't look very happy to see me."

"Are you alone?"

"What do you think?" He lifted his right hand, aimed it at my heart. It was only then I saw the gun.

There was a loud bang, and in a blinding flash, the world exploded. I fell back, cried out, glanced toward my chest, waiting for the sight of my blood to seep through the whiteness of my uniform.

"My God, what's going on here?" Beverley exclaimed as my vision began to blur. "Who are you?" she demanded of K.C. as the taste of blood filled my mouth.

"Friends of Terry's," K.C. answered easily, and I was too weak to object.

And then Alison suddenly jumped into view. "Happy New Year!" she shouted.

"Happy New Year!" echoed Denise, popping up beside her.

"Welcome to the first day of the rest of your life," Lance announced from another corner, laughing as champagne gushed from the large bottle in his hand to spill across the floor. "That was one noisy cork. Anybody see where it went?"

"What's going on here?" Beverley asked again, although a smile was already creeping into her voice.

"New Year's celebration," Lance told her. "We didn't think you angels of mercy should miss out on all the fun."

"Well, aren't you sweet. I'm Beverley, by the way."

"Pleasure to meet you, Beverley. I'm Lance. This is Alison, Denise, and K.C."

"Any friends of Terry's"—Beverley began, then stopped when she saw the look on my face.

"You scared me half to death," I said, realizing I hadn't been shot after all.

Lance laughed. "A little scare's good for you. Gets the adrenaline pumping."

"We didn't mean to scare you," Alison apologized. "We just wanted to surprise you."

"Don't you like surprises, Terry?" Denise asked, approaching the nurses' station. Her black hair had outgrown its trendy cut, and as a result, its spikes had lost some of their sharp edges, collapsing around her pale face like ash from a cigarette. Her eyes were rimmed with black, making her look more ghoulish than sophisticated, an effect I don't think was intentional, although knowing Denise, perhaps it was.

"Please don't touch anything," I admonished, still trying to catch my breath.

"We brought glasses," Alison said, producing them from the large shopping bag in her hands.

"We thought of everything," K.C. added.

"Where do you keep the drugs?" Denise asked.

"What!"

"Just joking."

"What happened to your lip?" Alison asked.

I touched the side of my mouth where I must have bitten down. Immediately, Lance was beside me, licking the drop of blood from my finger with the exaggerated gusto of a movie vampire. "Hmm. Two thousand two. A very good year."

I pulled my hand away. "Save it, Bela Lugosi," I told him, struggling to keep everyone in my line of sight. Beverley already had a glass in her hand.

"Don't be upset with us, Terry," Alison pleaded. She was dressed all in white, her strawberry-blond curls falling loosely around her face, Botticelli's Venus removed from her shell.

"I'm just not sure this is such a good idea."

"It's a great idea," Beverley countered with a slap on my arm, as Lance began carefully measuring out equal amounts of champagne. I noticed that he too was dressed all in white.

"We couldn't let you spend New Year's Eve alone," K.C. said.

"That wouldn't have been very nice of us." Denise began rifling through a nearby stack of patients' charts.

I quickly moved them out of her reach. "You shouldn't be back here."

"Why not?"

"Denise," Alison said.

Denise promptly left the nurses' station, grabbing a glass of champagne from the counter as she brushed by. "Cheers, everybody."

"Wait. We have to make a toast." Alison waited to make sure we each had a glass.

"What are we drinking to?" Lance asked his sister.

"To the best year ever." Alison raised her glass into the air.

"The best year ever," we all agreed.

I didn't want to be considered a wet blanket, so I took one sip, then another. The champagne tasted surprisingly refreshing, so I took several more, the bubbles stinging the insides of my nose. "Good health," I said under my breath.

"And wealth," Denise added quickly.

"May we all get exactly what we want in the coming year," Lance continued.

"Everything that's coming to us," K.C. added, smiling at me from over the rim of his glass as everyone took another sip of champagne.

"Everything we deserve," Denise said.

"Everything we need," said Alison.

"And what exactly is that?" her brother challenged.

Alison buried her nose inside her glass of champagne and said nothing. I finished the last of my champagne in two quick gulps.

"Well, I know what I need," Denise said, laughing. "I need a change of scenery."

"Weren't you just in New York?"

"New York doesn't count. I was with my mother."

"What's wrong with your mother?"

"Nothing—if you like uptight, anal-retentive, old farts." Denise immediately doubled over with laughter.

"Alison likes uptight, anal-retentive, old farts," Lance said, looking directly at me. "Don't you, Alison?"

"I like everyone." Alison finished the contents of her glass and poured herself another. I could tell by the way she was swaying, by the way they were **all** swaying, that this wasn't the evening's first bottle of booze. "Terry, your glass is empty." Alison filled it to the top before I had time to object. "Drink up," she urged, watching as I lifted the glass to my mouth.

"I'm serious," Denise was saying. "I've had it with the East Coast. It's time for a change."

"Could this have anything to do with getting fired by your aunt?" K.C. asked.

"My aunt's an uptight, anal-retentive, old fart."

"Why'd she fire you?" Beverley asked, holding out her glass for a refill.

Denise shrugged. "Because she's jealous of me. She's always been jealous of me."

"I thought it was because she caught you stealing from the till."

Denise waved away K.C.'s unwanted explanation. "Wouldn't have happened if she wasn't such a damn tightwad. She was paying me next to nothing, for God's sake. And she has all this money. Plus, I'm family. You'd think she could afford to be more generous. I hate people like that. Don't you hate people like that, Terry?"

"I think people have a right to decide what to do with their own money." I took another long sip of champagne, struggled to stay focused.

"Yeah, well, I think she's—"

"—an uptight, anal-retentive, old fart?" Lance asked slyly.

"Exactly." Denise wobbled toward him, pushed her breasts against his chest. "I was thinking of trying New Mexico. Want to come with me?"

"Sounds like a plan." Lance put his arms around Denise's waist, stared over her wilting dark spikes at Alison. "I'm getting a little tired of South Florida myself."

Alison looked away, smiled in my direction, though her smile was tight, as if it were holding back a torrent of angry words.

A buzzer sounded.

"What's that?" Denise raised her head from Lance's chest.

I glanced at the wall behind the nurses' station. The button indicating Eliot Winchell's room was lit up. "It's one of my patients. I have to go."

"We'll come with you," Lance said.

I shook my head in an effort to clear it, watched the room spin instead. "No. You have to leave now."

The buzzer sounded again.

"Come on, guys. We should get going," Alison said. "We don't want to get Terry in trouble."

Denise shook her head. "Oh, come on. Don't be such an uptight—"

"—anal retentive —" K.C. continued.

"—old fart," Lance concluded, and they all laughed. Except for Alison, who had the decency to look both embarrassed and ashamed.

The buzzer sounded again.

"Persistent little bugger, isn't he?" Beverley said, making no move to respond to his call.

"Okay, guys, I appreciate your coming here, and bringing the champagne, and celebrating New Year's Eve with us, but I really have to go now. And so do you."

"We understand," K.C. said.

"We can show ourselves out," Lance offered, guiding the others to the elevator as the buzzer sounded yet again.

"Thanks for dropping by," I heard Beverley say as I headed down the hall. The floor was sliding under my feet, like a moving sidewalk, and I grabbed the wall for support, trying to control the spinning of my head. Was

I drunk already, on only two glasses of champagne? The only other time I'd gotten this drunk this fast, I realized, I'd also been with Alison.

I pushed open the door to Eliot Winchell's room. He was sitting up in bed, his covers bunched up around his ankles, the front of his pajamas wet with his urine. "Oh, Eliot. Have you had an accident?"

"I'm sorry," he said sheepishly.

"No. Don't be sorry. It's not your fault."

"Really?" Lance asked, pushing past me into the room, followed by Denise and K.C. Alison hung back in the doorway as the others approached the bed. "Then whose fault is it? Hello, I'm Dr. Palmay," Lance continued before I had time to react. "And these are my colleagues, Dr. Austin and Dr. Powers."

Denise laughed, and Eliot laughed with her, although I doubt he got the joke.

"He's so cute," Denise said. "What's his problem?"

"Obviously, he's wet his pants," Lance answered. "What kind of doctor are you anyway?"

"Oh, gross," Denise said.

"You have to leave now," I said when I could find my voice. My mouth was dry. Thoughts swirled helplessly around my brain, as if trapped in an unexpected eddy. I steadied myself against Eliot Winchell's bed.

"Yes, we do," Alison agreed from the doorway. "Come on, Doctors. We have to go now and let Terry do her job."

"Looks like Terry could use a bit of help," K.C. said. "She's looking a little green around the gills."

"I'm sorry, Terry," Alison said. "I didn't know they were going to do this."

"What are you talking about?" Lance shot back angrily. "This whole thing was your idea."

And then they were gone. In the merciful silence that followed, I changed Eliot into another pair of pajamas and settled him back in his bed. I did all this by rote, my head spinning, my vision impaired by a cluster of bright neon bubbles exploding before my eyes. Had my glass contained something more potent than champagne?

I clung to the walls as I navigated the moving hallway back to the nurses' station, my concerns swept away in an unexpected fit of adolescent giggles that burst from my throat like kernels of corn from a popper. Seconds later, I collapsed into my chair, wondering at what precise moment I'd lost control of my life, knowing it was exactly the moment Alison had shown up at my door.

# 20

They were waiting for me in the parking lot at the end of my shift.

I saw Denise first. She was sitting on the trunk of a car, drinking wine directly from a bottle and kicking her feet into the air, as if she were lounging at the end of a dock on the Intracoastal. A small gold loop flashed at me from the side of her right nostril. I didn't remember seeing it earlier.

K.C. was standing beside her, his hands crammed into the pockets of his tight jeans, his eyes on the ground. He looked as if he'd just been sick or was about to be, although when he raised his head in my direction, I saw he was smiling. Surprisingly, I smiled back, as if I were no longer in charge of my own reflexes, as if I'd been reduced to a puppetlike state, and I went wherever my strings pulled me. I'd expected the champagne to have worn off by now, but if anything, I was feeling even more discombobulated than before. Strange images were dancing around my head, refusing to settle long enough for me to identify them. Bright colors continued to float, like loose balloons, across my line of vision. It required all my concentration just to put one foot in front of the other.

Alison and Lance were sitting, half-in, half-out of the white Lincoln that was parked several empty spaces away, its doors open to the early-morning air. Lance was in the front seat, Alison the back, and when she leaned forward, balancing her elbows on her knees, I saw that her eyes were puffy and wet, as if she'd been crying. Or maybe she was just stoned, I realized, as the unmistakable odor of marijuana wafted toward my nose, and I saw the rich orange glow of a hand-rolled cigarette dangling casually from Lance's fingers.

"Well, look who's here," Denise said.

"About time." K.C. straightened up, lifted his arms above his head in a prolonged, catlike stretch, as if he were getting ready to pounce.

"What are you still doing here?" I looked around, the scenery blurring as I strained to see whether anyone else was in the parking lot, but there was no one. Great security, I thought, wondering who would hear me if I screamed.

Alison climbed out of the rented Lincoln, swiped at

her eyes with the back of her hand. "I didn't want you driving home alone on New Year's Eve."

Lance took a long drag of his cigarette. "Party's just beginning."

"Party's over," I told them, trying to remember where I'd parked my car. "I'm exhausted. I just want to go home and crawl into bed."

"Now that's a plan," Lance said, as he had said earlier. He extended the marijuana cigarette in my direction. Smoke filled my nostrils, like a too sweet perfume.

I shook my head no, although I had to admit the sensation was not altogether unpleasant.

"For strictly medicinal purposes, of course." Denise slid off the trunk of the car and inhaled deeply from the smoldering joint in Lance's fingers.

"K.C., you and Denise take my car," Lance instructed. "Alison and I'll go with Terry." Without asking, he lifted my purse from my hands and extricated the keys to my car. "I'll drive," he said, the words crawling around the joint now pressed between his lips.

"I'm not sure this is such a good idea."

"You shouldn't be driving in your condition." Lance laughed, as if he knew something I didn't, and I felt my legs buckle beneath me. They **had** put something in my champagne. Probably a hallucinogen, I decided, trying to hang on to reality, like a child clinging to the handlebars of a runaway bicycle. **Let go,** a little voice urged inside my head. Give in and let go.

I felt a wave of euphoria wash over me as I released

my grip on the here and now. I pictured myself flying backward through the air without a helmet, the wind whipping at my hair. Instead I found myself squashed beside Alison in the passenger seat of my car, her arm around me in a protective, almost smothering embrace. The oppressive smell of marijuana circled my head like an errant halo, forcing its way up my sinuses, like wads of cotton batten. "What exactly did you put in my drink?" I heard someone ask, understanding it was me only by the echo bouncing between my ears.

"You mean aside from the rufies and the LSD?" Lance laughed as we sped out of the parking lot and turned onto Jog Road, the white Lincoln following close behind.

"Shut up, Lance," Alison said. "She'll think you're serious."

"I **am** serious. I'm a very serious fellow. Come on, Terry." He waved what was left of the marijauna ciga-rette in front of my face. "In for a penny, in for a pound. Isn't that what they say?"

"She said she doesn't want any," Alison said.

"No, that's all right," I surprised us all by saying. What the hell, I remember thinking. My life was no longer my own. Whatever was going to happen was no longer up to me. I'd been excluded from the decision-making process, and instead of feeling threatened and afraid, I felt relieved, even excited. I was walking a tightrope without a safety net. I was free.

So I laughed as I accepted the joint from Lance's waiting fingers, then raised it to my lips and inhaled deeply, holding it in my lungs the way I'd seen Denise do in the parking lot, until my throat burned and my chest threatened to explode.

"Look at that." Lance laughed. "She's an old pro."

I took another drag, this one longer than the first, watching dispassionately as the thin paper burned its way down to the tips of my fingers. Unfamiliar stirrings of well-being whooshed through my body, like a fresh transfusion of blood. I'd never smoked marijuana before, although I'd been tempted as a teenager. This had less to do with any great moral integrity on my part than it did with my greater fear of my mother finding out.

I drew another long drag into my lungs, then sank into a deep well of complete and utter calm, realizing I never wanted to resurface. I clung to the sensation, as a drowning woman clings to a life buoy, pressing the smoke against my lungs like a branding iron, exhaling only the faintest puff, and only when I could no longer hold my breath.

"Easy does it," Lance warned as I inhaled again, a small tower of ash replacing the paper in my hand.

I gasped as the cigarette burned into my fingers.

"Are you all right?" Alison asked. "Did you burn yourself?"

"Let me see that." Lance grabbed my right hand, forced my index and middle fingers into his mouth, sucked greedily on their tips.

"Oh, for God's sake." Alison slapped her brother's

hand with such force, his teeth scraped my knuckles. "Terry, are you okay?"

I stared at my tingling fingers.

"That's first-rate weed, isn't it?" Lance asked proudly.

"Where'd you get it?" I asked in return.

"Trust me. The drug trade still thrives in Delray Beach."

I looked around, trying to make sense of what was once familiar territory. "Where are we?" I asked as we turned onto Linton Boulevard.

"Lakeview Golf Course," Lance announced, reading the large sign on our left. "You ever play golf, Terry?"

I shook my head, not sure whether I'd answered him out loud.

"I tried it once," Lance said, "but it was a disaster. Balls splaying all over the damn place. It's not as easy as it looks on TV, I'll tell you that."

"I think it's the sort of thing you need lessons for," I heard myself say, remarkably self-assured for someone who had no idea what she was talking about.

"I have no patience for lessons."

"Lance has no patience for anything." Alison turned toward the window. Were there tears in her eyes?

"Are you okay?" I wondered if Lance had another of his magic cigarettes to give to his sister, get her to relax. Why was she so uptight?

Alison nodded without looking back. "You?"

"Fine." I lay my head against her shoulder, snuggled into the crook of her arm, closed my eyes.

"Terry?" Lance said. "Terry, are you asleep? Is she asleep?" he asked Alison before I could formulate a response.

I felt Alison swivel toward me, her breath warm on my face as she spoke. "I hope you're proud of yourself," she said in my mother's voice, and I jumped up, startled, sure she was speaking to me.

"So, you're not asleep," Lance said. "Trying to trick us, were you?"

"Where are we?" I asked again. How many times had I asked that already? "Where are we going?"

"Thought we'd go for a little New Year's dip in the ocean," Lance answered.

"Are you crazy?" Alison asked. "It's the middle of the night. It's pitch-black out there."

A sudden disquiet gnawed at my newfound serenity, like a mouse on a piece of rope. I pushed myself up in my seat and rubbed my forehead, as if trying to clear it. Maybe a dip in the ocean was exactly what I needed. Just what the doctor ordered, I thought, then laughed.

"What's so funny?" Lance asked, laughing with me.

Alison was the only one who didn't laugh. Worry clung to her eyes like wraparound shades. What's **her** problem? I thought with growing irritation.

I looked out the car window at the largely deserted thoroughfare. Where was everybody? It was New Year's Eve, for God's sake. Where were all the drunken revelers, not to mention all the extra police cars supposedly trolling the streets? Here we were, three plastered partiers crowded into the front seat of a car heading for the Atlantic Ocean. Surely we deserved a citation for that, I thought, giggling at the convoluted absurdity of my reasoning.

"Maybe we should just go home," Alison said. "I think Terry's had enough excitement for one night."

"Every party needs a pooper," Lance began singing. "That's why we invited you."

"Party pooper," I joined in, laughing so hard now I could barely catch my breath. Whatever twinge of trepidation I might have felt earlier had vanished as quickly as it had appeared, carried away by wave after wave of intense euphoria. I would ride those waves right into the middle of the sea, I thought as the ocean miraculously appeared before us, and Lance pulled to a stop at the side of the road, the white Lincoln stopping right behind.

In the next instant, four doors opened as one and both cars emptied. We raced each other toward the deserted beach, so dark it was almost impossible to see where the sand ended and the water began. In the distance, several lonely firecrackers exploded, and I looked up to see a spray of brilliant pink and green burst briefly across the sky. Aside from that, and the low growl of a passing motorcycle, it was quiet. I suppressed a shudder as the cool night air blew through my hair, then wrapped itself tightly around my neck, like a tourniquet.

"This is so great," Denise exclaimed, throwing her arm over my shoulder and dragging me across the sand. "Isn't this so great, Terry?"

"Let's get naked." Lance was already kicking off his shoes and pulling his shirt over his head.

"Let's not," Alison quickly countered. "What are you trying to do, Lance?" she asked above the roar of the ocean. "Draw as much attention to us as possible?"

"Not a good idea," Lance agreed quickly. "Okay, everybody. Clothes back on." He tried dragging his shirt back over his head, but his head got caught in one of the sleeves, and he gave up, throwing the shirt to the ground in frustration, then laughing as he stomped it into the sand with his bare feet. "Never did like that stupid shirt," he said, and we all laughed, as if he'd just told the funniest joke in the world.

Except Alison. She wasn't laughing.

I pulled off my clumsy nurse's shoes and surveyed the ocean stretched out before me—cold, dark, hypnotic. It beckoned me forward, pulling me like a giant magnet, and I rushed toward its angry waves as if possessed, the sand cold against my stockinged feet, the icy water rushing over my toes.

"Way to go, Terry!" Lance yelled from the darkness.

"Wait for us," Denise called out as a wave, like an oversize boxer's glove, pummeled my back.

I looked toward the shore, saw several vague shapes lumbering toward me, hands waving in the air, like delicate tree branches swaying in the wind. I waved back, lost my balance, and stumbled over a rock. Struggling to maintain my footing, I saw the darkness swirling around me and wondered briefly what in God's name I was doing. Hadn't I pulled this stunt once before? Hadn't I almost drowned?

"Terry, be careful," Alison cried out, fighting her way through the surf. "You're out too deep. Come back."

"Happy New Year," I shouted, splashing at the water with my hands.

"Somebody's stoned," Lance said, drawing closer, his voice a singsong.

I pushed myself to my feet, only to be slapped down on all fours by another wave. The taste of salt filled my mouth and I laughed, remembering the time I'd mistakenly sprinkled salt, instead of sugar, on my breakfast cereal, and my mother had insisted I eat it anyway. A lesson, she'd said, so I wouldn't make the same mistake again. But I was always making the same mistakes again, I realized, laughing even louder.

Once again, I tried to stand up, but my feet could no longer find the ocean floor, and I was drifting farther and farther away from the others. "Help!" I cried as the water crept above my head, and unseen hands reached for me in the dark.

Strong hands pulled at my clothing. "Stop struggling," Lance ordered, his voice as cold as the ocean. "You only make things worse by struggling."

I lunged into Lance's arms, the wet hairs of his bare chest rough against my cheek, his heartbeat resonating against my ears. I gasped for breath, my hands flailing wildly in the air as another wave tore us apart, then crashed over my head like a collapsing tent. I screamed, my mouth filling with water, as my fingers reached across the darkness for something solid to grab on to. I felt a large fish slap against my calves and I kicked it away.

"What are you doing?" Lance yelled above the sound of the angry surf. "Stay still."

"Help me!" The cold water swirled around my legs, tugging at my feet like heavy weights, pulling me under. I felt Lance close beside me and struggled through the darkness toward him.

It was then that I felt a weight on the top of my head, pushing me back under, holding me down. "No," I cried, although no sound emerged. I opened my eyes underwater, saw Lance beside me, his hands somewhere above my head.

Was he trying to save me or kill me?

"Stop fighting me," Lance ordered gruffly.

I reached frantically for the water's surface, but my body was growing weak, and my legs were constrained by the tightness of my uniform. My lungs felt as if they were about to burst, the sensation eerily similar to the one I'd enjoyed earlier with my first marijuana cigarette. So this is what it feels like to drown, I thought, remembering the fate of those unfortunate kittens at my mother's cruel hands. Had they been scared? I wondered. Had they fought back, clawed at her murderous fingers? Or had they quietly accepted their fate, as Lance was urging me to do now. "Damn it! Stop struggling," he bellowed as my head finally shattered the surface of the water, like a fist through glass.

And suddenly a bright light was shining toward me, and for one insane second, I wondered if I was already dead, if this was the white light patients who'd suffered near-death experiences sometimes talked about. And then I heard the distant voice—"Police," the voice announced. "What's going on out there?"

"Goddamn it," Lance said, pulling me up and securing me underneath his arm, pushing me roughly toward the shore.

"What's going on here?" the police officer asked again as I collapsed on the sand by his feet, gulping wildly at the air, unable to speak. Alison was immediately on her hands and knees, hugging me to her side. K.C. and Denise hovered silently nearby.

"Sorry, Officer," Lance said, shaking the water from his hair, like a dog. "Our friend forgot she doesn't know how to swim."

"You all right?" the officer asked me. I could tell by the timbre of his voice that he was young and more amused than concerned.

"She's fine," Lance said with another shake of his head. "I'm the one you should be worrying about. She almost killed me out there. Last time I play hero, I'll tell you that."

"Pretty stupid stunt, lady," a second officer admonished, looking directly at me, and I understood by his tone that it was the end of a long shift, and the last thing he wanted was unnecessary overtime. I noted that he was about the same height and weight as his partner, with the same thick neck and square chest. "You better get this lady home," he advised. "I think she's done enough celebrating for one night."

I opened my mouth and tried to speak, but no sound emerged. What could I tell them after all? That I was drunk on champagne and high on marijuana? That I suspected I'd been slipped some LSD? Did I really think that? Truthfully, at that moment, I didn't know what to think. I wasn't certain of anything, not what had happened earlier, not what was happening now.

"Thank you, Officers," Lance was calling after the already retreating policemen. "Happy New Year." When they were out of sight, he turned back to me as Alison's arm tightened around my waist. "You heard what the man said. Time to get you home."

# 21

The rest of the night is a blur.

I remember images—Lance's knuckles, white against the black of the steering wheel; Alison's wet hair clinging to the gaunt crevices of her face as tears continued spilling from her eyes; my uniform, wet and cold, riding high on my thighs, my sheer stockings ripped and speckled with sand.

I remember sounds—the wetness of our clothes against the leather of the seats; a horn blasting as a car sped past us on the inside lane; the nervous tapping of Lance's foot on the brake as we waited for a light to change from red to green.

I remember the silence.

And then we were home, and everyone was talking at once.

"What a night!"

"How is she?"

"What happens now?"

I remember being half-carried, half-dragged toward my front door.

"What are you going to do to me?" I recall whispering.

"What did she say?"

"What do you think we're going to do to you?"

"What's she babbling about?"

Alison's voice, as clear as the proverbial bell: "You guys should go now. We can handle it from here."

I remember stumbling up the steps, Alison's hand loosely on my elbow, Lance's arm tight now around my waist. My bedroom swirled around me, as if I were on an ocean liner during stormy seas. I fought to stay upright as Alison slipped from my side, ended up on her knees beside my bed.

"What the hell are you doing?" Lance demanded, gripping me tighter, as if afraid I might bolt, his fingernails carving small niches into my flesh.

"You know what I'm doing," Alison answered defensively, pushing herself back to her feet.

Checking for bogeymen, I told him silently, then laughed out loud.

"Jeez, two lunatics," Lance said, his fingers at the front of my uniform, struggling with the top button, as Alison left the room.

"Don't," I protested weakly.

"You want to go to bed soaking wet?"

"I can get undressed by myself."

Lance took a step back. "Suit yourself. I'm happy to watch."

"I think you should leave."

"Now, that's not very hospitable," Lance said, managing to sound hurt. "Especially after I saved your life."

Had he? I wondered again. Or had he tried to end it?

Alison reentered the room, several large white towels in her hands. She threw one at Lance. Were they going to tie me up, gag me, then smother me with my own pillow?

I felt the towels in my hair, at my breasts, between my legs. My wet uniform was scraped from my body, a dry nightgown lowered over my head, like a shroud.

"Hold still," Lance said.

"I'll do it," Alison instructed.

Strong hands guided me toward the bed, pushed me down on top of it, covered me with a blanket.

"Think she has any clue what's going on?" Lance asked as I buried my head in the pillow and curled into a fetal ball.

"No. She's really out of it," Alison said.

"So, what do we do now?"

I felt them watching me from the foot of the bed, as if considering my fate, weighing the alternatives. I feigned sleep, hinted at a snore.

"I should probably stay with her overnight," Alison said.

"What for? She's not going anywhere."

"I know. But I'd still like to keep an eye on her."

"Fine. I'll keep you company."

"No. You go. Get some sleep."

"You know I don't sleep well when you're not beside me."

I felt him move to her side.

"Lance, don't."

"Come on, Sis. Don't be like that."

I tilted my chin, opened my eyes just enough to peek through the layers of lashes, see two forms merging at the foot of my bed.

"Don't," Alison said again, this time with less conviction, as Lance, standing behind her, reached around to caress her breasts.

I felt a gasp building in my throat, held my breath to keep it from escaping my lips.

"I saw you, you know," Alison continued as Lance began nuzzling her neck. "Flirting with Denise. Don't think I didn't see you."

"What's the matter, Sis? You jealous?"

"This isn't right," Alison said as he twisted her around, kissed her right on the lips.

"We're gonna burn in hell," he agreed, kissing her again.

I buried my face in the pillow, smothered the fresh scream building in the pit of my stomach.

"Not here," Alison said huskily, taking her brother's hand, leading him from the room.

I waited until I knew they were gone before opening my eyes. Were they still in the house, making love on the downstairs sofa? In the next room? I listened for sounds of their voices, fearful of what other noises I might hear. I lay there in the semidarkness for what felt like an eternity, afraid to move, the first moon of the new year filtering through the ivory curtains. I was trapped inside my own house, tied to my bed by invisible wires. There was no escape.

I closed my eyes, opened them again, found myself staring into the blank eyes of the ladies' head vase that sat on my night table, the vase Alison had bought me for Christmas. Keeping an eye on me, I thought, and might have laughed had I not been so sickened by everything I'd seen. I pushed myself into a sitting position, determined to make a run for it.

But even as I watched myself in my mind's eye, climbing out of bed and getting dressed, phoning for a taxi, getting the hell out of my own house, I knew I didn't have the strength to go anywhere. My arms and legs were useless. They hung from my sides like anchors. My head felt as if some insane dentist had pumped it full of Novocain. Already I was losing consciousness, drifting in and out of reality. I knew I had only seconds left before I fell into whatever void was waiting.

I threw myself off the bed, my arms flailing about madly, as if I were still in the ocean and unseen hands were pressing into the top of my head, holding me down. My hand smacked against the lamp on the night table, and I heard something shatter. The sound bounced off the walls, whizzed by my ear like a bullet. I looked toward the door, expecting Alison and her brother to come bursting through, restrain me. But no one came, and I collapsed back into bed, my strength gone. I closed my eyes, abandoned myself to whatever fate had in store.

I AWOKE TO BRIGHT SUNSHINE and the sound of Alison's voice. "Good morning, sleepyhead. Happy New Year!"

She advanced toward me, wearing a pink sweater over matching pink jeans, looking like a long stick of cotton candy. I pushed myself up in bed, trying to clear my head, the events of the night before coming to me in fits and starts, like a videotape skipping in midreel.

What had happened last night?

"What time is it?"

"It's after twelve. I guess I should have said, 'Good afternoon.'" Alison deposited a tray of freshly squeezed orange juice, hot coffee, and croissants across my lap. "Breakfast in bed," she said, then laughed. "Or lunch. Whatever. The croissants are nice and fresh. Lance went to Publix."

Lance poked his head around Alison's shoulder. "How you feeling?"

I stared at him, unable to speak. Had he tried to drown me in the ocean last night or had he saved my life? Had I really seen him and Alison embracing at the foot of my bed? Had I dreamed the whole damn thing? Was that possible?

"Oh, no!" Alison cried suddenly. "What happened here?" Alison knelt beside the bed and began picking up the broken pieces of the china head vase she'd bought me for Christmas. "What happened?" she repeated, trying to fit the pieces back together.

I fought to remember, the back of my hand tingling with the memory of having smacked against something the previous night.

"Maybe we can fix it."

"Don't bother," Lance said, removing the shards from Alison's hands. "Couldn't have happened to a nicer girl, if you ask me." He shuddered visibly. "These ladies give me the creeps." Then he carried the pieces out of the room.

"Terry, are you all right?" Alison asked. "Terry? Is something wrong?"

"I know," I said to her under my breath.

"Know what?"

"I saw you," I continued boldly. "Last night. With your brother."

"Oh, God," Alison said as Lance returned to the room, smiling broadly, one broken lady easily disposed of.

Was I next?

"So, has Terry recovered from her excellent adventure?"

"She saw us," Alison said, her voice a monotone.

"Saw us?" The smile slowly faded from his face as his eyes moved rapidly between us.

"I saw you kissing," I said flatly.

"You saw us kissing?" The smile returned to Lance's eyes, played with the corners of his lips. "What else did you see?"

"Enough." I pushed the breakfast tray aside, climbed out of bed, not sure whether my legs would hold me. Immediately, something stabbed at the bottom of my foot. I cried out, fell back against the bed, hugged my knee to my chest, saw a small sliver of china sticking out from between my toes.

"Looks like the lady bites," Lance said, taking my injured foot in his hands.

"Don't," I said, as Alison had said last night, weakly, without much conviction. Alison ran from the room, returned seconds later with a wet towel.

"Be still," Lance said. "Relax."

I watched as he gently plucked the piece of china from my foot, drawing only a drop of blood, then patting it away with the towel.

"Seems like I'm always coming to your rescue," he said without a trace of irony.

I tried to remove my foot from his grasp, but he held on tight. "I'd like you to leave."

"Please, Terry," Alison said from somewhere beside me. "I can explain."

"I don't need any explanations."

"Please. It's not what you think."

"And what do I think?" Again I tried to remove my leg from Lance's sturdy hands, but his fingers had begun expertly massaging the sole of my foot, and I realized with no small degree of shock that I didn't want him to stop.

"You think he's my brother," Alison said.

Lance's knuckles moved to the base of my toes, kneeding my calloused flesh, manipulating my muscles as easily as Alison manipulated my emotions.

"He's not my brother."

**My husband used to give the best foot massages. It's probably why I married him. Certainly it would explain why I kept going back to him. He had the best hands. Once he started massaging my feet, I was a goner.**

"He's your husband," I said, my voice free of inflection. Why hadn't I realized it earlier? Why had it taken me so long to figure out what should have been obvious all along?

"Ex-husband," Alison qualified.

"Lance Palmay," he said, extending his right hand. "Pleasure to meet you."

I ignored him, concentrated on Alison. "You lied to me," I said, stating the obvious. "Why?"

"I'm so sorry. I didn't know what else to do."

"Have you ever heard of the truth?" I reclaimed my foot from Lance's grasp, pushed past him toward my closet, where I threw a robe over my nightgown, drew it tight around me. Never had I felt more vulnerable, more exposed.

"I wanted to tell you the truth," Alison protested, "but I was afraid."

"Afraid of what exactly?"

"Afraid you'd think I was some stupid, weak-willed bimbo who falls to pieces every time her no-good ex-husband shows up."

"Hey——" Lance interrupted.

"I wanted you to think well of me. I wanted you to like me."

"By lying to me?"

"It was stupid. I can see that now. But——"

"It seemed like a good idea at the time?" Lance interjected.

"Shut up, Lance."

"You're sure that's his real name?" I said.

Alison looked stricken, as if I'd slapped her across the face. "I phoned him after Thanksgiving. You were after me to call my family. . . ."

"You're saying this is my fault?"

"No, of course not. I'm just saying that in a moment of weakness, I called Lance and told him where I was. I didn't know he'd come to Florida. Or maybe I did. I don't know. I only know that when he showed up at my door, I couldn't help myself. He promised he'd only stay a few days. And I didn't want to upset you. I knew your rules about no roommates. I knew how skittish you were. Skittish," she repeated softly, smiling hopefully at me. "Good word."

I felt a familiar tug, the unwanted urge to take her in my arms and reassure her everything was going to be all right. God, I was as bad where she was concerned as she was with regard to her former husband. If he **was** her former husband, I thought, wondering why I should believe anything she said. Alison changed stories as easily as she changed clothes. What made me think she wasn't lying to me now?

"So I lied to you," Alison continued, as if reading my thoughts, "told you Lance was my brother. It just seemed easier that way."

"You don't have a brother," I stated more than asked.

"No, I do," Alison said quickly. "I do," she repeated unnecessarily, looking toward the floor, as if afraid to let me see her face.

"There's something you're not telling me."

"No. Nothing. I've told you everything."

She was lying. I knew it, and she knew I did. It was the reason she couldn't look me in the eye.

"I thought we were friends," I said weakly, not sure what else to say.

"We **are** friends," she pleaded.

"Friends don't lie to each other. They don't keep secrets. They don't have hidden agendas."

Alison's eyes shot to mine. For a second it looked as if she were about to break down and tell me everything, reveal the whole ugly truth of what she was really up to, confess her part in last night's mayhem, unravel the entire charade. But she said nothing, and the moment passed.

"I think you should leave now," I told her.

She nodded, turned to go. "I'll call you later."

"No, you don't understand. I want you to leave—for good."

"What?"

"I want you out of here."

"You can't mean that."

"Hey, Terry," Lance interjected. "Don't you think you're overreacting?"

"Was I overreacting last night when you tried to kill me?" I shot back.

"What!" Lance said.

"What!" Alison echoed.

"What the hell are you talking about?" The look Lance gave me was equal parts amusement and fury. "You're out of your fucking mind. You know that, lady?"

"I want you out of my cottage," I insisted. "Out of my life."

"No, please," Alison cried.

"I'll give you till the end of the day," I said.

"But that's so unfair."

"I think the law says you've got to give us at least a month's notice," Lance said lazily. "And I don't know about you, Terry, but I don't react too well to ultimatums."

"If you don't leave, I'll call the police. How's that for an ultimatum?"

"Pretty lame," Lance said. "Think you better call your lawyer too."

"Lance will be gone within the hour," Alison said forcefully.

"What!" Lance exclaimed. "You can't be serious."

"Just go," Alison told him, her eyes never leaving mine. "Now."

Lance shifted uneasily from one foot to the other, his hands slapping his sides in frustration. Then he stormed from the room,

"If you could just give me a few days to find another place," Alison said softly, "I promise I'll be out of your hair, if that's what you still want."

In truth, I didn't know what I wanted. Part of me wanted Alison gone immediately; part of me wanted her to stay. I said nothing for several seconds, waiting for her to fill in the empty spaces, the way she usually did, to offer even a semiplausible explanation I could latch onto. Even after everything that had happened, I was still looking for a reason to believe her.

"Fine." I spit out the word as if it were a piece of rotten meat. "You have till the weekend. If you're not gone by then, I'll call the authorities."

"Thank you." Alison breathed a deep sigh of relief. Then she spun around, her face disappearing inside a blur of strawberry curls. I heard her footsteps retreating down the stairs, the kitchen door opening and slamming shut. I watched her from the bedroom window as she ran toward the cottage, then stopped, turned back toward the house. I thought I saw her smile.

# 22

I didn't see Alison at all during the next several days. Nor did I see Lance, although I doubted he was really gone. I knew the matter was far from resolved, that they weren't likely to leave empty-handed, not with all the time and effort invested in me so far. I lay in bed that first night trying to figure out how much of what Alison had told me was true, wondering where the lies ended and the truth began, if indeed there'd been any truth to anything she'd said. Ever.

What difference did the truth make anyway?

Looking back, I see that Alison's great gift was her uncanny ability to make me doubt myself, to make me question what was beyond question, to make me see things that weren't really there.

To not see things that were.

In spite of everything, I had to keep reminding myself that Alison was not the sweet young woman I'd welcomed into my life, but a liar, a con artist, and quite possibly, a cold-blooded killer. I wasn't her friend—I was her target, a carefully selected one at that. And judging by what I'd read in her journal, I wasn't the first unsuspecting woman she'd duped. What had happened to the others?

And why?

That was the part I couldn't get past, the part that kept me awake at night, tossing restlessly back and forth in my bed. Not **when** Alison and her cohorts might strike again, but why?

**Why?**

What was she after?

**What do you want from me?** I should have demanded of her. **Why did you seek me out, work so hard to make me your friend? What is it you think I have that's of any value?**

What was the point?

**What do you mean?** would have come her inevitable response, green eyes wide with confusion, expressive hands aflutter. **I don't know what you're talking about.**

In my lighter moments, I told myself I was out of danger, that by confronting Alison and ordering her to vacate the premises, by threatening to call the police if she wasn't gone by the end of the week, I'd effectively put the kibosh to her little scheme. But in my darker moments, I recognized that the only thing I'd accomplished was a slight delay, a modest retooling of her plans, that Alison was simply biding her time, waiting for just the right moment to come at me again.

At any rate, several days passed without further incident. Alison made no further attempts to talk to me; the white Lincoln disappeared from my street. I went to work, tended to my patients, and almost managed to convince myself that the worst was over.

On the morning of January 4, I was getting ready for work when the phone rang. I knew that Josh had returned from California the night before, and I'd been eagerly anticipating his call all morning. I glanced in the mirror over my dresser, trying to see myself through Josh's eyes, noting the cut Alison had given me was growing out and I was in need of a trim. Impatiently pushing my hair behind my ears, I pinched my cheeks to give them needed color, then walked to the phone and, not wanting to appear too anxious, waited one more ring before answering it. "Hello," I said huskily, as if freshly roused from sleep, although I'd been up for hours.

"Erica says to wish you a happy New Year," the voice announced.

"Go to hell!" I shot back, about to hang up the phone.

"I believe you have something that belongs to her," the voice continued, undeterred.

"I don't know what you're talking about."

"I think you do."

"You're wrong. I have no idea what you want."

"She'd like it back."

"Like what back?" I felt the line go dead in my hands. "Wait! What do you mean, I have something of Erica's? Wait!" I continued shouting long after I knew the caller had hung up.

What could I possibly have of Erica's?

The necklace, I realized with a start. The heart-shaped pendant Alison had found beneath her bed and worn proudly around her neck, until I'd bought her one all her own. But it couldn't be worth more than a few hundred dollars, and Erica owed me far more than that in back rent. Erica had never struck me as the sentimental type. But then I was a lousy judge of character, I reminded myself. Look how easily I'd allowed myself to be duped by Alison.

My mind was racing, thoughts crashing into one another, like ocean waves. What was Erica's connection to Alison? Had Erica left behind more than the necklace, something valuable she'd hidden inside the cottage? And was that something the reason Alison had shown up on my doorstep, gone out of her way to befriend me? What did she think I had?

"Good God," I said, my head swimming as I grabbed my purse and ran down the stairs and out the front door. Did I really think Alison had any intention of vacating my cottage by the end of the week? That she and Lance would depart empty-handed?

I stood paralyzed by the side of my car, not knowing what to do, knowing only that time was running out, that I couldn't continue to stay in my house, that I had to talk to someone.

I had to talk to Josh.

I returned to the house, full of fresh resolve, locking the door behind me and marching purposefully to the phone in the kitchen. I punched in the familiar numbers, then waited while the phone rang once, twice, three times, before someone picked it up.

"Fourth-floor nurses' station. Margot speaking."

"Margot, it's Terry." There was desperation in my voice, as if someone had pushed it from a high ledge.

"What's the matter? You sound awful."

"I don't think I can come in today."

"Don't tell me you've got that horrible flu bug that's making the rounds."

"I don't know. Maybe. Can you manage without me?"

"Guess we'll have to. Don't want you coming in sick."

"I'm so sorry. It just hit all of a sudden."

"That's how these things work."

"I felt fine last night," I embellished, knowing I should stop while I was ahead, that the more lies I told, the more likely I was to trip myself up. Wasn't that what had happened to Alison?

"Well, get back into bed, take two Tylenol, and drink plenty of fluids. You know the routine."

"I feel really bad about this."

"Just feel better," Margot instructed.

I raced up the stairs to my bedroom, where I swapped my nurse's uniform for a pair of navy pants and matching jersey. I packed the uniform, along with another change of clothes and some underwear, into the large overnight bag I kept at the back of my closet. I wasn't sure how long I'd be gone, or where I'd be staying, but one thing was now crystal clear—I couldn't stay here.

Would Josh insist I stay at his place? I wondered, throwing in my yellow dress with the plunging neckline, in case he suggested somewhere nice for dinner. Or maybe I'd stay in one of those funky little art deco hotels in South Beach. Maybe Josh would stay with me, I projected giddily, opening the bottom drawer of my dresser and removing the slinky, lavender nightgown Lance had given me for Christmas. I tossed it into the bag, thinking how ironic it would be to wear a gift from my would-be killer to a tryst with my would-be lover, recognizing I was beyond giddy and was now verging on outright hysteria.

I took a series of long, deep breaths, trying to calm myself down. I knew I was behaving foolishly, even irrationally. But it was as if, in finally deciding to take action, I'd unleashed a part of me I'd repressed for far too long—the part that was determined to enjoy life, take risks, have fun. The part that was tired of being surrounded by death. The part that wanted to live.

I finished packing, debated whether to call Josh, tell

him I was coming, then decided to surprise him instead. I told myself I didn't have time for unnecessary phone calls, but maybe I was just afraid he'd tell me not to come, that he was too busy to see me. And I couldn't risk that. I needed Josh to be there for me.

I was at the car when I realized I'd left my nurse's shoes on the floor by the bed. I knew I'd need them if I chose to return to work the next day. So I tossed my overnight bag into the backseat and reluctantly returned to the house, taking the stairs two at a time. I was doubled over and gasping for air when I reached my bedroom and saw my shoes standing by the foot of the bed, as if waiting for me. I was leaving the room when a cursory glance out the bedroom window revealed Alison emerging from the cottage.

I raced downstairs, coming to an abrupt halt at my front door, fighting to catch my breath. I couldn't appear panicky. It was imperative everything appear normal. Alison couldn't suspect I was poised to take flight.

"Going somewhere?" she asked, waiting by the side of my car, her head tilting toward the overnight bag on the backseat.

"I joined a gym. Thought I'd work out before going to the hospital." I held up my nurse's shoes for added credibility.

She seemed to accept my explanation. "Terry—"

"I'm going to be late." I opened the car door, threw my shoes inside, walked around to the driver's side of the car.

"Please, I need to talk to you."

"Really, Alison, I don't see the point."

"Just hear me out. Then, if you still want me to leave, I will. I promise."

"I've already rented out the cottage," I told her, watching her eyes widen in alarm. "A nurse at the hospital. She's moving in on Saturday."

Alison's head snapped toward the cottage. A gasp caught in her throat.

"Look," I backtracked, suddenly afraid she might try to restrain me if she thought she'd run out of time. "If you really want to talk, we'll do it when I get home from work."

Relief flooded Alison's face. "That'd be great."

"It might be quite late."

"That's fine. I'll wait up."

"Okay." I climbed into the car and started the engine. "I'll see you later."

"Later," she agreed, tapping on the hood of the car as I backed out of the driveway.

Later, I thought.


I'M NOT SURE WHY I CHOSE I-95 over the turnpike. **Always take the turnpike,** I recalled Myra Wylie's advice to her son. **You get in an accident on 95 and you can be stuck all day.**

Which was exactly what was happening, I realized, opening my window and craning my neck to see what was causing the prolonged delay. But all I saw were long lines of cars, like brightly colored snakes, stalled and going nowhere. "God, get me out of here," I whispered, flicking the dials of the car radio, trying to find a traffic report. "I don't have time for this."

I heard Alan Jackson singing about lost love on one station, and Janet Jackson singing about finding it on another. Maybe it was the same love, I thought, a laugh catching in my throat. Maybe Alan and Janet Jackson were brother and sister. Or husband and wife. Just like Alison and Lance. I laughed out loud, catching the worried glance of the driver in the car beside me.

"I am not going to think about Alison," I whispered through barely parted lips, then flipped to another station, listening as a male announcer swapped inane banter with his female counterpart.

"So, Cathy, how many New Year's resolutions have you broken so far?"

"I never make New Year's resolutions, Dave."

"Why, Cathy?"

"Because I always break them."

I flipped to another station. "A four-car collision just south of the exit to Broward Boulevard is holding up traffic on I-95," the newscaster announced with the practiced calm of someone used to detailing disasters. "Ambulances are on the scene—"

"Great." I turned off the radio, not wanting to hear more. A four-car collision, complete with ambulances and police cars, meant I wasn't going anywhere for some time. There was nothing I could do about it, so there was no point in getting upset about it. Too bad I hadn't packed a book, I thought, swiveling around to check the backseat. Maybe there was a magazine on the floor. . . .

That's when I saw him.

"Oh, God."

He was several cars behind me, in the row to my right, and after the initial shock, I told myself I must be mistaken, that my eyes were playing tricks on me again, that the sunlight and my overactive imagination had combined to produce an image that couldn't possibly be real, that when I looked again, the image would be gone.

Except that when I looked again, he was still there.

Tall, even sitting down, his skinny frame was hunched over the wheel of his car, small brown eyes peering over the top of his strong, hawklike nose. He was staring straight ahead, as if unaware of my existence. Was it possible he didn't know I was there? That our being on the same stretch of highway at the same time was nothing but a strange coincidence?

And then he leaned forward, rested his chin on the top of his steering wheel, and turned his gaze purposefully to mine, his narrow lips creasing into a slow smile. **Why, Terry Painter,** I could almost hear him say. **As I live and breathe.**

"Shit!" I cursed out loud, watching as K.C. emerged from his car and sauntered lazily between the intervening cars toward me, his fingers hooked into the pockets of his tight jeans. What was I going to do? What **could** I do? Make a run for it? Where would I go? Damn it! Why didn't I have a cell phone? I was probably the only person left on the planet who didn't own one, who hated their mounting proliferation, their intrusion into every facet of our lives. Was I the only person who bristled at the sight of teenagers walking down the street, phones dangling from their ears like earrings, the person on the other end of the line more important than the person right beside them? I loathed the selfishness, the weird antisocialness of it all. Besides, it wasn't as if I got that many calls, I thought, as a shadow fell across the side window of my car.

I heard a tapping at my head and turned to see K.C. staring at me through the tinted glass. He signaled for me to roll down my window, and I complied. It was unlikely he'd try to harm me here, I reasoned, in the middle of a traffic jam, with so many witnesses.

"Well, well, well," he said. That was all. **Well, well, well.**

"Do you think it's a good idea to get out of your car?"

He shrugged. "Doesn't look like we're going any-where."

I nodded, turned away. "Where are you headed?" I asked, not looking at him, pretending to be concentrating on the traffic ahead.

"Nowhere in particular. You?"

"Nowhere in particular," I repeated.

"Thought you might be going to see Josh," he said, catching me by surprise. I'd forgotten they'd met at my house over Thanksgiving.

I noticed him looking at my overnight bag on the backseat, ignored the snide grin that crept into his eyes, as if he could see the silk lavender nightgown inside.

"So, I take it you're all recovered from your little New Year's Eve swim?"

A shiver traveled the length of my spine. What exactly was K.C.'s role in all this? "Yes, I'm fine now. Thank you."

"You had us pretty worried."

"I'm fine."

"Yeah, well, you should be more careful. Wouldn't want anything to happen to you, would we?"

"I don't know. Would you?"

His grin spread from his eyes to his lips. He said nothing.

"Are you following me?" I demanded suddenly.

The grin overtook his entire face. "Why would I be following you?"

"You tell me."

He shook his head. "You're imagining things, Terry." Then he straightened up, slapped his open palm on the side of my car and took a step back, as all around me, cars began inching forward.

I heard the approaching roar of a motorcycle, held my breath as first one, then two more motorbikes whizzed by. My eyes followed them as they weaved in and out of the stalled traffic, shiny black helmets hiding their riders' faces. Was the man in the red bandanna among them?

"Be sure to give Josh my regards," K.C. called as he returned to his car. Minutes later, when I finally worked up the nerve to check in my rearview mirror, I could still see him, sitting behind the wheel of his car, watching me.

# 23

We crawled along I-95 for the better part of an hour. By the time we reached Broward Boulevard, the four cars involved in the accident had been moved to the side of the road and the ambulances had already gone. Judging by the mangled remains of two of the automobiles, one a bright red Porsche that now resembled nothing so much as a squashed tomato, and a puddle of what appeared to be blood beside one of the tires, I suspected serious injuries, possibly even fatalities. I wondered briefly whether any of the victims would eventually find their way to my ward at Mission Care, prayed we'd all be spared. Several police cars remained on the scene, their officers trying to persuade motorists not to waste time gawking, but, of course, everyone did. We couldn't help ourselves.

"Keep moving," one of the officers directed as I again checked my rearview mirror. Immediately, K.C. waved his fingers at me in greeting, as if he knew I was looking at him, as if he'd been watching all along, waiting for our eyes to meet.

On impulse, I lowered my window, beckoned the policeman forward.

"Keep moving," he repeated, louder this time, his large hands waving the traffic forward.

"Please, can you help me? I'm being followed," I ventured timidly, trying to make out the features beneath the officer's protective helmet, seeing only his dark glasses and the impatient set of his jaw.

"Sorry, ma'am," the policeman said, his eyes darting back and forth among the cars, clearly oblivious to what I'd said. "I'm afraid I have to ask you to move along."

I nodded, raised the window, glanced into the rearview mirror in time to see K.C. shaking his head and laughing, as if he understood what I'd tried to do and was amused by my audacity. Or my stupidity.

What had I hoped to accomplish? Under the circumstances, had I really expected the officer to listen to me, let alone take my concerns seriously? And even if he had, what could he have done? Questioned K.C. on the spot, thereby causing further traffic jams and longer delays? Then what? Would he have arrested him? Highly doubtful. At best, he would have hauled both of us off to the station. A lot of good that would have done me.

Excuse me, sir, but this woman claims you were following her.

Following her? Terry, did you tell the officer I was following you?

Do you two know each other?

We're friends, Officer. She had me over to her house for Thanksgiving dinner.

Is this true, ma'am?

Yes, but . . .

To tell you the truth, Officer, she's been acting very strangely lately. All her friends are worried about her.

I felt the officer's judgmental nod. Still, I reminded myself, no matter how strong K.C.'s denials, my complaint would be a matter of record. At the very least, it might buy me some time. Again I lowered my window, waved the officer over. "Please, Officer, can you help me?"

"Is there a problem, ma'am?" He leaned in toward me, removing his dark glasses with an impatient hand.

I saw that he was young, younger than I, maybe even younger than K.C. I also heard by his tone, by the way he said "ma'am," that he would have a hard time believing a young man like K.C. would waste his time following a middle-aged woman like me. The thought now occurred to me that I would be dismissed as a troublemaker, that by mouthing off prematurely, I would effectively destroy any credibility I might need in the future. No, I decided, I would accomplish nothing by crying wolf. And I would miss seeing Josh, who was my only real hope. "Was anybody hurt?" I asked.

" 'Fraid so," the officer said, pushing his sunglasses back across the bridge of his nose, backing away.

"I'm a nurse. If there's anything I can do . . ."

But the policeman wasn't interested in my offer of help. "It's been taken care of" came his curt reply. "Keep moving, please."

The traffic thinned out after that, and by the time we reached Hollywood Boulevard, it was back to its normal pace. I picked up my speed, zigzagging between lanes whenever possible, trying to escape K.C., but he remained stubbornly on my tail. In an effort to shake him, I almost took the exit at Miami Shores, then decided against it. I didn't know the area, and if I was going to try to lose K.C., it was probably better to do it somewhere I wouldn't get lost myself.

He was still behind me when I transferred onto U.S. 1, heading south. Somewhere between Coconut Grove and Coral Gables, where Josh lived, K.C. vanished. This wasn't due to any clever maneuvering on my part. On the contrary—one minute he was behind me; the next minute he was gone.

I checked my rearview mirror at each stoplight. I saw a woman in a black Accord talking animatedly on her cell phone, a woman in a cream-colored minivan trying to subdue a backseat of unruly children, and a man picking his nose in a green BMW.

K.C. and his maroon-colored Impala were nowhere to be seen. Which didn't mean he wasn't lurking about, I realized, repeatedly swiveling around in my seat, scanning my surroundings for anyone remotely suspicious. Both the make and color of K.C.'s car told me it was likely a rental. Again, I wondered how he fit into Alison's plan.

The sound of a car horn brought me back to the here and now. The light had turned green and I was being urged forward. I continued driving north along U.S. 1, repeatedly checking my rearview mirror, twisting around in my seat at each subsequent red light, but it appeared my efforts had been successful. "I lost him," I announced triumphantly, turning to the car next to me in time to see a well-dressed, middle-aged man jam his index finger high inside his left nostril. "Wonderful," I said, entering the town of Coral Gables and continuing past the grand, geometrically designed entertainment and shopping complex known as Paseos, in the heart of the tidy Miami suburb. I deliberately avoided the famous Miracle Mile District, turning left, then right, then right again, looking for Sunset Place. I took several wrong turns, found myself back where I started, and almost had a heart attack when I saw a maroon-colored Impala pull up behind me. But one peek at the wizened, gray-haired man stooped over the steering wheel quickly brought my heart rate back to normal. I laughed at my paranoia and shook my head, continuing on.

Eventually I found myself on the right street, albeit at the wrong end. Sunset Place was typical of many streets in the area, a palm-lined avenue full of small Spanish-style bungalows in all the colors of the rainbow. Josh lived with his children at number 1044, a neat, white house with a sloping brown-tile roof, and a beautiful front garden filled with coral and white impatiens, as well as a variety of other flowers whose blooms I recognized, but whose names always eluded me.

I parked on the street directly across from Josh's house, then sat for several minutes trying to decide my next move. How had I come this far without a plan? What was I doing, showing up at his door, uninvited and unannounced, at just after one o'clock on a Friday afternoon?

My stomach was rumbling as I opened the car door and climbed out. Black rain clouds hovered ominously overhead, like bruises on an otherwise blue sky, and I debated whether I should go somewhere for lunch before seeing Josh, then decided to wait. Maybe Josh would suggest lunch at his favorite neighborhood café.

Unless he wasn't alone, I thought, stopping in the middle of the road. School didn't start till Monday. It was entirely possible his children would be at home. What was I going to say to them? **Hi, it's your aunt Terry, come for an extended stay?**

And what if Josh wasn't there? I asked myself, returning to the sidewalk. His car wasn't in the driveway, so it was entirely possible that, despite his having just returned from his vacation, he was already off visiting clients. Or maybe he was in Delray seeing his mother, I realized with a start. It was Friday, after all. Didn't he always visit his mother on Fridays? Of course he was in Delray! What a fool I was, coming all this way when all I'd had to do was go to work as usual. What was the matter with me? What in the world had I been thinking?

And then the wood-paneled front door to Josh's house opened, and suddenly Josh was standing in the doorway, looking tanned and unbearably handsome in a dark, short-sleeved shirt and faded denim jeans. He looked up and down the street, glanced at the increasingly menacing clouds, and was about to go back inside when his gaze drifted across the street toward me. "Terry?" he mouthed in obvious surprise, crossing the street in several long, quick strides. "It **is** you!"

"Josh, hello."

"Has something happened to my mother? Is she all right? What is it?" The questions toppled from his mouth like a line of dominoes.

"Nothing's happened to your mother. She's fine."

"I talked to her less than an hour ago," he said as if I hadn't spoken.

"Josh, your mother's fine."

His shoulders relaxed, although tension still narrowed his eyes. "Then I don't understand. What are you doing here?"

"I need to talk to you."

"About my mother?"

What was the matter with him? Hadn't I already explained my visit had nothing to do with his mother? "No, Josh. Your mother is doing remarkably well for a woman with both cancer and heart disease. She's been a little depressed lately, yes, but that's pretty normal during the holiday season. She'll bounce back. In fact, I'm beginning to think she'll outlive us all."

He smiled, the lines on his forehead releasing slowly, like an elastic band. "Well, that's a relief anyway. I've been feeling so guilty these last weeks."

"Nonsense," I said in my mother's voice, before biting down on my tongue, allowing a softer voice to emerge. "You weren't gone long enough to feel guilty." I lay my hand on his arm, trying to reassure him.

He flinched, as if I'd burned him with a match, and pulled away, coughing into his hand. He stared in the direction of his open front door. Was he thinking of inviting me inside or making a run for the house? "Feel like a cup of coffee?" he asked, surprising me with the sudden warmth of his smile.

"Coffee sounds good."

Actually lunch sounded even better, but he didn't suggest it, and since he already seemed spooked by my showing up on his doorstep without prior notice, I didn't want to appear too presumptuous. Maybe we'd go for an early dinner, I thought hopefully, as he led me into the rose marble foyer.

The interior of the house was surprisingly spacious, consisting of one large common area that encompassed living, dining, and family rooms. The kitchen was at the back, as were two small bedrooms. I caught only a brief glimpse of the master bedroom suite at the front, noticed the bed was unmade, and felt a slight weakening of my knees. "Your home is lovely," I remarked, leaning against the tan ultrasuede of the living room sofa for support, eyeing the clean lines of the modern, minimalist furniture throughout the house.

"How do you take your coffee?"

"Black," I reminded him, a smile masking my disappointment that he hadn't remembered.

"Be right back. Make yourself at home." He disappeared into the kitchen.

I crossed the white-tiled floor, punctuated at irregular intervals by a series of muted needlepoint rugs. The room surprised me. It didn't seem to reflect the Josh Wylie I knew at all. Not that I knew him that well, but I'd always assumed that Josh's tastes would be closer my own, that they leaned more toward comfort than style, more toward tradition than trends. I reminded myself that this was the house Josh had shared with his former wife, decided that the decor was probably more to her taste than his. He just hadn't gotten around to changing it, I concluded. Perhaps out of respect for his children's feelings.

The walls were white and largely bare. A few unimpressive lithographs hung at either side of the dining room table, and a large abstract painting of what looked to be a bowl of fruit occupied the far wall of the family room. I thought how nicely my own paintings would go in these rooms, the lush flowers replacing the anemic bowl of fruit, the unimaginative mirror by the front door usurped by the girl with the large hat on the beach.

Why had Alison given me such an expensive gift? I wondered suddenly, feeling my stomach cramp, as if I'd been sucker punched. I'd let my guard down for only a fraction of a second, and Alison had used it to sneak inside my head. Go away, I warned her. You're not welcome in this house. I'm safe here.

Still, experience had shown me that once Alison had her foot in the door, she was remarkably difficult to dislodge. Thoughts of her now swirled about my head: the first image of her in my doorway; the magic way she'd twirled about the cottage; her wondrous hair on my pillow as she slept; Erica's necklace around her neck; the necklace I'd given her at Christmas to replace it. And all the gifts she'd given me—the earrings, the head vase, the painting. So extravagant! Had she paid for it at all, or had Denise simply removed it from her aunt's inventory? And what exactly was Denise's part in all this? Was it possible the women had known each other all along, that Denise Nickson and Erica Hollander were two pieces of the puzzle that was Alison Simms?

**You're a stupid, stupid girl,** I heard my mother say.

"I hope the coffee's still good. It's been brewing all morning," Josh announced, returning to the room with two steaming mugs, coming to an abrupt stop when he saw me. "Terry, what's wrong? You look like you've just seen a ghost."

I raised my hands in the air, felt them shake. I opened my mouth, but no words came. Tears filled my eyes. Until this moment, I hadn't realized how scared I really was, how long I'd been denying my anxieties, suppressing my fears, and how desperately lonely I'd been and for how long. I was tired of being brave, rational, and independent. I was none of those things, and I couldn't survive this on my own. I needed someone to stand beside me, someone to protect me from harm. I needed Josh.

It took all my resolve to keep from throwing myself into his arms, to refrain from telling him what was in my heart—how much I needed him, wanted him, loved him. Yes, loved him, I realized, catching my breath in my lungs, holding the words tight against my chest, like smoke from a marijuana cigarette. "Hold me," I whispered, my voice a plea.

Immediately, I felt Josh's arms around me, his lips in my hair. "I'm sorry I haven't called you," he was saying.

"You've been away." I wiped the tears from my eyes, raised my lips to his. "You're here now."

"I'm here now," he repeated, pressing his lips to mine, lifting me into his arms and into the air, carrying me toward the master bedroom, like Clark Gable carrying Vivien Leigh, grappling with my clothes as he fell on top of me across the unmade bed.

Except he did none of those things, said nothing of the sort.

While my imagination was busy sweeping me into his arms and into his bed, he was already pulling out of my arms and out of my reach.

"Please," I heard myself say in a desperate bid to hold on to him.

"Terry, listen . . ."

"I'm so glad you're back. I've missed you so much."

"Oh, God. Terry, I owe you an apology."

"An apology? No. There's nothing to apologize for." Please tell me there's nothing to apologize for.

"So much has happened," Josh said, retreating to the other side of the glass table that held our coffee. The steam from the mugs wafted into the still air, like delicate streamers, creating a scrim between us.

"What do you mean? What's happened?"

"I'm so sorry if I've misled you in any way."

"I don't understand. How have you misled me?"

"I should have told you earlier. Actually, I assumed my mother already had."

"Told me what?"

He lowered his head as if he were ashamed. "Jan and I are back together."

His words slammed against my ears. "What?"

"Jan and I," he began, as if he actually thought I hadn't heard him the first time.

"When?" I interrupted, feeling sick to my stomach.

"Just before Christmas."

"Before Christmas?" I echoed, as if only the repetition of the words would make them sink in.

"I wanted to tell you."

"But you didn't."

"I'm a coward. It was easier to just keep canceling our dates. And, to be honest, I wasn't sure if things would work out with Jan."

"So, what are you saying? That you were using me as backup, in case your reconciliation didn't take?"

"I didn't mean it that way."

"How exactly did you mean it?"

"The kids are so happy," he said after a pause, as if this explained everything.

A numbness was creeping steadily into my arms and legs, buzzing about my head, like a pesky mosquito. "So, Thanksgiving meant nothing to you."

"That's not true. Thanksgiving was wonderful."

"The kiss . . . kisses . . . they were meaningless."

"They were beautiful."

"But meaningless."

Another pause, longer than the first. "Terry, let's not do this."

"Let's not do what?"

"I'd like us to stay friends."

"Friends don't lie to each other." Hadn't I just said the same thing to Alison?

"It was never my intention to lie." Then: "Listen, I have a little something for you." He walked quickly to the bedroom at the front of the house, returned seconds later with a package wrapped in bright blue foil. "I meant to give it to you earlier." He dropped the package into my hands.

"What's this?"

"I wanted to thank you again for taking such good care of my mother."

"Your mother." I felt a stab of humiliation so deep I almost doubled over. "I take it she knew you and Jan were back together?"

"Why do you think she's been so depressed?"

"She didn't tell me."

"She's not too happy about it."

"She's your mother. She'll come around."

"Aren't you going to open your present?"

I tore at the paper without enthusiasm. "A journal," I said, turning it over in my hands, thinking of Alison.

"I wasn't sure if you kept one or not."

"Guess I'll have to start."

"I'm really sorry, Terry. I never meant to hurt you." He broke off, looked toward the front door.

"Expecting company?" I asked coldly.

"Jan and the kids are at the mall. They should be home pretty soon." He looked anxiously at his watch.

"I guess your wife wouldn't be too happy to find me here."

"It would probably just confuse things."

"Well, we certainly wouldn't want anyone to be confused," I said, walking to the door. Had I really expected him to protect me from anyone?

"Terry," he called after me.

I stopped, turned around.

**Don't go. I need you. I'll find a way out of this mess. I love you.**

"Do you think you might talk to my mother, try to get her to understand? She loves you like a daughter. I know she'd listen to you."

Again I nodded, thinking this whole scene might be funny if it weren't so mind-numbingly awful. "I'll see what I can do."

"Thank you."

"Good-bye, Josh."

"Take care of yourself."

"I'll try," I said, closing the door behind me.

# 24

Goddamn you, you stupid, stupid girl!" I railed at myself in my mother's voice. "How could you be so dumb? Have you no pride? No self-respect? You're forty years old, for God's sake. Have you learned nothing in all that time? Do you know so little about men? Ha!" I laughed, ignoring the not-so-furtive glances of other drivers as I banged down on the steering wheel, inadvertently blasting the horn. "Why stop with men? You know nothing about anyone. There isn't a worse judge of character in the entire world. All someone has to do is show you a little kindness, the tiniest bit of interest, and you can't do enough for them. You open your house, you open your heart." You open your legs, I continued silently, too ashamed to say the words out loud, even in the closed confines of my car. "A man takes you out for one measly little lunch and already you have him marching down the aisle. You're a stupid, stupid girl! You deserve to be taken advantage of. You deserve to lose everything. You're too damn stupid to live!"

**You're a stupid, stupid girl,** I heard my mother say.

I thought of the unmade bed in Josh's bedroom. Had he and Jan had sex this morning before she'd left for the mall? Were the crumpled sheets still redolent with the scent of their lovemaking?

"You're an idiot!" I shouted, my words bouncing off the car windows to slap me in the face. "People as stupid as you are don't deserve to live."

I looked into the rearview mirror, saw my mother's eyes. I didn't need the sound of her voice to know what she was thinking: **How could you do this?** Her eyes burned into mine, until my own eyes clouded over with so many tears she was no longer visible. Who needed my mother's harsh pronouncements when I was doing such a good job on my own?

"You're a stupid, stupid girl," I was still repeating as I pulled into my driveway and fumbled in my purse for my house keys. "You deserve whatever happens to you." I checked the street for Lance's white Lincoln. "Come and get me," I cried at the quiet street, the threat of rain still hovering overhead. "Game over. I give up."

But a quick glance told me Lance's car was nowhere in sight. Probably had it parked somewhere around the block, I decided, pushing the tears away from my swollen eyes with the palms of my hands, and running toward my front door, repeatedly jabbing the key into the lock until I heard the familiar click. The door fell open.

I marched into the living room, roughly pushing the Christmas tree out of my way, then watched it teeter precariously on its stand before falling against the wall. Its ornaments dropped from its branches and burst into delicate slivers of silver and pink on the hard floor. "Should have taken this stupid thing down days ago." Should never have put it up in the first place. "Stupid, stupid, stupid!" I ripped a handful of festive bows from the tree's drying limbs, then stomped on them. To imagine that Alison had ever really liked me. To think Josh had ever really cared. "Why would anyone want you? Why would anyone want to be your friend, your lover?"

My mother was right. She was always right. I was nothing but a stupid, **stupid** girl. I deserved everything that happened to me.

**How could you do this?** my mother demanded, sneaking up behind me as I entered the kitchen.

"Go away," I cried. "Please, go away. Leave me alone. You did your job well. I don't need you anymore."

From their lofty position, my mother's collection of ladies' head vases sneered at my naïveté, my mother's words continuing to assault me through their empty eyes and forced smiles. I watched in horror as my arm suddenly shot out and swept across the bottom shelf. Instantly the line of china heads went flying in all directions, like a swarm of angry bees. And then the next row, and the next. I grabbed the head that Alison had admired her first time in this room, the one that resembled my mother, with her judgmental, imperious gaze, **like some snooty society matron, looking down her nose at the rest of us,** Alison had said. I held the china head high into the air, then flung it with all my might across the room.

It exploded upon contact with the wall, bursting into the air like a firecracker. I laughed as colorful shards of porcelain flew about the room, covering the floor like confetti.

"Terry!" a voice cried out from outside the kitchen door. "Terry, what's happening? Let me in. Please, let me in!"

The doorknob twisted frantically from side to side. I took a second to catch my breath, then pulled open the kitchen door.

"My God, Terry!" Alison exclaimed, a look of horror overwhelming her sweet face. "What's going on here? What are you doing? Look at you. You're bleeding."

I raised a hand to my forehead, felt blood on my fingers.

"Terry, what's wrong? Did something happen?"

A wail, like an ancient chant, began building in my gut, filling my mouth like water, until it poured from my lips, spilled onto the floor, and eventually flooded the room. I fell to my knees, the sound of bottomless grief bouncing off the walls, pieces of broken china piercing my clothing, attaching themselves to my skin like burrs.

Instantly Alison was at my side, rocking me in her arms, kissing my bloodied forehead, begging me to tell her what was wrong. Almost immediately, I felt myself being sucked back into her orbit, falling under her spell. Even now, after all the lies and deceit, after everything I knew to be true, and everything I knew to be false, I wanted nothing more than to believe she was truly concerned about me, that no matter what was about to happen, she wouldn't let any harm come my way.

"I'm such a fool," I whispered.

"No. No, you're not a fool."

"I am."

"Tell me what happened. Please, Terry. Tell me."

I looked into her eyes. Through the thick veil of my tears, I was almost able to convince myself of her sincerity. Might as well tell her what happened, I decided, wincing at the sight of my blood on her lips. She and her friends could have a good laugh about it later.

"Josh is back with his wife," I said simply, then almost laughed myself.

"Oh, Terry, I'm so sorry."

This time I actually did manage a strangulated chuckle. "That's what he said."

"You saw him?"

I told her the whole pathetic story of my visit with

Josh, knowing K.C. had probably already phoned her, informed her of my plans. Had she been sitting by the window, anxiously awaiting my return?

"Bastard," she uttered now, giving my shoulder a gentle squeeze.

"No. It's my fault."

"How is it your fault?"

Because it always is, I thought but didn't say. "Because I'm such a fool," I said instead.

"If you're a fool, that must make me a full-out moron."

I laughed, as I did so often when I was with her.

"I mean, look at me and Lance, for heaven's sake," Alison continued without prompting. "After everything I've been through with him, after all my resolutions about not letting him back into my life, what do I do the first time he shows up at my door? I invite him in. Hell, I practically drag him inside the house. It doesn't matter that I know he's no good for me, that I know, sooner or later, he's going to break my heart, screw things up, the way he always does."

"What things?" I interrupted.

She shrugged sadly. "Things. Like he did with you."

I waited, feeling the tension in her arms, wondering if she was about to open up, tell me everything. But she didn't, and the moment passed.

"Where **is** Lance?" I looked toward the back door, half-expecting him to be standing there.

"Gone."

"Gone where?"

Alison shook her head, her hair tickling the side of my face. "Don't know. Don't care."

"You mean he's gone back to Chicago?"

"Don't know," Alison said again. "I guess he'll go wherever Denise tells him to."

"He's with Denise?"

"Should have seen that one coming, I guess." She hit her forehead with her hand, as if trying to knock some sense into it. "What the hell—it was over anyway. Finally. About time," she added for emphasis.

I nodded, although I doubted Lance was really gone.

"Men," she said, as if the word were a curse. "Can't live with 'em—"

"Can't shoot 'em," I said, recalling the words to an old country song.

"I'm so sorry about everything. If I could just go back to the beginning, start over again . . ."

"What would you do?"

"I wouldn't give Lance the time of day, that's for sure. I'd run for the hills the minute I saw him. Before it was too late."

"It's never too late," I said, as if pleading my case.

"Do you really believe that?"

I shrugged. Who knew what I believed anymore? "I've been such a fool."

Alison's eyes probed mine, as if she were reaching into my soul. "He's the fool. How could anyone not want you?"

I studied her face for signs of ridicule, but all I saw were fresh tears welling up in those enormous green eyes. Her lips quivered as I rubbed her tears away, the blood from my finger staining her skin, like an errant brushstroke, as I took her cheeks in my hands and drew her face gently toward mine.

I don't know what it was—fear, disillusion, longing—maybe a combination of all those things—that brought my lips so close to hers. I wondered only briefly what I was doing, then closed my mind to further thought as I shut my eyes, grazed her lips with my own.

Instantly, Alison pulled back, as Josh had earlier. Out of my arms. Out of my reach. "No! That's not what I meant. You don't understand."

"My God," I said, scrambling to my feet, my hand covering my mouth. "My God, oh my God."

Alison was on her feet beside me. "It's all right, Terry. Please, it was a misunderstanding. It's all my fault."

"What have I done?" I stared down at all the shattered women at my feet, at their lost earrings and broken strands of pearls, pieces of their smiles mixed with stiff strands of their hair. All the king's horses, and all the king's men, I thought, seeing my reflection in Alison's horrified eyes, knowing we were all broken beyond repair, that nothing could be done to put any of us back together again. "I have to get out of here," I cried, fleeing the carnage, racing for the front door.

Alison was right behind me. "Terry, wait! Let me come with you."

"No, please. Just leave me alone. Leave me alone." I was in my car before she could stop me, the doors locked, the engine running, the car in reverse, my foot on the gas.

"Terry, please, come back."

I backed out of the driveway and onto the street, mowing over the grass of the corner lot and almost colliding with Bettye McCoy and her stupid dogs two blocks away. In response, she gave me the finger and called me a name, although it was my mother's voice I heard.

I drove through the streets of Delray for the better part of an hour, drawing comfort from the little seaside town that had somehow managed to retain its quaint, thriving downtown without falling prey to the towering office buildings and ugly strip malls of most of Florida's older cities. I drove past the small, old homes of the historic marina district, past the newer oceanfront condominiums and luxury estates along the coast, then doubled back, headed for the gated communities, retirement enclaves, and country clubs that existed west of the city limits. I drove until my legs were stiff and my hands felt welded to the steering wheel. I drove until the dark black clouds spreading above my head exploded in a thunderous rage, flooding the thoroughfares with sheets of angry rain. Then I pulled the car over to the side of the road and quietly watched the rain as it pounded against my windshield, an eerie calm settling over me, like a warm blanket. My tears stopped. My head cleared. And I was no longer afraid.

I knew exactly what I had to do.

*    *    *

TWENTY MINUTES LATER, I pulled my car into the parking lot of Mission Care and ran through the continuing downpour into the lobby, shaking the water from my hair as I headed for the stairwell. I kept my head down, not wanting anyone to see me. I was supposed to be in bed with the flu after all, not gallivanting around in the rain. Besides, my visit was personal, not professional. There was no reason for anyone to know I was there.

I climbed the steps to the fourth floor, stopping at the landing to catch my breath before cracking open the door and peeking my head around. No one was there, so I proceeded cautiously down the corridor. I was halfway down the hall when one of the staff doctors emerged from a patient's room, heading right for me. I thought of lowering my head, stooping to pick up an invisible penny from the floor, maybe even ducking into a nearby room, but I did none of those things. Instead I gave the young doctor a shy smile, preparing to tell him how much better I was feeling, thank him so much for asking. But the vacant smile he offered in return announced he had no idea who I was, that I was as faceless to him in my street clothes as I was in my nurse's uniform. I could have been anyone, I realized.

In fact, I was no one.

Myra Wylie was lying in bed staring at the ceiling when I pushed open the door to her room and stepped inside. "Please go away," she said without looking to see who it was.

"Myra, it's me, Terry."

"Terry?" She turned her cheek to me, smiled with her eyes.

"How are you today?" I walked to her side, grasped the bruised hand she extended toward me.

"They told me you were sick."

"I was. I'm feeling much better now."

"Me too. Now that you're here."

"Has the doctor been in to see you yet?"

"He was here a little while ago. He poked and prodded, lectured me about eating more if I want to keep up my strength."

"He's right."

"I know. I just don't seem to have much of an appetite these days."

"Not even for a piece of marzipan?" I produced a small candied apple from the pocket of my navy pants. "I stopped at the bakery on my way over."

"In this rain?"

"It's not so bad."

"You're a darling girl."

I opened the wrapping, broke the small piece of candy into two pieces, placed one on the tip of her tongue, enjoyed the pleasure that filled her eyes. "I saw Josh today," I said.

Immediately her eyes darkened, like the sky. "Josh was here?"

"No. I drove to Coral Gables."

"You went to Coral Gables?"

"To his house." I deposited the remaining piece of marzipan on her tongue.

"To his house? Why?"

"I wanted to see him."

"Is there something wrong? Something the doctors haven't told me?"

"No," I reassured her quickly, as I'd reassured her son only hours ago. "This wasn't about you. It was about me."

Concern swam through the milkiness of her eyes. "Are you all right?"

"I'm fine. I just needed to talk to Josh."

Myra looked puzzled. She waited for me to continue.

"He told me he's back with his wife."

"Yes."

"He says you're not very happy about it."

"I'm his mother. If that's what he wants, then I'm happy."

"It seems it is."

"I'm just an old worrywart, I guess. I don't want to see him get hurt again."

"He's a big boy."

"Do they ever really grow up?" she asked.

"How long have you known?"

"I think I've always known they'd get back together. He never stopped loving her, even after the divorce. The minute she started making reconciliation noises, I knew it was only a matter of time." Myra twisted her head from side to side, no longer able to find a comfortable position.

"Here, let me fluff that up for you."

"Thank you, darling." She smiled, lifted her head, allowed me to extricate one of the meager pillows from behind her head.

"I wish you'd told me," I said, kneading it with my fingers.

"I wanted to. But I felt a bit foolish after the things I'd said about her. I hope you understand."

"It would have saved me a lot of embarrassment."

"I'm sorry, dear. I didn't think it would be a big deal."

"I drove all the way down there, made a complete fool of myself." A sound, halfway between a laugh and a cry, escaped my lips. "How could you let me do that?"

"I'm so sorry, dear. I had no idea. Please forgive me."

I smiled, smoothed several fine strands of hair away from her forehead. "I forgive you."

Then I lowered the pillow I was holding to her face and held it over her nose and mouth until she stopped breathing.

# 25

It's such a strange sensation, killing another person.

Myra Wylie was surprisingly strong for someone so frail. She fought me with a determination that was stunning in its ferocity, her long, skeletal arms flailing blindly toward me, gnarled and brittle fingers clawing helplessly toward my throat, the muscles in her neck warring with the pillow in my hands as her desperate lungs screamed silently for air. Such stubborn tenacity, the instinct to survive in the face of certain, even longed-for, death, caught me temporarily off-guard, and I almost lost my grip. Myra seized that split second's hesitation with all the strength left in her, twisting her head wildly from side to side and kicking frantically at her sheets.

I quickly refocused, pressing down harder on the pillow, patiently watching as her feet twitched to an almost graceful stop beneath the tightly tucked hospital corners of her narrow bed. I listened to her last desperate intake of breath and smelled the pungent odor of urine as it leaked from her body. Then I counted slowly to one hundred and waited for the unmistakable stillness of death to overwhelm her. Only then did I remove the pillow from her face, fluffing it out before returning it to behind her head, careful to arrange her hair the way she liked it. It was damp with the sweat of her exertion, and I blew gently on the matted strands at her forehead in an effort to dry them, watching as Myra's thin eyelashes fluttered girlishly in my warm breath, as if she were flirting with me.

Watery blue eyes stared up at me in frozen disbelief, and I closed them with my lips, my hands trembling toward the exaggerated, open oval of her mouth, contorted in a way to suggest that, even now, she was still trying to suck air into her withered, broken frame. My fingers quickly molded her lips into a more pleasing shape, as if I were an artist working with fast-drying clay. Then I stood back and observed my handiwork. She reminded me of one of those floats people buy for their pool, stretched out and waiting to be inflated. Still, I was satisfied that Myra looked peaceful, even happy, as if she'd simply slipped away from life in the middle of a pleasant dream.

"Good-bye, Myra," I told her from the door. "Sleep well."

I proceeded briskly down the hall toward the exit, confident no one would notice me. I even smiled at a young man on his way to visit his father, the blank look I received in return reassuring me I was still invisible—a ghost haunting the hallowed hospital halls, as insubstantial and fleeting as a whisper in the wind.

How did I feel?

Energized, relieved, possibly a little sad. I'd always liked and admired Myra Wylie, considered her a friend. Until she'd betrayed me, abused the many kindnesses I'd shown her. Until I realized she was no better than any of the others who'd abused and betrayed me over the years, and that, like those others, she was the author of her own misfortune, responsible for, and deserving of, her fate.

Not that I enjoyed being the minister of that fate. The truth is that I've never liked watching people die, never really gotten used to it, no matter how many times I've borne witness. Maybe that's what makes me such a good nurse, the fact that I genuinely care about people, that I want nothing but the best for everyone. The idea of taking a life is genuinely abhorrent to me. As a nurse, I've been trained to do everything in my power to sustain life. Although, some might argue, why sustain a life void of purpose, a life that is increasingly more parasitic than human?

Besides, whom am I kidding? Nurses have no power. Even doctors, whose exalted egos we stroke daily and whose daily mistakes we're constantly covering up, have no real power when it comes to matters of life and death. We're not the caregivers we claim to be. We're care**takers**. Janitors, really—that's all we are—looking after the leftover detritus of all the people who've exceeded their "best before" dates.

Lance was right.

I pictured Alison's ex-husband, if that's who he truly was, tall, slim-hipped, irredeemably handsome, and wondered if he was really gone. Or was he still in Delray, squatting among the obscene appendages of an over-grown screw palm, biding his time, waiting for just the right moment to leap out at me from the darkness?

Time's up, I thought with a smile.

I walked calmly down the four flights of stairs to the exit, grateful to see the rain had stopped, and that the storm clouds that had carpeted the sky all day had given way to the cautiously optimistic sun of twilight. Happy hour, I thought, checking my watch as I climbed into my car, debating whether to stop on my way home for a celebratory drink, deciding that it was still too early to celebrate, that much still required my attention. It was important that I be fully alert for the night ahead, that I not let down my guard in any way.

A siren was wailing as I turned my car into the rush-hour traffic along Jog Road, and I watched an ambu-lance speed by on the outside shoulder, probably on its way to the Delray Medical Center. I wondered how long it would be before one of the nurses looked in on Myra, checked her vital signs, and realized she was dead. I wondered if anyone would call me to relay the sad news. She was my patient after all. **Where's my Terry?** she would say, the first words out of her mouth every morning, as if I weren't entitled to a few hours away from her side, as if I weren't entitled to a life of my own.

**Where's my Terry? Where's my Terry?**

Everyone always thought it was so cute.

"Here's your Terry," I said now, gripping the steering wheel as if it were a pillow, pushing on it with all my strength, hearing the loud blast of the horn as it spun out into the traffic, then crashed into the dying afternoon. Instantly, half a dozen other horns began polluting the air with their mindless bleating. Like lambs to the slaughter, I thought, smiling at the motorist in the car ahead of mine as he extended the middle finger of his right hand into the air without even bothering to turn around.

Why should he turn around? What was there to see? I was invisible.

There would be no autopsy. There was no need. Myra's death had been expected, even anticipated. It was long overdue. There was nothing remotely surprising or suspicious about it. An eighty-seven-year-old woman with both cancer and heart disease—her death would be considered a blessing. The nurses would acknowledge her passing with a collective nod of their heads and a brief notation in their charts. The doctors would record the time of death and move on to the next cadaver-in-waiting. Josh Wylie would quietly arrange for his mother's burial. A few weeks from now, he might even send the staff an arrangement of flowers in appreciation of the excellent care his mother had received during her stay at Mission Care. Soon a new patient would occupy Myra's bed. After eighty-seven years, it would be as if she'd never existed.

An old song by the Beatles—**She loves you, yeah, yeah, yeah!**—came on the radio, and I sang along loudly with it, surprised to discover I knew all the words. This made me feel strangely exhilarated, even elated. The Beatles were followed by Neil Diamond, then Elton John. "Sweet Caroline," "Goodbye Yellow Brick Road." Long a devotee of golden oldies, I knew every word, every beat, every pause. **"Soldier boy!"** I belted out along with the Shirelles. **"Oh, my little soldier boy! Bum bum bum bum bum. I'll—be—true—to—you."**

I'm not sure why I decided not to park in my driveway, why I chose to drive past my house, circle back around the block instead, and park around the corner. Was I looking for Lance's car? If so, I didn't see it. Was it possible he was really gone? That I was truly safe?

I scoffed at my own naïveté, rechecking the street before getting out of my car and continuing briskly on foot, careful to stay in the shadows of the growing darkness, the hovering palm fronds above my head shaking in the wind, like giant castanets.

When I reached Seventh Avenue, I slowed my pace, hunched my shoulders, lowered my gaze, approached my house as if I were about to pass it by, then turned with seeming nonchalance at the last possible second and hurried up the path to the front door, my key already secreted in my hand. I pushed open the door, locking it immediately behind me, then ran to the living room window, my heart thumping against my chest, perspiration from my forehead forming a small puddle on the glass as I pressed my flesh against it, my eyes racing up and down the quiet street. Was anyone watching?

"It's okay," I said out loud. "You're okay." I nodded, as if to reassure myself further, ignoring the toppled Christmas tree and shattered ornaments as I walked into the kitchen, listening to the crunch of broken china heads beneath my feet as I approached the back door, my total focus on the small cottage behind my house.

The lights in the cottage were on, which meant Alison was probably home. Undoubtedly waiting for my car to turn into the driveway, so that she could put the final phase of her plan into operation. "Listen to me," I said with a laugh. "Final phase of her plan," I repeated, this time out loud, and laughed again at the sound of it.

I sank into a kitchen chair and surveyed the mess of broken women's heads coating the floor. My mother's pride and joy. "What's the matter, girls? PMS got you down?" I kicked at the shards with my feet, watching the jagged pieces skate across the floor and collide with other fragments—an ear here, a bow there, an upturned collar, a wayward hand. "I don't know what you have to complain about, ladies. You already had big holes in your heads." I pushed myself off my chair and swept the mess into the center of the room, first with my hands, then with a broom.

It took the better part of half an hour to gather together and dispose of all the women—I was working in the dark, remember—but ultimately I threw the whole mess into the garbage bin under the sink, then went over the entire floor with a Dustbuster, and then again with a damp cloth. When I was finished, I was starving, so I made myself a sandwich of leftover roast beef, then washed it down with a tall glass of skim milk.

Women need their calcium, I remember thinking. Even invisible ones like me.

I returned to the window, stared through the deepening veil of night at the tiny cottage that had once been my home. A home for wayward girls, I thought, picturing first Erica and then Alison. What was the matter with me that I was drawn to such people? Where was my judgment, my common sense? Why was I constantly putting myself in such danger? Hadn't experience taught me anything at all?

My mother's silent scorn leaked through the ceiling from the upstairs bedroom, like battery acid from a car engine, and I felt it burning a hole in the top of my scalp.

Another stupid woman with a gaping hole in her head, I thought, pulling at my hair as my mother's voice whispered in my ear, **You never learn. You belong in the garbage with the others.**

A sudden movement caught my eye, and I flattened my back against the wall just as Alison pulled back her living room curtain to stare outside. She peered toward the driveway, her face full of worry. Wondering where I am, I realized. Wondering when I'm coming home.

She lingered at the window for several long seconds, then backed away, the curtains hiding her continuing vigil. I had to be careful, keep to the corners, not let her know I was home until I had everything in place. There was still so much to be done.

I pushed myself toward the kitchen counter, reached for the shelves, began gathering together the ingredients I would need: Duncan Hines yellow cake mix, a small box of instant chocolate pudding, a cup of Crisco oil, a package of chopped walnuts, a quarter cup of chocolate chippets, four eggs, and a cup of sour cream from the fridge. Terry's magic chocolate cake. My mother's favorite. I hadn't made it in years.

Not since the night she died.

**Terry!** I could still hear her yelling at me from upstairs, her voice strong despite the stroke that had rendered her body useless.

**I'll be up in a minute, Mother.**

**Now!**

**I'm coming.**

**What's taking you so long?**

**I'll be right up.**

I stirred the ingredients together in a large bowl, dropping the eggs onto the top of the cake mix, instant pudding, Crisco, and sour cream, then mixing them in by hand so that I wouldn't make any noise. There was always the chance that Alison might sneak out of the cottage without my noticing, hear the whir of an electric mixer, interrupt me before I was ready. I couldn't take that chance. I watched the yolks of the eggs separate from the whites and spill across the light brown of the pudding. Then I wove my spatula through the mix, producing vibrant yellow swirls, like paint on a canvas. Creating my own masterpiece.

Still life.

**Terry, for God's sake, what are you doing down there?**

**I'm almost done.**

**I need the bedpan. I can't hold it any longer.**

**I'll be right there.**

I folded the chopped nuts and the chocolate chippets into the rest of the mix, then ran my index finger along the top of the bowl, lifting a large gob of batter to my mouth and greedily sucking it from my fingertip. Then I did it again, this time using two fingers. A loud groan inadvertently escaped my throat as I slowly manipulated my fingers in and out of my mouth.

**What are you doing down there?** my mother cried.

When I was a little girl, I used to watch my mother in the kitchen. She was always baking something, and I often pleaded with her to let me help. Of course, she always refused, told me I'd only make a mess. But one afternoon when she was out, I decided to surprise her by making a cake of my own. I gathered up the necessary ingredients and mixed them together, careful to beat out all the lumps, just as I'd watched her do week after week. Then I baked the whole thing for an hour at 350 degrees.

When my mother came home, I presented her with my beautiful chocolate cake. She surveyed the neat countertop, checked the floor for spillage, then silently sat down at the table and waited to be served. With great pride, I cut into the cake and produced a perfect slice, then watched eagerly as my mother raised her fork to her lips. I waited for her words of praise, the tap on the top of my head that told me she was pleased. Instead, I recoiled in horror as her face began collapsing in on itself, her cheeks hollowing, disappearing into the sides of her mouth as she spit the cake into the air, shouting, **What have you done, you stupid girl? What have you done?**

What I'd done was use bitter chocolate instead of sweet. A careless mistake no doubt, but I was only nine or ten, and surely the look on my mother's face, the knowledge that she'd been right about me all along, was punishment enough.

Except that it wasn't. And I knew it. It was never enough.

Even now I can feel my body tense as I waited for the

blow to strike the side of my face, the blow that would send my head spinning and my ears ringing. But the blow never came. Instead came an eerie calm, a misplaced smile. My mother simply pointed to the chair beside her and instructed me to sit down. Then she took the knife and cut into my cake, producing a perfect piece similar to the one I'd cut for her, pushed it toward me, and waited for me to take a bite.

I can still feel my hands shaking as I pushed the cake into my mouth. Instantly, the bitter taste settled on my tongue, combining with the bitter salt of my tears as they fell down my cheeks and ran between my lips.

She made me eat the entire cake.

Only when I was sick and vomiting on the floor did she stop, and only then to make me clean it up.

**Terry, for God's sake, what are you doing down there?**

**Coming, Mother.**

I glanced back at the cottage, then preset the oven to 350 degrees and lightly greased a large Bundt pan. I poured the batter inside it, then added my secret ingredient.

**What on earth took you so long? I need the bedpan.**

**It's right beside you. No need to get so upset.**

**I've been calling you for forty-five minutes.**

**I'm sorry. I was baking you a cake.**

**What kind of cake?**

**It's chocolate. Your favorite.**

When the oven reached 350 degrees, I put the cake inside, then licked the bowl free of whatever batter remained. "You never let me lick the bowl, did you, Mother?" The best part, I've always thought. "I always missed out on the best part."

**I know you blame me.**

**I don't blame you.**

**Yes, you do. You blame me for the way your life has turned out, for the fact you never married or had children. That whole episode with Roger Stillman. . . .**

**That was a long time ago, Mother. I've let it go.**

**Have you? Have you really?**

I nodded, cut her a large slice of cake, pressed a forkful to her lips.

**You know that everything I did, I did for your benefit.**

**I know that. Of course I know that.**

**I didn't mean to be cruel.**

**I know.**

**It's the way I was raised. My mother was the same with me.**

**You were a good mother.**

**I made a lot of mistakes.**

**We all make mistakes.**

**Can you forgive me?**

**Of course I forgive you.** I kissed the flaky, dry skin of her forehead. **You're my mother. I love you.**

She whispered something unintelligible, maybe "I

love you," maybe not. Whatever it was, I knew it was a lie. Everything she said was a goddamn lie. She didn't love me. She wasn't sorry about anything except that she was the one in that bed, and not me. I pushed another forkful of cake into her stupid, eager mouth.

My reveries were interrupted by a loud knocking and I raced to the kitchen door. A man was standing outside the cottage, his back to me. Suddenly Alison opened her door, the light from inside the cottage throwing a spotlight on the now familiar figure.

"K.C.!" Alison exclaimed as his profile came clearly into view. "Come in." She cast a furtive glance around the cottage before ushering him inside and closing the door.

**Look at the lowlife you've allowed into my home,** I heard my mother hiss.

"**My** home," I corrected her now. "You died, remember?"

With the help of Terry's magic chocolate cake and a favorite pillow.

"Taste buds failed you that time, didn't they, Mother?" Whoever said that Percodan and chocolate pudding didn't mix?

I smelled the aroma of freshly baking cake, glanced at the oven, then back to the cottage in time to see the door reopen, and Alison step outside behind K.C. "Terry should be home soon," she was saying. "I can't be gone long."

I ran through the kitchen to the front of the house,

watched through the living room window as Alison and K.C. marched purposefully down the front path to the street, then turned the corner, their arms brushing up against one another as they walked. Were they going to meet Lance and Denise? How long before they'd be back? And would Erica's biker friend be with them?

I wasted no more time. Clutching the spare key to the cottage between my fingers, and carefully sliding the foot-long butcher knife with its tapered two-inch blade from its wooden slot, I opened the back door and stepped into a night redolent with whispers and lies.

# 26

I'm not sure what I was looking for, or what exactly I thought I'd find.

Maybe I was checking to make sure Lance was really gone. Or maybe I was looking for Alison's journal, something I could take to the police, point to as proof positive that my life was at risk. I don't know. As I stood in the middle of the brightly lit living room, my hands trembling, my knees all but knocking together, I had absolutely no thought in my head as to what to do next.

I had no idea how long Alison and K.C. would be gone. And how did I know Lance wasn't hiding in the bedroom, watching and waiting for my next stupid move? Hadn't I parked my car around the block to avoid discovery? Couldn't he have done exactly the same thing?

Except there was no sign of him anywhere: no rumpled clothing strewn carelessly on the floor; no wayward creases in the furniture where he might have sat; no stray masculine smells permeating the air, disturbing the scent of baby powder and strawberries. I tiptoed toward the bedroom, the handle of the large butcher knife clutched tightly in the palm of my hand, the blade protruding from my body like the thorn of a giant rose.

But nothing in the bedroom indicated Lance might still be in residence. No shirts in the drawers, no suitcase in the closet, no shaving kit in the medicine cabinet. I even checked under the bed. "Nothing," I said to the reflection that flickered at me from the long, sharp blade of the knife. Was it possible he was really gone, that he'd taken off with Denise, just as Alison had claimed?

If so, then why was K.C. still around? What was his connection to Alison?

I laid the knife across the top of the white wicker dresser, watched it wobble against the uneven surface as I rifled through each drawer. But the drawers were mostly empty—a few push-up bras from Victoria's Secret, half a dozen pairs of panties, several uncomfortable-looking thongs, and a pair of yellow cotton pajamas decorated with images from **I Love Lucy**.

Where was her journal? Surely that would tell me something.

Only after searching through every drawer several times did I spot the damn thing sitting on the night table beside the bed. "Stupid," I said in my mother's voice. "It was right there the whole time. Open your eyes." I marched to the nightstand, grabbed the journal, turned swiftly to its final entry.

**Everything's falling apart,** I read.

As if on cue, a series of loud bangs, like small explosions, erupted from the street, followed by an even louder voice, then more banging. "Terry!" the voice shouted. "Terry, I know you're in there. Terry, please! Open the door!"

I dropped the journal onto the bed, raced to the side window, watched as Alison came running around the side of my house from the front to the back door, K.C. at her heels.

"Terry!" she persisted, banging repeatedly on my back door with her open palm. "Terry, please. Open up. We have to talk."

"She's not there," K.C. said.

"She **is** there. Terry, please. Open the door."

Suddenly Alison was vaulting toward the cottage. Had she seen me watching from the window? I spun around in helpless circles, knowing there was nowhere for me to go.

I was trapped.

I ran toward the closet, noting only at the last second the journal I'd carelessly dropped on Alison's bed. I hurried back, scooped it up, and returned it to its rightful place on the nightstand, then scrambled across the bed toward the closet, bringing the door closed after me just as Alison's key turned in the front lock.

It was then, my fingers tightly curled around the doorknob, that I realized I'd left the knife—the foot-long behemoth with its tapered two-inch blade—lying on top of the dresser. **Stupid, stupid girl!** my mother whispered in my ear. **She's not likely to miss that, is she?**

"Maybe it wasn't her car," K.C. was saying from the next room. "There are lots of black Nissans."

"It **was** her car," Alison insisted, confusion bracketing her words. "Why would she park it around the block and not in the driveway?"

"Maybe she's visiting a friend."

"She doesn't have any friends. I'm the only friend she's got."

"Doesn't that strike you as strange?"

There followed a long pause in which we all seemed to be holding our breath.

"What are you talking about?" Alison asked.

I heard the shuffling sounds of two wary people walking around in circles. How long before one of them stepped into the bedroom, saw the knife? How long before Alison checked the closet for bogeymen?

"Look, Alison, there are some things I have to tell you."

"What kind of things?"

Another pause, this one even longer than the first. "I haven't been very honest with you."

"Welcome to the club," Alison muttered. "Listen, on second thought, I don't think I'm up for this discussion right now."

"No—you need to hear me out."

"I need to pee."

Dear God, I thought, as I shot from the closet like a yo-yo on a string. I grabbed the knife, the blade slicing across my palm as my fingers closed around it. Then I leaped back inside the closet, the door closing after me just as Alison entered the room.

I stuffed my wounded hand inside my mouth, sucked at the steady stream of blood issuing from my palm, and tried not to cry out. From the bathroom, I heard Alison grumbling as she relieved herself. "What in the world is going on here?" she kept repeating over and over. "What in the world is going on?"

Alison flushed the toilet, washed her hands, and reentered the bedroom, then stopped, as if not sure of her next move. Or had something suspicious caught her eye? A drop of blood on the dresser? A suspicious footprint in the carpet? Was her journal lying wrong-side up? I raised my knife, steeled my body for her approach.

"Alison?" K.C. called from the living room. "Are you all right?"

"That depends." A pronounced sigh of resignation. "What is it you want to tell me?"

K.C.'s voice drew closer. I felt him standing in the doorway. "Maybe you should sit down."

Alison obediently plopped down on her bed. "I'm liking this less and less."

"For starters, my name isn't K.C."

"It isn't," Alision said, more statement than question.

"It's Charlie. Charlie Kentish."

**Charlie Kentish?** Where had I heard that name before?

"Charlie Kentish," Alison repeated, as if thinking the same thing. "Not K.C., short for Kenneth Charles."

"No."

"No wonder nobody ever calls you that," she observed wryly, and I almost laughed. "I don't understand," she continued in almost the same breath. "Why would you lie about your name?"

"Because I didn't know if I could trust you."

"Why wouldn't you trust me?"

I felt him shrug. "I'm not sure where to start." Another shrug, perhaps a shake of his head.

"Then maybe you shouldn't bother." Alison jumped to her feet. I felt her moving around, pacing back and forth in front of the bed. "Maybe it's not important who you really are or what you have to tell me. Maybe you should just leave, so that you can get on with your life, whose ever it is, and I'll get on with mine, and we can all live happily ever after. Don't you think that's a good idea?"

"Only if you come with me."

"Come with you?"

"You're in danger if you stay here."

"I'm in danger?" Alison laughed. "Are you completely nuts?"

"Please listen to me——"

"No," Alison said resolutely. "You're starting to scare me, and I want you to leave."

"It's not me you have to worry about."

"Listen, K.C., or Charlie, or whoever the hell you really are—"

"I'm Charlie Kentish."

**Charlie Kentish,** I repeated. Why was that name so damn familiar?

"I don't want to have this conversation. If you don't leave, I'm going to call the police."

"Erica Hollander is my fiancée."

"What?"

"The woman who used to live here."

"I know who Erica Hollander is."

So that's where I knew the name. Of course. Charlie Kentish. Erica's fiancé, the one she was always going on about. **Charlie this. Charlie that. Charlie's so handsome. Charlie's so smart. Charlie's got this great job in Japan for a year. Charlie and I are getting married as soon as he comes home.**

"Your precious fiancée ran out on Terry in the middle of the night, owing several months' rent," Alison said.

"She didn't go anywhere."

"What do you mean?"

"I mean, she didn't go anywhere," he repeated, as if that explained everything.

"I don't understand. What are you saying?"

"I was hoping you could tell me."

"Tell you what? I don't have a clue what you're talking about."

"Maybe if you'd stop pacing for two minutes and sit down . . ."

"I don't want to sit down."

"Please. Just hear me out."

"And then you'll leave?"

"If that's what you want."

I heard the bed squeak as Alison resumed her former position. "I'm listening," she said in a tone that indicated she'd rather not be.

"Erica and I had been living together for about six months when I got this great job offer to work in Japan for a year. We decided I should go, and she'd stay here, move into a cheaper apartment, and we'd save our money so we could get married as soon as I got home."

"I thought you were from Texas."

"Originally, yes. I moved here after college."

"Okay, so off you went to Japan," Alison said, getting back on track.

"And Erica e-mailed me about finding this great little place, a small cottage behind a house belonging to a nurse. She was thrilled."

"I'm sure she was."

"Everything seemed perfect. I'd get these glowing E-mails telling me how wonderful Terry was, how she was always inviting Erica over for dinner, doing little things for her. Erica's mother died a couple of years ago, and her father had remarried and moved to Arizona, so I guess she was just really grateful to have someone like Terry in her life."

"So she could take advantage of her."

"Erica wasn't like that. She was the sweetest—" His voice cracked, threatened to break. "Then things started to change."

"What do you mean? What things?"

"The letters stopped being so positive. Erica wrote that Terry was starting to behave strangely, that she seemed fixated on some biker Erica once said hello to in a restaurant, that she was getting paranoid."

"Paranoid? In what way?"

"She never went into detail. She just said that Terry was starting to make her feel uncomfortable, that she was afraid she might have to start looking for another place."

"So she skipped out in the middle of the night."

"No. I was due back in a few months. We decided she might as well stay put until I got back to Delray and we could look for a place together. But then, the E-mails suddenly stopped. I tried calling her cell phone, but no one ever answered. That's when I started calling Terry. She told me Erica had moved out."

"You didn't believe her?"

"It seemed odd that Erica would move out without telling me, let alone go anywhere without leaving a for-warding address."

"Terry told me she was hanging out with a bad crowd."

"No."

"That she met someone else."

"I don't believe it."

"Things like that happen every day."

"I'm sure they do. But that's not what happened here."

"Did you check with her employer?"

"Erica didn't have a regular employer. She worked for Kelly Services. They hadn't heard from her in weeks."

"Did you go to the police?"

"I called them from Japan. There wasn't much they could do long-distance. They contacted Terry. She gave them the same story she gave me."

"Which you can't accept."

"Because it isn't true."

"Did you go to the police when you got back home?"

"As soon as I got off the plane. They reacted pretty much the same way you are now. 'She found somebody else, buddy. Move on.'"

"But you can't."

"Not till I find out what happened to her."

"And you think Terry is somehow involved? That **I'm** involved?"

"I thought that in the beginning."

"The beginning?"

"When you first moved in."

I could almost feel the quizzical look on Alison's face.

"I'd been watching the house for about a month at that point," K.C. explained. "After you moved in, I started following you. You got a job at that gallery, and I started hanging around. I almost had a heart attack when I saw you wearing Erica's necklace. I gave her that necklace."

"I found it under the bed," Alison protested.

"I believe you. But in the beginning, I didn't know what to think. I had to find out the extent of your involvement, how much you knew. I tried flirting with you, but you weren't interested, so I hit on Denise, convinced her to let me tag along for Thanksgiving dinner. I realized pretty quickly that you had nothing to do with Erica's disappearance. But the more I got to know Terry, the more convinced I became she did."

"And why is that?"

"Because there's something very weird about that lady."

"Don't be ridiculous."

"I've been watching her for months, phoning her, following her in my car, trying to spook her, anything to get her to slip up. And she's starting to crack. I can feel it."

So it hadn't been my imagination. Someone **had** been watching me. And not just today. K.C. was the shifting shadow outside my window, the anonymous, yet strangely familiar, voice on my telephone. That subtle Texas twang he couldn't quite disguise—how had I failed to recognize it before now?

"You've been harassing her for months," Alison stated, "and you're surprised she's acting strangely?"

"Terry knows what happened to Erica. Damn it, she's responsible."

"Are you finished? Because if you're finished, then it's time for you to leave."

"Haven't you heard anything I've said?"

"You haven't said anything," Alison shot back. "Your girlfriend pulled a disappearing act. I'm sorry. I know being dumped is a hard thing to accept. But what you're suggesting is outrageous. And I've heard quite enough, thank you. I want you to go now."

There was a second's silence, then the sound of feet shuffling reluctantly toward the front door.

"Wait!" Alison called out, and I held my breath, inched forward, leaned my head against the closet door. "You should have this." She walked around the side of the bed, pulled open the drawer of the night-stand. "You said you gave it to her. You should have it back."

I pictured Alison walking toward him, Erica's thin gold necklace dangling from her fingertips.

"Come with me," he urged. "It's not safe for you to stay here."

"Don't worry about me," she told him flatly. "I'll be fine."

I heard the front door open as I crept out of the closet and inched along the side of the dresser, my palm leaving a bloody trail on the white wicker as I balanced against it.

"Be careful," the man calling himself K.C. warned the young woman who called herself Alison Simms.

And then he was gone.

# 27

I don't know how long I stood there, my breath caught somewhere between my lungs and my mouth, my hand pulsating with pain as I pressed the handle of the knife against my torn flesh, like a branding iron. Could I really use this knife against Alison, even in self-defense?

"What the hell is going on here?" Alison demanded suddenly, and I lunged forward in response, my arm instinctively arcing into the air, while blood from my palm streaked down my arm, as if someone had out-lined the path of one of my veins in red ink.

But Alison hadn't been speaking to me, and she was already out the door and on her way to the main house when I emerged from the shadows, her anguished, unanswered question vibrating against the still air, like smoke from a discarded cigarette. "Terry!" I heard her shouting, as once more she pounded on my kitchen door. "Terry, open the door. I know you're in there."

I watched as she backed away from the door, her head tilted toward my bedroom. "Terry!" she shouted, her voice targeting my window like a well-aimed stone, before she gave up in defeat. What now? I wondered, swallowing what little air I could find, holding it hostage against my lungs.

Alison stood very still for what seemed an excruciatingly long time. Weighing her options, I thought. Just like me. Ultimately she decided to give it one last try, turning on her heels and running around the side of the house to the front. Only then did I push open the cottage door and creep into the night, a sudden breeze scratching at my neck, like the tongue of a cat. As Alison banged on the front door, I was opening the back.

In the next instant, I was inside my kitchen, the aroma of freshly baked chocolate cake settling about my head, like a bridal veil. I slid the bloody knife back into its triangular wooden holder, then wrapped my bleeding palm inside a dishcloth as Alison returned to the back door, her eyes widening with shock as I flipped on the light and opened the door to let her in.

"Terry! What's going on? Where have you been? I've been so worried."

"I was taking a nap," I answered sleepily, in a voice

not quite my own. Hell, K.C. wasn't the only one capable of disguising his voice.

"Are you all right?"

"I'm fine." I waved my hand into the air, as if to dismiss her concerns.

"My God, what happened to your hand?"

I glanced at my injured arm, as if seeing it for the first time. Blood had already soaked through the thin, cotton towel. "I cut it. It's nothing."

"It's not nothing. Let me have a look at it." She unwrapped the towel before I could protest further. "Oh, my God! This is awful. Maybe we should go to the hospital."

"Alison, it's just a little cut."

"It's not just a little cut. You might need stitches." She pulled me toward the sink, ran the cold water, guided my hand under the steady stream. "How long has it been bleeding like this?"

"Not long." I winced as the water hit my palm, pushing the blood aside, and exposing the fragile white line of my wound. My wounded lifeline, I thought, as blood continued to wash across the inside of my hand.

"What's that smell?" Alison looked toward the stove.

"Terry's magic chocolate cake," I said with a shrug.

Confusion brought her eyebrows together at the bridge of her nose. "I don't understand. When did you have time to bake? I've been waiting for you for hours. When did you get back? And what's your car doing parked around the corner?" The questions were coming faster now, out of her mouth as soon as they entered her head, one piled on top of the other, like pancakes. Alison shut off the water, grabbed a handful of paper towels from the roll on the wall, and pressed the absorbent white towels into my cupped hand. "Tell me what's going on, Terry."

I shook my head, trying to gather my thoughts together, to give order to my lies. "There's not that much to tell."

"Start with when you left here. Where did you go?" Alison prompted. She didn't have to say any more. She didn't have to mention the aborted kiss.

I noted a small red circle metastasizing in the middle of the white paper towels, like menstrual blood, I thought, watching it grow wider and darker, reach toward the edges. "I'm so embarrassed about what happened," I whispered as she led me to a chair. "I don't know what came over me."

"It was all my fault," Alison interjected immediately, sitting down beside me. "I obviously gave you the wrong impression."

"I've never done anything like that before in my life."

"I know. You were just upset about Josh."

"Yes," I agreed, thinking this was probably true. "Anyway, I'm not sure where I went after I left here. I was pretty confused, so I just drove around for a while, tried to clear my head."

"And you parked around the corner because you didn't want me to know you were back," Alison stated quietly, traces of guilt bracketing her words.

"I was feeling pretty shaky. I thought it was best if we didn't see each other right away."

"I was so worried about you."

"I'm sorry."

"Don't be."

I looked around the room. It felt so bare, so empty, without the women watching. "Baking's always been a kind of therapy for me," I continued, glancing from the shelves to the oven. "So, I decided, why not bake a cake? I don't know. It seemed like a good idea at the time. Isn't that what they say?"

She nodded. "Seems like they're always saying something."

I smiled. "You like chocolate cake, don't you?"

Her turn to smile. "Is that a rhetorical question?"

I patted her hand. It felt ice-cold. "It should be ready in a few minutes."

"Is that how you cut your hand? Baking?"

"It was stupid," I began, the lie wiggling around the tip of my tongue, like a worm on a fisherman's hook. "I was reaching for something in a drawer, and I sliced it on a small paring knife."

Alison clutched her own hand in sympathy. "Ooh, that hurts."

"It's a bit better now." I glanced back at the oven, smiled. "Cake should be ready. Feel like a piece?"

"Don't you have to let it cool off for a while?"

"No. It's best fresh out of the oven." I rose from my seat, walked to the stove, opened the oven door with my left hand. A gust of heat rolled toward me like an ocean wave as I bent forward and inhaled the rich chocolate perfume. I reached for my oven mitts on the counter.

"I'll do it," Alison offered immediately, sliding her hands inside the waiting pink mitts, then gingerly transferring the cake to a nearby trivet. "This looks as good as it smells. Should I make some coffee?"

"Coffee sounds wonderful."

"You sit. Keep that hand still. Raise it above your heart." She rolled her eyes. "Listen to me—you're the nurse, and I'm telling you what to do." She shook her head, laughed with what I recognized was relief—relief that I seemed to have a reasonable explanation for everything, relief that I seemed no longer angry with her, relief that things seemed back to normal.

**Seemed,** I thought, sitting back in my chair. Good word.

I smiled as I watched Alison prepare the coffee. It was amazing how comfortable she was in my kitchen, among my things. She knew without asking that I kept the coffee in the freezer and the sugar in the cupboard to the left of the sink. "There's whipped cream in the fridge," I told her as she measured out the coffee and poured the water into the back of the coffeemaker.

"You're amazing," she said. "You're always prepared for everything."

"Sometimes it pays to be prepared."

"I wish I was more like that." Alison leaned against the counter. "I've always acted more on impulse."

"That can be pretty dangerous."

"Tell me about it." There was a moment's silence. Alison glanced at the floor, then at the empty shelves, an impish grin spreading across her face. "Smashing all those heads was a pretty impulsive thing to do."

I laughed. "I guess it was."

"Maybe we're more alike than you think."

"Maybe." Our eyes locked, and for a moment, neither of us moved, as if we were daring each other to be the first to look away. Of course I was the one to blink first. "What say we have some of that cake?"

"You stay right where you are. Keep that hand up. I'll do everything." Alison removed two small plates from the cupboard, along with two sets of cups and saucers, and set them on the table beside several paper napkins, the sugar, and the bowl of whipped cream. Then she returned to the counter and reached for a knife. "Remember the first day I was here, and I grabbed the wrong knife," she said, pulling the giant butcher knife from its wooden block as my breath froze in my throat, "and you said, 'Whoa! Overkill, don't you think?' Whoa!" she repeated now, staring with openmouthed wonder at the blood-encrusted blade. "What's this? Is this blood?" Her focus shifted to the shaft of the knife. "And it looks like there's blood on the handle too." She stared at her palm.

"More like blood on the brain," I said, rising quickly from my chair and removing the knife from her hands, then dropping it into the sink and running hot water over it. "It's not blood," I told her.

"What is it?"

"Just a stubborn case of strawberry jam."

"Jam? On the handle?"

"Are you going to cut me a piece of cake, or what?" I asked impatiently.

Alison grabbed another knife and proceeded to slice into the warm cake. "Oh, no, it's starting to crumble. You're sure it's not too soon to do this?"

"The timing is perfect," I said as she slid a large piece of cake onto a plate. "Give me one half that size."

"You're sure?"

"I can always come back for more."

"Don't count on it." Alison returned to her seat and eagerly stuffed a heaping forkful of cake into her mouth.

I watched the crumbs form a dark outline around her lips. Like a clown's mouth, I thought, as she licked the errant crumbs into her mouth with the flick of her tongue. A snake's tongue, I thought, watching her swallow.

"This is absolutely the best cake you have ever made. The best." She swallowed another forkful. "Will you teach me how to bake one day?"

"It's really very easy."

"Don't worry. I'll find a way to make it difficult." Alison laughed self-consciously, quickly finishing what was left on her plate. "This is so yummy delicious. Why aren't you eating?"

"Thought I'd wait for the coffee."

Alison glanced at the coffeemaker. "Looks like it'll be a few more minutes. 'A watched kettle never boils,'" she reminded me, looking away. "You told me that."

"Do you remember everything I say?"

"I try to."

"Why?" I asked, genuinely curious.

"Because I think you're smart. Because I admire you." Alison hesitated, as if there was more she wanted to say, then obviously thought better of it. "Can I have another piece? I can't wait for the coffee."

"Be my guest. Try it with some whipped cream."

Alison cut herself another, even larger slice of cake, then spooned a large dollop of the whipped cream on top of it. "This is heaven," she enthused, filling her mouth. "Absolute heaven. You have to taste this." She extended her fork toward me.

I shook my head, pointed toward the coffee.

"You have such willpower."

"It won't be long now." I watched as she wolfed down the second piece of cake. A human Garburetor, I thought, with something approaching awe. "Ready for thirds?"

"Are you kidding? One more piece and it won't be just the china heads exploding around here." She hesitated. "Although maybe I have room for one more very tiny piece. With my coffee." She laughed. She lowered her gaze to her lap, closed her eyes. "I'll miss this," she whispered, her body swaying.

I leaned forward, wondering if she was about to fall,

thinking that even a strong sedative like Percodan needs more than a few minutes to work its magic.

Instead of falling over, Alison bolted upright in her chair, her eyes popping open, as if she'd just awakened from a bad dream. "Please don't make me leave."

"What?"

"I know you said you've already rented out the cottage to someone at work, but I'm really praying you'll change your mind and give me another chance. I promise I won't mess up this time. I'll do everything you say. I'll follow all your rules. I won't screw up again. Honest."

She sounded so sincere that I almost found myself believing her. In spite of everything, I realized I **wanted** to believe her. "What about Lance?"

"Lance? That's over. Lance is gone."

"How do I know he won't come back?"

"Because I give you my solemn vow."

"You lied to me before."

"I know. And I'm so sorry. It was stupid. **I** was stupid. Stupid to think Lance would ever change, that things would be any different this time."

"What about the next time?"

"There won't be a next time. Lance knows he went too far, that he crossed the line when he came on to you."

"Why am I any different than anyone else?"

She paused, looked up, then down, as if searching for just the right words. "Because he knew how important you are to me."

"And what makes me so important?"

Another pause. "You just are." Alison jumped to her feet, then grabbed for the table.

"Alison? Are you all right?"

"Yeah. I just got a little dizzy there for a minute. I guess I must have moved too fast."

"Are you still dizzy?"

She shook her head slowly, as if she wasn't sure. "I think I'm okay now. Kind of scary though."

"Have some coffee. Coffee's a good antidote to dizziness."

"It is?"

"I'm the nurse, remember?"

She smiled. "Two cups of coffee coming right up." She poured the freshly brewed coffee into each cup, then added three heaping spoonfuls of sugar and a large dollop of whipped cream to hers.

"Cheers." I clicked my cup against hers.

"To us."

"To us," I agreed, watching as she took a long sip.

She made a face, lowered the cup to its saucer. "Kind of bitter."

I took a sip from my own cup. "Tastes fine to me."

"I think I made it too strong."

"Maybe you need more sugar," I teased.

Alison added a fourth spoonful, took another sip. "No. Still not quite right." She brought her hand to her head.

"Alison, are you okay?"

"I don't know. I feel a little strange."

"Drink some more coffee. It'll help."

Alison did as she was told, throwing back the coffee as if it were a glass of tequila, then taking a long, deep breath. "Is it warm in here?"

"Not really."

"Oh, God. I hope I'm not getting a migraine."

"Is this how they usually start?"

"No. Usually I get this kind of tunnel-vision thing going, and then this horrible headache takes over."

"I have some more of those pills." I got up from my chair and pretended to fish around in a drawer. "Why don't you take a couple? Strike a preemptive blow." I handed her two little white pills, returned the bottle of Percodan to the drawer.

She took the pills without even bothering to examine them. "So, what do you think?" she asked, pushing her hair away from her forehead.

I noticed she was beginning to perspire. "I think you'll start to feel better soon."

"No. I mean about me staying."

"You can stay as long as you like."

Tears immediately appeared in the corners of each eye. "Really? You mean that?"

"Absolutely."

"You're not kicking me out?"

"How could I? This is your home."

Alison brought her hands to her mouth, muffled a gasp of pure joy. "Oh, thank you. Thank you so much. You won't be sorry. I promise you."

"But no more lies."

"I promise I'll never lie to you again."

"Good. Because lies destroy trust, and without trust . . ."

"You're right. Of course you're right." She ran her hand through her hair, rolled her neck from side to side, wet her lips with her tongue.

"Are you all right, Alison? Would you like to lie down?"

"No. I'll be okay."

"What was K.C. doing here before?" I asked, slipping the question in casually as her eyes struggled to stay focused.

"What?"

"No more lies, Alison. You promised."

"No more lies," she whispered.

"What was K.C. doing here?"

She shook her head, then raised her hands to her temples, as if to steady her head, prevent it from rolling off altogether. "His name isn't K.C."

"It isn't?"

"No. It's Charlie. Charlie something-or-other. I don't remember. He was Erica Hollander's fiancé."

"Erica's fiancé? What was he doing here?"

"I don't know." Alison's eyes struggled to find my face. "He was talking crazy."

"What did he say?"

"Nothing that made any sense." She laughed, but the weak sound wobbled, then died in her throat. "He says that she didn't run off, that she never went anywhere. He has this ridiculous idea that you know where she is."

"Maybe it's not such a ridiculous idea."

"What? What are you saying?"

"Maybe I **do** know where she is."

"Do you?" Alison tried to stand up, stumbled, collapsed back in the chair.

"I really think you'd be much more comfortable lying down. Why don't we go into the living room?" I helped Alison to her feet, lifting one long, slender arm over my shoulder, and guiding her from the kitchen, her feet shuffling along the floor, like whispers from a crowd.

"What happened to the Christmas tree?" she asked as we entered the living room.

"It had a little accident." I directed her to the sofa and sat down beside her, lifting her feet into my lap.

"Are you going to give me a pedicure?" she asked with a smile that refused to settle.

"Maybe later."

"I feel so strange. Maybe it's the pills."

"And the cake," I said, removing her sandals, massaging her bare feet the way I knew she liked. "And the coffee."

She regarded me quizzically.

"I believe you had four spoonfuls of sugar this time. Not a good idea, Alison. They say sugar's poison for your system."

"I don't understand." For the first time, a look of fear

flashed through Alison's beautiful green eyes. "What are you talking about?"

"You thought you had me, didn't you, Alison? You thought all you had to do was smile and pay me a few stupid compliments, and I'd fall under your magic spell all over again. Except it didn't work. This time I'm the one with all the magic: Terry's magic chocolate cake; Terry's magic sugar; Terry's magic pills."

"What are you talking about? What have you done to me?"

"Who are you?" I demanded.

"What!"

"Who are you?"

"You know who I am. I'm Alison."

"Alison Simms?" I didn't give her a chance to answer. "I doubt that. There is no Alison Simms." I watched her flinch, as if I'd raised my hand to strike her. "Just like there's no K.C."

"But I didn't know about K.C. I didn't know—"

"Just like there's no Rita Bishop."

She rubbed her mouth, her neck, her hair. "Who?"

"Your friend from Chicago. The one you were looking for at Mission Care when you just happened to stumble across my notice."

"Oh, God."

"Let's play our little game. Three words to describe Alison."

"Terry, please. You don't understand."

"Let's see. Oh, I know: liar, liar, liar."

"But I haven't lied. Please, I haven't lied."

"You've done nothing **but** lie since the moment I met you. I read your journal, Alison."

"You read my journal? But then you know—"

"I know you're coming here was no accident. I know you and Lance have been plotting for months to get rid of me."

"Get rid of you? No!" Alison swung her legs off my lap, tried to get up, only half-succeeded before her knees gave out and she teetered to the floor. "Oh, God. What's happening to me?"

"Who are you, Alison? Who are you **really?**"

"Please help me."

"The Lord helps those who help themselves," I said coldly, in my mother's voice.

"It's all a huge misunderstanding. Please. Take me to the hospital. I promise I'll tell you everything as soon as I feel better."

"Tell me now." I pushed her back on the sofa, watching her disappear into the deep, down-filled cushions, their pretty pink and mauve flowers threatening to swallow her whole. I settled into the striped Queen Anne chair directly across from her and waited. "The truth," I warned her. "Don't leave anything out."

# 28

"Can I have a glass of water?" Alison asked.

"Later. After you tell me."

Tears fell the length of Alison's face. Her color was ashen, a once vibrant photograph fading before my eyes. "I don't know where to start."

"Start with who you really are. Start with your name."

"It's Alison."

"Not Simms," I said matter-of-factly.

"Not Simms," she repeated dully. "Sinukoff." A sudden spark of interest. "Does that name mean anything to you?"

"Should it?"

She shrugged. "I wasn't sure if it would or not."

"It doesn't."

"I didn't know if it would. I had to be sure."

"Sure of what?"

"I didn't want to make another mistake."

"What are you talking about? What kind of mistake?"

Alison's head rolled back across her shoulders, swayed precariously, as if it might fall off. "I'm so tired."

"Why did you come to Florida, Alison?" I demanded. "What were you after?"

"I came to find you."

"I know that. What I don't know is why. I'm not rich. I'm not famous. I have nothing that could possibly interest you."

She steadied her head, concentrated all her attention on my face. "You have everything," she said simply.

"I'm afraid you'll have to explain that one."

Her eyes fluttered to a close, and for a moment I thought she might have succumbed to all the sedatives in her system, but then she started to speak, slowly at first, and with obvious effort, as if trying to keep track of her words, as one thought merged with another, and one word slurred into the next. "I'd been looking for you for a while without any luck. I decided to hire a private detective. The first one didn't work out, so I hired someone else. He said you were working in a hospital in Delray. So I went there to see for myself. That's when I saw your notice at the nurses' station. I couldn't believe my luck. I made up the story about Rita Bishop. I thought it would give us a chance to get to know one another before . . ."

"Before what?"

"Before I told you."

"Told me what, for God's sake?"

"Don't you know?"

"Know what?"

"I don't understand. You said you read my journal."

"Know what?" I repeated, my voice a low roar, like the sound of an approaching wave.

Her eyes locked on mine, snapped into focus, as if seeing me for the first time. "That you're my mother."

For an instant I didn't know whether to laugh or cry, so I did both, the strangled sound emerging from my mouth foreign even to my own ears. I jumped to my feet, began pacing back and forth in front of her. "What are you talking about? That's impossible. What are you talking about?"

"I'm your daughter," she said, fresh tears forming in her eyes.

"You're crazy! Your mother lives in Chicago."

"I'm not from Chicago. I'm from Baltimore, like you."

"You're lying!"

"I was adopted as an infant by John and Carole Sinukoff. Did you know them?"

I shook my head vigorously, distant images flashing through my mind like a strobe light. I shielded my eyes, struggled to keep unwanted memories at bay.

"They already had a son, but they couldn't have any more children, and they wanted a daughter, so they picked me. A mistake," she acknowledged, licking at her lips. "I was this awful kid. Pretty much like I told you. I never felt I belonged. I was so different from everyone else. And it didn't help that my perfect older brother kept reminding me I wasn't really part of the family. One Christmas when he came home from Brown, he told me that my real mother was a fourteen-year-old slut who couldn't keep her legs together."

"Oh, God."

"I kicked him where it counts. He certainly didn't have any trouble keeping **his** legs together after that." She attempted a laugh, wheezed instead.

"But what you're saying is impossible," I told her, my head spinning as much as hers. Images of the past snuck through decades-old defenses to assault my brain: Roger Stillman clumsily pushing his way inside me in the backseat of his car; my frantic eyes checking my underwear every day after that for signs of a period that stubbornly refused to come; my child's belly growing more distended every day, no matter how baggy the clothes I wore. "It's impossible," I repeated, more force-fully this time, trying in vain to frighten the images away. "Do the math. I'm forty. You're twenty-eight. That would have made me twelve—"

"I'm not twenty-eight. I'm twenty-five. I'll be twenty-six . . ."

On February 9, I mouthed silently as she spoke the words out loud. I covered my ears with my hands in an effort to block out her voice. When had it gotten so loud, so strong?

"I was afraid if I told you my real age, you might figure everything out before you had the chance to get to know me. And I didn't know how you'd feel about having me back in your life. I wanted so much for you to like me. No, that's a lie," she said, correcting herself. "I wanted more than that. I wanted you to **love** me. So you wouldn't be able to give me up again."

I sank back into the Queen Anne chair. She was crazy, of course. Even if some of what she said was true, it was impossible for her to be my daughter. She was so tall, so beautiful. Just like Roger Stillman, I thought. "It's not true," I insisted. "I'm sorry. You've made a mistake."

"No. Not this time. The first detective I hired found some woman in Hagerstown he thought was you. I got so excited, I went to see her, but it turned out he was wrong. Then I found you. Lance said I was crazy to come all the way down here, that I was only going to get hurt again, but I had to see you. And the minute I did, the minute I talked to you, I knew I was right. Even before you told me about Roger Stillman, I knew you were my mother."

"Well, I'm sorry, but you're wrong."

"I'm not wrong. You know I'm not."

"The only thing I know is that you're a stupid, stupid girl!" I heard myself shout.

My mother's voiced bounced off the walls.

**You're a stupid, stupid girl!**

"No, please don't say that."

How could you do this? How could you let some ridiculous boy stick his awful thing inside you?

I'll take care of the baby, Mommy. I promise I'll take good care of it.

Don't think for one minute that I'm going to allow a bastard child into this house. I'll drown it in a basin, just like I drowned those damn kittens!

"Terry," Alison was whispering. "Terry, I'm not feeling very well."

I moved swiftly to her side, wrapped her in my arms. "It's all right, Alison. Don't worry. You won't throw up. I know how much you hate throwing up."

"Please take me to the hospital."

"Later, sweetheart. After you've had a little nap."

"I don't want to fall asleep."

"Ssh. Don't fight it, darling. It'll all be over soon."

"No! Oh, God, no! Please. You have to help me."

We heard the noise at the same moment, our heads twisting in unison toward the kitchen door. Pounding, yelling, ringing. "Alison!" a voice bellowed over the cacophony of sounds. "Alison, are you in there?"

"K.C.!" Alison exclaimed, her voice scarcely audible. "I'm here. Oh, God, help me! I'm in here."

"Terry!" K.C. hollered. "Terry, open this door right now or I'm calling the police."

"Just a minute," I called back calmly, gently extricating myself from Alison's side, hearing her groan as she toppled over, too drugged to move. I walked quickly to the back door. "I'm coming. Hold your horses."

"Where is she?" K.C. pushed roughly past me into the house. "What have you done with her?"

"Who are we talking about?" I asked him pleasantly. "Erica? Or Alison?"

But K.C. was already in the living room. "Alison! My God! What has that lunatic done to you?"

I reached into the sink and carefully removed the butcher knife from the white enamel basin. It fit comfortably into the center of my hand, as if it belonged there. I squeezed it, felt it damp against my tender skin as the cut reopened in my palm. Then I returned to the living room, watching from behind the dying branches of the Christmas tree as K.C. struggled to lift Alison to her feet.

"Can you walk?"

"I don't think so."

"Put your arms around my neck. I'll carry you."

How can I describe what happened next?

It was as if I'd been handed the starring role in a play. No, not a play. More like a ballet, full of grand gestures and exaggerated mime, each move carefully planned and choreographed. As Alison raised her arms, so did I. As K.C. was bending to scoop her up, I was swooping down. As he took the first of several awkward steps, I was flying across the room with savage grace. As Alison was resting her head against K.C.'s shoulder, I was plunging the foot-long blade into his back with such force the handle snapped off in my hands.

K.C. staggered forward, Alison dropping from his

arms and landing with a dull thud on the floor. K.C. spun around in a sloppy pirouette, his hands losing their graceful rhythm and flailing about for the blade that was buried deep in his back. The growing swell of Alison's screams filled the air, like a third-rate orchestra, as K.C. balanced on his toes, his arms extended toward me, as if asking me to join him for one final twirl around the room. I declined his silent invitation, taking a step back as he fell forward, his disbelieving eyes glazing over with the approach of imminent death. He hit the floor, the top of his head just missing the base of the overturned tree.

It took a few seconds for me to realize that Alison had stopped screaming, that she was no longer sprawled carelessly across the floor, that she had somehow managed to gather whatever strength she still possessed and was making a desperate scramble for the front door. That she actually succeeded in getting it open and was halfway down the front steps before I caught up to her is a great tribute to her strength and determination.

The instinct for survival, the will to live, is an amazing thing.

I remembered having had similar thoughts about Myra Wylie. Only Erica Hollander had gone quietly, dozing off within minutes of finishing the late-night snack I'd prepared. The pillow I'd subsequently held over her nose and mouth had brought only token resistance.

"No!" Alison was screaming as I reached for her arm.

"Alison, please. Don't make a scene."

"No! Don't touch me! Leave me alone!"

"Come back inside, Alison." I grabbed her elbow, dug my fingers into her flesh.

"No!" she screamed again, wresting her arm away from me with such force I almost lost my balance. She made it halfway to the street before her legs simply gave out, and she collapsed like the proverbial rag doll. Even then, she refused to give up, crawling on her hands and knees toward the sidewalk.

It was then we heard the barking, followed immediately by the click of high heels on pavement. Bettye McCoy and her two lunatic dogs, I realized, trying to drag Alison to her feet.

"Help me!" Alison cried as the third Mrs. McCoy wiggled around the corner in a pair of leopard-print capri pants. "Help me!"

But Alison's cries were drowned out by the angry yapping of the dogs.

"It's okay," I called to the aging Alice in Wonderland. "She's just had a bit too much to drink."

Bettye McCoy tossed her overly teased blond mane disdainfully over her shoulder and gathered the two dogs into her arms before crossing the street and walking briskly in the opposite direction.

"No, please!" Alison called after her. "You have to help me! Help me!"

"You really need to sleep this off," I said loudly, in case anyone was listening.

"Please," Alison begged the now empty street. "Please, don't go."

"I'm right here, baby," I told her, gathering her into my arms, guiding her toward the house. "I'm not going anywhere."

When we reached the door, she stopped fighting. Whether it was the drugs or the realization that such struggles were useless, I don't know. She simply sighed and went limp in my arms. I carried her across the threshold, as a new husband lovingly transports his bride.

Do they even do that anymore? I don't know. I doubt I'll ever have the opportunity to find out. It's too late for me, just as it was too late for Alison. And it's too bad, because I think I would have made a fine wife. That's all I ever really wanted. To love someone, to be loved in return, to make a home, have a family. A child on whom I could lavish all the tenderness I'd been denied. A daughter.

I've always wanted a daughter.

I carried Alison to the sofa, cradled her in my arms. **"Too-ra-loo-ra-loo-ra,"** I sang tenderly. **"Too-ra-loo-ra-lie . . ."**

Alison raised her eyes slowly to mine. Her mouth opened. Whispers filled the air. I think I heard the word **Mommy.**

# 29

Of course, I don't believe for a minute that Alison was my child.

She probably heard about how I'd disgraced my family from the Sinukoffs. The name sounds vaguely familiar. Perhaps they were neighbors. Perhaps not. Baltimore's a big city. You can't know everyone, despite my mother's assertion that the whole town knew about my condition, that she was a laughingstock, too ashamed ever to show her face in public again.

That's why we moved to Florida. Not because my father's job demanded it. Because of me.

I stayed in school until my condition became too obvious to ignore, then I was asked to leave. Nothing happened to Roger Stillman. My shame was his badge of honor, and he was allowed to remain in school and graduate with his classmates.

I endured almost twenty hours of labor before my mother let my father drive me to the hospital. It was another ten hours before the baby—weighing in at an impressive eight pounds, seven ounces—was born. I never got the chance to hold her. Never even got the chance to see her. My mother made sure of that.

Of course she was right. What else could she have done? I was only fourteen years old, after all, a baby myself. What did I know of life, of looking after another human being? It was a ridiculous notion, one I'm sure I would have lived to regret.

And yet, maybe not. Would I have been such a bad mother? I've often wondered. I'd secretly loved that little baby growing inside me from the first minute I felt her moving around. I talked to her when no one was home, sang to her when we were alone in my room, assuring her that I would never lose my temper with her, never hit her or disparage her in any way, that I would shower her with kisses, assure her each and every day how very much she was loved. "I'll take care of you," I promised her when no one was listening. Instead, she was pulled from my body and banished from my side before her sweet little face had time to register, and I spent my whole life taking care of other people instead.

Of course Alison wasn't my child.

She'd undoubtedly heard about "the fourteen-year-old slut who couldn't keep her legs together" from someone back in Baltimore, possibly even her older brother, as she'd claimed. Then she and her friends had concocted this elaborate scenario, determined to insinuate themselves into my life. **I wanted you to like me. No. I wanted you to** love **me,** Alison herself had admitted shortly before she died.

I miss her terribly, of course, think of her often, and always with great affection, even love. So maybe Alison got what she came for after all.

She didn't suffer. She simply fell asleep in my arms. The rest was easy. There were so many drugs in her system, I doubt she was even aware of the pillow I held against her face for the better part of two minutes. Later, I dressed her in her pretty blue sundress—the one she had been wearing the first day we met—and then buried her in the garden beside Erica. The flowers are especially lush in that corner of the yard, and I think she would have approved.

K.C. was a different story. I'd never killed a man before, never used a knife, never had to resort to such brutality. It took days for the vibrations to stop echoing through my hand, weeks till I was finally able to scrub all the blood from my living room floor. Of course, I had to get rid of the rug. It was ruined. Alison was right—a white rug in the living room hadn't proved very practical. At any rate, it was time for a change.

I didn't want K.C. polluting my garden, so I waited until the middle of the night, then bundled him into the trunk of my car and drove all the way to the Everglades, where I tossed him into a slime-covered swamp. It seemed fitting, and I'm sure the alligators appreciated my efforts.

It's been three months since Alison died. The season is almost over. Every day there are fewer cars on the roads, fewer tourists prowling the streets. It's easier to get into restaurants now. There are shorter lines at the movies. Bettye McCoy still walks her two lunatic dogs down the street several times a day, and occasionally one breaks away from her, makes a bee-line for my backyard. I've erected a small fence to keep them out. Hopefully, that will suffice. Should one of those mangy mutts manage to get into my yard again, I won't be chasing it out with anything as gentle as a broom.

Occasionally, I wonder what would happen if Lance and Denise came back, looking for Alison. But so far, there's been no sign of either of them, so maybe Alison was telling the truth about their taking off together, about her relationship with her ex-husband being over once and for all. I hope so. Still, I can't let down my guard.

My job at the hospital continues much as it always has. Myra's bed has been filled by an elderly gentleman with advanced Parkinson's. I take very good care of him. His family think I'm the greatest thing since sliced bread.

Incidentally, I was right about Josh. He did send flowers to the staff several weeks after his mother's funeral. Actually, the flowers were from both him **and** his wife. The note thanked everyone on the ward. No one was singled out for special mention.

The journal he gave me has proved useful, however. It's nice to have somewhere to record my thoughts, as I'm doing now. A place to set the record straight.

And who knows? Maybe one day I'll find true love. Just because Josh proved both weak and unworthy doesn't mean there isn't someone out there who's right for me. It's not too late. I'm only forty. I'm still reasonably attractive. I could meet someone tomorrow, get married, have the family I've always craved. Many women over forty are having babies. It could happen. I'm praying it does.

And that's about it. Life goes on, as they say.

**Who are** they **anyway?** I can hear Alison ask, her voice never very far from my ear.

I turn around, look the other way. She's right beside me.

**Describe your life since I went away,** she whispers playfully. **Three words.**

"Uneventful," I reply obediently. "Unexciting." I survey the empty shelves that line the kitchen walls, thinking that perhaps the time has come to start rebuilding my collection. "Lonely," I admit, choking back tears.

I stare out my back window at the small, empty cottage behind my house. It has been unoccupied for three months now and is starting to look a little neglected. It needs someone as much as I do. Someone who will love it and take care of it, who will show it the love and respect it deserves. After the debacles with Erica and Alison, I'm not sure such a person even exists. But maybe it's time to find out. Maybe it's time to bury the whispers and lies of the past, time to start afresh.

"Afresh," I repeat out loud in Alison's voice, deciding to place an ad in the weekend paper. "Good word."